D0992196

BEAUCHAMPE

BEAUCHAMPE

OR

THE KENTUCKY TRAGEDY

A SEQUEL TO CHARLEMONT

By W. GILMORE SIMMS, Esq.

"Maid of Lulan," said Fingal, "white-handed daughter of Grief! a cloud, marked wit..
streaks of fire, is rolled along thy soul. Look not to that dark-robed moon : .ook not to those
meteors of Heaven. My gleaming steel is around thee, the terror of thy foes."....
"I rose, like a stalking ghost. I pierced the side of Corman-trunas. Nor did Forna-
Bragäl escape. She rolled her white bosom in blood. Why, then, daughter of heroes,
didst thou wake my rage ?"—OSSIAN. *Cath. Loda.*

NEW AND REVISED EDITION

AMS PRESS
NEW YORK

Reprinted from the edition of 1856, New York
First AMS EDITION 1970
Manufactured in the United States of America

S 592 be

International Standard Book Number: 0-404-06006-4

Library of Congress Catalog Card Number: 68-54296

AMS PRESS, INC.
NEW YORK, N.Y. 10003

ADVERTISEMENT.

"BEAUCHAMPE; or the Kentucky Tragedy," is the sequel to the story of "Charlemont." The story supposes some little interval of time between its opening, and the close of its predecessor. The connection between the two is sufficiently intimate, though the sequel introduces us to new persons — the hero among them — who do not figure in the first publication. I do not know that anything farther need be added by way of explanation. In regard to moral and social characteristics, the preface to "Charlemont" will suffice. A few words, perhaps, in regard to the *materiel*, may not be amiss in the present connection, to prevent mistakes, and save the critic from that error, which he occasionally makes, of substituting his own point of view for that of the author — an error which usually results in a mere game or cross purposes between the parties, which is profitable to neither. The reader may find or fancy some occasional differences of fact and inference, date, place, and period, between this and other narratives relating to Beauchampe, and the famous Kentucky tragedy of which he was the unhappy hero. But, as a man of sagacity, he will naturally discard all bias derived from any previous reading, in

deference to that which is now submitted him. Ours, as
the language of the quack advertisements, is the only gen
uine article. We alone have gone to the fountain head for
our materials. We have good authority for all that is here
given. We can place our hand on the record at any moment, and we defy all skepticism. Newspapers are lying
things at best—they have told sundry fibs on this very
subject. Pamphlets—and our melancholy history has induced several—are scarcely better as authorities;—even
the dusty files of the court should make nothing against the
truth of our statements where they happen to differ. At
all events, the good reader may be assured that our disa-
greements are not substantial. They affect none of the
vital truths of the narrative. We agree in all wholesome
aspects. Our morals are the same—our results very nearly so; and if we have made a longer story of the matter
than they have done, it only proves that we had so much
more to say. We need say no more by way of preparative,
and we forbear saying anything by way of provocative.
Fall to and welcome! The fare is solid enough, and, as
for the spices and the dressing—say nothing in disparagement of these, if you would not incur the maledictions of
the cook. We Anglicise in this sentence a homely proverb,
which would scarcely tell so well in the original.

BEAUCHAMPE.

CHAPTER I.

THE RUINED HAMLET.

Time does not move with the less rapidity because his progress is so insensible. His wings may be compared to those of the owl and other birds who fly by night. Their feathers are fined off to such exquisitely-delicate points, that they steal silently through the air, as swiftly as stealthily, and strike their object without alarming it. So with that "subtle thief" whom men personify as Time. He moves like the pestilence, without beat of drum, without pomp of banners, with no pageantry of state or terror, which might warn the victim to prepare his defences. He fans us to sleep as the fabled vampire, with dark wing slowly waving over our slumbers, while his sharp tooth is penetrating the vital places in our bosoms.

Five years have elapsed since the period of those melancholy events, which furnished us with the materials for our village-chronicle of "Charlemont." The reader of that legend will not require that we should remind him of its sorrowful details. Enough that we tell him that its inhabitants are all dispersed — scattered variously in remote regions — some silent in the grave — all changed; all undergoing change; and that the village itself is a ruin! The

1*

vicissitudes of life have told in various ways upon all t
parties to our former story. Some of them have been *key*
wretched ; others, made so ; while others again, have he
a sensible progress—onward, upward—to prosperity and
honorable distinction. Perhaps, we shall gather something
more definite on this head from the discourse of the two
travellers, whom we behold alighting from their horses, and
seating themselves upon one of the hills by which the valley of Charlemont is overlooked.

Here, on this very spot, more than five years before, two
other travellers had paused to survey the natural beauties
of the village, and to feast their eyes upon the rural aspect
of its innocent society. At that period, it was comparatively innocent. There was peace within its borders, and
Plenty sat beside its winter fires, fully solaced by Content.
But the gaze of those two travellers brought blight upon
several of its sweetest homes. One of the two. a good old
man, went on his way, dreaming with delight upon the
simple beauties and felicities of the little hamlet. He little
dreamed that the other, his favorite nephew, had surveyed
it with far less loving, yet more rapacious eyes—that he
would steal back, alone, in disguise, and penetrate the little
sanctuary of peace, hiding among its flowers, as a serpent,
and leaving taint in the place of innocence. The reptile's
mission was successful. The home was polluted, the hope
destroyed, and the little village was no longer the abode of
peace or happiness. Now we see that it is in ruins—that
it is deserted of its people—that its old familiar homes are
solitary, and sinking fast into decay. We may not say that
all this melancholy change was the fruit of this serpent's
visit, but who shall say that it was not ? Who shall measure the suffering and loss to a little rustic hamlet from the
shame and sorrow which defile and degrade one of its
favorite families. The shadow upon one sweet cottage-
home casts a darkening atmosphere, in some degree over
all around it, and lessens the charm which was once enjoyed

all in common, and takes from the beauty of the general landscape. Where the resources of society are drawn from natural and simple causes, we all share in the loss which proves fatal only to the single individual.

But, in place of the two former travellers, whose inauspicious gaze was thus full of mischief to the universal beauties of Charlemont, we see two very different persons. They occupy the same point of survey; they both gaze from the same eminence which erewhile unfolded the charm of a most lovely landscape. One of these strangers, as in the former instance, is a tall, finely-built, noble-looking old gentleman, whose white head declares him to be fast approaching the ordinary limits of the natural life. He was between sixty and seventy years of age, though you would arrive at this conclusion chiefly from the snowy whiteness of his hair, and the serene benevolence of his countenance, showing that the more violent passions were now wholly overcome, and not from any appearance of decrepitude. On the contrary, his bearing is that of a man still vigorous in bone and muscle. He carries himself erectly, alights promptly from his steed, with the freedom and ease of the practised hunter, and there is still, in his movement, the evidence of very considerable physical power, if not of energy. His eye is still of a bright and earnest blue; his cheeks are but little wrinkled, nowhere much seared by either suffering or time, and the ruddy hue which clothes them declare equally for health and vigor.

His companion is a young man who might be twenty-five or thereabouts. In respect to frame, size, bearing, he might be the son of the former. He is of noble figure and stature, of firm, dignified, and easy carriage, and wears a fine, frank expression of countenance. The face, though without one feature like that of the senior, is also quite a handsome one, marked with great serenity, though of a gravity which seemed to declare the presence of emotions of a nature much more serious than any of those which are

caused by thought and study. Though full of intellige
and a fine spirit, the expression is shadowed by a look of
sadness approaching to melancholy. There is a fixedness
and depth in his eyes—an intensity of gaze—which pene-
trates you with a sense of suffering and mystery; suffering
which has been overcome, but which has left its traces, as
the fire which has been extinguished, yet leaves the scorch-
ing proofs of its wing upon the roof and sides of the bright
dwelling over which it once has swept. His mouth, in its
rather close compression, confirms the story of his eyes,
and the beauty of the well-cut lips is somewhat impaired
by the sternness resulting from this additional evidence of
trial, and vexing passions. The mystery which you see
written in the young man's visage is one that invites to the
study of that character, which a single glance persuades
you must be worthy of examination. His movements are
deliberate, his voice is low in tone, quiet, gentle, musical,
yet capable of great and sonorous utterance. There is no
sign of feebleness or indecision of purpose in the movements which are yet slow. On the contrary, every step
which he takes is significant of strength—of powers that
only wait the proper motive, or the sufficient provocation,
to declare themselves with commanding, and even startling
effect. As he stands awhile, after fastening the two horses
in the thicket, and leaning slightly forward, gazes down
intently upon the valley slope, dotted with the decaying
cottages, you read in his look and action a further secret
in which you conjecture a something, which links the fate
of the lonely hamlet with his own fortunes, and confirms,
with a deeper meaning, the sorrowful thought, and saddening memories, which loom out, darkly bright, in all the
lines of his strongly-expressive countenance.

The old man is already seated upon the cliff and looking
forth in silence. The young one joins him with quiet movement, and takes his seat beside him. And thus they sat
together, for some time, without speaking. It would seem

as if they enjoyed a communion of thought and sympathy —that neither needed to speak of reminiscences which were cherished in equal degree by both, and that, whatever the cause of melancholy reflection, it was shared between them.

A considerable interval of time, speaking comparatively, was thus yielded up in silence, to sad if not bitter thought. At length the old man said:—

"We are here, again, William. It is the same, yet not the same. Nature is ever young. Trees, rocks, hills, valleys—these rarely change. Here, without a single companion, as of old! yet how many of our old companions are about us. I feel the former life, if not the ancient feelings. Yet what a change. And five years have done it all! What a brief period! Yet, what an eternity!"

The other did not immediately answer. When he did, he said musingly:—

"I see no sign of human life. I doubt if there be a single inhabitant left."

"Indeed, it looks as if there were none. How strange is it, that, feeling with the place as we both did, and do, we should have so entirely forborne to keep up any communication with it. We know not a syllable of the occasion of these changes. How strange that they should have been so altered! Can there have been any epidemic here? I have heard of none. The village was always healthy. The place is sweet and beautiful. The people were mostly in good circumstances, had few wants which they could not satisfy, and seemed happy enough and contented enough in these abodes. What was the sad necessity, what the vexing appetite which prompted their abandonment. Shall we descend into the valley and inquire further? It may be that we shall find some lingering occupant in some one of the farther cottages. These are evidently abandoned. What say you, William? Shall we feel our way once more along the old familiar places?"

"Ah! sir, with what reason? Shall we behold anything more grateful in a nearer approach. Here, it seems to me, we can behold enough for melancholy thought; and none other can we borrow from the associations with this place. You see yonder the ruins of my father's house. It has evidently been destroyed by fire—the work, no doubt, of some passing incendiary. Yet, among these ruins, I first drew the breath of life; there, I first enjoyed delicious hopes, which the same house saw blasted. My father and mother are wanderers in the far south, and—I had abandoned them. I would see no more. I wonder at the strange anxiety which has prompted me to seek thus much; to come hither, after so long an interval, merely to behold a ruin! I might have known that I should gain nothing from such a survey, but the resurrection of mocking dreams, and delusive fancies, and foolish hopes—upon which, as upon this little hamlet—we may write nothing but the one word—ruin!"

A big tear stood in the young man's eye—a single drop —the outburst of emotions that even manhood, filled with noble ardor, and moved by great energies, could not utterly repress. And again a deep silence, for a while, succeeded to this brief dialogue. At length, the old man laughed with a subdued chuckle—mixed mirth and melancholy.

"Strange, William, that the hovel should so frequently outlast the stately hall and tower. Such is the process by which Time mocks at pride. Look, where my old schoolhouse stands as it did five years ago. There you see the roof, almost black with age, glooming out beneath the shelter of green trees. My favorite oaks, William, still stride about, like ancient patriarchs, spreading great arms as in benediction. Ah! I could embrace them, every one, with the feeling of a son or brother! How much do they recall! It was under their shade that we brooded over the chronicles of old Vertot and Froissart together. They have grown together in my mind with these old chronicles, and

I could fancy the knights of the temple and the hospital all pleasantly encamped beneath their friendly shelter."

" How strange, sir, that the imagination should thus speak out with you, rather than with me. The sight of that wild retreat for our rustic muses brings me other images and aspects, which appeal only to the affections. My fancies, at the sight, bring me glimpses of boyish forms, that leap and run along beneath the shadows. Instead of the trumpets of chivalry, I hear only the merry shouts of boyhood, such as made this little valley ring with the genuine music of the heart in those happy, happy days."

" Music! ah! my dear boy, I little thought it so, when they made my ears ring too, with clamors, which made me pray, a thousand times, for the dreamy and sad silence, such as the scene affords us now. That I should now feel this silence so painfully oppressive, is more profoundly in proof than any other sign, of the terrible character of the human change which the passing time has brought. Where are all these merry children now? The memory of those clamorous shouts, and that happy uproar of boyhood, comes now with a sensible pleasure to my heart, and arouses it with a delicious thrill. And I, who bemoaned the fate which fettered me so long in this obscure hamlet — dead to the world, and wholly unfruitful — even I could be persuaded to entreat of Heaven that the season might return once more. I was not sufficiently grateful, my son, for the peace — with all its boy-clamors — of that rustic solitude. Now, that all is gone, and all is ruin which I see, I feel, for the first time, how very precious and beautiful was it all."

" You have made all this sacrifice for me, my father!" said the young man, while his hand rested fondly upon the arm of the other.

" It was fit I should, William; and you have more than requited me, my son. But, in truth, there was no sacrifice. There was need of change — for me as for you. My own

heart required it. I had grown a discontent. This unper
forming life of simple peace and rustic content, is not to
be allowed to those who have burning thoughts in their
brains, and earnest desires in their hearts. It is for such,
only to snatch moments of this sort of life, as it wore, for
rest and refreshment after toils, and that they may recover
strength for new fields of wrestle, and trial, and performance.
I had lived in it too long. I *was* rapidly sinking
into all sorts of unbecoming dotages. I have grown
stronger, and wiser, and better, from the change. I do not
deplore it, though I may look with sorrow over the mournful
ruins of the once familiar and favorite retreat. It is,
indeed. a melancholy spectacle."

"And how very strange that so short a period should
destroy every vestige of the life and pleasure of the place!"

"Shall we wonder, when we see how brief a term is
needed here to substitute desolation for life, that the great
cities of the past should leave so few vestiges—that the
very sites of so many should be forgotten? Were we now to
descend among the old thoroughfares, we should possibly
lose our way, familiar as was once the path—we should
find ourselves wondering at the decreased or increased
length of distances, at the great size or the smallness of
places, the measure of which seems to have been taken on
our very hearts. We never think of the change in ourselves!'

"But the fate of the place is still so very curious a mystery.
One would think, from what we knew, that every
day would only contribute to its utility, and growth, and
beauty. Here were health, security, sweetness, innocence
—every possible charm—all that should make a village
dear to its inhabitants."

"Ah! my son, but its inhabitants lacked the all-in-all,
content. You, for example, to whom this peaceful dell was
so beautiful, you were one of the first to leave it."

"Yes! But not willingly. I was expelled from it by

cruel necessities, by a harsh and brutal fate. It was with
no exulting desire that I left its sacred abodes. They
refused any longer to entertain me. I was driven ruth-
lessly from the sanctuary which denied me refuge any
longer."

"And I am one of those who rejoice that you were so
driven. The necessity which expelled you from the sanctuary was the mother of a glorious future. It brought out
the manhood that was in you. It taught you to know your
strength and muscle—forced you to their exercise, and
will crown your name with honor!"

"And yet, sir, I would gladly exchange all that I am—
all that I hope to be—for the restoration of that hope and
home of boyhood, which I was thus driven to abandon."

"No, Willie, you would not. This is only the sentiment
of a passing mood, which you will not rationally seek to
encourage. It is better as it is! *You* are better as you
are; and, to-morrow, when you return to your duties, your
performances—the toils you have grappled with so man-
fully—the field into which you have so nobly sunk the
shaft—you will feel how idle is the sentiment which seems
so natural to you now. If this was the scene of your boyish sports and hopes, my son, you are not to forget that it
was also the scene of your disappointments—your sorrows
—your first strifes—your bitter humiliations! Would you
go over that period of doubt, and strife, and scorn, and
shame? Would you feel anew the pang of denial—the
defeat and disappointment of every youthful hope?"

"Do not—do not remind me! It is as you say! And
yet, sir, returning to the subject with which we began, how
strange that all should have abandoned the village. I was
the only *involuntary* exile. I was the only one whom the
fates seemed resolute to expel. Why should *they* fly also,
and so soon after me? Where should my poor old father,
John Hinkley, and my mother, for example, find the motive
for leaving the home where they had so long dwelt happily,

and, in the decline of life, why seek an abode upon the
Choctaw borders? It could not be the love of gain; they
had enough!"

"You forget that your father had become something of a
monomaniac. He followed the ministry of John Cross.
Your departure, too, my son, had probably something to do
with it. His stubborn pride of heart naturally kept him
from making any admissions; but I have no doubt he felt
keenly the wrong that he had done you. The discovery of
the true character of Alfred Stevens must have done a great
deal toward disabusing him of his *superstitions*—for they
were superstitions really—in respect to both of you. What
does your mother say in her last letter?"

"They are well; but she mentions, particularly, that my
father never mentions my name, and avoids the subject."

"A proof that he broods upon it, and with no self-satis-
faction. Your departure, his, and that of the Coopers, are
easily accounted for; and did we know the secret history
of all the other villagers—their small, sweet, deceptive
hopes; each man's petty calculations, and petty projects—
all grounded in some vexing little discontent; there would
be no difficulty, I fancy, in finding sufficient reasons, or at
least motives, for the flight of all."

"Still, sir, there seems to be a fate in it!"

"Why, yes; if by this word, Fate, you mean a Providence. I have no doubt that these sparrows are all, in
some degree, the care of Providence; and, whether they
fall or fly, the omniscient eye sees, and the omnipresent
finger points. Your error, perhaps, lies in the very natural
assumption that mere place, itself, becomes an essential of
humanity. These wandering hearts do not cease to beat
with hope, because they no longer beat in the cottage of
their boyhood. Their limbs do not cease to labor, nor their
minds to think, because they break ground and plant stakes
in remote forests of the south and west. Mere locality is,
after all, a very small consideration, in any question of the

interests of humanity. It is the man that makes the place what it is or should be!"

"I am inclined to think, sir, that we something undervalue the social importance of place. A population loses something of its moral when it wanders. It substitutes a savage wildness for domestic virtues."

"Granted! For a time this is certainly the case. But, on the other hand, an old locality is liable to suffer from the worse evil of moral stagnation; and the cure of this demands the thunder-storm. The extreme conditions usually work out precisely the same consequences in the end; and, in the case of society, the locality is altogether a subordinate condition. My old trees, there, were very grateful to both of us; but I became an imbecile under them, in the enjoyment of the *dolce far niente*—that luxury which has destroyed the very nation from whom we borrow the phrase! And the same delightful condition of *non*-performance, continued for five years, would have ruined *you*, also, for any career of usefulness and manhood. And this would have been a crime, my son, as well as a shame. Neither you nor I, believe me, were designed for the slavish employment—however sweet—

> "To sport with Amaryllis in the shade,
> Or with the tangles of Neæra's hair."

"I know not, sir, I know not! Fame is something—something charming and fascinating—having its uses no doubt; and designed for the natural and gradual elevation of the race as well as individual. But the heart ought not to be sacrificed for the brain—the sensibilities and affections for the genius. There should be a life for each, for all; and to surrender the one up entirely to the other, works dismay in the soul, and decay in the sympathies, and leaves ashes only upon the hearth of home!"

"But why the sacrifice of either, my son? Who says surrender the affections to the genius—sacrifice the heart

to the brain! It is *not* the counsel of Miltom. It is far
from my wish that you should do so. Nourish both. The
heart, in fact, the sensibilities, are the absolute necessities
of genius. The brain, so far from demanding t h e annihilation of the affections and sympathies, actually draws constant food from their abundant sources, by which its own
strength and vitality are cherished for performance. No
intellect is in perfect symmetry unless it maintains a con
stant intercourse with the warmest human affections. It is
altogether a mistake to suppose that they can maintain a
separate existence, or that one can preserve its integrity
without due co-operation with the other. The most health·
genius is that which never surrenders its humanity. It
may suffer disappointment—nay, agony—but it is in the
very moment of the heart's worst sufferings that the intellect is most needed, and it furnishes adequate he l p for support and relief, provided the training of both has been com-
mensurate to their mutual wants and necessities. ”
    "Ah! my dear sir," said the younger shaking his head
mournfully—" you forget my fortunes."
    "Do I? No, indeed! I repeat, my son, that your for-
tunes have been equally beneficial to your head and your
heart. You mistake, altogether, when you confound a disappointment—the defeat and denial of a boyish hope--
with the annihilation of the heart. A hope and fancy are
repeatedly crushed out of existence; but we should err
very greatly to suppose that *the life* of the affections— the
heart—had suffered serious hurt. No! no! Believe me.
your heart is quite as sound as ever. What are the proofs?
In my sight, they are hourly present, if not in yours. You·
disappointments have saddened your fancies, but have they
impaired your strength? They have rendered your thoughts
graver in hue than is usual with your years, but have they
not acquired in vigor what they may have lost in brightness?
You do not *play* now with thought, but you can *work* with
it, as you never did before. You do not sport and trifle

now with life, but you feel it as a circle spreading everywhere, connecting you with all the links of existence, making you sympathize with all its pulses and vibrations, and
sensibly lifting your mood to the contemplation of all its
higher offices and duties. In short, you have made a sudden spring from the dreaming, uncaring, unheeding, nature
of the boy—as it were in a single night—into the active
consciousness of all the responsibilities, glorious though
saddening, which belongs to a proper manhood. Now
men possess real manhood only in degree with their capacity to perform. Had you been still a dweller in Charlemont—had you gained the objects of your boy desires in
that place, you would have sunk into the habitual torpor of
the place. You would never have found out what is in you
—would have been nothing and done nothing."

"I might have been happy!" answered the other gloomily.

"No! my son. You would have gratified a youthful fancy,
and, would have survived it! This is a common history of
what is vulgarly called youthful happiness. What would
have remained to you then? Misanthropy. The graver
necessities of the mind take the place very soon of its boyish fancies, and demand stronger food. Fancy is but the
food of a thought just beginning to develop. It requires
strong meat very soon after, and this can be afforded only
by earnest grappling with care and toil, and trial and pain
—those angel overseers, whom God appoints, to goad the
truant and the idle nature to its proper tasks. I repeat
that your loss in Charlemont is the most fortunate of all
your gains."

"Would I could think so, my father. Yet her image
passes before me ever with so pleading a face. I see her
now, as I have seen her a thousand times among those old
groves; treading those crags; gliding, with eager and fearless step down those precipices which conduct to the silent,
sad, and beautiful tarn, where we were once so fond to

brood. In my mind's eye I shall never cease to behold that
beautiful yet mournful memory — two images, so unlike each
other, of the same being; one proud, and brave, and noble,
like the eagle soaring up in the sunshine; the other gloomy,
dispirited, made ashamed, like the same brave bird, with
wing broken, the film over his eyes, close fettered in a cage
of iron, and with curious fingers pointing to the earth-spots
on breast and pinion."

"A pitiful contrast, in sooth, my son, and such as it is
very natural that your imagination should frequently depict before your eyes. But both of these images will gradually fade from sight. A newer world will supersede your
past; new forms and aspects will take the places of the old;
new affections will spring up in your soul; nay, fresh fancies will wing their way to your heart, and a nobler idea
of love itself will possess your affections. The heart has
resources not less fertile than the fancy. God has not
decreed it to isolation. You will see and feel new plants
of verdure suddenly appearing upon the waste places; nay,
the very heat and ashes of former passions prepare the
ground for superior plants of more verdure, strength, and
beauty The time will come when you will wonder that
you ever felt the pang and privation which trouble you
now. Five years hence you will be unwilling to believe
me when I describe, as I hope playfully to do, the fierce
troubles of your soul at present."

The youth shook his head negatively, as he said—

"Impossible!"

"One thing is certain, William. You are now confes
sedly one of the first lawyers in Kentucky. Our little world
acknowledges your power. If politics were your aim, the
field is open to you, and it invites you. Yet, five years
ago, you were desponding on the subject of your capacity.
Then, you had misgivings of your strength, and fancied that
your powers but imperfectly seconded your wish. Your
ambition was then regarded as the dream of a foolish van-

ity, which was destined only to rebuke and disappointment.
Look at your position now—behold your own performances. It was but the other day, when Harry Clay said
to me: ' He is the most promising of our young men. I
would not counsel him to politics; yet, if he should desire
that field, he will conquer in it. He has the steadfastness,
the enlarged view, the industry, and the endowment, which
will give him rank among the highest whenever he shall be
disposed to fling off the mere lawyer, and embark on the
troubled sea of politics.' "

" In truth, a troubled sea."

" Yes ; but so far a persuasive one to ambition, as, just
now, it needs such a good helmsman for the ship of state.
I counsel politics no more than our friend Clay ; but the time
approaches when no man of mark will be allowed to withhold his seamanship. Keep to the law for the present, and
wait your time. I would have no son of mine—no friend
—undertake state affairs of any sort till he is fairly thirty
or thirty-five. A democracy is the very world in which to
break down premature young men. It is the very world
for strong men — naturally strong — who have allowed themselves to harden into perfect manhood before they attempt
a province in which the wrestle is beyond their strength.
You are naturally too well endowed and too well trained
to sink into the mere lawyer. You will never forego the
nobler powers of generalization in the practice of a petty
detail. The very troubles of your affections have thrown
the proper burdens upon your mind ; and you will go on
conquering, my son, until you have equally purged your
heart and your understanding of all these delusions. You
will forget, among other dreams of boyhood, the very one
which has had such an effect, for good upon your fortunes,
and for evil, as *you* think, upon your heart. The image of
Margaret Cooper will fade from your fancy, or remain only
as a study, in which you will be just as likely to wonder at
your delusion as to cherish it fondly. There will come a

season when your heart will open to a wiser, and purer and nobler affection — when you will seek and find an object of attachment, who will be more worthy of your love, and will be better able to requite your desires."

"Never! never!—no, sir, no! I freely tell you that, promising as are my social prospects now, honorable as is the reputation which I have acquired, grateful as the future promises to be to my ambition, I would gladly forego all, were I once more restored to that one hope of my boyhood — could I attain now, in her original purity, the one being who filled all my desires, and might have satisfied all my cravings of heart."

"You think so now ; but wait. Five years have wrought the most wonderful changes in your mind. Another five years will work other changes, quite as wonderful, in your affections. The destiny before you will not be defrauded. After all, the heart of man keeps very much in the track of his intellect; and the charm that satisfies the one at first, requires in the end to satisfy the other. You will forget—"

Here a sudden start and exclamation of the young man arrested the remarks of the aged speaker, who, the next moment, was confounded to behold his companion rise up at a single bound, and rush almost headlong down the hill He called to him :—

"What is the matter, William ? What do you see?"

The youth did not answer, but, throwing out his arms as he ran. he pointed to the opposite end of the valley, where following with his eyes, the senior caught a glimpse—but a single glimpse—of a female figure, in widow's weeds, re tiring from sight. In another moment the figure was hidden from view by the crags of the range of heights beyond The young man, meanwhile, kept a headlong course, still downward, pursuing his way into the valley of the settle ment, with the fleetness of a deer.

"Can it be Margaret Cooper whom he has seen ?" mur

mured the old man to himself, as he slowly rose up, and prepared to follow, but more slowly, down the hill.

"Can she be here? can she be living? and how has she contrived to elude all inquiry? If it be she, how unfortunate! It will revive, in full force, all his wild anxieties. It will arrest him in the nobler course he is now pursuing. But no, no! I have better hopes. God will not suffer this defeat!"

CHAPTER II.

THE UNEXPECTED MEETING.

THE five years of lapsing events which, in the career of William Hinkley, had brought him to distinction in his profession, the esteem of society, the love and admiration of friends, had been productive of very different results to the woman he had once loved with all the ardor of ingenuous passion, and for whom, as we have seen, he still entertained emotions, if not affections, of the most tender regard and interest. She had sunk from the heights of self-esteem to the lowest depths of self-abasement. She, the village-beauty, proud equally of her intellect and personal charms, had, in this to her dreary interval, been fettered in an obscurity as impenetrable by others as it was deep, dark, and humiliating, to herself. Of the cruel sorrows of this period it is impossible to make any adequate record. The gnawing misery of hopelessness; the consciousness of sin and weakness; the bitterness of defrauded hopes, and aims, and powers; the loss of name, position, love; the forfeiture of all those precious regards which are so necessary to the life of the young, the beautiful, and the ambitious—these had worked their natural consequences, in the thought perpetually brooding over the ruin, in which every flower of hope, and pride, and love, had been stifled in dust and ashes.

Yet she lived! She would willingly have died. She prayed for death. She meditated death by her own hands; and it was the indulgent providence of God alone—by almost direct interposition—that saved her from this last dreadful method of escape from the terrible soul-suffering of those last five years.

Strange that she should thus live—with her pride, and all her passions, rendered mad by disappointment, preying perpetually upon her heart! For a time, there was a weary blank in her existence, in which she did not even dream. Her vitality seemed utterly suspended. When she recovered from this condition, which was meant as a merciful alleviation of her acuter sufferings, it was to endure the active gnawings of her grief. For another period, her life was a long spasm—a series of spasms—in which she was conscious of no security from hour to hour—in which all in her soul was in wild uproar and confusion—storm and calm alternating ever—and no certainty of life or sanity for a single day. That was the period of her greatest peril. It had been easy for her then, by a single blow, to end the terrible history; and a thousand times, during this period, did she murmur to herself—

"It is surely not so difficult to die!"

But they watched her! The deed was prevented. She lived, and lived for another passion—darker even than suicide, and more deadly. To this she bent all her thoughts. To this she gave all her prayers. Shame, defeat, overthrow—the utter annihilation of all her ambitious dreams—those brought her none of those humiliations of pride in which the prayer for grace and mercy find their origin, and realize the blessed fruits of penitence. The blow, which humbled her for ever in society, had only wounded her pride, not crushed it; only stung her brain to madness, not soothed it with a sense of feebleness and dependence, making it a fit home for gentle thoughts, and subdued desires, and a strengthening humility. Her prayers, for a long season, were addressed only to the gratification of that wild justice which infuses the savage soul with the dream of vengeance!—

"Being mortal still, [she] had no repose,
   But on the pillow of revenge! Revenge —
Who sleeps to dream of blood; and, waking, glows
   With the oft-baffled, slakeless thirst!—"

There was but one victim. But the fates interposed for his safety—and her own. She was in no situation to gratify her desires. She knew not how to name—knew not where to seek—the spoiler of her happiness. She was a woman, and must wait her time—wait on circumstance and chance, and the favoring succor of that subtle demon whom she called upon in place of Deity. And he finally responded to her call.

But there was a dreary interval to be overcome and endured.

In this period, her whole person, as her soul, had undergone a curious change. The fair, white skin became jaundiced. The fine, dark, expressive eye had assumed a dull, greenish hue, and seemed covered with a filmy glaze. Her frame became singularly attenuated, her limbs feeble; she frequently sunk from exhaustion, and would lie for hours, gasping upon her bed, or upon the dried leaves of the forest, in the shades of which she perpetually sought escape from the sight of human eyes. That she survived the long strain upon her faculties of mind and body, was wonderful to all. Yet she did survive.

More! she gradually threw off the feebleness and suffering of the frame. She was again endowed with a noble hardihood of constitution. She had a proud, steadfast, enduring will. The very working of her passions, now concentrated upon a single object, seemed, after a certain period of prostration, to work for her relief. Gradually another change followed. Her skin became cleared. The jaundice disappeared. Her eyes became healthy in expression — bright as before—but not happy in their brightness; luminous, yet wild; of a gloomy beauty, in which the whole face shared. She did not smile again, or, if she did, it was

in a manner to mock the smile with bitterness. Her mind
resumed its activity, though it still pursued what the mor-
alist may well call an insane direction, fixed only upon a
single object, which seemed to supersede all others. For-
merly, she had felt, and dreamed, and imagined, poetry;
now she wrote it—wild, dark, spasmodic fancies glowing
in her song, which was wholly impulsive, not systematic—
the effusion of blood and brain working together intensely,
and relieving themselves by sudden gushes which were like
improvisations.

It was sometime after she had reached this condition,
when, one day, she declared her intention to revisit Charlemont. Her retreat was only seven miles from this spot, in
an obscure farm to which no public road conducted.

Her mother somewhat wondered at this desire, but did
not oppose it. They were both well aware of the change
which five years had wrought in the fortunes of this once
beautiful village. It had been productive of sore loss to
them in money. They had sold their little cottage, under
mortgage, and the purchaser had abandoned the property,
leaving the debt unpaid. Something was said by Margaret
of the necessity of seeing that the building was kept in repair, but the suggestion was only made as a sort of pretext
justifying the visit. The mother very well knew that the
daughter had another motive. Though by no means a sagacious interpreter of heart or mind, she yet readily understood that the proposed visit was the fruit of some morbid
fancy; but she did not see tha any evil would result from
suffering Margaret to indulge ner mood; and, in fact, she
had long since learned that opposition was by no means the
process by which to effect her objects with her daughter, or
to bring her mind into the proper condition in which it usually regards the social requisitions as the natural law. She
offered no objection accordingly.

The little family *carry-all*—a snug, simple box, drawn
by one horse—was got in readiness, the negro driver

mounted, and the girl departed upon her secret mission of
sad thought, and melancholy revery, in a region which had
been the source of all her sorrows.

She sought the old cottage, penetrated its silent chambers, and busied herself for awhile in a search of closets
which seemed to afford her nothing. Her search led her to
sundry bundles of old papers. These she pulled apart and
examined in detail. From these she extracted some scraps
which she put away carefully in her bag, and after this, she
scarcely looked at the dwelling, which already needed the
regards of locksmith and carpenter.

How soon the favorite place goes to ruin if left to itself.
There shall be a snug simple house, in which your heart
first found its want, your soul its first speech, your dearest
joy its first satisfaction, and five years after you have abandoned it, it will be desolate—the lichen will glide over its
walls; the door will fall from its hinges; the shutter, the
sash, drop to fragments. Shall time spare us any more
than our dwellings?

Yet can he not utterly destroy!

The heart recognises a soul in the lonely and desolated
ruin. There is a subtle spirit appealing to you from every
corner. Nay, you will surely hear voices in the lonely
rooms which call upon all the affections to restore, rebuild
—return!

Poor Margaret heard these voices all around her. They
startled her. They seemed to mock her fall—to depict
the state from which she had fallen—to compare her own
with the desolation of the scene around her. And finally,
they spoke in the well-remembered tones of her betrayer.
She fancied she heard Alfred Stevens close beside her,
whispering his subtle eloquence—those snares of fancy and
passion which he had so successfully woven for her ruin.

And this voice lifted her into strength. Then she remembered that she had an oath of vengeance; and she went
forth from the lonely dwelling, only half conscious that she

went, and almost heedless of her steps, she took her way up the rocky heights to the lonely tarn whither she had so often wandered with *him*.

And the past returned to her, memory, and filled her imagination with all its chronicles of mixed sweet and bitter—pride and shame—and keen was the agony that followed, and terrible the oath which she now renewed, of vengeance for the wrongs she had suffered and the degradation which she must perforce endure. She had no future, but in the accomplishment of this one terrible oath; and she renewed it with fearful brevity and solemnity in the shadows of those towering rocks, above the deep dark waters of the silent lake—by the very scenes which had witnessed her overthrow, she called for witnesses to confirm her oath!

And what a picture to mind and eye did she present at that moment—still young, still beautiful—of noble figure, commanding form, bright haughty eye, and a face gloomily lovely—as she stood forward on the edge of the precipice, and looked forth to sky and rock, her hand slowly rising in adjuration, as simple as it was stern and imposing.

What witnesses, of her wrongs and sufferings, her wild hopes and haughty aims, and their cruel defeat, were all the objects which encompassed her. They were a part of herself. They had taught, informed, encouraged her nature. She had lived in and with them all, and all, in turn, had infused their nature into hers. These rocks had taught her height and hardihood; these waters, depth and contemplation, and the tender nursing of solitary fancies; the woods had lessoned her heart with repose; and the skies, with their eagles ever going upward, had taught her aspiration.

Very mournful were they now in her eyes, assembled as witnesses of her fate. She was their child. Their sad aspects were those of loving parents defrauded of every hope. They might well attest with sympathetic sternness of brow,

and sadly echoing voices, her brief, savage oath of vengeance.

" Yes," she murmured, " ye were all the witnesses of my
wrongs, my blindness, my madness, my simple faith, and
cruelly-abused confidence. Here it was, that I listened to
the subtle voice of the beguiler, even as the drowsing
eagle, to the spells of the serpent, while he winds himself
fatally about the neck of the free bird of the mountain !

" Oh ! why did ye not fall upon me, rocks—upon both
of us—ere I hearkened to the lying tempter—who deluded
me with my own hopes, and made my own daring aspirations
the very spells by which to destroy me !

" Why, waters, when I fell headlong into your embrace,
did ye not engulf me for ever. Any fate had been better
far than this !

" Cruel wast thou, that day, in thy loving-kindness, William Hinkley, when thou drew'st me forth from their abys-
ses !

" Verily, thou hadst *thy* vengeance, William, for all the
scorn which I gave thee in return for love, in the misery
for which thou hast preserved me !

" Oh ! thinking of all that time—of the fond, foolish
vanity which so uplifted me, only to fling me down for ever
from my pride of place and hope—I could weep tears of
blood, tears of blood !

" But mine eyes are dry. Would I could weep !

" Alas, the sorrows that deny the heart its tears are such
only as fill it with gall and venom ! Wonder not, Alfred
Stevens, when I face thee with death and terror !—Oh,
when we meet ! when we meet !

"And we *shall* meet ! I feel that we shall meet. There
is a whisper, as that of a fate, or a demon, that breathes in
mine ears the terrible promise. We shall meet !—thou,
and I—and—Death !—"

And she crouched down upon the boulder upon which
she had been standing, on the very brink of that dark and

silent lake, and buried her face within her hands, as if to shut out from sight the images of horror which that promised meeting had raised up before her imagination.

Poor, desolate woman! There was still a strife in her heart, of contending hate and tenderness. The woman who has once loved, however mistakenly, unwisely, and to her own ruin, never altogether loses the sentiment which even her destroyer has inspired. It is still a precious sentiment. It pleads in his behalf; and if he be not heartless, and cold, and cruel, it will not wholly plead in vain. Mercy will interpose against hate, and the hand of vengeance will be apt to fall nerveless, even when about to strike fatally.

But mercy does not plead for Alfred Stevens. He had shown no redeeming tenderness. He had proved himself heartless — wantonly cruel — indifferent to the desolating doom which his guilty passions had brought upon her. Margaret Cooper could feel tenderness still, but it was not for him. Here, her soul was resolute, her will iron. She did not recoil from the horrible deed on his account, but her own. It was the recoil of the feminine nature alone, and not pity, that made her shrink from the fearful images of blood which were conjured up by her excited fancy.

But, suddenly, in the midst of her dream of terror and revenge, she starts — she starts to her feet, with a bound that makes the rock vibrate and quiver beneath her, on the very edge of the precipice.

A voice is calling to her from the opposite side of the lake. But a single word she hears:—

"Margaret!"

She looks beyond the water, and on a cliff above the lake she sees the figure of a man — a noble, graceful figure — whom she recognises in a moment.

"God of heaven! it is William Hinkley!"

The words are only murmured. She waves her hand out involuntarily, as if to say:—

2*

"Away! we must not meet! There must be no speech between us!"

And then she starts, recedes from the stream, and, with hasty steps, glides into the cover of rock and forest. She was gone from sight in another moment, hurrying down the cliffs to the road where her carriage had been left at a little distance.

William pursued—without any purpose, except to meet, to see, to speak once more to the woman whom he had loved, but with whom, as a single moment of thought would have assured him, he could have no closer communion.

He pursued, but at disadvantage. He was compelled to compass the lake which lay between them. He pursued with the fleet bounds of the practised mountaineer, over the cliffs, and through the umbrage; but in vain. She had reached the carriage ere he had descended from the heights. She had leaped in, and, with stern, low words, through closely-compressed lips, she said to the negro driver:—

"Drive fast!—fast as you can!"

When the young man descended to the valley-road, she was gone. He could only catch the faint echoes of the receding wheels.

CHAPTER III.

PHILOSOPHIES OF AGE AND YOUTH.

"Now should we make moral anatomies
Of these two natures — hostile, yet so like."

AND thus they met—and thus they parted!

Both creatures seeking the ideal; born for other things than mere bread and meat; born for love, for performance, for triumph; neither satisfied — both desponding : the one with the half-fanciful griefs of youth, which are designed to strengthen, even as the obstruction which taxes and strains yet expands and improves the muscle ; the other with shame, which depresses the energies that it may refine them, and humbles the pride that it may waken the heart to becoming sensibilities.

The one retires from the fruitless interview sad, disappointed, but, just in the same degree, better prepared to pursue one steady aim to right and complete achievement; the other, having her aim also, but one of a kind still further to humble pride, awaken sensibility, and, through agony, to conduct to peace !

Very different their objects, desires, performances ; but both working out results for humanity, such as, in the progress of the life-ordeal, gradually inform society with new aspects and properties in man, and unfold the exactions of a progress in the ages, whose necessities evolve, through vice itself, the true conditions of all virtue.

Shall they ever meet again, and how ? Shall they realize

the vague hopes and objects that now persuade both minds? shall they ever become to each other more than they are now? shall *he* attain greater triumphs of intellect—better securities of the heart? shall *she* find the peace which she yearns for, even more than the wild justice which she seeks? will she regain the wing of her youth and innocence, and steadily develop the gradual powers of that ambitious genius which, in the very daring and pride of its aim, blinded her wholly to the dangers of her flight? We can not prescribe the course and conditions of their progress: we must be content simply to follow, and record them. They are in the hands of a self-made destiny, and must, because of will, and passion, and peculiar aims, determine their own fates. It is not for art to pass between, to interpose, to prevent, or pervert, or in any way alter, the fortunes of those whose own characters constitute the arbitrary necessities governing equally their lives and our invention.

Sad, silent, full of roused thoughts and conflicting emotions, Margaret Cooper drove home to her obscure farm stead, musing to herself, and murmuring within her soul of the past and of the future.

That single glance of an old and rejected lover—that one imploring word from his lips—smote on her heart with a sense of agonizing self-reproach. Her thoughts, framed into speech, might have run as follow:—

"With him I might have been happy. He was young, truthful, honorable. He loved me: that I felt then—that I know now. He would have cherished me with affection, as he approached me with devotion! Yes! I might have been happy with him!—

"But I knew him not! I undervalued him. I regarded him as the obscure peasant—having no high purpose—no mind—no great thoughts and ambitious fancies—such as should properly mate with mine!

"Even in this was I mistaken! He had the faculties, but I was not wise enough to see them. I was blinded by

my own wandering visions — that miserable vanity which
relished no spectacle that did not present me with some
image of myself — which, in perpetual self-delusion, could
see nothing in the qualifications of another!

"Yet, how bravely and nobly did that young man declare himself at last! how wisely did he speak! how clearly
did he see the dangers gathering about me! how, with what
instinct, did he pierce the secret of that cunning serpent!—
while I, who despised him for the very humility of his aims
— the very modesty of his passion — I could see nothing.
I was a fool! a fool!—blind, deaf, mad! But for this, we
might have been happy together. It might have been! it
might have been!

"Oh, mournful words!—'It might have been!'

"Too late! too late!

"Love is impossible to me now. The dream is gone!
the hope — every hope! Even ambition is impossible!
Alas, what a dream it was! how wild, how impossible from
the first! Yet, I believed it all. Fool! fool! as if such
could be the fortune of a woman! Here, too, in this savage region of shadow and obscurity, a woman conquering
position, high place, high honors, great distinction! And
I believed it all!—believed him, that treacherous serpent,
when he crept with the subtle, sweet, lying whisper to my
heart! O fool! fool! fool!

"But I am awake now! I no longer delude myself!
None can delude me now!

"Yet, to lose this so precious delusion! Oh, the misery
of this conviction, for in losing this I have lost all!

"Yet, was it a delusion? Could I not have achieved
this distinction? Is it true that there is no field for woman's genius? is it true that, of all this great country,
there is no one region where the wisdom and the inspiration of woman can compel faith and find tribute? is she to
be a thing of base uses always, as the malignant Iago has
declared her? God, thou hast not designed this — else

wherefore hast thou given her the will to soar, the faculty
to sing, the genius to conceive, the art to refine and beau-
tify, the sensibilities which make the beautiful her dream
and her necessity alike!

"It is a mystery—a mystery!

"And I am hopeless! lost! losᵤ! All lost—lost to all!
Nothing left me but—"

She buried her face in her hands; she shuddered. The
terrible images, thronging about the one vindictive passion
which her soul now entertained and fostered, seemed to
gather before her eyes, and she covered them as if to shut
out the fearful spectacle. She murmured audibly, after a
brief pause:—

"I would I had not seen William Hinkley to-day! The
sight of him has weakened me. His voice seems to ring
even now so mournfully in my ears—'Margaret!'

"How often have I heard that name upon his lips—so
tenderly—so pleadingly always—with so much sweetness
and humility!

"I despised him then. I looked down upon him then—
with scorn—with contempt. O Margaret, Margaret! and
thou darest not look upon him now! Shame, shame! my
cheek burns with shame, as I think of him, and remember
the calling of his voice.

"Yes! yes! we might have been happy together!

"Too late! too late! I can be happy no more!"

We need not listen any longer to these mournful memories of ruined hopes and lost honors, defeated ambition, defrauded affection, bitter self-reproach, and still-sleepless
and ever-goading passions. We need not follow her to the
obscure retreat where she has striven for five dreary years
to bury out of sight the secret of her shame. Enough that
we have put on record the condition of her moods—her
broken spirit, her almost purposeless intellect, and the one
hope—the only one—which she seems to entertain. These
will suffice as clues for the future, showing the *motif*, the

key note, of much that prevails in the melancholy history which follows.

Let us return to the young man whose disappointment we have just witnessed. He, too, as we have seen, has his griefs and trials ; but, unlike hers, they are not of a sort to bring humiliation in their train.

When he found his pursuit was vain, and when the last faint echoes of the receding carriage-wheels came to his ears, he clasped his hands spasmodically together.

" She would not see me ! she would not even speak with me ! She feels the old scorn ; she knows not that I am no longer the obscure peasant that she knew me once !"

Foolish youth ! as if the fact, even if known to her, that he had won successes, and was glowing with the prospects and promises of fame, would have made her more tolerant of his presence.

It was shame, not scorn, which made her fly from that meeting.

It was a wild and stifling sense of agonizing humility that made her wave him off, in despair, as one of the most knowing witnesses of her fall from the proud heights where he had once loved to behold and do her honor.

Scorn now for him, on the part of Margaret Cooper, was impossible. It was fear, shame, horror, terror—nay, a sense of justice, and a new feeling of respect, if not reverence—that made her shrink before his face.

Brooding sadly upon his disappointment, with bewildering thoughts and conflicting feelings, the young man slowly made his way back through the valley of Charlemont, going unconsciously among the deserted dwellings, in the direction of the heights where he had left his venerable companion. As he passed the schoolhouse, he heard the voice of the senior calling to him from the shade of the great oaks by which it was overhung.

He joined him in silence.

The old man was sitting upon the turf beneath the trees.

a thoughtful smile upon his countenance. He was once more in the well-remembered places in which so many years of his life had been spent. Here he had himself mused and meditated, from a safe distance, the capricious changes and frauds of busy life among the crowd. Here he had given the first lessons, in the humanities, to the young man who now made his way in silence and sat down beside him.

"Well," said the elder, "did you overtake her, William?"

"You saw her, then?" was the indirect reply.

"Yes, I saw a female, in widow's weeds, but only for a moment. She disappeared among the rocks in an instant after. I concluded, from the wild haste of your movement, that you had recognised her as Margaret Cooper. Was I right?"

"Yes!"

"Did you speak with her?"

"No, sir; she fled from me — waved me off as I called to her, and disappeared in the thicket. When I succeeded in getting round the lake where I saw her, she was gone. I could just catch the sounds of carriage-wheels. She still scorns or hates me as much as ever."

"She does neither, my son. On this subject you seem to lose all your usual powers of reasoning. Margaret Cooper would not see, or speak with you, from very shame and humiliation. Why should she speak with you? Have you anything of a pleasant kind to communicate to each other? Why should she see you? To be reminded only of a history full of mortification to her! You are unreasonable, my son."

The other had no answer.

"And now, William, pray tell me why you desired to see her. You have, no doubt, some of your old feelings for her; but is it really in your thought to marry Margaret Cooper?"

"Oh, no, sir!—no! How could you suppose such a thing?"

"I do *not* suppose such a thing, and therefore I say that you are very unreasonable, nay, more, unkind and cruel, in your attempt to see her. You have no business with her; you have no reason to suppose that you can help her in any way; and your passion for her—whatever of it now remains—is not such as to prompt you to make her your wife. You obeyed only a youthful impulse in desiring to see her, without reflecting upon the cruelty of the proceeding. It was this blind impulse only; for I know you too well to think that you would be thus moved by a merely wanton, and, in respect to her, a cruel curiosity."

"You are right, sir. It was a blind impulse. I am a boy still. I shall never be wise."

"Nay! nay! you do yourself wrong. If to be wise required that we should never be wrong—should never feel an impulse, and in the moment obey it—I should agree with you, and argue against your intellect and moral with yourself. But, you are simply young, ardent, sensitive, with a free gush of blood from the heart to the brain, such as time and training only will enable you to regulate. We must learn to wait on youth. All in due season. It is enough for me to see that you are in the right course, generally, though sometimes, like a young and fiery Arabian, you bolt the track. But, the present opportunity for a lesson must not be foregone. I hope that you will never again repeat this cruelty to this unhappy woman. She has shown you always, as well in the day of her pride as in that of her shame, that she does not sympathize with your affections. You yourself admit that, even were she to do so, you could never offer yourself to her in marriage. She has in no way given you to believe that she needs your services either as man or lawyer. We know that, though in moderate circumstances, she needs no succor in money. Now, on what pretence of reason would you seek to see her? What pretext of humanity, or law. of manhood, or sympathy of any sort, can be urged for your thrusting yourself upon a person who distinctly shows you that she desires no communion with you. I repeat, she does not scorn or hate you, William, but the meeting with you must necessarily be painful to her. Why should you inflict this pain ?"

" No more, sir, please say no more. I will not err in this manner again."

The young man spoke with a choking effort, and his head hung down, and a great drop fell from his eyes.

" Impulse, by a law of nature, is necessarily a selfishness. Our duty, for this reason is to curb it. Impulse rarely allows us to recognise the rights of others, their situation or their sensibilities. It is humanity only, that requires that we should set reason on perpetual watch, as a good house-dog, to see that this outlaw, impulse, does not break down the door, and break into the close, to the terror, if not the destruction, of the trembling flock within."

" Enough on this head, sir. I will not err again."

" Another, my son, of quite as much importance to yourself and of even more importance to others. You have chosen a profession. A profession, once chosen, constitutes a pledge to the Deity for the proper working out of your human purposes, and the exercise of your peculiar gifts. Passions, and fancies, and desires, which keep us away from our duties — which make us work sluggishly at them, and without proper sympathy and energy, are indulged sinfully. You must fight against them, Willie. You must not only give up the pursuit of Margaret Cooper — as I know you will — but you must give up the very thought of her."

" How is that possible ?"

" It *is* possible. It must be done. You have but to resolve, Willie ; and be equally resolved upon the law ! You must give up Eros, and all the tributary muses of that god.

They still too much employ your thought. Look at what I copied last night from the fly leaf of your docket."

The senior produced a sheet of paper, and in somewhat lackadaisacal accents, read the following verses: —

SING NOT OF FAME.

I.

"Sing not of Fame! There was a time
Such song had suited well mine ear,
When passion had sought, perchance through crime,
Ambition's laurelled pomps to wear;
The wild desire, th' impetuous thirst,
The wing to soar, the will to sway,
Had led me on, through fields accurst,
On all life's precious things to prey.
Sing not of Fame.

II.

"Oh! rather sing of lonely hours,
And sleepless nights and mournful sighs,
When on his couch of blasted flowers,
Despair looks up with loathing eyes;
In vain, with visions straining far,
Hope seeks dear shape and baffled dream;
And wandering on, from star to star,
Finds mockery in each golden gleam.
Sing not of fame!"

"Now, Willie, these are what the newspapers would call very good verses; nay, there are some moralists. even in the pulpit, who, regarding the one proposition only, which rebukes ambition, would hold them to contain very proper sentiments. Yet they are all wrong."

"Oh! sir, waste no more words upon such a theme. It is a poor trifle. I did not mean that you should see it. Give it me, sir, or tear it up if you please."

"Nay, nay, I will do neither, Willie. They will better represent my sentiment than yours. It is for him whose own struggles of ambition have resulted in vanities, to declare ambition itself a vanity; but if it be such. it is one which is at once natural and of the best uses to humanity. Were it not for ambition, ours would be a brute world merely. There would be little in life, worth more than a good grazing patch to a hungry buffalo. It is ambition that puts in exercise all the agencies of art and civilization. It is ambition that sires all public virtues. I do not now mean that poor drivelling vanity, which foolish people call ambition, but that glorious builder and destroyer, who makes great empires, and achieves great results, and wrestles and toils for the victory, and is never so well satisfied as in the toil and the conflict, without one moment considering the results to self. Its presence implies strength for achievement, courage to dare new paths, enthusiasm to sustain against defeat, power to conceive and create agencies, and art to work out all the processes of great and bold and novel performance. This is my notion of ambition, and the fame which follows, or should follow such performances, is a legitimate object of human desire—but only where the endowment really exists."

"Ah, sir, this brings me to my particular trouble, and, no doubt, justifies the sentiment of my ballad. ˙ What if I really lack the endowments which, alone, have the right to crave the laurel? It is your affectionate interest, alone, I fear, which holds them to be in my possession."

"Not so, my son. I have no doubts of your possessions —nay, have little of the use which you are destined to make of them. I know, too, that your song is but the fruit of a temporary despondency—the voice of a momentary mood, in which the sensitive nature rather rests herself than desponds. We are all more or less liable to these fits of despondency, and they have their uses. They fling the mind back upon the heart, and contribute to check its froward tendencies. They counsel due caution and humility to progress. They teach modesty to conquest. I do not fear them in your case, though I counsel you against too great indulgence of them. You would feel them even if you had never been denied by Margaret Cooper. They are signs, in fact, of the ambitious nature which thus deplores

Its own slow progress. But too much encouraged—and they have their beguiling attractions to a nature such as yours—they are apt to enfeeble. They encourage revery, which is always a dangerous pleasure, as it induces inaction. In our world, the demands of society require sleepless activity and vigilance. If we pause too long for rest—if we too much dream—we wake to find some other person in possession of our conquests. You are now with hand upon the plough, and there must be no misgiving—no hesitation. To-morrow, as Milton hath it—' to fresh fields and pastures new.' And you will feel this new impulse to-morrow. You will forget your disappointment of heart—I should say fancy rather—in fresh motives to struggle. You will one day wonder, indeed, that Margaret Cooper should have been so dear to you."

"Never! never!"

"Ay, but you will, and forget her beauties and charms, her bold talent and commanding nature, in still superior attractions."

The youth shook his head with mournful denial.

"So will it be, Willie. That the boy should love at seventeen or eighteen—that he should *insist* upon loving at that period—nay, *fancy* the charms which inspire passion—is his absolute necessity. But the passion of this period is still but a boy passion only. His heart will rarely be touched by it. I would not have your passion absorbed by your ambition. I would only use the one passion to restrain and regulate the choice of the other. Do you suppose that God has made us so inflexible that but one woman in all the world should satisfy the longings of the heart? If so, and you never should meet with this one woman? Besides, do you not see how perfectly childish it is to suppose, at twenty five—when youth is all vigor; when every muscle is a conscious power; when the heart and head are full of powers; all demanding exercise; when the fancy is on perpetual wing; when the imagination daily communes with some ideal, bringing out the wing into the sunshine—how childish then to fancy that life can be without purposes, and hope no longer a thing of aim, filled with generous desires! Your ballad, as I have said, declares only for a temporary mood which another day will dissipate. You have only read too much of Byron. This mood was his *rôle*. It was at once true and false. True, as it illustrated a temporary mood; false, as it insisted upon this mood as a fatality; making that a life, which was only a passing cloud over the face of life."

The subject had led the old man on much farther than he had designed. The youth submitted patiently to his ancient teacher. It was thus that his youth had been lessoned: thus that his heart and fancy had been trained; so that, with all his seeming impulse and despondency, his aims were really more in harmony with his powers, than is usually the case with most young men.

We have dwelt longer upon this sort of teaching than is necessary to our story—*as a story*. But we have had our object in our desire for the proper characterization of both parties. The novel only answers half its uses when we confine it to the simple delineation of events, however ingenious and interesting.

There was a brief pause in the dialogue, when the elder, without leaving the subject of conversation, presented it to his young companion's mood through another medium. He had his objects, we may say, in thus familiarizing the *mind* of the youth with the annoying topic. Could he transfer the case from the courts of the affections to those of the brain—we do not mean to say, from the lower to the upper courts—he felt that he should work very considerably toward the relief of moods which were a little too much indulged in for propriety, and, perhaps, safety.

"It is somewhat surprising, William, that Margaret Cooper never once detec ed your sympathies with poetry, and your own occasional wooings of the muse. Had she

done so, it would, I think, have greatly helped your wooings of herself. Did you ever show her any of your verses ?"

" Never, sir."

" And you never once, I suspect, betrayed any desire to
see her verses ?"

" Never, sir ! I thought only of *her*."

" Had you been a worldling, William, with a better
knowledge of human nature, and *woman* nature, you might
have been more successful. Alfred Stevens knew better.
He simply held the mirror before the eyes of her vanity.
He showed her her own portrait even as she desired to see
it — as she was accustomed to see it. He pleased her *with
herself*. He confirmed her notions of herself. He gave
his sympathies to her ambition, and never troubled himself
about her affections, which he soon discovered were properly approachable only through her ambition. The great
secret of conquest over such persons is to become a necessary minister to their most passionate desires. The devil
worked thus cunningly with Eve. He works, in this very
wise, with all our passions. You might have succeeded as
Stevens did, had you been a student of humanity — had you
been capable of the painful study of its weaknesses, and
willing to descend to the mean occupation of stimulating
them into excesses. This poor girl lived only in her ambition. Her affections were all bonded to her brain. This
made her bold — made her confident of strength. She did
not fear her affections — she did not crave sympathy for
them. She could only do so, after her fall from place and
purity. Had your sympathies been given to her intellect,
and had you shown her your capacity to sympathize fully
with, and appreciate the objects of her own desire, you
could have won all the affections that she was able to bestow. You would be more successful in pursuit now."

" But you can not think, sir, that I have *now* any purpose — any wish ——"

He paused.

"No! that is impossible now, I know. Your own pride,
your own ambition, if nothing else, would preserve you from
any such desire. I am speaking, now, only of the natural
change in her, such as her changed condition necessarily
works. In her fall, her mind became humanized. Her
heart is even purer, and truer now, in its shame—has more
vitality, more sensibility, more delicacy, more sympathy
with the really true and good—than she had when her name
was without spot. Margaret Cooper did not fall through
vicious inclinations, but a wilful pride. I regard her as
far more really virtuous, *now*—as now conscious of the
value of virtuous sympathies—conscious, in other words,
of a heart-development—than she was in the day of her
insolent pride, when her vanity stood unrebuked by any
consciousness of lapse or weakness. The humility which
follows shame is one of the handmaids employed to conduct
to virtue."

And thus, resting upon the hill-side, and looking down
upon that ruined hamlet, age and youth discoursed of the
past, as if life had no future. But the future hath its germ
in the past, and the present is a central point of survey,
from which the wise may behold both oceans. We shall see,
in our progress, what was the result of this serious discourse, which places in our hands certain of the clues to the
tale which follows—which sounds the preluding notes, and
prepares us, in some degree, for the social tragedy which
the rude chronicle of the border-historian has yielded to
the purposes of art.

The sun was rapidly passing down the slope of heaven.
The valley of Charlemont began to look colder and darker
in the eyes of our two companions. They had turned aside
from their appointed road to take a last look, and a final
farewell of the old-remembered places. This done, they
prepared to depart. In another hour they were slowly
riding through the paths of the forest. directing their course
for the dwelling of Edward Hinkley a cousin of William,

who was now a thriving young farmer, in a beautiful tract of country, some twelve miles farther on. While they sat at his cheerful fireside that night, they discoursed of everything but their mournful visit, and the encounter that day with Margaret Cooper. Her name was not once mentioned in William's presence. Ned's fiddle enlivened the family circle after supper, and while the buoyant young man played for his sombre cousin, and the more ancient guest, the thought of William wandered off to the unknown dwelling of Margaret.

Where was she then? How employed? With what hopes, in what condition?

Could he have seen her brooding that night over the meeting of that day! Could he have heard her mournful exclamations of self-reproach—seen with what dreary aspect, she mused on the terrible words: "Too late—too late!" his sympathies would have made him forgetful of all the counsels of his venerable friend. As it was, he heard but little of his cousin's violin. The gay sounds were lost upon his senses. His revery depicted still mournfully enough, though inadequately, the condition of the unhappy woman, isolated by her own intellect as by her defeat and shame. There she sat, in her own lonely chamber, with but one companion—the muse—brooding over her fate until the gloomy thought took the form of verse—the only process left her by which to relieve the over-burdened brain. We shall assert a privilege denied to William, and look over her as she writes. Her verses, singularly masculine as well as mournful, will constitute a sufficient and appropriate prelude, to the sequel of her unhappy story.

> " 'Tis meet that self-abandoned I should be,
> Whom all things do abandon! Where is Death?
> I call upon the rocks and on the sea:
> The rocks subside—the waters backward flee—
> The storm degenerates to the zephyr's breath,
> And even the vapors of the swamp deny

Their poison! It is vain that I would die!
Earth hath not left one charity for me!
Fate takes no shape to fright me — none to save,
Or stifle, and I live as in a grave
Where only death is wanting.
                       Oh! the gall,
And bitter of a life where this is all!
Where one can neither drink, nor dream, nor choke,
And freedom's self is but a bond and yoke,
And breath and sight denial!
                  Why the light,
When the life's hope is sightless? Why the bloom,
When naught of flavor's left upon the taste?
Why beauty, when the earth refuses sight,
Leaving all goodliest things to go to waste? —
And why not Death when Life's itself a tomb!"

CHAPTER IV.

LAW IN DESHABILLE.

"Fun is your true philosophy : the laugh
Still speaks the winning wisdom."

WITH change of scene, we change the nature of the action. Life shows us hourly all the rapid transitions of the kaleidoscope : now we share the bright, now the dark ; now the scintillating gleams of a thousand tiny sparklers, in wreaths, and roses, stars, and beautiful twinings, that seem as endless in variety of form as color — and anon the cold formality of cross and square, and the solemn significance of the perpetual circle, which leaves the eye no salient beauty upon which to rest. The youth weeps to-day, with a grief that seems altogether too hard to bear ; and he laughs to-morrow with a joy that seems as wild, and capricious, and as full of levity and hum, as the life in the little body of a humming-bird. And so, we pass, *per saltem*, from gay to grave, from lively to severe, and if reason be the question, in either change, with quite as little justification in any ! We are creatures of a caprice which might be held monstrously immoral and improper, were it not that caprice is just as essential to the elasticity and tone of humanity, as it is to the birds and breezes.

But, whatever, the changing phase of the mood and the moment, the *motif* of the performance is the same. We get back, all of us, to the old places in our circle. We set

our figures in our drama, and they laugh or weep, droop
or dance, are sad or merry, as the case may be ; but never
materially, or for any length of time, to baffle the fates,
which are just as arbitrary in the world of art, as in that of
humanity. If therefore, we, who have so recently been
dwelling on very gloomy topics—presenting only dark and
sombre, and even savage aspects to the mirror—now show
ourselves in quite other characters and costume, this is no
fault in us, nor does it conflict with the absolute law in our
progress. *That* is written, as indelibly as were the laws
of Mede and Persian, and the *decrees* of court undergo no
fluctuation, though there may be a burst of mistimed merriment during the course of the trial. The change of scene
will make a difference—change of costume, and the intro-
duction of new characters. Besides, as we have already
gravely taught, the moods of mind have no permanent influence, or but very little, on the real nature, the true character of the subject, which has its own atmosphere, and
tends inevitably to decreed results, which, to be legitimate,
must be systematic throughout, and arbitrary in all their
workings. We can not help it, if, while the mournful pro-
cession is in progress to the grave, and the bolt strikes
down the noble, and the gloomy pall hides the bright and
beautiful from loving eyes—if fools laugh the while, and
the cold, the base, the cruel, pursue each their several little, sneaking, scoundrelly purposes, working against the
sweetest humanities of life and culture !

With this *caveat* against any mistakes of assumption, we
raise the curtain upon other scenes and characters.

The city of Frankfort, in the noble state of Kentucky,
is very beautifully situated upon the banks of the river of
that name. It is overlooked by a cluster of steep hills, but
occupies an elevation of its own, at a point where the river
curves gracefully before it, in a crescent figure. The city,
itself, of moderate dimensions at the period of which we
write, is a capital ; handsomely built, laid out in rectangu-

lar sections, and presenting, altogether, a view at once
pleasing and promising, scanned from any of the numerous eminences which look down upon it. A place, now, of
considerable opulence, and tolerably large population, it
was even then distinguished by its numerous men of talent
and people of fashion. Of the former, at this and suose-
quent periods, it has furnished to the Union abundant
proofs; of the latter, the charm will be remembered with
freshening interest, by all who have ever enjoyed the grace
and hospitality of its society.

Upon the resources of this young and promising capital,
however, it is not our purpose to dwell. We are permitted
to glance at its circles only, and to detach, from the great
body of the community, a few only of its members, and such
of its haunts only as can but imperfectly illustrate its virtues. We proceed to introduce them.

The reader will please suppose himself for the time,
within one of those dark, obscure tabernacles—sanctuaries
dare we call them?—which, in the silent, narrow streets
and portions of a city which are usually most secluded from
the uproarious clamors of trade, have been commonly assigned to, or rather chosen by, the professors of the law,
in which to carry on their mysteries in appropriate places
of concealment. Like the huge spiders to which the satirist
has so frequently likened them, these grave gentlemen
have always exhibited a most decided preference for retreats
in dismal and dusty corners. They seem to find a moral
likeness for the craft in the antique, the obscure, and the
intricate ; and with a natural propriety! They seem to
shrink, with a peculiar modesty, from the externally attrac-
tive, the open, the transparent, and the graceful; as calculated to attract too curious eyes, if not admiration ; and
whether it is that their veneration for the profession demands the nicest preservation of the antiquities which it so
loves to enshrine and cherish, even after their uses have
utterly departed, or whether it is that the wisdom which

they practise, is of the owl-like sort which will tolerate no
excess of light, it is very certain that you will find them
always in the most dingy and out-of-the-way dwellings,
in the most dismal and obscure lanes and crannies of a
city. The moral usually determines the externals. It
would seem, among most of the practitioners whom it is my
fortune to know, that anything like a conspicuous situation,
and neat, well-fitted, and cleanlily-painted rooms, would
incur the reproach of professional dandyism. These might
argue, perhaps, against the profundity, the gravity, the dignity, the obscurity, of the sage professor. They might break
the effect of that Burleigh nod which means so much, and
is of such prodigious emphasis, so long as the shaker of the
head shows nothing else, and keeps as dumb as dark!
Such is the prescriptive necessity of these externals, that
you will rarely happen upon the young student who will
readily fall into the levities of clean lodging, decent exte-
rior, and a modern-looking set of chambers.

The office to which we now repair, is one which evidently
belongs to a veteran ; one, at least, who knows what are
the excellent effects upon the vulgar superstition, of the
rust and dust of antiquity. If ever dirt and dismals could
make any one spot more sacred than another, in the eyes
of a grave and learned lawyer — who understands the full
value of mere externals, and of authority upon the vulgar
mind — this was the place. Here dullness was sainted ;
obscurity jealously insured and protected ; dust consecrated
to sacred uses and respect ; and law preserved in maxims
which it would be worse than heresy to question Here,
darkness and doubt were honored things ; and mere accumulation grew into a divinity, whose chaotic treasures no
one ever dreamed to distrust. Authority, here, wielding
her massy tomes, as Hercules his club, craved no succor
from digestion ; knocking reason over with the butt of the
pistol, according to Johnson, when failing to do execution
from the muzzle. One breathed an atmosphere of dust at

the mere sight of these chambers: the dusty desks, dirty books, grimy walls; all inspiring solemn thoughts of the tombs of Egypt and the Assyrian, merely to behold them. The two small apartments, such as a lawyer would regard as snug, were dimly lighted by a single window in each, and these looked out upon a dismal and crowded little court. The panes of the two windows, wretchedly small as they were, had, evidently, never once, since fashioned in their frames, been opened, or subjected to the impertinent agency of soap and water. The sun grew jaundiced as he looked through the sombre glasses. Shelves of cumbrous volumes, all of that uniform vulgar complexion which distinguishes the books of a lawyer's office—a uniform as natural as drab to the quaker, white neckwrappers to the priest, and black to the devil—increased the lugubrious aspect of the apartments. Plaster casts of Coke and Bacon, and sundry other favorite authorities, stood over the book-cases, smeared with soot, and fettered with the cobwebs of three lives, or, possibly, as many generations. The rooms had little other furniture of any sort, except the huge table covered with baize, now black, which had once been green, and which also bore its century of dingy volumes. Rigid cases of painted pine occupied the niches on each side of the chimney, divided into numerous sections, each filled with its portly bundles of closely-written papers:—

"Strange words, scrawled with a barbarous pen."

In short, the picture was that of a law-office, the proprietor of which was in very active and successful practice.

But the gravity which distinguished the solemn fixtures, and the silent volumes, did not extend to the human inmates of this dim lodging-house of law. Two of these sat by the table in the centre of the room. Their feet were upon it at opposite quarters, while their chairs were thrown back and balanced upon their hind legs, at such an angle as gave most freedom and ease of position to the person.

Something of merriment had inspired them, for the room was full of cachination from their rival voices, long before our entrance. Of the topics of which they spoke, the reader must form his own conjectures. They may have a significance hereafter, of which we have no present intimation. It may be well to state, however, that it is our present impression that we have somewhere met both of these persons on some previous occasion. We certainly remember that tall, slender form, that sly, smiling visage, and those huge bushy whiskers. That chuckling laugh enters into our ears like a well-remembered sound; and, as for the companion of him from whom it proceeds, we can not mistake. Every word and look is familiar. It is five years gone, indeed, but the impression was too strongly impressed to be so easily obliterated.

Our companions continued merry. The conversation was still disjointed—just enough being said to renew the laughter of both parties. As, for example:—

"Such an initiation!" said one.

"Ha! ha! ha!" roared the other, at the bare suggestion.

"And did you mark the uses made of old Darby, Warham?"

"No: I missed him before eleven. Did he not escape? Where was he?"

"Quiet as a mouse, unconscious as a pillow, under the feet of Barnabas. Barnabas used him as a sort of footstool. First one foot, then another, came down upon his breast; and you know the measure of Barnabas' legs. Ha! ha! ha!"

"Ha! ha! ha!"

"Hundred-pounders each, by Jupiter. Whenever they came down you could hear the squelch. Poor Darby did not seem to breathe at any other time, and the air was driven out of him with a gush. Ha! ha! ha! It was decidedly the demdest fine initiation I ever saw at the club."

" But Beauchampe !"

" Ah! that was a dangerous experiment. He can't stand the stuff."

" No, Ben, and that's not all. It will not do to put it in him, or there will be no standing him. What passions! Egad, I trembled every moment lest he should draw knife upon the pope. He's more a madman when drunk than any man I ever saw."

" He's no gain to the club. He has no idea of joking. He's too serious."

" Yet what a joke it was, when he took the pope by his nose, in order to show how a cork could be pulled without either handkerchief or corkscrew."

" Ha! ha! ha! I thought he'd have wrung it off."

" That was the pope s fear also : but he was too much afraid of provoking the madman to do worse, to make the slightest complaint, and he smiled too, with a desperate effort, while the water was trickling from his eyes."

" Ha! ha! ha!" and the chuckling was renewed, until the sound of footsteps in the front room induced their return to sobriety.

" Who's there ?" demanded one of the merry companions.

" Me !—the pope," answered the voice of the intruder.

" Ha! ha! ha!" was the simultaneous effusion of the two, concluded, however, with an invitation to the other to come in.

" Come in, pope, come in."

A short, squab, but active little man, whose eyes snapped continually, and whose proboscis was of that truculent complexion and shape which invariably impresses you with the idea of an experienced bottle-holder, at once made his appearance.

" Ha! ha! ha! Your reverence, how does your dignity feel this morning—your nose, I mean ?"

3*

"Don't talk of it, Warham, I was never so insulted in all my life."

"Insulted! How? By what?"

"By what! why, by that d——d fellow pulling my nose."

"Indeed, why that was universally esteemed a compliment, and it was supposed by every one to give you pleasure, for you smiled upon him in the most gracious manner, while he was most stoutly tugging at it."

"So I did, by the ghost of Naso, but reason good was there why I should? The fellow was mad—stark mad."

"Oh, I don't think he would have done you any harm."

"Indeed, eh! don't you. By the powers, and if you have your doubts on that point, get your nasal eminence betwixt his thumb and finger, as mine was, and you will be ready enough to change your notion, before the next sitting of the Symposia. D—n it, I have no feeling in the region. It's as perfectly dead to me ever since, as if it were frozen."

"It certainly does wear a very livid appearance, eh, Ben?" remarked the other, gravely.

"Do you think so?" responded the visiter, with some signs of disquiet.

"Indeed, I do think so. Will you pass Dr. Filbert's this morning? if so, take his opinion."

"I will make it a point to do so. I will."

"It's prudent only. I have heard of several disastrous cases of the loss of the nose. Perhaps there is no feature which is so obnoxious to injury. The most fatal symptom is an obtuseness — a sort of numbness — a deficiency of sensibility."

"My very symptom."

"Amputation has been frequently resorted to, but not always in season to prevent the spread of mortification."

"The devil, you say — amputation!"

"Yes, but this is a small matter."

"What! to lose one's nose — and such a nose!"

" Yes, a small matter. Such is the progress of art that noses of any dimensions are now supplied to answer all purposes."

" Is this true, Warham? But dang it, even if it were, there's no compensating a man for the loss of his own. No nose could be made to answer my purposes half so well as the one I was born with."

"But you do not suppose that you were born with that nose."

" Why not?"

" You were born of the flesh. But that nose is decidedly more full of the spirit."

" That's an imputation. But I can tell you that a man's nose may become very red, yet he be very temperate."

" Granted. But temperance, according to the club, implies anything but abstinence. Besides, you were made perpetual pope only while your nose lasted, and color, size, and the irregular prominences by which yours is so thickly studded, were the causes of your selection. The loss of your nose itself would not be your only loss. You would be required to abdicate."

" But you are not serious, Warham, about the susceptibility of the nose to injury."

" Ask Ben!"

" It's a dem'd dangerous symptom, you have, your reverence."

" Coldness — at once a sign of disease, though latent perhaps, and of inferior capacity, for it is the distinguishing trait of cat and dog."

" And the dem'd numbness."

" Ay, the want of sensibility is a bad sign. Besides, I think the pope's nose has lost nearly all its color."

" Except a dark crimson about the roots."

" And the bridge is still *passable*."

" Yes, but how long will it be so in the club? That has grown pale also."

"To a degree, only, Ben: I don't think it much faded."

"Perhaps not; and now I look again, it does seem to me that one of the smaller carbuncles on the main prominence keeps up appearances."

"Look you, lads, d—n it, you're quizzing me!" was the sudden interruption of the person whose nose furnished the subject of discussion, but his face wore a very bewildered expression, and he evidently only had a latent idea of the waggery of which he was the victim.

"Quizzing!" exclaimed one of the companions.

"Quizzing!" echoed the other. "Never was more dem'd serious in all my life!" and he stroked his black, bushy whiskers in a very conclusive manner. The visiter applied his fingers to the nasal prominence which had become so fruitful a source of discussion, and passed them over its various outline with the tenderness of a man who handles a subject of great intrinsic delicacy.

"It feels pretty much as ever!" said he, drawing a long breath.

"Ay, to *your* fingers. But what is its own feeling? Try now and snuff the air."

The ambiguous member was put into instant exercise, and such a snuffing and snorting as followed, utterly drowned the sly chuckling in which the jeering companions occasionally indulged. They played the game, however, with marvellous command of visage.

"I can snuff—I can draw in, and drive out the air!" exclaimed the pope, with the look of a man somewhat better satisfied.

"Ay, but do you feel it cut—is it sharp—does the air seem to scrape against and burn, as it were, the nice, delicate nerves of that region."

"I can't say that it does."

"Ah! that's bad. Look you, Ben. There's a paper of snuff, yellow snuff, on the mantelpiece in t'other room. Bring it—let the pope try that."

The other disappeared, and returned, bringing with him one of those paper rolls which usually contain Sanford's preparation of bark. Nor did the appearance belie the contents. The yellow powder was bark.

"Now, pope, try that! The test is infallible, that is the strongest Scotch snuff, and if that don't succeed in titillating your nostrils, run to Filbert with all possible despatch. He may have to operate!"

The pope's hand was seen to tremble, as a portion of the powder described as so very potent, was poured into it by the confederate. He put it to his nose, and, in his haste and anxiety, fairly buried his suspected member in the powder. His cheeks shared freely in the bounty, and his mouth formed a better idea of the qualities of the " snuff," than ever could his proboscis. The application over, the patient prepared himself to sneeze, by clapping one hand upon the pit of his stomach, opening his mouth, and care fully thrusting his head forward and his nose upward.

"Oh! you're trying to sneeze!" said one of the two. "You shouldn't force the matter."

"No, I don't. But is the snuff so very strong?"

"The demdest strongest Scotch that I ever nosed yet."

"I can't sneeze!" said the pope, in accents of consternation.

His companions shook their heads dolefully. He looked from one to the other as if not knowing what to do.

"A serious matter," said one.

"Dem'd serious! There's no telling, Warham, what sort of a looking person the pope would be without his nose."

"Difficult, indeed, to imagine. A valley for a mountain! It's as if we went to bed to-night with the town at the foot of the hills, and rose to-morrow to find it on the top of them. There's nothing more important to a man's face than his nose. Appearances absolutely demand it. The uses of a nose, indeed, are really less important than its presence "

" I can't agree with you there, Warham ; a sneeze—"

" Is a joy, Ben — a luxury; but a nose is a necessity.
What show could a man make without a nose ?"

" Rather what a show he would make of himself without
it! A monstrous show !"

" You're right. Besides, the pope's loss would be greater than that of most ordinary men."

" Much, much ? Let us take the dimensions, pope.
Three inches from base to apex — from root to the same
point — "

" Four at least — the dromedary's hump alone calls for
two."

And in the spirit of unmeasured fun, the person who is
called Ben by his companion, arming himself with a string,
was actually about to subject the proboscis of the pope to
rule and line, when the eyes of the latter, which had really
exhibited some consternation before, were suddenly illumi-
nated. He caught up the paper of supposed snuff which
Ben had incautiously laid down upon the table and read the
label upon it.

" Ah! villains !" he exclaimed, " at your old tricks. I
should have known it. But I'll pay you," and starting up
he proceeded to fling the yellow powder over the merry-
makers. This led to a general scramble, over chairs and
tables from one room to another. The office rang with
shouts and laughter — the cries of confusion and exultation,
and the tumbling of furniture. The atmosphere was filled
with the floating particles of the medicine, and while the
commotion was at its height, the party were joined unexpectedly by a fourth person who suddenly made his appearance from the street.

" Ha, Beauchampe! that you ? You are come in time.
Grapple the pope there from behind, or he will suffocate us
with Jesuit's bark."

" And a proper fate for such Jesuits as ye are," exclaimed
the pope, who, however, ceased the horse-play the moment

that the name of the new-comer was mentioned. He turned round and confronted him as he spoke, with a countenance in which dislike and apprehension were singularly mingled and very clearly expressed.

"Mr. Lowe, I am very glad to see you here," said Beauchampe respectfully but modestly ; "it saves me the necessity of calling upon you."

"Calling upon me, sir ? For what ?"

"To apologize for my rudeness to you last night. I was not conscious of it, but some friends this morning tell me that I was rude."

"That you were, sir ! You pulled my nose ! you did !"

"I am sorry for it."

"No man's nose should be pulled, Mr. Beauchampe, without an object. If you had pulled my nose with an intention, it might have been excused ; but, to pull it without design, is, it appears to me, decidedly inexcusable."

"Decidedly, decidedly !" was the united exclamation of the two friends.

"I am very sorry, indeed, Mr. Lowe. It was, sir, a very unwarrantable liberty, if I did such a thing, and I know not how to excuse it."

"It is not to be excused," said the pope, or Lowe, which was his proper name, whose indignation seemed to increase in due proportion with the meekness and humility of the young man.

"A nose," he continued, "a nose is a thing perhaps quite as sacred as any other in a man's possession."

"Quite !" said the jesters with one breath.

"No man, as I have said before, should pull the nose of another, unless he had some distinct purpose in view. Now, sir, had you any such purpose ?"

"Not that I can now recollect."

"Let me assist you, Beauchampe. You had a purpose. You declared it at the time. The purpose was even a benevolent one ; nay, something more than benevolent. The

corkscrew had been mislaid, and you undertook to show to
the pope — remember, the presiding officer of the society —
that a cork might be drawn without any other instrument
than the ordinary thumb and forefinger of a free white man.
You illustrated the principle on the pope's proboscis, and
so effectually, that everybody was convinced, not only that
the cork might be drawn in this way from every bottle, but
that the same mode would be equally effectual in drawing
any nose from any face. If this was not a purpose, and a
laudable one, then I am no judge of the matter."

"But, Sharpe, my dear fellow," said Lowe, "you over-
look the fact that Beauchampe has already admitted that
he had no purpose."

"Beauchampe is no witness in his own case, nor is it
asked whether he has a purpose now, but whether he had
one when the deed was done."

"It was a drunken purpose then, colonel," said Beau
champe gravely.

"Drunk or sober, it matters not," said the other; "it
was not less a purpose, and I say a good one. The act
was one *pro bono publico;* and I, moreover, contend that
you did not pull the nose of our friend except in his official
capacity. You pulled the nose, not of Daniel Lowe, Esq.,
but of the supreme pontiff of our microcosm; and I really
think that the pope does wrong to remember the event in
his condition as a mere man. I am not sure that he does
not violate that rule, seventeenth section, seventh clause,
of the ' ordinance for the better preservation of the individ-
uality of the fraternals,' which provides that ' all persons,
members, who shall betray the discoveries, new truths, and
modern inventions, the progress of discovery and prosely-
tism, the processes deemed essential to be employed,' &
You all remember the section, clause, and penalty."

"Pshaw! how can you make out that I violate the clause?
What have I betrayed that should be secret?"

"The new mode of extracting a cork from a bottle, which

our new member, Beauchampe, displayed last evening, to the great edification of every fraternal present."

" But it was no cork! My nose—"

" Symbolically, it was a cork, and your nose had no right to any resentments. But come, let us take the back room again and resume our seats, when we can discuss the matter more at leisure."

The motion was seconded, and the dusty particles of Jesuit's bark having subsided from the atmosphere of the adjoining room, the parties drew chairs around the table as before, with a great appearance of comparative satisfaction.

CHAPTER V

STUMP TACTICS.

"Our village politicians, how they plan
    Their pushpin practice — for the rights of man!"

The name of Beauchampe, of which our readers have
heard nothing until this period, though it confers its name
on our story, renders it necessary that we should devote a
few moments in particular to him by whom it is borne.   He
was a young man, not more than twenty-one, tall, and of
very handsome person.   His eye was bright, and his whole
face full of intelligence.   His manners and features equally denoted the modesty and the ingenuousness of youth.
There was a gentleness in his deportment, however, which,
though natural enough to his nature when in repose, was
not its characteristic at other periods.   He was of excitable constitution, passionate, and full of enthusiasm; and,
when aroused, not possessed of any powers of self-govern-
ment or restraint.   At present, and sitting with the rest
about the table, his features were not only subdued and
quiet, but they wore an air of profound humility and self-
dissatisfaction, which was sufficiently evident to all.

   "Our new member," said one of the party, "does not
seem to have altogether got over the pains of initiation.
Eh, Beauchampe! how is it?   Does the head ache still?
Are the nerves still disordered?"

   "No, colonel, but I feel inexpressibly mean and sheep-
ish.   I am very sorry you persuaded me to join your club."

"Persuade! it was not possible to avoid it. Every new graduate at the bar, to be recognised, must go through the initiation. Your regrets and repentance are treasonable."

"I feel them nevertheless. I must have been a savage and a beast if what I am told be true. I never was drunk before in my life, and, club or no club, if I can help it, never will be drunk again. Indeed, I can not even now understand it. I drank no great deal of wine."

"No, indeed, precious little—no more than would dash the brandy. You may thank Ben there for his adroitness in mingling the liquors."

"I *do* thank him!" said the youth with increased gravity, and a glance which effectually contradicted his words, addressed to the offender. That worthy did not seem much annoyed, however.

"It was the demdest funny initiation I did ever see! Ha! ha! ha! I say, pope, how is your reverence's nose?"

"Let my nose alone, you grinning, big-whiskered, little creature!"

"Noses are sacred," said Sharpe.

"To be pulled only with a purpose. Warham."

"Symbolically," pursued the first.

"By way of showing how corks are to be drawn."

"Oh, d—n you for a pair of blue devils!" exclaimed Lowe, starting to his feet, and shaking his fist at the offenders.

"What, are you off, pope?" demanded Sharpe.

"Yes, I am. There's no satisfaction in staying with you."

"Call at Filbert's on your way, be sure."

"For what, I want to know?"

"Why, for his professional opinion. The worst sign, you know, is that numbness—"

"Coldness."

"Insensibility to Scotch snuff."

"And remember, though your nose was pulled officially,

it may yet be personally injured. The official pulling simply acquits the offender: the liability of the nose is not lessened by the legalization of the act of pulling."

"The devil take you for a pair of puppies," cried the victim with a queer expression of joint fun and vexation on his face. "Of course, Mr. Beauchampe," he said, turning to the young man, "of course I don't believe what these dogs say about my nose having suffered any vital injury; but I must tell you, sir, that you hurt me very much last night; and I feel the pain this morning."

"I am truly sorry, Mr. Lowe, for what I have done. Truly, sincerely sorry. I assure you, sir, that your pain of body is nothing to that which I suffer in mind from having exposed myself, as I fear I did."

"You did expose yourself and me too, sir. I trust you will never do so again. I advise you, sir, never do so again—never, unless you have a serious and sufficient motive. Don't let these fellows gull you with the idea that it was any justification for such an act that corks might be drawn from bottles in such a manner. Corks are not noses. Nobody can reasonably confound them. The shape, color, everything is different. There is nothing in the *feel* of the two to make one fancy a likeness. You are young, sir, and liable to be abused. Take the advice of an older man. Look into this matter for yourself, and you will agree with me not only that there is no likeness between a nose and a cork, but that, even admitting that your plan of drawing a cork from a bottle by the thumb and forefinger is a good one, it would be impossible to teach the process by exercising them upon a nose in the same manner. These young men are making fun of you, Mr. Beauchampe—they are, believe me!"

"Ha! ha! ha!" roared the offenders. "Very good, your reverence."

"He! he! he! you puppies. Do you think I mind your cackling!" and shaking his fist at the company, Mr. Lowe took his departure, involuntarily stroking, with increased affection the nasal eminence which had furnished occasion for so much misplaced merriment.

"Well, Beauchampe," said one of the companions, "you still seem grave about this business, but you should not. If ever a man may forget himself and be mad for a night, after the fashion of old Anacreon, it is surely the night of that day when he is admitted to the temple — when he takes his degree, and passes into the brotherhood of the bar."

"Nay, on such a day least of all."

"Pshaw, you were never born for a puritan. Old Thurston, your parson teacher, has perverted you from your better nature. You are a fellow for fun and flash, high frolic, and the complete abandonment of blood. You look at this matter too seriously. Do I not tell you — I that have led you through all the thorny paths of legal knowledge — do I not tell you that your, offence is venial. 'A good sherris-sack hath a twofold operation in it.'"

"Beauchampe found it fourfold," said the bush-whiskered gentleman — "that is, fourth proof; and he showed proofs enough of it. By Gad! never did a man play such pleasant deviltries with his neighbor's members. The nose-pulling was only a small part of his operations. It was certainly a most lovely initiation."

"At least it's all over, Mr. Coalter; and as matters have turned out, nothing more need be said on the subject; but were it otherwise, I assure you that your practice upon my wine would be a dangerous experiment for you. I speak to you by way of warning, and not with the view to quarrel. I presume you meant nothing more than a jest?"

"Dem the bit more," said the other, half dissatisfied with himself at the concession, yet more than half convinced of the propriety of making it. "Dem the bit more. Sharpe will tell you that it's a trick of the game — a customary trick — must be done by somebody, and was done by me, only because I like to see a dem'd fine initiation such as

yours was, my boy. But, good morning, Beauchampe—
good morning, Sharpe—I see you have business to do—
some dem'd political business, I suppose; and so I leave
you. I'm no politician, but I see that Judge Tompkins is
in the field against your friend Desha. Eh! don't you
think I can guess the rest, Warham—eh?"

"Sagacious fellow!" said Sharpe as the other disappeared; "and, in this particular, not far from the mark.
Tompkins is in the field against Desha, and will run him a
tight race. I too must go into the field, Beauchampe. The
party requires it, and though I have some reasons not to
wish it just at this time, yet the matter is scarcely avoida-
ble. I shall want every assistance, and I shall expect you
to take the stump for me."

"Whatever I can do I will."

"You can do much. You do not know your own abilities on the stump. You will do famous things yet; and
this is the time to try yourself. The success of a man in
our country depends on the first figure. You are just admitted; something is expected of you. There can be no
better opportunity to begin."

"I am ready and willing."

"Scarcely, *mon ami*. You are going to Simpson. You
will get with sisters and mamma, and waste the daylight.
Believe me this is no time to play at mammets. We want
every man. We will need them all."

"You shall find me ready. I shall not stay long at
Simpson. But do not think that I will commit myself for
Desha. I prefer Tompkins."

"Well, but you will do nothing on that subject. You
do not mean to come out for Tompkins?"

"No! I only tell you I will do nothing on the subject of
the gubernatorial canvass. You are for the assembly. I
will turn out in your behalf. But who is your opponent?"

"One Calvert—William Calvert. Said to be a smart
fellow. I never saw him, but he is spoken of as no mean

person. He writes well. His letter to the people of ——
lies on the desk there. Put it in your pocket and read it
at your leisure. It is well done — quite artful — but rather
prosing and puritanical."

Beauchampe took up the pamphlet, passed his eyes over
the page, and placed it without remark in his pocket.

" Barnabas," continued Sharpe, " who has seen this fellow
Calvert, says he's not to be despised. He's a mere country
lawyer, however, who is not known out of his own precinct.
In taking the field now, he makes a miscalculation. I shall
beat him very decidedly. But he has friends at work, who
are able, and mine must not sleep. Do I understand you
as promising to take the field against him ?"

" If he is so clever, he will need a stronger opponent.
Why not do it yourself ?"

" Surely, I will. I long for nothing better. But I can
not be everywhere, and he and his friends are everywhere
busy. I will seek him in his stronghold, and grapple with
him tooth and nail ; but there will be auxiliary combatants,
and you must be ready to take up the cudgel at the same
time with some other antagonist. When do you leave
town ?"

" To-day — within the hour."

" So soon ! Why I looked to have you to dinner. Mrs
Sharpe expects you."

" I am sorry to deprive myself of the pleasure of doing
justice to her good things ; but I wrote my sisters and they
will expect me."

" Pshaw ! what of that ! The disappointment of a day
only. You will be the more welcome from the delay."

" They will apprehend some misfortune — perhaps, my
rejection — and I would spare them the mortification if not
the fear. You must make my compliments and excuse to
Mrs. S."

" You *will* be a boy, Beauchampe. Let the girls wait a
day, and dine with me. You will meet some good fellow

and get a glimpse into the field of war—see how we open
the campaign, and so forth."

"Temptations, surely, not to be despised; but I confess
to my boyhood in one respect, and will prove my manhood
in another. I am able to resist your temptations—so much
for my manhood. My boyhood makes me keep word with
my sisters, and the shame be on my head."

"Shame, indeed; but where shall we meet?"

"At Bowling Green—when you please."

"Enough then on that head. I will write you when you
are wanted. I confess to a strong desire, apart from my
own interests, to see you on the stump; and if I can ar-
range it so, I will have you break ground against Calvert."

"But that is not so easy. What is there against him?"

"You will find out from his pamphlet. Nothing more
easy. He is obscure, that is certain. Little known among
the people. Why? For a good reason—he is a haughty
aristocrat—a man who only knows them when he wants
their votes!"

"Is that the case?"

"Simple fellow! we must make it appear so. It may
be or not—what matter? That he is shy, and reserved,
and unknown, is certain. It's just as likely he is so, because of his pride, as anything else. Perhaps he's a fellow
of delicate feelings! This is better for us, if you can make
it appear so. People don't like fellows of very delicate
feelings. That alone would be conclusive against him. If
we could persuade him to wear silk gloves, now, it would
be only necessary to point them out on the canvass, to turn
the stomachs of the electors, and their votes with their
stomachs. They would throw him up instantly."

Beauchampe shook his head. The other interpreted the
motion incorrectly.

"What! you do not believe it. Never doubt. The fact
is certain. Such would be the case. Did you ever hear
the story of Barnabas in his first campaign?"

" No!—not that I recollect."

"He was stumping it through your own county of Simpson. There were two candidates against him. One of them stood no chance. That was certain. The other, however, was generally considered to be quite as strong if not stronger than Barnabas. Now Barnabas, in those days, was something of a dandy. He wore fine clothes, a long-tail blue, a steeple-crowned beaver, and silk-gloves. Old Ben Jones, his uncle, saw him going out on the canvass in this unseasonable trim; told him he was a d——d fool; that the very coat, and gloves, and hat, would lose him the election. ' Come in with me,' said the old buck. He did so, and Jones rigged him out in a suit of buckskin breeches; gave him an old slouch tied with a piece of twine; made him put on a common homespun roundabout; and sent him on the campaign with these accoutrements."

" A mortifying exchange to Barnabas."

"Not a bit. The fellow was so eager for election, that he'd have gone without clothes at all, sooner than have missed a vote. But one thing the old man did not remember—the silk-gloves—and Barnabas had nearly reached the muster-ground before he recollected that he had them on his hands. He took 'em off instantly, and thrust 'em into his pocket. When he reached the ground, he soon discovered the wisdom of old Jones's proceedings. He was introduced to his chief opponent, and never was there a more rough-and-tumble-looking ruffian under the sun. Barnabas swears that he had not washed his face and hands for a week. His coat was out at the elbows, and though made of cloth originally both blue and good, it was evidently not made for the present wearer. His breeches were common homespun; and his shoes, of yellow-belly, were gaping on both feet. He had on stockings, however. Barnabas looked and felt quite genteel alongside of him; but he felt his danger also. He saw that the appearance of the fellow was very much in his favor. There was al-

4

ready a crowd around him; and, when he talked, his words were of that rough sort which is supposed to indicate the true staple of popular independence. As there was nothing much in favor or against any of the candidates, unless it was that one of them—not Barnabas—was suspected of horse-stealing, all that the speakers could do was to prove their own republicanism, and the aristocracy of the opponent. Appearances would help or dissipate this charge; and Barnabas saw, shabby as he was, that his rival was still shabbier. A bright thought took him that night. Fumbling in his pockets while they were drinking at the hotel, he felt his silk-gloves. What does he do, but, going to his room, he takes out his pocket inkstand and pen, and marks in large letters the initials of his opponent upon them. This done, he watches his chance, and the next morning when they were about to go forth to the place of gathering, he slips the gloves very slyly into the other fellow's pocket. The thing worked admirably. In the midst of the speech, Joel Peguay—for that was his rival's name —endeavoring to pull out a ragged cotton pocket-handkerchief, drew out the gloves, which fell behind him on the ground. Barnabas was on the watch, and, pointing the eyes of the assembly to the tokens of aristocracy, exclaimed—

" ' This, gentlemen, is a proof of the sort of democracy which Joel Peguay *practises.*'

" A universal shout, mixed with hisses, arose. Peguay looked round, and, when he was told what was the matter, answered with sufficient promptness, and a look of extraordinary exultation :—

" ' Fellow-citizens, ain't this only another proof of the truth of what I'm a-telling you ?—for, look you, them nasty fine things come out of this coat-pocket, did they ?'

" ' Yes, yes! we saw them drop, Joel,' was the cry from fifty voices.

" ' Very good,' said Joel, nowise discomfited, ' and the

coat was borrowed, for this same occasion, from Tom Meadows. I hain't a decent coat of my own, my friends, to come
before you—none but a round jacket, and that's tore down
in the back—and so, you see, I begged Tom Meadows for
the loan of his'n, and I reckon the gloves must be his'n too,
since they fell out of the pocket.'

"This explanation called for a triumphant shout from
the friends of Peguay, and the affair promised to redound
still more in favor of the speaker, when Barnabas, shaking
his head gravely, and picking up the gloves, which he held
from him as if they had been saturated in the dews of the
bohon upas, drew the eyes of those immediately at hand to
the letters which they bore.

"'I am sorry,' said he, 'to interrupt the gentleman; but
there is certainly some mistake here. These gloves are
marked J. P., which stands for Joel Peguay, and not Tom
Meadows. See for yourselves, gentlemen—you all can
read, I know—here's J. P. I'm not much of a reader,
being too poor to have much of an education; but I know
pretty much what you all do, that if these gloves belonged
to Tom Meadows, they would have been marked T. M.:
the T for Tom, and the M for Meadows. I don't mean
to say that they are not Tom's; but I do say that it's very
strange that Tom Meadows should write his name Joel
Peguay. I say it's strange, gentlemen—very strange—
that's all!'

"And that was enough. There was no more shouting
from the friends of Peguay. He was completely confounded. He denied and disputed, of course; but the
proofs were too strong, and Barnabas had done his part of
the business with great skill and adroitness. Joel Peguay
descended from the stump, swearing vengeance against
Meadows, who, he took for granted, had contrived the exhibition secretly, only to defeat him. No doubt a fierce
feud followed between the parties, but Barnabas was elect-
ed by a triumphant vote."

" And do you really think, colonel," said Beauchampe, " that this silly proceeding had any effect in producing the result ?"

" Silly, indeed ! By my soul, such silly things, Master Beauchampe, have upset empires. The tumbling of an old maid's cap has done more mischief. I can tell you, from my own experience, that a small matter like this has turned the scale in many a popular election. Barnabas believes to this day that he owes his success entirely to that little *ruse de guerre*."

" I know not how to believe it."

" Because you know not yet that little, strange, mousing, tiger-like, capricious, obstinate, foolish animal, whom we call man. When you know him more, you will wonder less."

" Perhaps so," said Beauchampe. " At all events, I can only say that, while I will turn out for you and do all I can to secure your election as in duty bound, I will endeavor to urge your claims on other grounds."

" As you please, my good fellow. Convince them that I am a patriot, and a prophet, and the best man for them, and I care nothing by what process it is done. And if you can lay bare the corresponding deficiencies of mine opponent—this fellow Calvert—it is a part of the same policy, to be sure."

" But not so obviously," replied the other, " for as yet, you remember, we know nothing of him, and can not accordingly pronounce upon his deficiencies."

" You forget—his aristocracy !"

" Ah ! that is conjectural, you know."

" Granted," said the other, " but what more do you want ? A plausible conjecture is the very sort of argument in a popular election."

" But scarcely an honorable one."

" Honorable ! poh ! poh ! poh ! Old Thurston has seriously diseased you, Beauchampe. We must undertake your treatment for this weakness—this boyish weakness. It is a boyish weakness, Beauchampe."

"Perhaps so, but it makes my strength."

"It will always keep you feeble—certainly keep you down in the political world."

The young man smiled. The other, speaking hastily, continued :—

"But this need not be discussed at present. Enough that you will take the field, and be ready at my summons. Turn the state of parties in your mind, and that will give you matter enough for the stump. Read that letter of Calvert; I doubt not it will give you more than sufficient material. From a hasty glance, I see that he distrusts the people; *that*, as a stern democrat, you can resent happily. I leave that point to you. You will regard that opinion as a falsehood; I think it worse—a mistake in policy. It is to this same people that he addresses his claims. How far his opinion is an impertinence may be seen in his appeal to the very judgment which he decries. This, to my mind, is conclusive against his own. But this must not make us remiss. I will write to you when the time comes, and at intervals, should there be anything new to communicate. But you had better stay to dinner. Seriously, my wife expects you."

"Excuse me to her—but I must go. I so long to see my sisters, and they will be on the lookout for me. I have already written them."

With a few words more, and the young lawyer separated from his late legal preceptor. When he was gone, the latter stroked his chin complacently as he soliloquized :—

"He will do to break ground with this fellow Calvert. He is ardent, soon roused; and if I am to judge of Calvert from his letter, he is a stubborn colt, whose heels are very apt to annoy any injudicious assailant. Ten to one, that, with his fiery nature, Beauchampe finds cause of quarrel in any homely truth. They may fight, and this hurts me nothing. At least, Beauchampe may be a very good foil for the first strokes of this new enemy. Barbanas says he is to be feared. If so, he must be grappled with fearlessly. There is no hope else. At all events, I will see, by his issue with Beauchampe, of what stuff he is made. Something in that. And yet, is all so sure with this boy? He has his whims; is sometimes suspicious; obstinate as a mule when roused; and has some ridiculous notions about virtue, and all that sort of thing. At least, he must be managed cautiously — very cautiously!"

We leave the office of Colonel Warham P. Sharpe for a while, to attend the progress of the young man of whom he was speaking.

CHAPTER VI.

BEAUCHAMPE AT HOME.

BEAUCHAMPE was on his way to the maternal ma sion. We have already endeavored to afford the reader some idea of the character of this person. It does not need that we should dilate more at large on the abstract constituents of his nature. We may infer that his mind was good, from the anxiety which his late teacher displayed to have it put in requisition in his behalf during the political campaign which was at hand. The estimate of his temperament by the same person will also be sufficient for us. That he was of high, manly bearing, and honorable purpose, we may also conclude from the share which he took in the preceding dialogue.

Of his judgment, however, doubts may be entertained. With something more than the ardor of youth, Beauchampe had all of its impatience. He was of that fiery mood, when aroused, which too effectually blinds the possessor to the strict course of propriety. His natural good sense was but too often baffled by this impetuosity of his temper; and, though in the brief scene in which he has been suffered to appear, we have beheld nothing in his deportment which was not becomingly modest and deliberate, we are constrained to confess that the characteristic of much deliberation is not natural to him, and was induced, in the present instance, by a sense of his late elevation to a new and exacting profession; the fact that he was in the presence of his late teacher; and that he had, the night before, participated, however unconsciously, in a debauch, of the performances of which he was really most heartily ashamed. His manner has therefore been subdued, but only for a while. We shall see him before long under very different aspects; betraying all the ardor and impetuosity of his disposition, and, as is usual in such cases, not always in that way which is most favorable to the shows of judgment.

Beauchampe was the second son of a stanch Kentucky farmer. He had received quite as good an education as the resources of the country at that time could afford. This education was not very remarkable, it is true; but, with the advantage of a lively nature and retentive memory, it brought into early exercise all the qualities of his really excellent intellect. He became a good English speaker, and a tolerable Latin scholar. He read with avidity, and studied with industry; and, at the age of twenty-one, was admitted to the practice of law in the courts of the state. This probation over, with the natural feeling of a heart which the world has not yet utterly weaned from the affections and dependencies of its youth, he was hurrying home to his mother and sisters, to receive their congratulations, and share with them the pride and delight which such an occasion of his return would naturally inspire.

Hitherto, his mother and sisters have had all his affections. The blind deity has never disturbed his repose, diverted his eyes from these objects of his regard, or interfered with his mental cogitations. Dreams of ambition were in his mind, but not yet with sufficient strength or warmth as to subdue the claims of that domestic love which the kindnesses of a beloved mother, and the attachments of dear sisters, had impressed upon his heart. He had his images of beauty, perhaps, along with his images of glory, but they were rather the creations of a lively fancy, in moments of mental abstraction, than any more real impressions upon the unwritten tablets of his soul.

These were still fair and smooth. His life had not been touched by many griefs or annoyances. His trials had been few, his mortifications brief. He was not yet conscious of any wants which would induce feelings of care and anxiety; and, with a spirit gradually growing lighter and more elastic, as the number of miles rapidly diminished beneath the feet of his horse, he forgot that he was alone in his journeyings; a light heart and a lively fancy brought him pleasant companions enough, that beguiled the time, and cheered the tediousness of his journey. The youth was thinking of his home—and what a thought is that in the bosom of youth! The old cottage shrunk up in snug littleness among the venerable guardian trees, and the green grass-plat and the half-blind house-dog, and a thousand objects besides, forced themselves, through the medium of his memory, upon his delighted imagination. Then he beheld his sisters hurrying out to meet him—Jane running for dear life, half mad, and shouting back to Mary, the more grave sister, who slowly followed. Jane shrieking with laughter, and Mary with not a word, but only her extended hand and her tears!

Strange! that even at such a moment as this, while these were the satisfying images in his mind, there should intrude another which should either expel these utterly, or should persuade him that they were not enough to satisfy his mind or confer happiness upon his heart. Why, when, in his dreaming fancy, these dear sisters appeared so lovely and were so fond, why should another form—itself a fancy— arise in the midst, which should make him heedless and forgetful of all others, and fixed only on itself! The eye of the youth grew sadder as he gazed and felt. He no longer spurred his steed impatiently along the path, but, forgetful in an instant of his progress, he mused upon the heart's ideal, which a passing fancy had presented, and

4*

all the bright sweet domestic forms vanished from his sight.

The feeling of Beauchampe was natural enough. He felt it to be so. It was an instinct which every heart of any sensibility must feel in progress of time; even though the living object be yet wanting to the sight, upon which the imagination may expend its own colors in seeking to establish the identity between the *sought* and the *found*.

But was it not late for him to feel this instinct for the first time? Why had he not felt it before? Why, just at that moment—just when his fancy had invoked around him all the images which had ever brought him happiness before—forms which had supplied all his previous wants—smiles and tones which had left nothing which he could desire—why, just then, should that foreign instinct arise and expel, as with a single glance, the whole family of joys known to his youthful heart. Expelling them, indeed, but only to awaken him to the conviction of superior joys and possessions far more valuable.

It was an instinct, indeed; and never was youthful mind so completely diverted, in a single instant, from the consideration of a long succession of dear thoughts, to that of one, now dearer perhaps than all, but which had never made one of his thoughts before.

He now remembered that, of all his schoolmates and youthful associates, there had not been one, who had not professed a passionate flame for some smiling damsel in his neighborhood. Among his brother students-at-law, that they should love was quite as certain as that they should have frequent attacks of the passion, and of course, on each occasion, for some different object.

He alone had gone unscathed. He alone had run the gauntlet of smiles and glances, bright eyes and lovely cheeks, without detriment. The thought had never disturbed him then, when he was surrounded by beauty; why should it now, when no apparent object of passion was nigh

him, and when but a small distance from his mother's farm
he had every reason to think only of that and the dear relatives which there awaited him? There was a fatality
in it!

At that moment he was roused from his reveries by a
pistol-shot which sounded in the wood a little distance before him.

The circumstance was a singular one. The wood was
very close and somewhat extensive. He knew the spot
very well. It was scarcely more than a mile from his mother's cottage. He knew of no one in the neighborhood who
practised pistol-shooting; but, on this head, he was not capable to judge. He had been absent from his home for
two years. There might—there must have been changes.
At all events no mischief seemed to be afoot. There was
but one shot. He himself was safe, and he rode forward,
relieved somewhat of his reveries, at a trifling increase of
speed.

The road led him round the wood in which the shot had
been heard, making a sweep like a crescent, in order to
avoid some rugged inequalities of the land. As he followed
its windings he was suddenly startled to see, just before
him, a female, well-dressed, tall, and of a carriage unusually firm and majestic. Under her arm she carried a small
bundle wrapped up in a dark silk pocket-handkerchief.

She crossed the road hastily, and soon buried herself out
of sight in the woods opposite. She gave him but a single
glance in passing, but this glance enabled him to distinguish features of peculiar brilliancy and beauty. The moment after, she was gone from sight, and it seemed as if
the pathway grew suddenly dark. Her sudden appearance and rapid transition was like that of a gleam of summer lightning.

Involuntarily he spurred his horse forward, and his eyes
peered keenly into the wood which she had entered. He
could still see the white glimmer of her garments. He

stopped, like one bewildered, to watch. At one moment
he felt like dismounting and darting in pursuit of her. But
such impertinence might receive the rebuke which it merit-
ed. She did not seem to need any service, and on no other
pretence could he have pursued.

He grew more and more bewildered while he gazed, and
mused upon the incident. This vision was so strange and
startling; and so singularly in unison with the fancies
which had just before possessed his mind. That his heart
should now, for the first time, present him with an ideal
form of attraction and delight, and that, a moment after, a
form of beauty should appear, so unexpectedly, in so unusual a place, was at least a very strange coincidence.

Nothing could be more natural than that the fancy of the
young man should find these two forms identical. It is an
easy matter for the ardent nature to deceive itself. But
here another subject of doubt presented itself to the mind
of Beauchampe. Was this last vision more certainly real
than the former? It was no longer to be seen. Had h
seen it except in his mind's eye, where the former brigh.
ideal had been called up? So sudden had been the appearance, so rapid the transition, that he turned from the
spot now half doubting its reality. Slowly he rode away,
musing strangely, and we may add sadly — often looking
back, and growing more and more bewildered as he mused,
until relieved and diverted by the more natural feelings
of the son and brother, as, the prospect opening before his
eyes, he beheld the farmstead of his mother.

In the doorway of the old cottage stood the venerable
woman, while the two girls were approaching, precisely as
his fancy had shown them, the one bounding and crying
aloud, the other moving slowly, and with eyes which were
already moist with tears. They had seen him before he
had sufficiently awakened from his reveries to behold them.

" Ah, Jane — dear Mary !" were the words of the youth,
throwing himself from the horse and severally clasping

them in his arms. The former laughed, sang, danced, and capered. The latter clung to the neck of her brother, sobbing as heartily as if they were about to separate.

"Why, what's Mary crying for, I wonder?" said the giddy girl.

"Because my heart's so full, I must cry," murmured the other. Taking an arm of each in his own, Beauchampe led them to the old lady, whose crowning embrace was bestowed with the warmth of one who clasps and confesses the presence of her idol.

We pass over the first ebullitions of domestic love. Most people can imagine these. It is enough to say that ours is a family of love. They have been piously brought up. Mrs. Beauchampe is a woman of equal benignity and intelligence. They have their own little world of joy in and among themselves. The daughters are single-hearted and gentle, and no small vanities and petty strifes interfere to diminish the confidence in one, and another, and themselves, which brings to them the hourly enjoyment of the all-in-all content. It will not be hard to fancy the happiness of the household in the restoration of its tall and accomplished son—tall and handsome, and so kind, and so intelligent, and just now made a lawyer too! Jane was half beside herself, and Mary's tears were constantly renewed as they looked at the manly brother, and thought of these things.

"But why did you ride so slow, Orville?" demanded Jane, as she sat upon his knee and patted his cheek. Mary was playing with his hair from behind. "You came at a snail's pace, and didn't seem to see anybody; and there was I hallooing to make you hear, and all for nothing."

"Don't worry Orville with your questions, Jane," said the more sedate Mary. "He was tired, perhaps—"

"Or *his* heart was too full also," said Jane, interrupting her mischievously. "But it's not either of these, I'm sure, Orville, for I know horseback don't tire you, and I'm sure your heart's not so very full, for you hav'n't shed a tear yet. No, no! it's something else, for you not only rode slow, but you kept looking behind you all the while, as if you were expecting somebody. Now, who were you looking for? Tell me, tell Jane, dear brother!"

Now you hit it, Jane! The reason I rode slowly and looked behind me — mind me, I rode pretty fast until I came almost in sight of home — was, because I *did* expect to see some one coming behind me, though I had not much cause to expect it either."

" Who was it?"

" That's the question. Perhaps you can tell *me;*" and, with these words, the young man proceeded to relate the circumstance, already described, of the sudden advent of that bright vision which had so singularly taken the place, in our hero's mind, of his heart's ideal.

"It must be Miss Cooke, mother," said the girls with one breath.

" And who is Miss Cooke?"

" Oh! that's the mystery. She's a sort of queen, I'm thinking," said Jane, " or she wants you to think her one, which is more likely."

" Jane! Jane!" said Mary, who was the younger sister, in reproachful accents.

" Well, what am I saying, but what's the truth? Don't she carry herself like a queen? Isn't she as proud and stately as if she was better than anybody else?"

" If she's a queen, it's a tragedy-queen," said the graver sister. " I don't deny that she's very stately, but then I'm sure she's also very unhappy."

"I don't believe in her unhappiness at all. I can't think any person so very unhappy who carries herself so proudly."

" Pride itself may be a cause of unhappiness, Jane," said the mother.

" Yes, mamma, but are we to sympathize with it, I want to know?"

" Perhaps ! It is not less to be pitied because the owner
has no such notion. But your brother is waiting to hear
something of Miss Cooke, and, instead of telling him *who*
she is, you're telling him *what* she is."

" And no better way, perhaps," said the brother. " But
do you tell me, Mary : Jane is quite too much given to
scandal."

" Oh, brother !" said Jane.

" Too true, Jane ; but go on, Mary, and let us have a key
to this mystery. Who is Miss Cooke ?"

" She's a young lady—"

" Very pretty ?"

" Very ! She came here about two years ago—just after
you went from Parson Thurston to study law—she and
her mother, and they took the old place of Farmer Davis.
They came from some other part of Simpson, so I have
heard, and bought this place from Widow Davis. They
have a few servants, and are comfortably fixed ; and Mrs.
Cooke is quite a chatty body, very silly in some things, but
fond of going about among the neighbors. Her daughter,
who is named Anna, though I once heard the old lady call
her Margaret—"

" Margaret Anna, perhaps—she may have two names,"
said the brother.

" Very likely ; but the daughter is not sociable. On the
contrary, she rather avoids everybody. You do not often
see her when you go there, and she has never been here
but once, and that shortly after her first arrival. As Jane
says, she is not only shy, but stately. Jane thinks it pride,
but I do not agree with her. I rather think that it is owing
to a natural dignity of mind, and to manners formed under
other circumstances ; for she never smiles, and there is such
a deep look of sadness about her eyes, that I can't help
believing her to be very unhappy. I sometimes think that
she has probably been disappointed in love."

" Yes, Mary thinks the strangest things about her. She

says she's sure that she's been engaged, and that her lover
has played her false, and deserted her."

"Oh, Jane, you mistake; I said I thought he might have
been killed in a duel, or—"

"Or that he deserted her; for that matter, Mary, you've
been having a hundred conceits about her ever since she
came here."

"She is pretty, you say, Mary?" asked the young man,
who by this time had ejected Jane from his knee, and trans-
ferred her younger sister to the same place.

"Pretty? she is beautiful."

"I can't see it for my part," said Jane, "with her solemn
visage, and great dark eyes, that seem always sharp like
daggers ready to run you through."

"She is beautiful, brother, very beautiful, but Jane don t
like her because she thinks her proud. She's as beautiful
in her face as she is noble in her figure. Her stateliness,
indeed, arises, I think, from the symmetry and perfect proportion of her person; for when she moves, she does not
seem to be at all conscious that she is stately. Her movements are very natural, as if she had practised them all her
life. And they say, mother, that she's very smart."

"Who says, sister?" cried Jane—"who but old Mrs.
Fisher, and only because she saw her fixing a bushel of
books upon the shelves at her first coming!"

"No, Jane; Judge Crump told me that he spoke to her,
and that he had never believed a woman could be so sensible till then."

"That shows he's a poor judge. Who'd take old
Crump's opinion about a woman's sense? I'm sure I
wouldn't."

"But Miss Cooke is very sensible, brother. Jane does
dislike her so!"

"Well, supposing she is sensible, it's only what she ought
to be by this time. She's old enough to have the sense of
two young women at least."

"Old!" exclaimed Beauchampe. "The lady I saw was not old, certainly."

The suggestion seemed to give the young man some annoyance, which the gentle-hearted Mary hastened to remove.

"She is *not* old, Orville. Jane, how can you say so? You know that Miss Cooke can hardly be over twenty-one or two, even if she's that."

"Well, and ain't that old? You, Mary, are sixteen only, and I'm but seventeen and three months. But I'm certain she's twenty-five if she's a day."

The subject is one fruitful of discussion where ladies are concerned. Beauchampe, having experience of the two sisters, quietly sat and listened; and, by the use of a moderate degree of patience, soon contrived to learn all that could be known of that neighbor who, it appears, had occasioned quite as great a sensation in the bosoms of the sisters, though of a very different sort, as her momentary presence had inspired in his own. The two girls, representing extremes, were just the persons to give him a reasonable idea of the real facts in the case of the person under discussion. It may be unnecessary to add that the result was, to increase the mystery, and heighten the curiosity which the young man now felt in its solution.

CHAPTER VII.

PROGRESS OF DISCOVERY.

WHEN the first sensations following the return of our hero to his home and family had somewhat subsided, the enthusiastic and excitable nature of the former naturally led him to dwell upon the image of that strange lady, whose sudden appearance seemed to harmonize so singularly with the ideal of his waking dream. The very morning after his arrival, he sallied forth at an early hour, with his gun in hand, ostensibly with a view to birding, but really to catch some glimpse of the mysterious person. For this purpose, as all the neighborhood and neighboring county was familiar to him, he traversed the hundred routes to and from the farmstead of old Davis, which the stranger now occupied, and wasted some precious hours, in which neither his heart nor his gun found game, in exploring the deep wood whence the pistol-shot, the day before, had first challenged his attention.

But no bright vision blessed his search that day. He found nothing to interest his mind or satisfy his curiosity, unless it were a tree which he discovered barked with bullets, where some person had evidently been exercising, and —assuming the instrument to have been a pistol—with a singular degree of success. The discovery did not call for the thought of a single moment; and, contenting himself with the conjecture that some young rifleman was thus "teaching the young idea how to shoot," he turned off, and, with some weariness, and more disappointment, made his way, birdless, to his cottage.

But the disappointment rather increased than lessened his curiosity; and, before two days had passed, he had acquired boldness enough to advance so nearly to the dwelling of Miss Cooke, as, sheltered beneath some friendly shade-trees, to see the passers by the window, and on one or more occasions to catch a glimpse of the one object for whom all these pains were taken.

These glimpses, it may be said, served rather to inflame than to satisfy his curiosity. He saw enough to convince him that Mary was right, and Jane wrong; that he was not deceived in his first impression of the exceeding loveliness of the mysterious stranger; that she was beautiful beyond any comparison that he could make—of a rare, rich, and excelling beauty: and slowly he returned from his wanderings, to muse upon the means by which he should arrive at a more intimate knowledge of the fair one, who was represented to be as inaccessible as she was fair—like one of those unhappy damsels of whom we read in old romances, locked up in barred and gloomy towers, lofty and well guarded, whose charms, if they were the incentives to chivalry and daring, were quite as often the cruel occasion of bloody strife and most unfortunate adventure.

The surpassing beauty of our heroine, so strangely coupled with her sternness of deportment and loneliness of habit, naturally enough brought into activity the wild imagination and fervent temperament of our young lawyer. By these means her beauty was heightened, and the mystery which enveloped her was made the parent of newer sources of attraction. Before three days had passed, his sisters had discovered that his thought was running only on their fair, strange neighbor; and at length, baffled in his efforts to encounter the mysterious lady in his rambles, he was fain to declare himself more openly at home, and to insist that his sisters should call upon Miss Cooke and her mother, and invite them to tea.

This was done accordingly, but with only partial success. Mrs. Cooke came, but not the daughter, who sent an excuse. Beauchampe paid his court to the old lady, whom he found very garrulous and very feeble-minded ; but though she spoke with great freedom on almost every other subject, he remarked that she shrunk suddenly into silence whenever reference was made to her daughter.

On this point everything tended to increase the mystery, and, of course, the interest. He attended the mother home that night, in the hope to be permitted to see the daughter ; but though, when invited to enter, he did so, he found the *tête-à-tête* with the old lady — a half-hour which curiosity readily gave to dullness — unrelieved by the presence of the one object for whom he sought. But a well-filled bookcase, which met his eyes in the hall, suggested to him a mode of approach in future of which he did not scruple to avail himself. He complimented the old lady on the extent of her literary possessions. Such a collection was not usual at that time among the country-houses of that region. He spoke of his passion for books, and how much he would be pleased to be permitted to obtain such as he wanted from the collection before him.

The old lady replied that they were her daughter's, who was also passionately fond of books ; that she valued her collection very highly — they were almost her only friends — but she had no doubt that Mr. Beauchampe would readily receive her permission to take any that he desired for perusal.

Beauchampe expressed his gratitude, but judiciously declined to make his selection that night. The permission necessarily furnished the sanction for a second visit, for which he accordingly prepared himself. He suffered a day, however, to pass — a forbearance that called for the exercise of no small degree of fortitude — before repeating his visit. The second morning, however, he went. He saw the young lady, for a brief instant, at the window, while making his approaches—but that was all! He was admitted, was received by the mother, treated with great kindness, and spent a full hour—how we say not—in company with the venerable and voluble dame. She accorded him the permission of her daughter to use any book in the collection, but the daughter herself did not appear. He mustered courage enough to ask for her, but the inquiry was civilly evaded. He was finally compelled, after lingering to the last, and hoping against hope, to take his departure without attaining the real object of his visit. He selected a volume, however, not that he cared to read it, but simply because the necessity of returning it would afford him the occasion and excuse for another visit.

The proverb tells us that grass never grows beneath the footsteps of true love. It is seldom suffered to grow beneath those of curiosity. Our hero either read, or pretended to have read, the borrowed volume, in a very short space of time. The next morning found him with it beneath his arm, and on his way to the cottage of the Cookes. The grave looks of his mother, and the sly looks of his sisters, were all lost upon him; and, pluming himself somewhat upon the adroitness which disguised the real purpose of his visits, he flattered himself that he should still attain the object which he sought, without betraying the interest which he felt.

Of course, he himself did not suspect the real motives by which he was governed. That a secret passion stirring in his breast had anything to do with that interest which he felt to know the strange lady, was by no means obvious to his own mind.

Whatever may have been the motive by which his conduct was influenced, it did not promise to be followed by any of the results which he desired. His second morning-call was not more fortunate than the first. Approaching, he saw the outline of Miss Cooke's person at an upper window, but she instantly disappeared; and he was received below, and wholly entertained, by the good old mother.

It may readily be imagined that, with a fervent, passionate nature, such as Beauchampe's, this very baffling of his desires was calculated to stimulate and strengthen them. He was a man of equally strong impulses and indomitable will. The necessary creature of such qualities of mind is a puritan tenacity of purpose — a persevering energy, which ceases altogether, finally, to sleep in the work of conquest; or, at least, converts even its sleeping hours into tasks of thought, and wild, vague dreams of modes and operations, by which the work of conquest is to be carried on. The momentary glimpses of the damsel's person, which the ardent youth was permitted to obtain, still kept alive in his mind the strong impression which her beauty had originally made. We do not insinuate that this exhibition was designed by the lady herself for any such object. Such might be the imputation — nay, was, in after-days, by some of her charitable neighbors — but we have every reason for thinking otherwise. We believe that she was originally quite sincere in her desire to avoid the sight and discourage the visits of strangers. Whether this was also the desire of the mother, is not so very certain. We should suppose, on the contrary, that the course of her daughter was one that afforded little real satisfaction to her. If the daughter remained inflexible, the good mother soon convinced Beauchampe that she was not; and, saving the one topic — the daughter herself — there was none upon which good Mrs. Cooke did not expatiate to her visiter with the assured freedoms of a friend of a thousand years. Any approach to *this* subject, however, effectually silenced her: not, it would seem, because she herself felt any repugnance to the subject — for Beauchampe could not fail to perceive that her eyes brightened whenever the daughter was referred to — but her voice was hurried when she replied on such occasions, and her glance stealthily turned to the entrance, as if she dreaded lest the sound should summon other ears to the apartment.

The curiosity of Beauchampe was further stimulated by a general examination of the contents of the library. The selection was such as, in regions where books are more in requisition, and seem more in place, would testify considerably in behalf of the judgment and good taste of the possessor. They were all English books, it is true, but they were genuine classics of the best days of British literature, including the more recent writers of the day. There were additional proofs, in such as he took home with him, of the equal taste and industry of their reader. The fine passages were scored marginally with pencil-lines, and an occasional note in the same manner indicated the acquaintance of the commentator with the best standards of criticism. Beauchampe made another observation, however, which had the effect of leaving it still doubtful whether these notes were made by the present owner. They were all in a female hand. He found that a former name had been carefully obliberated in every volume, that of Miss Cooke being written in its stead. Though doubtful, therefore, whether to ascribe to her the excellent criticism and fine taste which thus displayed itself over the pages which he read, this doubt by no means lessened his anxiety to judge for himself of the attainments of their possessor; and fortune — we may assume thus much — at length helped him to the interview which he sought.

The mother, one day, with nice judgment, fell opportunely sick. It is easier to suspect that she willed this event than to suppose the daughter guilty of duplicity. It necessarily favored the design of Beauchampe. He made his morning visit, which had now become periodical, was ushered into the parlor, where, after a few moments, he was informed that Mrs. Cooke was not visible. She pleaded indisposition. Miss Cooke, however, had instructed the

servant to say to Mr. Beauchampe that he was at liberty
to use the library as before.

By this time the eager nature of Beauchampe was excited
to the highest pitch of anxiety. So many delays — such
baffling — had deprived his judgment of that deliberate action, without the restraint of which the boundaries of con-
vention are very soon overpassed. A direct message from
the mysterious lady, was a step gained. It had the effect
of still further unseating his judgment, and, without scruple,
he boldly despatched a message by the servant, soliciting
permission to see Miss Cooke. An answer was immediately
returned in which she declined seeing him. He renewed
the request with the additional suggestion that he had a
communication to make. This necessarily produced the
desired effect. In a few minutes she descended to the
parlor.

If Beauchampe had been fascinated before, he was certainly not yet prepared for the commanding character of
that beauty which now stood before him. He rose, trembling and abashed, his cheeks suffused with blushes, but his
eyes, though dazzled, were full of the eager admiration
which he felt. She was simply clad, in white. Her person, tall and symmetrical, was erect and dignified. Her
face was that of matured loveliness, shaded, not impaired,
by sadness, and made even more elevated and commanding
by an expression of intense pain which seemed to mingle
with the fire of her eyes, giving a sort of subdued fierce-
ness to her glance, which daunted quite as much as it dazzled him. Perhaps a something of severity in her look
added to his confusion. He stammered confusedly; the
courage which had prompted him to seek the interview,
failed utterly to provide him with the intellectual readiness
by which it was to be carried on. But the feminine instinct
came to his relief. The lady seated herself, motioning
her visiter to do the same.

"Sit down, sir, if you please. My mother presumes

that you are anxious to know how sue is. She instructs me to thank you for your courtesy, and to say that her indisposition is not serious. She trusts in another day to be quite restored."

By this time Beauchampe had recovered something of his confidence.

" It gives me pleasure, Miss Cooke, to hear this. I did fear that your mother was seriously suffering. But I can not do you and myself the injustice to admit that I came simply to see her. No! Miss Cooke, an anxiety to see you in person, and to acknowledge the kindness which has given me the freedom of your library, were among the objects of my visit."

The lady became instantly grave.

" I thank you, sir, for your compliment, but I have long since abandoned society. My habits are reserved. I prefer solitude. My tastes and feelings equally require it. I am governed so far by these tastes and feelings, which have now become habits, that it will not suit me to recognise any new acquaintance. My books are freely at your service, whenever you wish them. Permit me, sir, to wish you good morning."

She rose to depart. Beauchampe eagerly started to his feet.

" Stay, Miss Cooke. Do not leave me thus. Hear me but for a moment."

She resumed her seat with a calm, inflexible demeanor, as if, assured of her strength at any moment to depart, she had no apprehensions on the subject of her detention. The blush again suffused the cheeks of Beauchampe, and the rigid silence which his companion observed, as if awaiting his utterance, suddenly increased his difficulties in this respect. But the ice once broken, his impetuous temper was resolved that it should not freeze again.

" I know, Miss Cooke," he observed, " after what you have just said, that I have no right any longer to trespass

5

upon you, but I dare not do otherwise — I dare not depart — I am the slave of a passion which has brought me, and which keeps me here."

"I must not listen to you, Mr. Beauchampe," she replied, rising, as if to leave the room.

"Forgive me !" he exclaimed, gently detaining her — "forgive me, but you must."

'Must !" her eyes flashed sudden fires.

"I implore the privilege to use the word, but in no offensive sense. Nay, Miss Cooke — I release you — I will not seek to detain you. You are at liberty — with my lips only do I implore you to remain."

The proud woman examined the face of the passionate youth with some slight curiosity. To this, however, he was insensible.

"You are aware, Mr. Beauchampe," she remarked, indifferently, "that your conduct is somewhat unusual."

"Yes, perhaps so. I believe it. Nay, were I to think, Miss Cooke, I should perhaps, under ordinary circumstances, agree to pronounce it unjustifiable. But, believe me, it is meant to be respectful."

She interrupted him : —

"Unless I thought so, sir, I could not be detained here a moment longer."

"Surely, surely, Miss Cooke, you can not doubt my respect — my——"

"I do not, sir."

"Ah ! but you are so cold — so repulsive, Miss Cooke."

"Perhaps I had better leave you, Mr. Beauchampe. It will be better for both of us. You know nothing of me ; I nothing of you."

"You mistake, Miss Cooke, in assuming that I know nothing of you."

"Ha ! sir !" she answered, rising to her feet, her face growing like scarlet, while a blue vein, like a chord, divided the high white forehead in the midst. "What mean you, what know you!"

"Much! I know already that you are alone among women—alone in beauty—in intellect!"

He paused. He marked a sudden and speaking change upon her features which struck him as more singular than the last. The flush had departed from her cheeks, the blue vein had suddenly sunk from sight—a complete pallor overspread her face, and with a slight tremor over her frame, she sank upon the seat from which she had arisen. He sprang forward, and was at once beside her upon his knees. He caught her hand in his own.

"You are sick—you are ill!" he exclaimed.

"No! I am better now!" she answered in low tones.

"Thank God!" he exclaimed. "I feared you had spasms —I dreaded I had offended you. You are still so pale, Miss Cooke—so very pale!"—and he again started to his feet as if to call for assistance. She arrested him.

"Do not alarm yourself," she said with more firmness. "I am subject to such attacks, and they form a sufficient reason, Mr. Beauchampe, why I should not distress strangers with them. Suffer me now to retire."

"Bear with me yet awhile!" he exclaimed, "I will try not to alarm or to annoy you. You ask me what I know of you! nothing, perhaps, were I to answer according to the fashion of the world; everything, if I answer according to the dictates of my heart."

"It is unprofitable knowledge, Mr. Beauchampe."

"Do not say so, I implore you. I know that I am a rash and foolish young man, but I mean not to offend— nay, my purpose is to declare the admiration which I feel."

"I must not hear you, Mr. Beauchampe. I must leave you. As I said before, you are welcome to the use of my books."

"Ah! Miss Cooke, it is you, and not your books which have brought me to your dwelling. Suffer me to see you

when I come. Suffer me to know you—to make myself
known—to bring my sisters; to conduct you to them. They
will all be so glad to see and know you."

She shook her head mournfully, while a sad smile rested
upon her lips as she replied :—

"Mr. Beauchampe," she said, "I will not affect to misunderstand you; but I must repeat, as I have said to you
before, I have done with society. I am in fact done with
the world."

"Done with the world! Oh! what a thought! You,
Miss Cooke, you so able to do all with it!"

"You can not flatter me, Mr. Beauchampe. The world
can be nothing to me. I am nothing to it. To wear out
life in loneliness, forgot, forgetting, is the utmost of my
hopes from the world. Spare me more. It is not well, it
will not be desirable, that any intimacy should exist between me and your sisters."

"Oh! why not? they are so gentle, so pure!"

"Ah! no more, sir, I implore you;" her brow had suddenly become clouded, and she rose. "Leave me now, sir
—I must leave you. I must hear you no longer."

Her voice was firm. Her features had suddenly put on
their former inflexibility of expression. The passionate
youth at once discovered that the moment for moving her
determination was past, and every effort now to detain her
would prejudice his cause.

"You will leave me, Miss Cooke—you will drive me
from you—yet let me hope——"

"Hope nothing from me, Mr. Beauchampe. I would not
have you hope fruitlessly."

"The wish itself assures me that I can not."

"You mistake, sir—you deceive yourself!" she replied
with sterner accents.

"At least let me not be denied your presence. Let me
see you. I am not in the world, nor of it, Miss Cooke. Let
me sometimes meet you here, and if I am forbid to speak of

other things, let me at least speak and hear you speak of these old masters at whose feet I perceive you have been no idle student."

"Mr. Beauchampe, I can promise nothing. To consent to receive and meet you would be to violate many an internal resolve."

"But why this dreary resolution ?"

"Why!—but ask not, sir. No more from me now. You knew not, sir—and you meant not—but you have wakened in my mind this morning many a painful and dreary thought, which you can not dissipate. I say this to excuse myself for what might seem rudeness. I do not wish to excite your curiosity. I tell you, sir, but the truth, when I tell you that I am cut off from the world—it matters not how, nor why. It is so—and the less I see of it the better. When you know this, you will understand why it is that I should prefer not to see you."

"Ah! but not why I should not seek to see you. No Miss Cooke, your dreary destiny does not lessen my willingness to soothe—to share it."

"That can never be."

"Do not say so. If you knew my heart——"

"Keep its secrets, Mr. Beauchampe. Enough, sir, that I know my own. *That*, sir, has but one prayer, and that is for peace—but one passion, and that, sir——"

"Is—speak, say, Miss Cooke, tell me what this passion is ? Relieve me; but tell me not that you love another. Not that—anything but that."

"Love !" she exclaimed scornfully; "love! no, sir, I do not love. Happily, I am free from any such weakness—that weakness of my sex !"

"Call it not a weakness, dear Miss Cooke—but a strength—a strength of the heart, not peculiar to your sex, but the source of what is lofty and ennobling in the heart of man."

"Ay, he has a precious stock of it, no doubt; but no more

of this, Mr. Beauchampe. I have my passion, perhaps, but surely love makes no part of it."

"What then ?"

"Hate !" she cried with startling energy.

"Hate ! ha ! can it be that *you* hate, Miss Cooke ?"

"Ay, sir, it is possible. Hate is my passion, not the only one, since it produces another bearing its own likeness."

"And that ?——"

"Is revenge !—Ask yourself, with these passions reign-ing in my heart, whether there is room for anything more — for any other ! There is not, and you may not deceive yourself with the vain hope to plant any feebler passion in a spot which bears such poisonous weeds."

Thus speaking she left the room, and, astounded by her vehemence, and by the strange though imperfect revelation which she had made, Beauchampe found himself alone !

CHAPTER VIII.

DEVELOPMENTS OF PASSION.

HAD the words of the lady fallen from the lips of a ora-
cle, they could not have more completely fastened themselves on the ears of our hero. Her sublime beauty as she
spoke those wild accents was that of one inspired. Her
eye flashed with fires of a supernatural brightness. Her
brow was lifted, and her hand smote upon her heart, when
she declared what fierce passions were its possessors, as if
they themselves were impelling the blow, and the heart was
that of some mortal enemy.

Beauchampe was as completely paralyzed as if he had
suffered an electric stroke. He would have arrested her
departure, but his words and action were equally slow. He
had lost the power of hands and voice; and, when he was
able to speak, she had gone.

Confused, bewildered, and mortified, he left the house;
and sad and silent he pursued his way along the homeward
paths. Before he had gone far he was saluted with the
laughter of merry voices, and his sisters were at his side.
What a contrast was that which instantly challenged the
attention of his mind, between the girlish, almost childish
and characterless damsels beside him, and the intense, soul-
speaking woman he had left! How impertinent seemed the
levity of Jane! how insipid the softness and milky sadness
of the gentle-hearted Mary! The reflections of the brother

were in no wise favorable to the sisters, but he gave no
utterance to the involuntary thoughts.

"Why, the queen of Sheba has struck you dumb, Brother
Orville !" said the playful Jane. "You have seen her to-
day, I'm certain. That's the way she always comes over
one. She has had on her cloudy-cap to-day for your especial benefit."

"But have you seen her, brother ?" asked the more timid
Mary.

"To be sure he has—don't you see ? nothing less could
make Orville look on us as old Burke, the schoolmaster,
used to look on him when he put the nouns and verbs out
of countenance. He has seen her to be sure, and she came
out clothed in thunder, I reckon."

"Jane, you vex Orville. But—you did see her, brother ?"

"Yes, Mary, Jane is right."

"Didn't I tell you ? I could see it the moment I set
eyes on him."

"And don't you think her very beautiful, brother ?"

"Very beautiful, Mary."

"Yes, a sort of thunderstorm beauty, I grant you," said
Jane; "dark and dismal, with such keen flashes of lightning as to dazzle one's eyes and terrify one's heart !"

"Not a bad description, Jane," said the brother.

"To be sure not. Don't I know her ? Why, Lord love
you, the first time we were together I felt all crumpled up,
body and soul. My soul, indeed, was like a little mouse,
looking everywhere for a hole to creep into and be out of
the way of danger; and I fancied she was a great tigress
of a mouser, with her eyes following the mouse every which
way, amusing herself with my terrors, and ready to spring
upon me and end them the moment she got tired of the
sport. I assure you I didn't feel secure a single moment
while I was with her. I expected to be gobbled up at a
moment's warning."

"How you run on, Jane, and so unreasonably !" said the

gentle Mary. "Now, brother, I think all this description very unlike Anna Cooke. That she's sad, usually, and gloomy sometimes, I'm willing to admit; but she was very kind and gentle in what she had to say to me, and I believe would have been much more so, if Jane hadn't continually come about us making a great laughter. That she is very smart I'm certain, and that she is very beautiful everybody with half an eye must see."

"I don't, and I've both eyes, and pretty keen ones too."

"Well, girls," said Beauchampe, "I intend that you shall have a good opportunity to form a correct opinion of Miss Cooke—her talents and her beauty. I intend to carry you both to visit her to-morrow."

"Oh, don't, don't, brother, I beg you! she'll eat me up, the great mouser! I sha'n't be a moderate mouthful for her anger."

And the mischievous Jane darted from his side, and lifted up her hand with a manner of affected deprecation.

Mary rebuked her as was usual on such occasions, and her rebuke was somewhat seconded by one which was more effectual. The brother betrayed some little displeasure as well in words as in looks, and poor Jane contrived to make the *amende* by repressing some portion of that lively temerity of temper which is not always innocuous in its pleasantries.

In this way they proceeded to the cottage, where, in private, the young man contrived to let his mother know how much he was charmed with the mysterious lady, but not how much of his admiration he had revealed. On this head, indeed, he was as little capable as anybody else of telling the whole truth. He knew not, in fact, what he had said in the interview with Miss Cooke. He had felt the impulse to say many things, and in his conscience felt that he might have said them; but of the precise nature of his confessions he knew nothing. Something, indeed, he might infer from what he recollected of the language of

Anna Cooke to himself. He could easily comprehend that the freedom with which she declared her feelings must have been induced in great degree by the revelation of his own; but, as he had no right—and, by-the-way, as little wish—to betray her secrets, so he naturally spared himself the mortification of telling his own.

Thus matters stood with him. His mother listened gravely. She could see, in the faltering tongue and flushed face of her son, much more of the actual state of his feelings than his words declared. She was not satisfied that he should fall in love with Miss Cooke: not that she had anything against that young lady—she had none of the idle prejudices of her eldest daughter—but that the beautiful stranger—and she acknowledged her to be beautiful —did not impress her favorably. Mrs. Beauchampe was a very pious lady; and the feeling of society is so nearly allied to that of pure religion, that when she found Anna Cooke deficient in the one tendency, she naturally suspected her equal lack of the other. But, in the next place, if the old lady had her objections to the young lady, she, at the same time, was too fond of her son to resist his wishes very long or very urgently. She contented herself with suggesting some grounds of objection, which the ardency and eloquence of the latter found but little difficulty in overcoming. At all events, it was arranged that Beauchampe should take his sisters the next day to visit his fair, and, so far, tyrannical enslaver.

From this visit, Beauchampe, though without knowing exactly why, had considerable expectations. At least, he did not despair of seeing the young lady. The mother politely kept sick—much, it may be added, to the annoyance of her daughter. The day came, and breakfast was scarcely over before the impetuous youth began to exhibit his anxiety. But the sisters had to make their toilet, and something, he fancied, was due to his own. A country-girl has her own ideas of finery, and, the difference of taste aside, the only other differences between herself and the city-maiden are differences in degree. The toilet is the altar where Vanity not only makes her preparations, but says her prayers. We care not to ask whether Love be the image that stands above it or not. Perhaps there are few calculations of the young female heart in which Love does not enter as an inevitable constituent. Certainly, few of her thoughts are altogether satisfactory, if they bear not his figures in the woof.

Beauchampe's sisters fairly put his patience to the test; and, strange to say, his favorite sister Mary was much the most laggard in her proceedings. She certainly had never before made such an unnecessary fuss about her pretty little person. At length, however, all were made ready. The party sallied forth, reached the house of Mrs. Cooke, were admitted, and, after a brief delay, the daughter entered the room, to a very quick march beaten by the heart of our ardent hero.

But, though this accompaniment was so very quick, the entrance of Anna Cooke was calm, slow, and dignified, as usual. She received the party very kindly; and her efforts to please them while they stayed seemed as natural and unconstrained as if the business of pleasing had been a habit of her life. Jane's apprehensions of being eaten up soon subsided, and the gentle Mary had the satisfaction of bringing about, by some inadvertent remark of her own, an animating conversation between her brother and the lovely hostess. We say animated conversation, but it must not be supposed that it was a lively one. The animation of the parties arose from their mutual earnestness of character. The sanguine temperament thus readily throws itself into the breach, and identifies itself with the most passing occasions. It was in this way that Beauchampe found himself engaged in a brief and pleasant discussion of one of those topics, arising from books, in which the parties may engage with warmth, yet without endangering the harmony of the conference; even as a wild strain of music—from the rolling, rising organ, or the barbaric drum and Saracenic trumpet—will make the heart thrill and throb again, with a sentiment of awe which yet it would be very loath not to have awakened.

Beauchampe was perfectly ravished, the more particularly as he did not fail to see that Miss Cooke was evidently not insensible to the spirit and intelligence which he displayed in his share of the dialogue. The presence of the sisters, fortunately, had the effect of controlling the brother in the utterance of those passionate and personal feelings which had been forced, as it were, from his lips the day previous. Love was unspoken by either, and yet, most certainly, love was the only thought of one, and possibly, of both. But love is the most adroit of logicians. He argues his case upon the data and criteria of a thousand far less offensive topics. Religion, law, politics; art, science, philosophy; all subjects he will discuss as if he had no other purpose than to adjust their moot points and settle their vexing contrarieties. The only misfortune is that when he is done —nay, while he is going on, one is apt to forget the subject in the orator. Special pleader that he is, in what a specialty all his labors terminate!

When Anna Cooke and Orville Beauchampe separated that day, what of the argument did they remember? Each readily remembered that the speaker was most eloquent. Beauchampe could tell you that the fair debater was never so beautiful in person, so high and commanding in intellect before; and when Anna Cooke was alone, she found herself continually recalling to her mind's eye, the bright aspect and beaming eyes of the enthusiastic young lawyer—so earnest, so seemingly unconscious of himself, as he poured forth the overflowing treasures of a warm heart, and a really well-stored and naturally-vigorous intellect. She saw too, already, how deeply she had impressed herself upon his fancy. Beauchampe's heart had no disguises

Strange feelings rose into her own. Strange, terrible thoughts filled her mind ; and the vague musings of her wild and scarcely coherent spirit, formed themselves into words upon her tongue.

"Is not this an avenger!" she muttered. "Is not this an avenger sent from heaven! I have striven in vain. I am fettered. It is denied to me to pursue and sacrifice the victim. Oh! surely woman is the image of all feebleness. These garments are its badges; and sanction obstruction and invite injustice. As I am, thus and here, what hope is there that vengeance can be mine? The conquest of this enthusiastic youth will afford me the freedom that I crave, the agent that I need, the sacrifice for which only I dream and pray. With him the victim may be sought and found wherever he hides himself, and this crushed heart shall once more rise in triumph — this trampled pride be uplifted — the pangs of this defrauded and lacerated bosom be soothed by the sacrifice of blood!

"And why should it not be so? Why? Do I live for any other passion? Do I entertain any other image in my soul? What is love, to me, and fear, and hope, and joy — the world without and the world within — what but a dark abode in which there is but one light — one star, red and wild — a planet rising fiery at the birth of hate, only to set in blood, in the sacrifice of its victim. Here is one comes to me bearing the knife. He is mine, so declare his looks — he loves me, so equally speak his words and actions. Shall I not use his love for my hate? What is his love to me? His love — ha! ha! ha! His love, indeed — the love of a young ambitious lawyer. Is it not rather the perfection of vengeance that I should employ one of the tribe for the destruction of another!

"But no — no! why should I involve this boy in my fate? Why should I make him my instrument in this wild purpose? He is not of the same brood, though of that brotherhood. This youth is noble. He is too ardent, too impetuous, for a deliberate design of evil. His soul is generous. He feels—he feels!—he, at least, is no masked, no cold-blooded traitor, serpent-like, crawling into the open and warm heart to beguile and sting.

"No—no! I must not wrong him thus. He must be spared this doom. I must brood over it alone, and let the fates work it as they may. Though, were he but half less ardent—could I suspect him of a baseness—I should whet the dagger, and swear him to its use! Yes—at any altar, for that sacrifice—though that altar be the very one on which *I* am the sacrifice—though it bear the name of love, and hold above it *his* cruel and treacherous image!"

Such were the frequent meditations of the passionate and proud woman. Her mother prompted these not un-frequently without intending it. She, with the sagacity of an ancient dealer, soon discovered the sort of coin which Beauchampe was disposed to bring with him into Love's crowded market-place. She readily detected, in the unso-phisticated manners of Beauchampe, the proper material on which it would be easy for her daughter to work. The intense, inflammable, impetuous nature was such as a single glance of those dark, bright eyes—a single sentence from that mellow, yet piercing, sweet, yet deep-toned voice—might light up with inextinguishable flame—might prompt with irresistible impulses. Of course, the old lady had no knowledge of the one absorbing passion which had become a mania in the breast of her daughter. Her calculations went no farther than to secure a son-in-law—but of this the daughter had no thought, only as it might be necessary to effect other objects. *Her* purpose was to find an avenger, if anything; and, even for this object, we have seen, from her spoken meditations, she was yet too generous to seek for such an agent in one so unselfish, so true-hearted as Beauchampe had appeared.

But the rough-hewing of events was not to be left either to mother, or daughter, however resolved and earnest might

be the will which they severally or mutually exercised.
The strongest of us, in the most earnest periods of our
lives, move very much as the winds blow. It may hurt our
vanity, but will do our real interests no harm to declare,
that individual man is mostly, after all, only a sort of moral
vane on the world's housetop. If you find him stationary
for any length of time be sure it is less from principle than
rust.

CHAPTER IX.

LOVE AND LAW.

"Denial, which is death,
Hangs on her lips, and from her heart to mine
Sends the great agony, like an icy shaft!"

THE progress of Beauchampe, though in one respect nothing, was yet not inconsiderable as bringing about the development of his own tendencies and affections. In the results which his desires might have suggested to his mind,
there had been no sort of progress. He was pretty much
where he was at the beginning. His pursuit, begun in his
instincts, and seemingly from mere curiosity, had, however,
brought him to a better consciousness of the meaning of
that sudden fancy which had prompted him to dream of a
heart-ideal at the moment when love seemed to be the re-
motest thing from his thoughts. He now began to feel that
a fate had been busy to bring about the acquaintance between himself and the mysterious stranger. He had identified the vague image of his fancy with the fascinating
woman whose charms, for the first time, seemed to put his
passions into activity. Yet his thoughts gave him but little
encouragement. He had no such vanity as could persuade
him that his interviews with the object of his fancy had
been productive of any good to his cause; and his moments
of calmer reflection only taught him additional humility, as
he felt how very wide was the gulf that lay between his
hopes, his claims, and pretensions, and the very remarka-

able woman whom he had begun to worship. He did not deceive himself for a moment with the idea that he had made, or could make, any impression upon her. He felt that he had not done so; and while he was as eager in his desires as ever, he was full of despondency as he examined, with all the calmness possible to his nature, the very slender foundation for his hopes. The startling character of the scene which we have just described—her terrible declaration, so evidently earnest—the mysterious secret of her life, the existence of which it declared, but did not elucidate—all seemed to determine against the possibility of any progress with a nature at once so wild, so powerful, and so utterly unlike the ordinary characteristics of the sex as usually found in society.

But perseverance, where passion is the impelling power, will sooner or later work its way to the object which it seeks. It will bring about the issue, certainly, though it may be disappointed in its results. If hate be intense on the one hand, love, in the case of a determined will, is no feeble opponent; at all events, the one may be as tenacious of its object as the other: and the fiery passions of Beauchampe, if less matured and less concentrative than the hate which raged in the bosom of Anna Cooke, were yet in hourly training under the guidance of a fate, which, as she was now beginning to think, contemplated the union of both forces, for the gratification of at least one of the seemingly hostile passions!

We pass over numerous small details in the progress of the parties, which were yet, in some degree, important in bringing about the general result. They served gradually to break down the barriers, of a social kind, which had hitherto stood up as a wall between the two families. The impetuous nature of Beauchampe had succeeded in tearing away those which had been set up by his own. He was too much the object of warm affection with mother and sisters to suffer them very long to maintain their hostilities to

his obvious desires; and, without exactly apprehending that her son designed anything further than the communion with a young woman whose intellect had won the admiration of his own—without thinking it certain, or even probable, that this communion would ripen into love—for Mrs. Beauchampe felt that there was something repulsive to herself in the character of Anna Cooke, and naturally concluded that the same qualities would exercise antagonistic effects to passion on the part of her son—she at length gave fully in to his wishes that there should be a closer intimacy between her girls and the beautiful and mysterious stranger.

This concession won, the ardent nature of Beauchampe pushed his advantages with due celerity and earnestness. He suffered no day to escape without some approach to the mutual intercourse of the parties; and, with even pace, Mrs. Cooke, and even her daughter, became reconciled to the frequent presence of the Beauchampes within their household, while the visits of the strangers, though less frequent, were now stripped of nearly all constraint. Our young lawyer felt that he had compassed a considerable degree of ground when he found himself admitted to continual intercourse with the Cookes, as a friend of the family. Mrs. Cooke had some unproductive property, of which she desired to dispose. She had certain ancient claims, which were thought not beyond recovery. There were papers, and titles, and letters, which were to be examined professionally; and young Beauchampe was duly installed as the lawyer of the widow and her daughter.

Lawyer and lover! The combination promises rare results in logic. We shall see what they are to produce. Usually, the one sinks himself in the other character. Let the client understand that this is not certainly the fact, and he considers his case in bad condition. The lover will be apt to kill the lawyer, in his opinion. He will get out of such doubtful custody before next term, if this be possible. At all events, he will desire assistant counsel.

We doubt if Beauchampe ever fully surrendered his mind to the law-matters of Mrs. Cooke. We somewhat fear that he considered all the business a bore. At all events, he hurried over its details, whenever they conferred on the subject, with what Mrs. Cooke soon began to think a singular want of regard for her interests.

But neither did he seem to make much progress with his own. Though he turned away from the mother to the daughter, leaving the law to shift for itself, yet love with the latter was an interdicted subject.

But when, and for how long, will love stay interdicted?

Can you answer, gentle reader? What is your experience of the matter? As easily curb the tides, chain the winds, arrest the flight of birds in their season — do any other impossible thing — with the subtlest agencies of life and nature working with an indomitable will, and under the impulse of a law the secret of which no man can claim to fathom.

Beauchampe was under interdict of law.

Love was under interdict on Beauchampe's lips.

But love could not be put under interdict in Beauchampe's heart —

And the wild blood of Beauchampe was of such fiery impulse, that it never yet had bowed submissively to law.

What curbed him for a while, and made him submissive, in appearance, to the interdict, was awe, veneration, the humility of his hope, the fear lest he should prejudice and lose his case by precipitation. In brief, for the first time in his life, he called in Prudence to his aid.

Now, when Love makes an ally of Prudence, it becomes a very formidable power. It was the only ally who could possibly have served Beauchampe in his approaches to Anna Cooke. It disarmed her vigilance in the first place; it increased his own; and sap may enable one to overcome the fortress which resists the most terrible assault.

Time wrought favorably for Beauchampe. It enabled

him to show his resources of mind and character—above all, the ingenuous and impulsive, the frank and faithful, the solicitous and confiding, the dutiful and considerate — which, in spite of his fiery passions, were the predominant virtues of his mind and heart.

Anna Cooke gradually took pleasure in seeing him. She found him both abler in intellect and gentler of disposition than she had fancied him at first. His amenities, prompted as much by his fears of the loss of her favor, had greatly controlled the natural audacity of his blood, and the prudence of his approach gradually served to quiet her suspicions. She somewhat relaxed in that vigilant watch of eye and ear which she had maintained over his first approaches. She no longer looked for the equivocal in his speech; no longer encountered the doubtful with asperity. The way was gradually smoothing for the approach of other powers. The small pioneer virtues, which Passion so cunningly employs under the guidance of that great engineer Prudence, were doing wonders in the cause of a despot, who, as yet, judiciously kept his standard out of sight.

Anna Cooke was really getting to be quite pleased when Beauchampe looked in of a morning, or strolled in to tea, unaccompanied by his sisters, of an evening.

It is one of the natural arts of Love to excite the sensibilities into the most commanding activity, even while it refines and purifies the tastes; to subdue all the sharpnesses of character, even as it subdues the asperities of tone and accent in the voice; to throw into the eyes a mild, persuasive expression of entreaty and solicitude; a hesitating tenderness into the utterance; and, above all, so certainly, and even suddenly, to elevate the mind, that even the vulgar nature and the inferior understanding become modified and enlarged under its influence—and Ignorance itself seems, as if under inspiration, to receive such an increase of intelligence, that its speech shall rarely declare its deficiencies.

Now, though by no means a wise, learned, or greatly-gifted youth, Beauchampe was neither vulgar nor ignorant. Still, at the beginning of his intercourse with Anna Cooke, he was full of those salient points of character and manner which exhibit the lack of that refining attrition of society which no course of education can well supply. And some of these saliences grated upon Anna Cooke on his first interview with her.

But, in a single week, all this was altered. Love carries with it those instincts of good taste, those solicitous sensibilities, that refinement becomes inevitable under its presence; and without his own consciousness, perhaps, though it did not escape hers, the bearing, the whole carriage and deportment, tone and manner, of Beauchampe, underwent rapid transition. From the rough, sturdy, confident rustic —almost insolent in his independence, and very determined upon his objects—indifferent to, if not wholly ignorant of, the higher polish of the social world—he grew, in a single week, into the subdued and quiet gentleman, heedful always of the sensibilities of those whom he addressed, and tenderly considerate of the claims and rights of others. At a single bound he became a gentleman!

And that word "gentleman"—how few have ever weighed and properly taught its due significance! To acquire this character is one of the first processes by which we make a Christian. Certainly, no man can be a Christian who is not first a gentleman. And this involves no idle lesson for the clergy. Among writers, old Middleton, the dramatist, seems to have been almost the only one who seems fully to have caught a just conception of the character so as to define it. Incidentally, he gives a happy array of the virtues—not merely qualifications, graces, and manners—essential to the gentleman. His allusion to the MAN Christ will only be misconstrued by blockheads:—

> "Patience, my lord! why, 'tis the soul of peace;
> Of all the virtues, 'tis nearest kin to Heaven:

> It makes men like the gods. *The best of men,*
> That e'er wore earth about him, was a sufferer;
> A soft, meek, patient, humble, tranquil spirit,
> *The first true gentleman that ever breathed!"*

Beauchampe, under the tuition of Love, was making great progress toward becoming a gentleman. Love first made him gentle; Prudence then brought in the other allies, Patience, Forbearance, Conciliation, Solicitude — humble virtues, serving-brothers of the household, whose permitted tendance will make of the humblest dwelling —

> "A happy home, like heaven!"

Beauchampe's improvement, under the new course of tuition — under this new, potent, and almost unsuspected teacher — was wonderfully rapid. A few weeks had made the most surprising changes in bearing, sentiment, character, nay, in the very expression of his face. His features — and the fact belongs to the studies of the psychologist in especial, as significant of what the refining arts did for the Greek soul and character — his very features, though not wanting in a certain nobleness before, had become softened, sweetened, spiritualized as it were, in the wonderful progress which the gentler virtues had been making in his heart.

The result did not escape the attention of Anna Cooke. She was not insensible to the singular and interesting change in his features since the time when she first saw him. It surprised even her, who was ordinarily so indifferent to external aspects. It gradually affected her own feelings, as it conveyed an exquisite compliment to her own influence. She saw the beginning of this improvement of the young man, in the birth of his devotion to herself. She began to feel a certain sympathy with the progress of a sentiment which was so powerful and at the same time so unobtrusive, so little claiming or aspiring. Not that she dreamed to encourage it. How could she? That was impossible! So she said to herself, whenever she thought upon the subject. We have seen her expressed reflections.

She renewed them. Her mind was as unmoved as ever
The changes, whatever they might be, were confined wholly
to her tastes and sensibilities. But these, after all, are the
true provinces in which true love is decreed to work!

Her mental opinions and resolves had undergone no
change. Nay, they grew stronger, by a natural tendency,
as her interest in the young man increased. She resolved
that he should not be sacrificed; and this resolve was the
necessary parent of another. She could never give encouragement to the object of her present lover. She could
never be his wife. No! she already felt too much interested in the youth, to use her own energetic language, uttered in midnight soliloquy, "to dishonor him with her
hand!" She was not conscious of the sigh which fell from
her lips when this determination was spoken. She was not
conscious, and consequently not apprehensive, of the progress which a new passion was making in her heart. That
sigh had its signification, but this, though it fell from her
own lips, was inaudible to her own ears.

Laboring under this unconsciousness with regard to her
own feelings, it was perhaps not so great a stretch of magnanimity, on her part, to resolve that Beauchampe should
not be permitted to serve her brooding hatred, or to share
in her secret sorrows. Such was her determination.

One day, he grew more warm in his approaches. Circumstances favored his object, and the topics which they
had discussed, on previous occasions, insensibly encouraged
this. Suppressing his eagerness of manner, putting as much
curb as he could on the impatient utterance which was only
too habitual to him where his feelings were excited, he
strove, in the most deliberate form of address, to declare
his passion, and to solicit her hand.

"Mr. Beauchampe," she said firmly, "I thank you. I
am grateful for this proof of your regard and attachment;
and, in regretting it, I implore you not to suspect me of
caprice, or a wanton desire to exercise the power which

your unhappy preference confers on me. Nor am I insensible to your claims. Were it possible, sir, that I could ever marry, I know no one to whom I would sooner intrust my affections than to you. But there is an insuperable barrier between us—not to be broken—not to be overpassed. Never! never! never!"

"Do not speak thus, dearest Miss Cooke. Spare me this utterance. What is the barrier, this insuperable barrier, not to be broken, not to be overpassed? Trust me, it can be broken, it can be passed. What are the obstructions that true love can not remove?"

"Not these, not these! It is impossible, sir. I do not deceive myself—I would not deceive you—but I assure you, Mr. Beauchampe, that the truth I declare is no less solemn than certain. I can never listen to your prayer— I can never become your wife—no, nor the wife of any man! The barrier which thus isolates me from mankind is, I solemnly tell you, impassable, and can not be broken."

"Suffer me to strive—it is not *in me* that your objections arise?"

"No! but—"

"Then suffer me to try and overcome this difficulty— remove this barrier."

"It will be in vain, sir; you would strive in vain."

"Not so! declare it—say in what it consists—and, believe me, if such talents as are mine, such toils as man can devote, with such a reward awaiting him as that which my success would secure for me, can effect an object, I must succeed. Speak to me freely, Miss Cooke. Show me this obstacle—"

"Never! never! There, at once, the difficulty rises. I can not, dare not, reveal it. Ask no more, I entreat you. I should have foreseen this, and commanded it otherwise. I have suffered your attentions too long, Mr. Beauchampe: for your own sake, let me forbid them now. They can never come to good. They can have no fruits. Here, before Heaven, which I invoke to hear me, I can never be—"

"Stay!—do not speak it!" he exclaimed, passionately catching her uplifted hand, and silencing, by his louder accent, the word upon her lips.

"Stay, Miss Cooke! be not too hasty—be not rash in this decision; I implore you, for your sake and mine. Hear me calmly—resume your seat but for a few moments. *I* will strive to be calm; but only hear me."

He led her to a seat, which she resumed with that air of recovered dignity and stern composure which shows a mind made up and resolute. He was terribly agitated, in spite of all his efforts at composure. His eyes trembled, and his lips quivered, and the movements of his frame were almost convulsive. But he also was a man of strong will. But for his youth, he had been as inflexible as herself. He recovered himself sufficiently to speak to her in tones surprisingly coherent, and with a degree of thoughtfulness which showed how completely a determined will can control the utterance even of extraordinary passion.

"Hear me, Miss Cooke. I can see that there is a mystery about you which I do not seek to penetrate. You have your secret. Let it be so still. I love you, deeply, passionately, as I never fancied it was possible for me or any man to love. This passion rends my frame, distracts my mind—makes it doubtful if I could endure life in its denial. I have seen you only to worship you. Lost to me, I lose faith as well as hope. I no longer know my divinities; I no longer care for life, present or future. Do not suppose I speak wildly. *I* believe all that I say. It *must* be as I say it. Now, hear me: to avoid this fate, I am willing to risk many evils—dangers that might affright the ordinary man under the ordinary feelings of man. You spoke the other day of having but a single passion, which was not love!—"

"Hate!" she interrupted him to say.

"Hate, it was—and that gave birth to another not un-like it."

"Revenge! yes, revenge!" such was her second inter-ruption. He proceeded:—

"I understand something of this. You have been wronged. You have an enemy. I will seek him. I will be your champion—die for you if need be—only tell me that you will be mine!"

"Will you, indeed, do this?"

She rose, approached him, laid her hand on his arm, and looked into his eyes with a keen, fixed, fixing, and fascina-ting glance, like that of a serpent. Her tones were very low, very audible, but how impressive! They sunk not into his ear, but into his heart, and a cold thrill followed them there. Before he could reply, however, she receded from him, sunk again into her seat, and covered her face in her hands. He approached her. She waved him off.

"Leave me, Mr. Beauchampe—leave me, now and for ever. I can not hear you. I *will* not. I need not your help. You *can not* revenge me."

"I will! I can! Your enemy shall be mine. I will pur-sue him to the ends of the earth! But give me his name."

"No, you shall not!" she said with apparent calmness. "Thus I reject your offer—your double offer. I will not wrong your generosity—your love, Beauchampe—by a compliance with your prayer. Leave me now; and, oh, come not to me again! I would rather not see you. I feel for you—deeply, sincerely—but, no more. Leave me now—leave me for ever."

He sunk on his knee beside her. He clasped her hand, and carried it passionately to his lips. She rose, and with-drew it from his grasp.

"Rise, Beauchampe," she said, in subdued but firm ac-cents. "Let it lessen your disappointment to know that, if I could ever be the wife of any man, you should have the preference over all. I believe your soul to be noble. I do not believe you would be guilty of a baseness. Believing this, I will not abuse your generosity. You are young. You speak with the ardor of youth; and with the same ardor you feel, for the moment, the disappointments of youth. The same glow of feeling will enable you to overcome them. You will forget me very soon. Let me entreat you, for your own sake, to do so. Henceforward, I will assist you in the effort. I will not see you again."

A burst of passionate deprecation and appeal answered this solemn assurance, but did not affect her decision. He rose, again endeavored to grasp and detain her hand, but she broke away with less dignity of movement than usual; and, had not the eyes of the youth been blinded by his own weaknesses, he might have seen the big tear in hers, which she fled precipitately only to conceal.

CHAPTER X.

HOPE DENIED.

FROM this period Miss Cooke studiously withheld her presence from the eyes of her infatuated lover. In vain did he return day after day to her dwelling. His only reception was accorded by the mother, whose garrulity was considerably lessened in the feeling of disappointment which the course of her daughter necessarily inspired in her mind. She had had her own plans, which, as she knew the firmness of her daughter's character, she could not but be convinced were effectually baffled. To her Beauchampe declared himself, but from her he received no encouragement except that which was contained in her own consent, which, as he had already discovered, did not by any means imply that of the one object whose consent was everything. The old woman pleaded in secret the passion of the young man, but she pleaded fruitlessly. Her petition became modified into one soliciting only her daughter's consent to receive him as before; and to induce this consent the more readily, Beauchampe pledged himself not to renew the subject of love.

But Anna Cooke now knew the value of such pledges. She also knew, by this time, the danger to herself of again meeting with one whose talents and worth she had already learned to admire. The feeling of prudence grew stronger as her impressions in his favor were increased. This con tradiction of character is not of common occurrence. But the position of Anna Cooke was not only painful but a peculiar one. To suffer her affections to become involved with Beauchampe was only to increase her difficulties and mortifications. She felt that it would be dishonorable to accept him as a husband without revealing her secret, and that revealed, it would be very doubtful whether he would be so willing to take her as his wife. This was a dilemma which she naturally feared to encounter.

We do not say, that she did not also share in those feelings of disappointment and denial under which Beauchampe so greatly suffered. The sadness increased upon her countenance, and softened its customary severity. She felt the darker passions of her mind flickering like some sinking candle-flame, and growing daily more feeble under the antagonist feeling of another of very different character. The dream of hate and vengeance which for five years had been, however baneful to her heart, a source of strength to her frame, grew nightly less vivid, and less powerful over her imagination; and, hopeless as she was of love, she trembled lest the other passions which, however strangely, had yielded her solace for so long a time, should abandon her also.

For such a nature as that of Anna Cooke, some strong food was necessary. There must be some way to exercise and employ those deep desires and earnest spiritings of her mind, which else would madden and destroy her. It became necessary to recall her hates, to renew her vows and prayers of vengeance, to concentrate her thoughts anew on the bloody sacrifice which she had so long meditated in secret.

But this was no easy task. The image of Beauchampe came between her eyes and that of the one victim whose destruction alone she sought. The noble, generous, devoted countenance of the one, half obliterated the wily, treacherous visage of the other. The perpetual pleadings of the mother contributed to present this obstacle to her mind.

To escape from this latter annoyance, and, if possible, evade the impression, which, in softening her feelings, had obliterated some of her hates, she renewed a practice which she had for some time neglected. She might be seen every morning stealing from the cottage and taking her way to the cover of the adjacent forests. Here, hidden from all eyes, she buried herself in the religious solitude. What feelings filled her heart, what fancies vexed her mind, what striving forms of love and hate, conflicted in her fancy, we may perhaps conjecture ; but there, alone, save with the images of her thought, she wasted the vacant hours ; drawing her soul's strength from that bitter weed of hate, the worst moral poison which the immortal soul can ever cherish.

With Beauchampe the sorrow was not less, and there was less to strengthen ; but that little was not of so dangerous a quality. He felt the pang of denial, but the bitterness of hate had never yet blighted the young, green leaves of his youthful affections. He was unhappy, but not desperate. Still he could not but see, in the course taken by Anna Cooke, a character of strength and inflexibility, which rendered all prospects of future success, which looked to her, extremely doubtful. There had been no relaxing in her rigor. The mother, whose own sympathy with his cause was sufficiently obvious, had shown its hopelessness, even when she most encouraged him to persevere. Perseverance had taught him the rest of a hard lesson — and the young lover, in his first love, now trembled to find himself alone !

Alone ! and such a loneliness. The affections of mother and sisters no longer offered solace or companionship to his heart. They no longer spoke to his affections. Their words fell upon his ears only to startle and annoy ; their gentle smiles were only so many gleams of cold, mocking

moonlight scattered along the dreary seas of passion in
his soul. He felt that he could not live after this fashion,
for he had still a hope—a hope just sufficiently large to
keep him doubtful. Anna Cooke had declared that her
scruples were not to him. The bar which severed her from
him was that which severed her from man. But for that—
such was her own assurance—" he should be preferred to
all others whom she knew."

That bar! What was it? Beauchampe was not sufficiently experienced in the history of the passions, to conjecture what that obstacle might be. He fancied, at the
utmost, that her affections might have been slighted ; he
knew—but chiefly from books which are not always correct in such matters—that women did not usually forgive
such an offence. Betrothed, she might have been deserted
—perhaps with insult—and this, he readily thought, might
amply justify the fierce spirit of vengeance which she
breathed. Or, it might be that she had been born to fortune, and had been wronged and robbed, by some wily villain, of her possessions. Something of this he fancied he
had gathered from the garrulous details of the mother.

But, even were these conjectures true, still there was
nothing in them to establish such a barrier as Anna Cooke
insisted on, between his passion and herself. Blinded as
he was by his preference, and, in his own simple innocence
of heart, overlooking the only reasonable mode by which
such a mystery could be solved, the truly wretched youth
became hourly more so. Failing to find his way to her
presence, he resorted to that process of pen, ink, and paper,
which the Heloïse of Pope insists was designed by Heaven
expressly for the use of such wretches as Beauchampe and
herself, and his soul poured itself forth upon his sheet with
all the burning effluence of the most untameable affection.
Page after page grew beneath his hands—every line a keen
arrow from the bended bow of passion, and shot directly
at the heart. To borrow the phraseology of the old Span-

ish teachers of the *estilo culto*, if his tears wet the paper, the heat of his words dried it as soon. Beauchampe spoke from his soul and it penetrated to hers. But though she felt and suffered, she was unmoved. Her reply was firm and characteristic : —

"Noble young man, leave me and be happy. Depart from this place; seek me, see me, think of me, no more! Why should you share a destiny like mine? Obey your own. It calls you elsewhere. If it be just to you, yours will be lofty and honorable; if not, at least it will spare you any participation in one so dreary as is mine. Go, I implore you, and cease to endure the anguish which you still inflict. Go, forget me, and be happy. Yet, if not, take with you as the saddest consolation I can give, the assurance that you leave behind you a greater suffering than you bear away. If, as you tell me, the arrow rankles in your heart, believe me there is an ever-burning fire which encircles mine. I have not even the resource of the scorpion, not, at least, until my 'desperate fang' has done its work on another brain than my own. Then, indeed, the remedy were easy; at all events where life depends upon resolution, one can count its allotted minutes in the articulations of a drowsy pulse. Once more, noble young man, I thank you; once more 1 implore you to depart. I will not send you my blessings—I will not endanger your safety by a prayer of mine. Yet, I could pray for you, Beauchampe. I believe you worthy of the blessings, and perhaps you would not be injured by the prayer, of one so desolate as I am!"

This letter, so far from baffling his ardor, was calculated to increase it. He hurried once more to the dwelling of Mrs. Cooke; but only to meet a repulse.

"Tell him, I can not and will not see him!" was the inflexible reply; and the mother was not insensible to the struggle which shook the majestic soul and form of the speaker in uttering these few words.

In a paroxysm of passion, most like frenzy, Beauchampe darted from the dwelling. That day he rambled in the woods, scarcely conscious of his course, quite unconscious of any object. The next, taking his gun with him by way of apology, he passed in the same manner. And thus for two days more.

Somewhat more composed by this time, his violent mood gave way to one of a more contemplative character; but the shadows of the forest were even more congenial to the disconsolate than the desperate. They afforded him the only protection and companionship which he sought in either of his moods. Here he wandered, giving himself up to the dreary conviction which swells every young man's heart. when first loving, he seems to love in vain, and when the sun of hope seems set for him for ever; and henceforth. earth was little more than a place of tombs — the solemn cypress, and the Druid mistletoe, its most fitting decorations; while, under each of its deceptive flowers, care, and pain, and agony, lay harbored in the forms of gnat, and wasp, and viper, ready to dart forth upon any thoughtless hand that stoops to pluck the beauty of which they might fitly be held the bane.

But, it was not Beauchampe's destiny, as Anna Cooke had fancied, to escape from hers. In vain had she striven to save him from it. He was one not to be saved. Mark the event. To escape him — perhaps dreading that her strength might fail, at some moment, to resist his prayer to see and speak with her; and tired of her mother's constant pleading in behalf of her suitor — she fled from the house, and, as we have seen, stole away, day by day, to lonely places, dark, gloomy, and tangled, such as the wounded deer might seek out, in his last agonies, in which to die in secret.

We have seen already what has been the habit of Beau-

6*

champe in this respect. His woodland musings had not been without profit. Assured now of the hopelessness of his pursuit from the stern and undeviating resolution which the lady of his love had shown, at every attempt which he made to overcome her determination, he, at length, with a heavy heart, concluded to adopt her counsel, and to fly from a scene in which disappointment had humbled him, and where all of his most acute feelings were kept in a state of most painful irritation. But, before this, he again addressed her by letter. His words were brief:—

"I shall soon leave this place. I shall obey you. Yet, let me see you once more. Vouchsafe me one look upon which my heart may brood in its banishment. Let me see that dear image—let me hear that voice—that voice of such sweet sorrow. Do not deny me this prayer. Do not; for in leaving you, dearest, but most relentless woman, I would not carry with me at the last moment, to disturb the holier impression which you have made upon my soul, a feeling of the injustice of yours. With a heart hopeless and in the dust, I implore you. Do not reject my prayer. Do not deny me—let me once more behold you, and I will be then better prepared to rush away to the crowded haunts of life, or it may be the more crowded haunts of death. Life and death! ah! how naturally the words come together. You have rendered their signification little in my ears. You, you only. Yet I ask you not now to reverse the doom. Is not my prayer sufficiently humble! I ask you not to spare, not to save ; only to soothe the pangs of that departure which you command, and which seems little less than death to me. On my knees, I implore you. Let me see you but once—once more—let me once more hear your voice, though I hear nothing after."

To this, the answer was immediate, but the determination was unchanged. It said:—

"I may seem cruel, but I am kind to you. Oh! believe me. It will console me under greater suffering than any I can inflict, to think that you do believe me. I am a woman of wo—born to it—with no escape from my destiny. The sense of happiness, nevertheless, is very strong within me. Were it not impossible that I could do you wrong, I could appreciate the generous love you proffer me. I feel that I could do it justice. But terror and death attend my steps, and influence the fortunes of all who share in mine. I would save you from these, and—worse! You need not to be told that there are worse foes to the proud, fond heart, than either death or terror. Fancy what these may be, and fly from me as from one whose touch is contagion—whose breath is bondage—whose conditions of communion are pangs, and trials, and—shame! Do not think I speak wildly. No, Beauchampe, you little dream with what painful inflexibility I bend myself to the task of saying thus much. Spare me and yourself any further utterance. Go, and be happy. You are yet young, very young. Perhaps you know not that I am older than you. Not much—yet how much. Oh! I have so crowded moments with events—feelings, the events of the heart—that I am grown suddenly old. Old in youth. I am like the tree you sometimes meet—flourishing, green at the top—while in the heart sits death and decay, and, perhaps, gloomier tenants beside. These I can not escape—I can not survive. But you have only one struggle before you. You have suffered one disappointment. It will disturb you for a while, but not distress you long. You will find love where you do not seek it—happiness, which you could never find with me. Go, Beauchampe—for your sake, I deny your prayer. I will not see you. Do not upbraid me in your soul, nor by your lips. Alas! you know not how hard is the struggle, which I have, to say so much. You know not from what a bondage this struggle saves you. My words shall not call you back. No looks of mine shall beguile you. Be you

free, Beauchampe — free and happy ! If you could but guess
the temptation which I overcome — the vital uses which
your love could be to me, and which I reject, you would
thank me — oh ! how fervently — and bless me — would I
could say, how justly ! Farewell ! Let it be for ever,
Beauchampe ! Farewell ! farewell for ever !"

CHAPTER XI.

THE TERRIBLE SECRET.

BEAUCHAMPE sat, sad and silent, in a corner of one low cnamber in his mother's cottage. The family were all present. There was an expression in every face that sympathized with his own. All were sad and gloomy. A painful reserve, so strange hitherto in that little family of love, oppressed the spirits of all. They were aware of the little success which followed his course of wooing. They, perhaps, did not regret the loss so much as the disappointment of one whom they so much loved. With the exception of little Mary Beauchampe, Anna Cooke had not taken captive the fancy of either of the ladies. Jane positively feared and disliked her, with the natural hostility which a person of light mind always entertains for one of intensity and character. Mrs. Beauchampe's objections were of another kind; but she had seen too little of their object, and was too willing to promote her son's wishes, to attach much importance to them. She had derived them rather from the casual criticisms of persons *en passant*, than from anything which she herself had seen.

It would have been no hard matter for Beauchampe, had he been successful in his suit, to reconcile all the parties to his marriage. That he was unhappy in the rejection of his hand, made them so; and the feeling was the more painful as the event had made Beauchampe determine to depart on the ensuing day. He felt the necessity of doing so. Active life, the strifes of the politician, the triumphs of the forum, were at hand, offering him alternatives, if not atonements. In the whirl of successive performance, and in scenes that demand promptitude of action, he felt that he could alone dissipate the spell, or at least endure its weight with dignity, which the charms of Anna Cooke had imposed upon him. His resolution was declared accordingly.

It may be supposed that the distress of the little family made the scene dull. Much was said, and much of it was in the language of complaint. Poor Mary wept with a keen sense of disappointment, more like that of her brother than any one. Jane muttered her upbraidings of the " scornful, high-headed, frowsy Indian Queen, who was too conceited to see that Orville was ten thousand times too good a match for such as she ;"—while Mrs. Beauchampe, with the usual afflicting philosophy of age which has survived passion, discoursed largely on the very encouraging text which counsels us to draw our consolation from our very hopelessness. Pretty counsel, with a vengeance! Beauchampe thought it so.

The torturous process to which these occasional remarks and venerable counsels subjected him, drove him forth at an early hour after dinner. Once more he traversed the woods in moody meditation. He inly resolved that he should see them the last time. With this resolve he determined to pay a personal visit to the spot where, at his coming, he had obtained the first sight of the woman, who, from that moment, had filled his sight entirely. He followed the sinuous course of the woods, slowly, moodily, chewing the cud of sad and bitter thought alone.

His passion was in its subdued phase. There is a moment of recoil in the excited heart, when the feelings long for repose. There is a sense of exhaustion — a dread of further strife and excitement, the very thought of which makes us shudder; and the one conviction over all which fills the mind, is that we could willingly lay ourselves down in the shady places, none near, and sleep — sleep the long sleep, in which there are no such tortures and tumults.

Such were the feelings of Beauchampe, and thus languid, from this recoil, in the overcharged sensibilities, he went slowly forward, with a movement that denoted quite as much feebleness as grief.

He was already buried in the thick woods—he fancied himself alone—when, suddenly, he heard a pistol-shot. He started, with a sudden recollection of a like sound, which had attracted his ears on his first approach to the same neighborhood. The coincidence was at least a strange one.

He now determined to find out the practitioner. He paused for a few moments, and looked about him. He was not exactly sure of the quarter whence the sound proceeded; but he moved forward cautiously, and at a venture. Suddenly he paused! He discovered, at a distance, the person of the very woman whom he had been so long seeking—she whose obduracy denied him even the boon of a last look and farewell accent.

His first impulse was to rush forward. A second and different impulse was forced on him by what he saw. To his astonished eyes she bore in her hands a pistol. He watched her while she loaded it. He saw her level it at a tree, and pull the trigger with unhesitating hand. The bark flew on every side, betraying, by the truth of her aim, at a considerable distance, the constancy of her practice.

Beauchampe could contain himself no longer. He now rushed forward. A faint cry escaped her as she beheld him. She dropped the pistol by her side, clasped and covered her face with her hands, and staggered back a few paces.

But, before Beauchampe reached her, she had recovered, and, picking up the pistol, she came forward. Her eye sparkled with an expression which showed something like resentment. Her voice was abrupt and sharp.

"You rush on your fate!" she exclaimed. "Why, Beauchampe, do you thus pursue me, and risk your own destruction?"

"At your hand, it is welcome!" he exclaimed, mistaking her meaning.

"I mean not *that!*" she replied.

"But you inflict it!"

"No! no!" impatiently. "I do not. I have prayed against it—would spare you that and every risk; but you will it otherwise! You rush on your fate; and if you dare, Beauchampe—mark me! if you dare—it is at your option. Heretofore, I have striven *for you*, and against myself; but you have forced yourself upon my privacy—you have sought to fathom my secrets—and it is now necessary that you should bear the penalty of forbidden knowledge!"

"Have I not supplicated you for these penalties? Ah! what pain—inflicted by your hand—would not be pleasure!"

"You love me!—I believe you, Beauchampe; but the secret of my soul is the death-blow to your love! Ah! spare me!—even now I would have you spare me. Go—leave me for ever; press no farther into a mystery which must shock you to hear, shame me to speak, and leads—if it drives you not hence with the speed of terror—leads you to sorrow and certain strife, and possibly the cruelest doom."

"Speak! I brave all! I am your bondsman, your slave. Declare the service: let me break down these barriers which divide us."

He caught her hand passionately in his as he spoke, and pressed it to his lips. She did not withdraw it.

"Beauchampe!" she said, with solemnity, fixing her dark, deep-glancing eyes upon his face—"Beauchampe! I will not swear you! You shall hear the truth, and still be free. Know, then, that you clasp a dishonored hand!"

CHAPTER XII.

THE VOW OF VENGEANCE.

THE terrible words were spoken. The effect was instantaneous. He dropped the hand which he had grasped. A burning flush crimsoned the face of the woman; an instant after, it was succeeded by the paleness of death.

"I knew it!" she exclaimed, bitterly, and with cruel keenness of utterance. "I knew that it would come to this. God! this is thy creature man! In his selfishness he destroys—in his selfishness he shames us. He pries into our hearts, to declare their weakness—to point out their spots—to say, 'See how I can triumph over, and trample upon!'"

"Anna!" exclaimed Beauchampe, in husky accents— "speak not thus—think not thus. Give me but a moment's time for thought. I was not prepared for this."

The young man looked like one in a dream. A ghastly expression marked his eyes. His lips were parted; the muscles of his mouth were convulsed.

"Nay, sir, it needs not. Your curiosity is satisfied. There is nothing more."

"Yes," he exclaimed, "there is!"

"There is!" she answered promptly. "To clasp the dishonored hand, and take from its grasp the instrument of its vengeance. In a few words, Beauchampe, this hand can only be yours under one condition. Dishonored though it is, I tell you, sir, never yet did woman subject man to more terrible conditions as the price of her love."

"I take the hand," he said, "ere the condition is spoken."

"No, Beauchampe, that can not be. You shall never say that I deceived you. As I shall insist on the fulfilment of the condition, so it is but fair that you be not hooded when you pledge yourself to its performance."

She withdrew the hand, which he offered to take, from his contact.

"This dishonored hand is pledged to vengeance on him who blackened it with shame. Hence its practice with the weapon of death. Hence the almost daily practice of the last five years. Here, in these woods, I pursue a sort of devotion, where Hate is the deity — Vengeance the officiating priest. I have consecrated my life to this one object. He who takes my hand must adopt my pledge — must devote himself also to the work of vengeance!"

He seized it, and took the weapon from its grasp. With the pistol lifted to heaven, he exclaimed :—

"The oath !—I am ready !"

Tears gushed from her eyes. She spoke in subdued accents :—

"Five long years have I toiled with this delusive dream of vengeance! But what can woman do? Where can she seek—how find her victim? Think you, Orville Beauchampe, that if I could have met my enemy, I would have challenged the aid of man to do this work of retribution? In my own soul was the strength. There is no feminine feebleness of nerve in this eye and arm! I should have shot and struck—ah! Christ !"

She sunk to the ground with a spasm, which was the natural effect of such passions working on such a temperament. The desperate youth knelt down beside her in an agony of equal passion and apprehension. He drew her to his breast, he glued his lips to her cheeks, scarcely conscious that she was lifeless all the while.

Her swoon, however, was momentary only. She recov
ered even while he was playing the madman in his fondness.

Refusing his assistance, and pushing him from her, she
staggered up, exclaimed, in piercing, trembling accents :—

" What have I done ? what have I said ?"

" Given me happiness, dearest," he replied, attempting
to take her hand.

" No, Beauchampe," she answered, " let me understand
myself before I seek to understand you. I am scarcely
able, though !"—and, as she spoke, she pressed her hands
upon her eyes with an expression of pain.

" You are still sick !" he observed apprehensively.

" I am in pain, Beauchampe, not sick. I am used to
these spasms. Do not let them alarm you. They are not
deadly, and, if they were, I should not consider them dangerous. I know not well what I have said to you, Beauchampe, before this pain ; but as I never have these attacks
unless the agony of mind becomes too intense for one to
bear and live, I conclude that I have told you all. You
know my secret—my shame !"

" I know that you are the noblest-hearted woman that
ever lived !" he exclaimed rapturously.

" Do not mock me, Beauchampe," she answered mildly.
" Speak not in language of such extravagance. You can
not speak too soberly for my ears, you can not think too
soberly for your own good. You have heard my secret.
You have forced me to declare my shame ! You had no
right to this secret. Was it not enough that I told you
that the barrier was impassable between us ? Did I not
swear it solemnly ?"

" It is not impassable."

" It is !"

" No !" he exclaimed with looks and accents equally de-
cisive, " this is no barrier. You have been wronged —
your confidence has been abused. That I understand. I

care not to know more. I believe you to be all that is pure and honorable now ; and, in this faith, I am all yours. In this faith I pray you to be mine."

"Becauchampe, this is not all! Mere love, though it be such as yours — simple faith, though so generous and confiding — these do not suffice. The food is sweet, but it has little nutriment. My soul is already familiar with higher stimulants. It needs them — it can not do without them. I do not ask the man who makes me his wife, to believe only that I can be true to him — and will! — I demand something more than a confidence like this, Beauchampe : my husband must avenge my dishonor. This is the condition of my hand. Dishonored as it is, it has a heavy price. He must devote his life to the work of retribution. To this he must swear himself."

"I am already sworn to it. The moment which revealed your wrong, bound me as your avenger. You shall only point to your enemy—"

"Ah, Beauchampe, could I have done so, I should not have needed to stain your hands with his blood. But he eludes my sight. I hear nowhere of him. He is as if he had never been.

"His name!" said Beauchampe.

"You shall know all," she replied, motioning him to a seat beside her on the trunk of a fallen tree. "You shall know all, Beauchampe, from first to last. It is due to you that nothing should be withheld."

"Spare yourself, dearest," said Beauchampe tenderly. "Tell me nothing, I implore you, but the name of your enemy, and what may be necessary for the work of vengeance."

"I will tell you *all*. It is my pride that I should *not* spare myself. It is due to my present self to show that I am not blind to the weaknesses of my former nature. It is due to what I *am*, to convince you that I can never again be what I have been. O Beauchampe! I have meditated

often and sadly, since I have known you, the necessity of
making this revelation. At our first meeting, my heart
said to myself, 'The love by which I was betrayed has at
length sent me an avenger!' I saw it in your instant
glances—in the generous earnestness of your looks and
tones—in the fervent expression of your eye—in the
frank, impetuous nature of your soul! But I said to myself:—

"'I will deny myself this avenger. I will reject the instinct that tells me he is sent as one. Why should I involve
this noble young man in a fate so desperate and sad as
mine? It shall not be!' With this resolve, I strove against
you. Nay, Beauchampe, I confess to you farther, that,
even when my will strove most against you, my heart was
most earnest in your favor. With my increasing regard
for you, grew my reluctance to involve you in my doom.
The conflict was close and trying; and then, when the strife
in my mind was greatest, I meditated what I should reveal
to you. I went over that long and cruel memory in the
deep silence of these woods—in the deeper silence of midnight in my chamber: I could not escape from the stern
necessity which compelled the remembrance of those moments of bitterness and shame. By frequent recall, they
have been revived in all their burning freshness; every
art of the traitor—the blind steps by which I fell—the
miserable mockeries which deluded me—and the shame
which, like a lurid cloud, dusk and fiery, has ever since
hung before my eyes! All this I can relate—his crime
and my folly—nor omit one fraction which is necessary to
the truth."

"But why tell all this, dearest? Let it be forgotten—
let all be forgotten, except the name of the villain whom it
is allotted me to destroy."

"Forgotten? It can not be forgotten! Nay, more, it is
a duty to remember it, that the vengeance may not sleep.
Beauchampe, I have lived for years on this one thought.

By recalling these bitter memories, that thought was fed. Do not persuade me to forget them. You know not how much of life depends on the sustenance which thought derives from this copious but polluted fountain. Deprive me of this sustenance, and I perish. Deny me to declare all, and I can speak nothing. I can not curb my nature when I will; and where would you gather the fuel of anger, should I barely say to you that one Alfred Stevens — an artful stranger from a distant city — found me a simple, vain child among the hills, and, practising on my vanity, overcame my strength? This would serve but little in rousing that fierce fire of hate within you which sometimes, even in my own bosom, burns quite too faintly to be effectual. No, no! you shall witness the progress of the criminal. You shall see how he spun his web around my path —my soul!—by what mousing cunning he contrived to pull down a wing whose feeblest fancy, in those unconscious days, was above the mountains, and striving ever for the clouds. You shall see the daily records of its spasms, which my misery has made. To feel my struggle, you must share in it from the first."

He took her hand in his, and prepared to listen.

"You will feel my hand tremble," said she; "the flush may suffuse my cheek; for, oh! do not suppose I tell this tale willingly. No! I can not help but tell it. An instinct, which I dare not disobey, commands me; and truly, when I think of the instinct which told me that you *would* come — made you known to me as the avenger from the first moment when I saw you — and has thus forced you, as it were, in my own despite, upon my fearful secret — I almost feel that there is a divine, at least a fated compulsion, in the mood which now prompts me to tell you all. It is a necessity. I feel it pressing upon me as a duty. It is like that Fate which coerced the ancient mariner into the report of his marvellous progress, and compelled the listener to hear. It must be told; and you, Beauchampe, can not help but

hear. A power beyond mine own has willed it, and therefore you are here now. It chains us both. It wills that I
should speak, and speak nothing but the truth. I can even
suppress nothing. I am not able to control my own utterance. May the same power endue me with the strength to
speak the history of my bitter, bitter shame!"

And, in truth, Beauchampe, like herself, was under a
spell. He could not have torn himself away under any
conditions, or with any impulse. He was fastened to the
spot — not by her arts, for she sternly rejected any help of
art, save that which naturally belonged to her own remarkable genius — not by the charms of her beauty, for her face
now had more of terror in it than beauty — not by any sympathy which might arise from pity, for, as he looked into
the sombre grandeur of her eyes, and the stern power of
soul, and will, and mind, which declared itself in every
feature of her countenance, in every action of her form, he
felt that awe, not pity, was the most natural sentiment
which she inspired.

Under the spell he sat beside her. Under a like spell —
the imagination, in both, being the Prospero, the master
of the magic wand — she spoke. And how — the first choking effort at utterance being overcome — how clearly, simply, sternly, she laid bare the whole cruel history, even as
we have already told it — nothing suppressed, nothing obscured ; no idle apologies for weakness offered — no excuses
urged in behalf of sinful impulses. She spared herself in
nothing. She laid herself bare to discovery, to keen analysis, to the most critical inspection. Governed, as she felt
or fancied, by some supernatural influence, there was a terrible earnestness, an unequivocal intenseness and directness,
in all she revealed, that would have left the most captious
attorney at a loss for the opportunity to cross-examine.
There was no attempt at glozing artifice, at adroit insinua-
tion or suggestion, by which to soften the darker colors —
to relieve the doubtful — to conceal what had been her real

errors, weaknesses, and vicious desires.   All the characteristics of her soul—its follies, faults, foibles, vices—were
all made apparent: but through all, equally apparent, was
the proud spirit, falling chiefly through pride, the noble
nature, the ingenuous ambition, the lustrous and winged
genius!

7

CHAPTER XIII.

THE BETROTHAL.

"I drink of the intoxicating cup,
And find it rapture. Yet, methinks I feel
As if a madness mingled with the sweet,
And dashed it with a bitter."

WHAT a hush for a moment hung over the forest when she ceased to speak!

The story was ended.

For a few moments, Beauchampe sat immoveable, as if slowly recovering from a spell. Then suddenly he shook himself free, started up with a cry of mingled joy and pain, and clasped her in his wild embrace.

His passion had undergone increase. He was no longer master of his pulses. Her superior will had already made itself felt in all the sinews of his soul. Every beat and bound of his heart was full of the exquisite fascination.

She extricated herself from his grasp. Her breathing came with effort. She pressed her hand upon her side, as if with a sudden sense of pain; then looked up, and met his eager glance with eyes which were so fixed, so glassily stern, that he looked alarmed, and clasped her hands in his own.

She was, in truth, deadly pale — but, oh, how strong!

"Fear nothing," she said, in a whisper; "it is nothing. I shall soon be well."

And a brief silence ensued between them, he gazing still with apprehension into her eyes.

"Look not thus, Beauchampe. I am better now. The pain is gone. I am used to it. It always comes with any great excitement, and this to-day has been a terrible one. I feared I should not have strength for it. Thank God, it is over — and — and — I am better now."

And she laughed hysterically.

Anna Cooke was wonderfully strong, but she was yet a woman. She had overtasked herself. She sank, a moment after, in a fainting-fit, upon the sward.

Beauchampe was terrified. He called her name, and received no answer. He ran off to a well-remembered brooklet, some two hundred yards distant, over which a gourd was suspended from a tree. He hurried back with it full of water, and found her recovering. She drank freely, bathed her face and forehead in the liquid, and felt relieved.

"And now, Beauchampe — now that you have heard all — now that you see and understand the full nature of the conditions imposed upon you — the fearful nature of the penalty — the crime, and its terrible consequences — I release you from your pledge! Be free! Go — leave me! I would not have your young and generous soul burdened with the sting, the sin, the agony, and the resolve, of mine!"

This was said, how mournfully, but with what sincerity! — with that utter self-abandoment which denotes the recoil and the subsidence of powerful and now-exhausted energies!

"Oh! how can you speak thus!" he answered reproachfully. "I would not be released. I ask not even respite. Your cause is mine — your wrongs! I feel them all! Your vengeance — I have sworn to accomplish it. It is now my passion not less than yours. Nay, more, I would have you dismiss it from *your* soul! I would have it exclusively my own!"

"And you are still willing, burdened with this poor wreck of youth, and virtue, and beauty — and with this terrible necessity — to undergo the consciousness of the world's

mock—nay, to see its skinny pointing finger, and hear its
venomous tongue, as it mutters, while I pass, the cruel
story of my shame!"

"I will make that story yet a memorial of virtuous vengeance, to be remembered in Kentucky when we are both
in the dust!" was the vehement answer, while the eyes of
the speaker flashed fire, and his hand was outwaved as if
challenging the whole world's voice and ear. He continued :—

"If that story is to be told again, Margaret Cooper—
for so, this once, will I call you—it shall sound as an ominous voice of terror, speaking doom and sudden judgment
to the cold-blooded profligates who pride themselves on the
serpent conquest over all that is blessing and beautiful in
the world's Eden!"

The tears rolled down her cheeks. She had not thus
wept before—never once had such tears covered her
cheeks even in the moments of her bitterest remorse and
suffering.

"Do not weep!" he said; "I can not bear to see you
weep."

"It is for the last time," she answered, almost prophet-
ically.

"What, indeed, had she to do with tears? They could
not speak for passions, and such an agony as hers. Then,
timidly, he laid one hand upon her wrist, while the other
crept about her waist. And she shuddered. He felt the
convulsive shiver, and withdrew his grasp. He whispered :—

"You are now to be mine—mine—you remember!"

"Alas! for you, Beauchampe, that it is so. It is not too
late! You are still free to go. It is a ruin—not a heart,
that I can give you!"

"Be it so! The ruin shall be more precious to my soul
than the glory only born to-day.

"Leave me now, Beauchampe. Do not seek me again

until to-morrow. I would sleep to-day. I need sleep—
sleep—more than anything besides. I have not slept once
since I penned you that letter."

"Good Heavens! can it be possible? Oh! you must
sleep. Shall I not see you home at once?'

"No! leave me, Beauchampe. I will find my way home
after awhile. Leave me—will you not!"

"Yes—but Anna, let me take this weapon. It is *mine*
now, remember, not yours! Here, with this hour, Anna,
your practice ends—ends with the necessity."

"Take it. Hide it from my sight."

He possessed himself of the pistol, which he thrust hurriedly into his pocket, and then suddenly embracing and
kissing her, he cried :—

"This, Anna—this—seals every vow, whether of love
or vengeance!"

She waved him off, and as he disappeared slowly, she
hurried still deeper into the wood. What were her meditations there? Who shall say? They were entertained
for hours in deepest silence, were mournful, yet of uncer-
tain character—now marked by a sense of relief which was
momentary only, and still followed by a great cloud-like
doubt, and vague, dark terror which seemed to stretch and
spread over all the prospect.

And this cloud she could not disperse—she could not
penetrate. It was ominous, she fancied, of her future.

"Oh, God!" she exclaimed, "if I have erred—if I have
covered my soul with a new sin in thus involving this generous young man in my fate—in thus binding his soul with
my own to the blind fury of this wild revenge which I have
sworn."

Strange that she should doubt in this regard. Strange
that human being in a Christian land should really fancy for
a moment that God's sanction should hallow the purposes
of a bloody vengeance. But, even thus wild and mistaken
in their supposed sanctions are half the purposes of hu-

manity. The disordered judgment, governed by an imagination which the blood has wrought up to delirious dreams
and excesses, can always evoke a sanction for all its purposes, from some terrible demon wearing the aspect of
divinity!

And this false god whispered his encouragement audibly
to her senses, until she grew satisfied — calmer — resolved
— confirmed in all her purposes.

When she returned home and met her mother, she said,
as quietly as possible : —

"Your wishes are answered, mother. I have seen
Beauchampe. I have consented to be his wife!"

"Have you, indeed, Margaret! Oh! I am so glad. He
is such an excellent young man, and of such a good family.
Oh! you will be happy now, I know!"

"Happy!" exclaimed the girl with a look of scorn, mingled with surprise. "How can you fancy that there should
be happiness for *me*?"

"And why not, Margaret? Who knows of what's done
and past?"

"*He* knows! I have told Beauchampe the whole of my
history."

"What!" almost with a scream. "You don't mean to
say that you've been such a fool as to tell him about what
happened at Charlemont — about Alfred Stevens!——"

"All! I have withheld nothing!"

The old woman threw up her eyes and hands with a sort
of terror.

"And he consents to marry you after all!"

"Yes!"

"I don't believe it will ever come to that! No—no!
Men are not such fools! Oh! Margaret, what could possess you to tell him*that?*"

"Truth, justice! I could do no less. Had I not told
him, I had deserved my fate!"

She left the room as she said this, and hurried to the sol

itude of her own. The mother, when she was gone, expressed her horror and her wonder, at what she deemed the insane proceeding of her daughter, in more copious language than before.

"It's just like her. She was always different from everybody else. Now what woman of any sense would have told of such things to the very man that was offering her marriage. What a fool—what a fool! If Beauchampe comes back, then he's the fool! But he'll never come again. No—no! when he's cooled off, and begun to think over the matter, he'll go with a spur. That a daughter of mine should be such a fool. But she don't take a bit after me. All her foolishness comes from her father. Cooper was a fool too. He was for ever a-doing, a-thinking, and a-saying, things different from everybody else. And he, too, would call it truth, and right, and justice; as if anybody had any reason to think of such matters, when it's a clear case of interest and safety a-pinting all the other way. Such a fool-daughter as she is! We'll see if he comes again. And I reckon it's her only chance; and even if she had another, with as good a man, she'd be doing and telling the same thing over again. Such a fool— such a fool! But I'll put on my bonnet, and go over and see the Beauchampes, and see what they've got to say about it."

And she prepared herself; but just as she was about to sally forth, her daughter reappeared, and arrested her at the entrance. She had divined her mother's purposes, knowing something of *her* usual follies.

"Do not go to Mrs. Beauchampe's, mother."

"And why not, if all's true that you've been telling me?"

"You do not doubt its truth, mother, I know. Why I wish you not to go, is for a good reason of my own. I must only repeat that you must not go there now. A few days hence, mother, and only after some of them have come here."

"Ah! I see! You have your fears too, Margaret, that it's all a flash-in-the-pan, and that he'll be off; and that's the very reason why I would go. We must clinch the nail before it draws."

The face of Margaret was full of ineffable scorn.

"You must not go, mother. Beauchampe is not to be detained, should he desire to depart, by any argument that you can offer; and if he goes—well! I have no fear that he will go, and if such were really his inclination, I should be the first to encourage it. You do not understand either of us. Meddle not. You can make nothing—may mar everything, and will certainly mortify me! Wait! The Beauchampes must now seek you, not you them!"

The will of the daughter prevailed as usual, though her own will remained a grumbling discontent. Margaret, having attained her purpose, retired again to her chamber, wasting no unnecessary words in answer to the growling dissatisfaction, that still seemed inclined to pursue her. The old woman had set her mind upon the visit and yielded very reluctantly—perhaps would not have yielded but for the threat of Margaret, sternly expressed, that if she interfered one bit in the matter, she would herself break away from the engagement. The mother too well knew the imperious nature of the daughter, not to feel the danger of incurring her resentment, after such a warning. She contented herself with the reflection that:—

"Margaret was a fool always, and nothing seemed to better her sense. Beauchampe"—she was sure—"will be certain to bolt as soon as he gets cooler and thinks over the matter."

But Beauchampe did not bolt!

When he reached home, he hardly suffered himself to enter the house, before he cried out to his mother and sisters:—

It's all settled! I'm so happy, mother. O girls! all's

right. I sha'n't leave you now for a long time — perhaps never, and we shall all be so happy together."

"Why, what's the matter, Orville? What has so unsettled you?" demanded the mother.

"Do tell us, brother, what's made you so happy? What has so excited you?" demanded Jane.

But Mary, the more sagacious as the more sympathizing, said at once, while she flung her arms about the neck of her brother : —

"Ah! I know; Anna Cooke has consented!"

"She has — she has! What a good guesser. You are my dear little sister. Ah! Mary understands her brother better than you all."

"So! she has consented?" said the mother, somewhat deliberately. "And did she give you any explanation, Orville, of her previous refusal — so stern, so peremptory?"

"Yes, Orville, how did she excuse herself? What explanation did she give?" demanded Jane.

"Explanation!" exclaimed the brother, a cloud suddenly covering his brow. "Ay! she gave me full — ample explanation."

"Well! what was it?"

"Enough, mother, that it was perfectly satisfactory to me. I am satisfied. Let us say no more on that subject. You will believe me when I tell you that I am satisfied. Further, I do not mean to say. She is now mine! all mine! and I am happy."

"God grant, Orville, that it be so!" answered the mother in grave accents. "Yet these so sudden changes, Orville, are strange to me, at least. But I will not cloud your happiness with a single doubt. I trust in God that she will bring you happiness, my son."

"Oh! never doubt, dear mother. She is a glorious creature — noble, beautiful — all that should bring a man happiness."

Happiness is not a creature of wild impulses and of

7*

great excitements ; nor is the glory of beauty, however un-
paralleled, nor the fascinations of genius, however powerful, the best guaranty of happiness — which needs sympathy,
and security, above all things, and loves the shade rather
than the sun ; longing for quiet not turbulent waters, and
rather keeping the passions in leash, than goading them into
perpetual exercise by stimulating means.

Somehow, the wild joy of Beauchampe did not seem to
his mother the best guaranty for his happiness. There was
something prescient in the thoughts of the old lady, which
made her sigh over the unborn future.

CHAPTER XIV.

THE BRIDAL.

"Why, look you, sir, I can be calm as Silence
    All the while music plays.   Strike on, sweet friend,
    As mild and merry as the heart of Innocence:
    I prithee, take my temper.   Has a virgin
    A heat more modest?" — MIDDLETON.

A VAST change had certainly been wrought, within a very few hours, in the moods and feelings of Beauchampe.   He had gone forth weary, dispirited, humbled, hopeless: he had returned bounding, wild, excited to enthusiastic measures — assured, within himself, of the attainment of every mortal desire that was precious.

But we can not call him a happy man — or one, indeed, whose prospect of happiness was very promising.   We would not misuse that word, as we fear that it is too frequently misused.   It is one the necessity for which is very rare in the ordinary progress of society and life.   Its absolute significance is really to be found only in future conditions.   But we need not go into any analysis of its propriety in common parlance.   Enough that it deludes most people, at some period or another in their lives.

Beauchampe said he was happy — very happy — and he believed what he said, and his mother and sisters wished to believe, and Mary certainly did believe, quite as fervently as her brother himself.   Certainly, if a man in a state of pleasant delirium may be considered happy, then Beauchampe was!

But happiness is scarcely consistent with any very great intensity of passion, excited to sleeplessness in the absorbing pursuit of a single object, particularly when the condition of the conquest implies trials, and struggles, and fears, and dangers, the measure of which no mind can compass, the end of which no mind can foresee!

Beauchampe had won the consent of the woman whom he had sought with all the intensity of a first passion. All young men find it easy to persuade themselves that such a condition must satisfy all the longings of the heart.

But young men build on the sands, and kindle their fires too frequently with dry straw, which blazes fearfully at first, but dies out, leaves no warmth, and covers the landscape with blackened stubble and fine ashes.

Beauchampe was not deceived, in a single respect, by or with the woman he had won. She was the very person that she appeared and claimed to be. She had concealed nothing from him — worn no mask — put on no disguises — nay, piercing her own heart, and laying bare its most hidden places, she had shown him, so far as she herself could find and understand them, the very motives, moods, interests, impulses, of her soul — which had informed her actions, and might inform them still — as, perhaps, no woman had ever shown them to lover before. If he yet labored under any delusion in respect to her, she was not the cause of it. Her pride, as well as just sense of his claims, had been at pains to strip herself of all things which might be calculated to delude. The very secret of her dishonor was revealed only because she was sworn to honor.

And he acknowledged no delusions. He was satisfied — as he thought, happy — and at first his joy was a delirium. She was the peerless creature, the woman among a world of women, such as he had thought her at first.

But we can not govern or restrain the imperious thought which works its way in the brain and soul, secretly, even as the mole in the garden; and we never dream of what is going on below, even though the loveliest flower in our Eden is perishing at the roots.

After a few days, though Beauchampe still exulted, his mother fancied that his mind seemed jaded and wearied, his fancy had lost its wing, his eyes were heavy, yet wandering. He himself was quite unconscious of these external shows of the secret nature, but he too had a consciousness which disturbed his imagination. The very fact that his betrothal was so unlike that of any man of whom he had ever heard or read — that it was under such conditions — compelled his thought to a serious yet vague exercise of study, such as did not well comport with the unreasoning confidence which, perhaps, marks the presence of the most happy sort of love. Still, as yet, he did not exactly reason on the subject. He could not. The mind was exerting itself through the imagination, experimentally, as it were, sending out feelers into this or that region of the brain — sounding them — then withdrawing, to touch some other place.

The effect was, to bring into the otherwise bright atmosphere which surrounded him the perpetual presence of one small but dark and threatening cloud. He rubbed his eyes, but it was there. He looked away, but, when he turned his glance again upon the spot, it remained, steady and threatening as before.

Was there a Fate hidden in that cloud? Did it contain the evil principle, shadowing his progress, or was it simply the presentiment of evil — a benignant warning against the dangers yet wrapped in mystery? Was it the ominous sign of that fierce condition of hate which had been prescribed to him as the condition of love? Could Love prescribe such a condition — require such a sacrifice? Was it possible for that meek sentiment — so holy, so certainly from heaven — so celestial an element in the economy of heaven — was it possible for such a sentiment so openly to toil in behalf of its most deadly antipathy? Love laboring for Hate! It well might bring a cloud into the moral atmosphere of Beauchampe's soul, when he thought of these conditions.

And yet Anna Cooke had really learned to love Beauchampe. There is nothing contradictory or strange in this. We have painted badly, unless the reader is prepared for such a seeming caprice in her character as this. She is, whatever may be her boast, scarcely wiser than when she was eighteen. All enthusiasm and earnestness, she was all confidence then. She is so still. Her impressions are sudden and decided. She sees that Beauchampe is generous and noble-minded. She has discerned the loyalty of his character, and the liberality of his disposition. She finds him intellectual. His frankness wins upon her —his unqualified devotion does the rest. She sees in him the agent of that wild passion which had kept goading her without profit before; and Love, in reality, avails himself of a very simple artifice to effect his purposes. It is Love that insinuates to her, ' Here comes your avenger!'—and, deceived by him, she obeys one passion, when, at the time, she really fancies she is toiling in behalf of its antagonist.

See the further argument—felt, not expressed—of this wily logician!

He suggests to her that it is scarcely possible that Beauchampe will ever be called upon to fulfil his fearful pledges. For, where is the betrayer? For five years had the name been unspoken in the ears of his victim; for five years he had eluded all traces of herself and friends. He was gone, as if he had not been; and the presumption was strong that he was of some very distant region; that he would be very careful to avoid that neighborhood, hereafter, in which his crime had been committed: and as, in equal probability, the lot was cast which made this limited scene the whole world of Beauchampe s future life, so it followed that they would never meet; that the trial, to which she had sworn him, would never be exacted; and, subdued by time, and the absence of the usual excitements, the pang would be softened in her heart, the recollection would gradually fade from her memory, and life would once more be a progress of comparative peace, and probably of innocent enjoyment.

It is an adroit, and not an infrequent policy of Love, to make his approaches under the cover of a flag which none is so pleased to trample under foot as he. He knows the usual practices of war, and has no conscientious scruples in the employment of an ordinary *ruse*. The drift of his policy was not seen by the mind of Anna Cooke; but it was — though less obvious than some of her instincts — not the less an instinct. Nay, more certainly an instinct, for it was of the emotions; while those of which she had spoken to Beauchampe were nothing more than the suggestions of monomania. Her imagination, brooding ever on the same topic, was always on the watch to convert all objects into its agents; and never more ready than when Love, coming forward with his suggestions, lent that seeming aid to his enemy which was really intended for his overthrow. It was only when she had become the wife of Beauchampe that she became aware of the true nature of those feelings which had brought about her marriage. It was after the tie was indissolubly knit — after he had pressed his lips to hers with a husband's kiss — that she was made conscious of the danger to herself from the performance of the conditions to which he was pledged. The fear of his danger first taught her that it was love, and not the mere passion for revenge, which had wrought within her from the moment when she first met him. The moment she reflected upon the risk of life to which he was sworn, that moment awakened in her bosom the full appreciation of his worth. Then, instead of urging upon him the subject of his oath, she shuddered but to think upon it; and, in her prayers — for she suddenly had learned to pray — she implored that the trial might be spared him, to which, previously, her whole soul had entirely been surrendered.

But she prayed in vain — possibly because she had learned to pray so lately. Ah! how easy would be all lessons of good;— how easy of attainment and of retention — did we only learn to pray sufficiently soon! The habit of prayer is so sure to induce humility! and humility is, after all, and before all, one of the most certain sources of that divine strength, arising from love and justice, which sustains the otherwise falling and fearful world of our grovelling humanity.

The wife of Beauchampe prayed beside him while he slept. She prayed for mercy. She prayed against that fatal oath. Far better — such was her thought — that the criminal should escape for ever, than that her husband's hands should carry the dagger of the avenger. She now, for the first time, recognised the solemn force, the terrible emphasis, in the Divine assurance — "Vengeance is mine!" saith the Lord. She was *now* willing that the Lord should exercise his sovereign right.

But all this is premature. This change in her heart and mind was only now in slow and unsuspected progress. It required time, the actual formation of the new ties; the actual exercise of the feminine duties in an humble and as yet happy household. Up to the moment of her marriage, there had been no change in her heart or its purposes, such as moved her to any change in the conditions of the marriage. Far from it. When, on the contrary, the time approached, she summoned Beauchampe to a private interview the afternoon before the nuptials. They met, by appointment, in the same wood where the engagement had been made. Her sombre spirit was on her, wrapping her as in a pall; and, at his approach, she said abruptly and sternly:

"Beauchampe, the time has come. But it is not too late. You are at liberty, even now, to withdraw from these bonds. If you will it, Beauchampe, you are free from this moment, and shall never hear reproach of mine."

He rejected the boon proffered him, with indignant but loving reproaches.

" Have you summoned me for this, Anna ?"

" No! not for this only — in part. It was due to you to afford you a last opportunity of escaping the terrible conditions upon which only can my hand be given. This, you know, was my oath. It requires yours. If you persist in claiming my hand — swear to avenge its dishonor !"

And she lifted up her hands in solemn adjuration, and he obeyed her ; and there, in that silent solitude, he uttered audibly the oath to avenge her shame — to sacrifice her seducer, at bloody altars, the moment he should be found!

And it was as if the demons of the air which had inspired, trooped round to receive, the oath ; for the sky darkened above them, even as the vow was uttered, and the awful stillness of the wood was as if the spirits were all listening breathlessly.

" Enough, Beauchampe ! It is done. To-morrow I am yours !"

And, with these words, she left him — no kiss, no embrace, no look or word of tenderness.

But he looked for none — expected none. It was not a moment, nor were the moods of either suitable, for caresses. He looked up at the cloud as she went from sight, and enveloped in it, as he thought, for more than an hour he walked that wood, his fancies sublimed with the terrible oath which he had taken, and his whole soul shadowed as it were with the stately pall of velvet in some great solemnity.

The marriage followed the next day. The bride was calm and very pale, but firm and placid. Beauchampe's eye was eager and bright, and his cheeks flushed with hope and triumph. He felt sure that he was happy ; and the cloud seemed to disappear from before his sight, and, for the moment, his landscape was without a speck.

And, in the sight of his joy, the mother and the sisters forgot their apprehension ; and they took the bride to their

hearts as warmly as if they had never felt upon their souls
the shadow of a doubt.   But, even as the bridal vow was
taken, Fear took the place of Hate in the soul of the bride,
and she shuddered, she knew not why, at the kiss of her
husband, which, as it declared the warmth of his passion,
brought up in dark array before her eyes the images and
events of terror to which that kiss had pledged him for
ever!

CHAPTER XV.

THE HONEYMOON.

" What a delicious breath marriage sends forth,
    The violets bed's not sweeter."—MIDDLETON.

" Oh ! I distrust this happiness ; it seems
    Too exquisite to last. I fancy clouds
    Already gather on the sky of bliss."—*Old Play.*

THEY were now man and wife. The bond, for weal or
wo, was indissolubly fastened. But, for the present, we
must not speak of wo. It did not now seem to threaten
the happy household, of which Beauchampe was now the
lord. In the novel joy of his situation, the enthusiastic young
man lost sight of days and weeks and months. With very
happiness he grew idle — the mind conquered by the heart.
Law and politics were alike forgotten. He had no call to
them at present. He was in a dream — in a dream-land
like that of Eden, in which toil was a stranger, and care,
that ever-intriguing toad was kept off by the Ithuriel spear
of pleasure. He could have mused away life in this manner — never once conscious of the flight of time — there,
amid groves of unbroken shade, with the one companion.
And she — did she share the happiness which she imparted ?
Did the cruel fate relax in his persecutions ? In the em-
braces of that fond young heart, did she forget the sting
and agony of the past — did she lose herself a moment in
the new dream of a fresh and better existence ?

It is but reasonable to suppose that she did. She sang now, and her voice was a very rich and powerful one — combining the soul and strength of man with the sweetness and freedom of the bird. While her voice, in musing thought, subdued by humility to devotion, was full of a charming philosophy — social yet imaginative always — which would not have been unworthy of the lips of a divine priestess officiating among the oaks of Dodona, her soul, aroused by the sympathies of an ear which she wished to please, never poured forth strains of such sweet eloquence and song. She could improvise both verse and music. She resumed her pen and wrote as well as sang ; and her verses grew less and less sombrous daily.

Beauchampe was all happiness. He had found a muse and a woman in one! Surely, they were, neither of them, unhappy then!

But the fates were not satisfied, even if their victims were forgetful. It was decreed that our hero should be awakened from his dream of happiness. One day a letter was put into Beauchampe's hands. He read it with a cloudy brow.

"No bad news, Beauchampe?" was the remark of his wife, expressed with some solicitude.

"Yes," he answered tenderly. "Yes, for I am forced to leave you for awhile. Read."

He handed her the letter as he spoke. She read as follows: —

"DEAR BEAUCHAMPE: — The campaign has opened with considerable vigor, and we feel the want of you. The sooner you come to the rescue the better. We must put all our lieutenants into the field. This fellow, Calvert, is said to be doing execution among our pigeons. He is quite successful on the stump. At G—— he carried everything before him, and fairly swept Jenkins and Clemens out of sight. He is to address the people at Bowling-Green on the 7th, and you must certainly meet us there ; or, shall I take you on my way down ? Barnabas comes with me. He insists that we shall need every help, and is decidedly aguish. He has somehow contrived to make me a little apprehensive that we have been too confident, and accordingly a little remiss. He reports this man, Calvert, as a sort of giant, and openly asserts him to be one of the most able, popular orators we have ever had. He has a fine voice, excellent manners, is very fluent, and has his arguments at his finger-ends. I can not think that I have any reason to fear him whenever I can meet with him in person. But this, just now, is the difficulty. The difference between a young lawyer in little practice, and one with his hands full, is something important. Should I not join you on the 6th, you had better go on to the Green. He will be there by that time. I will meet you there certainly by the 8th ; though I shall make an effort to take the stump on the 7th, if I can. Should I fail, however, as is possible, you must be there to take it for me, and maintain it till I come. Barnabas and myself will then relieve you, and finish the game.

" Why do we not hear from you ? Whisker-Ben said at Club last night that he had heard some rumor that you were married or about to be married. We take it for granted, however, that the invention is his own. Barnabas flatly denied it, and even the pope (his nose, by the way, is thoroughly recovered) expressed his opinion that you were ' no such ass.' Of course, he suffered neither his own, nor my wife, to hear this complimentary opinion. One thing, however, was agreed upon among us, viz. : that you were just the man, not only to do a foolish thing, but an impolitic one ; and a vote was carried, *nem. con.*, in which it was resolved to inform you that, in ' the opinion of this club, marriage is a valuable consideration.' A word to the wise, etc. You know the proverb. Barnabas spoke to this subject. Whisker-Ben, too, was quite eloquent. ' What,'

said he, ' are the moral possessions of a woman ?   I answer,
bank-notes, bonds, sound stocks, and other *choses in action.*
Her physical possessions, I count to be lands and negroes,
beauty, a good voice, &c.   His distinction was recognised
as the true one by everybody but ZAUERKRAOUT, who now
wears the red hat in place of Finnikin.   He thinks that
negroes should be counted among the moral possessions,
or, at least, as of a mixed character, moral and physical.
I will not trouble you with more of the debate than the
summary.   An inquiry was made into your qualities, and
the chances before you, and you were then rated, and found
to be worth seventy-five thousand dollars, the interest of
which, at five per cent., being five thousand dollars, it was
resolved that you be counselled not to marry any woman
whose income is less.   A certificate of so much stock in the
club will be despatched you to assist in any future operations ; as a friend to yourself, not less than to the club, let
me exhort you to give heed to its counsels.   ' Marriage *is*
a valuable consideration.''   Marry no woman whose income is not quite as good as your own.   As a lawyer, in
tolerable practice, you may fairly estimate your capital at
thirty or forty thousand dollars.   If you have a pretty
woman near you, before you look at her again, see what
she's worth ; and lose sight of her as soon as you can, unless she brings in a capital to the concern, equal to your
own.   Be as little of a boy in these matters as possible.   In
no other, I think, are you likely to be a boy !   Adieu !   If
you do not see me on the 6th, start for the Green by the
7th.   I shall surely be there by the 8th.   Barnabas sends
his blessing, nor does the pope withhold his.   He evidently
thinks less unfavorably of you, since his nose has been pronounced out of danger.   " Lovingly yours,
     " J. O. BEAUCHAMPE, Esq.''   " W. P. SHARPE.

The wife read the letter slowly.   Its contents struck her
strangely.   It had something in its tone like that of one

whom she had been accustomed to hear. The contents of it were nothing. The meaning was obvious enough. Of the parties she knew nothing. But there was the *sentiment* of the writer, which, like the key-note in music, pervaded the performance — not necessarily a part of its material, yet giving a character of its own to the whole. That key-note was not an elevated one. She looked up. Her husband had been observing her countenance. A slight suffusion flushed her cheek as her eyes met his.

" Who is Mr. W. P. Sharpe," said she, " who counsels so boldly, and I may add so selfishly ?"

" He is the gentleman with whom I studied law — one of our best lawyers, a great politician and very distinguished man. He is now up for the assembly, and, as you see, thinks that I can promote his election by my eloquence. What think you, Anna ?"

" I think you *have* eloquence, Beauchampe — I should think you would become a very popular speaker. You have boldness, which is one great essential. You have a lively imagination and free command of language, and your general enthusiasm would at least make you a very earnest advocate. There should be something in *the cause* — the occasion — no doubt, and——"

She stopped.

" Go on," said he — " what would you say ?"

" That I should doubt very much whether the occasion *here*," lifting up the letter — " would be sufficient to stimulate you to do justice to yourself."

The youth looked grave. She noticed the expression, and with more solicitude than usual, continued : —

" I think I know you, Beauchampe. It is no disparagement to you to say I something wonder how such people as are here self-described should have been associates of yours."

" Strictly speaking they were not," he replied, with something of a blush upon his face. " I know but very little of them. But you are to understand that there is exag-

geration — which is perhaps the only idea of fun that our
people seem to have — in the design and objects of this
club.   It is a lawyers' society, and Colonel Sharpe insisted,
the day that I graduated, that I must become a member.
I attached no importance to the matter either one way or
the other, and readily consented.   I confess to you, Anna,
that what I beheld, the only night when I did attend their
orgies, made me resolve, even before seeing you, to forswear
the fraternity.   We do not sympathize, as you may imagine.
But no more, I fancy, does the writer of this letter sympathize with them.   Colonel Sharpe is willing to relax a little
from serious labors, and he takes this mode as being just as
good as any other.   These people are scarcely more than
creatures for his amusement."

The wife looked grave but said no more, and Beauchampe sat down to write an answer.   This answer as may
be supposed, confirmed the story of Whisker-Ben, legiti-
mated all the apprehensions of the club, and assured the
writer of the letter that his counsels of " moral prudence"
had come too late.   He had not only wedded, but wedded
without any reference to the possessions, such as had been
described as moral, at least by the philosophers of the fraternity.

" My wife," said the letter of the writer — " has beauty
and youth, and intellect — beauty beyond comparison — and
a grace and spirit about her genius that seem to me equally
so.   Beyond these, and her noble heart, I am not sure that
she has any possessions.   I believe she is poor; but really,
until you suggested the topic, I never once thought of it.
To me, I assure you, however heretical the confession may
seem, I care not a straw for fortune.   Indeed, I shall be
the better pleased to discover that my wife brings me nothing but herself."

The letter closed with the assurance of the writer that
he should punctually attend at the gathering, and do his
best to maintain the cause and combat of his friend.

"Is this Colonel Sharpe so very much your friend, Beauchampe?" demanded his wife when he had read to her a portion of his letter.

"He has been friendly — has treated me with attention as his pupil — has not spared his compliments, and is what is called a fine gentleman. I can not say that he is a character whom I unreservedly admire. He is a man of loose principles — lacks faith — is pleased in showing his skepticism on subjects which would better justify veneration; and, of the higher sort of friendships which implies a loyalty almost akin to devotion, he is utterly incapable. Seeking this loyalty in my friend, I should not seek *him*. But for ordinary uses — for social purposes — as a good companion, an intelligent authority, Colonel Sharpe would always be desirable. You will like him, I think. He is well read, very fluent, and though he does not believe in the ideals of the heart and fancy, he reads poetry as if he wrote it. You, who do write it, Anna, will think better of him when you hear him read it."

"Do you know his wife, Beauchampe?"

"No — strange to say, I do not. I have seen her; she is pretty, but it is said they do not live happily together."

"How many stories there are of people who do not live happily together; and if true, what a strange thing it is, that such should be the case. Yet, no doubt, they fancied, at the first, that they loved one another; unless, Beauchampe, they were counselled by some such club as yours. If so, there could be no difficulty in understanding it all."

"But with those, Anna, who reject the advice of the club?"

"Can it ever be so with them, Beauchampe? I think not. It seems to me as if I should never be satisfied to change what *is* for what might be. Are *you* not content, Beauchampe?"

"Am I not? Believe me it makes my heart tremble to

8

think of the brief separation which this election business
calls for.   Sharpe little knows what a sacrifice I make to
serve him."

"And if I read this letter of his aright, he would laugh
you to scorn for the confession."

"No! that he *should* not."

"You would not see it, Beauchampe.   You are perhaps
too necessary to this man.   But who is Mr. Calvert—is
he an elderly man?—I once knew a very worthy old gentleman of that name.   He too had been a lawyer and was
a man of talents."

"This is a very young man, I believe; not much older
than. myself.   He does not practise in our counties and I
have never seen him.   Judge Tompkins brings him forward.   You see what Sharpe says is said of him.   It will
do me no discredit to grapple with him, even should he
fling me."

"Somehow, I think well of him already," said the wife.
"I would you were with *him*, Beauchampe, rather than
against him.   Somehow, I do not incline to this Colonel
Sharpe.   I wish you were not *his* ally."

"What a prejudice!   But you will think better of the
colonel when you see him.   I shall probably bring him
home with me!"

The wife said nothing more, but there was a secret feeling at her heart that rendered this assurance an irksome
one.   Somehow, she wished that Beauchampe might *not*
bring this person to his house.   Her impression—which
was certainly derived from his letter—was an unfavorable
one.   She fancied, after awhile, that her objection was only
the natural reluctance to see strangers, of one who had so
long secluded herself from the sight of all; and thus she
rested, until Beauchampe was about to take his departure
to attend the gathering at Bowling-Green, and then the
same feeling found utterance again.

"Do not bring home *any* friends, Beauchampe.   I am

not fit, not willing to see them. Remember how long I have been shut in from the world. Force me not into it. Now we have security, husband — I dread change of any kind as if it were death. Strange faces will only give me pain. Do not bring any !"

" What! not Colonel Sharpe! I care to bring no other. I could scarcely get off from bringing him. At least I must ask him, Anna; and, I confess to you, I shall not be displeased if he does decline. The probability is that he will for his hands are full."

She turned in from the gate, saying nothing further on this subject, but feeling an internal hope, which she could not repress, that this would be the case. Nay, somehow, she felt as if she would prefer that Beau-'.ampe would bring any other friend than this.

How prescient is the soul that loves and fears! Talk of your mesmerism as you will, there are some divine instincts in our nature which are as apprehensive of the coming event, as if they were already a part of it. It is as if they see the lightning-flash which informs the event, long before the thunder-peal which, like the voice of fame, comes slowly to declare that all is over.

CHAPTER XVI.

STUMP PATRIOTS.

WERE we at the beginning of our journey, instead of being so far advanced on our way, it would be a pleasant mode of wasting an hour, to descant on the shows and practices of a popular gathering in our forest country. The picture is a strange, if not a startling one. Its more prominent aspects must, however, be imagined by the reader. We have now no time for mere description. The more decidedly narrative parts of our story are finished. As we tend to the denouëment, the action necessarily becomes more rapid and more dramatic. The supernumeraries cease to thrust in their lanthern-long images upon us. This is no place for meditative philosophers; and none are suffered to appear except those who *do* and *suffer*, with the few subordinates which the exigency of the case demands, for disposing the draperies decently, and letting down the curtain.

Were it otherwise — were not this disposition of the parts and parties inevitable — it would afford us pleasure to give a *camera-obscura* representation of the figures, coming and going, who mingle and dance around the great political caldron during the canvass of a closely-contested election:

> "Black spirits and white,
> Red spirits and gray;
> Mingle, mingle, mingle,
> You that mingle may.'

And various indeed was the assortment of spirits that assembled to hear liquid argument — and drink it too — on the present occasion. Fancy the crowd, the commotion, the sharp jest and the wild laughter, most accommodating of all possible readers, and spare us the necessity of dilating upon it. We will serve you some such scene, with all its lights and shadows, on some other more fitting occasion.

Something, however, is to be shown. You are to suppose a crowd of several hundred persons, shrewd, sensible people enough, after their fashion — rough-handed men of the woods, good at the plough and wagon — masters of the axe, tree-quellers and hog-killers — a stout race, rugged it may be, but not always rude — hospitable, free-handed — ignorant of delicacies, but born with a strong conviction that much is to be known, much acquired — that they are the born inheritors of much — rights, privileges, liberties — sacred possessions which require looking after, and are not to be intrusted to every hand. Often deceived, they are necessarily jealous on this subject; and, growing a little wiser with every political loss, they come to their patrimony with an hourly-increasing knowledge of its value and its peculiar characteristics. Not much learning have they, but, in lieu of it, they can tell " hawk from handsaw" in all stages of the wind ; which is a wisdom that your learned man is not often master of. You may cheat them once, nay, twice, or thrice, for they are frank and confiding ; but the same man can not *often* cheat them ; and one thing is certain — that they can extract the uses from a politician, and then fling him away, as sagaciously as the urchin who deals in like manner with the orange-sack which he has sucked.

Talk of politicians ruling the American people ! Lord love you ! where do you find these great rulers after five years ? Sucked, squeezed, thrown by, an atom in the dung-heap ! Precious few of these men of popular dimensions survive their own clamor. Even while they shout upon their petty eminences, the world has hurried on and left them; and there they stand, open-mouthed and wondering! Waking at length, they ask, like the shipwrecked traveller on the shore: "Where am I? where is my people?"* *My* people!—ha! ha! ha! There is something worse than mockery in that shout. It is *my* people that speaks, but the voice is changed. It is now *thy* people. The sceptre has departed. Ephraim is no longer an idol among them. They have other gods; and the late exalted politician, freezing on his narrow eminence, grows dumb for ever— stiff, stone-eyed—like the sphinx, brooding in her sinking sands, saying, as it were, "Ask me nothing of what I was, for *now* see you not that I am nothing?"

Precious little of such a fate dreams he, the high-cheeked, sunburnt orator, that now rallies the stout peasantry at Bowling-Green. He thinks not so much of perpetual fame as of perpetual office. He has a faith in office which shall last him much longer than that which he professes to have in the people. He hath not so much faith in them as in their gifts. But he fancies not—not he—that the shouts which now respond to his utterance shall ever refuse response to his summons. He assumes a saving exception in his own case, which shall make him sure in the very places where his predecessors failed. He hath an unctuous way with him which makes his faith confident; and his voice thunders, and his eye lightens; and he rains precious drops among them, which might be eloquence, if it were not balderdash!

"Who is this man?" quoth our young hero Beauchampe, as he listened to the muddy torrent, which, like some turbid river, having overflowed its banks, comes down, rending and raging, a thick flood of slime and foam, bringing along with it the refuse of nauseous places, and low flats, and swampy bottoms, and offal-stalls!

The youth was bewildered. The eloquent man was so

---

* Years after this was published, even Webster was heard to ask, in this very condition of bewilderment, "Where am *I* to go?"

sure of his ground and auditors—seemed so confident in his strength—so little like a doubting giant—that it was long before Beauchampe could discover that he was a mere wind-bag, a bloated vessel of impure air, that, becoming fixed air through a natural process, at length explodes and breaks forth with a violence duly proportioned to its noisomeness.

"This can not be the man Calvert!" soliloquized our hero. It was not. But, when the wind-bag was exhausted—which, by a merciful Providence, was at length the case—then arose another speaker; and then did Beauchampe note the vast difference, even before the latter spoke, which was at once evident between the two.

"This must be he!" he murmured to himself.

He was not mistaken. The crowd was hushed. The stillness, after those clamors which preceded it, was awful; but was it not encouraging? No such stillness had accompanied the torrent-rushing of those beldame ideas and bulldog words which had come from the previous speaker. Here was attention — curiosity — the natural curiosity of an audience about to listen to a new speaker, and already favorably impressed by his manner and appearance.

Both were pleasing and impressive. In person he was tall and well made—his features denoted one still in the green and gristle of his youth—not more than twenty-five summers had darkened into brown the light flaxen hair upon his forehead. His eyes were bright and clear, but there was a grave sweetness, or rather a sweet, mild gravity in his face, which seemed the effect of some severe disappointment or sorrow.

This, without impairing youth, had imparted dignity. His manner was unostentatious and natural, but very graceful. He bowed when he first rose before the assembly, then, for a few moments, remained silent, while his eye seemed to explore the whole of that moral circuit which his thoughts were to penetrate.

He began, and Beauchampe was now all attention. His
voice was at first very low, but very clear and distinct.
His exordium consisted of some general principles which
the subjects he proposed to discuss were intended to illustrate, to confirm, and at the same time to receive their own
illustration, by the application of the same maxims.

In all this there was an ease of utterance, a familiarity
with all the forms of analysis, a readiness in moral conjecture, a freedom of comparison, a promptness of suggestion, which betrayed a mind not only excellent by nature,
but admirably drilled by the severest exercise of will
and art.

We do not care to note his arguments, or the particular
subjects which they were intended to elucidate. These
were purely local in their character, and were nowise remarkable, excepting as, in their employment, the speaker
showed himself everywhere capable of rising to the height
of those principles by which the subject was governed. This
habit of mind enabled him to simplify his topic to the understanding of his audience; to disentangle the mysteries
which the dull brains and rabid tongue of the previous
speaker had involved in a seemingly inextricable mass; and
to unveil, feature by feature, the perfect image of that leading idea which he had set out to establish.

In showing that Mr. Calvert argued his case, it is not to
be understood, however, that he was merely argumentative.
The main points of difficulty discussed, he rose, as he proceeded, into occasional flights of eloquence, which told with
the more effect, as they were made purely subordinate to
the *business* of his speech. Beauchampe discovered, with
wonder and admiration, the happy art which had so arranged it; and from wonder and admiration he sank to
apprehension, when, considering the equal skill of the debater and the beauty of his declamation, he all at once recollected, toward the close, that it was allotted to him to
take up the cudgels and maintain the conflict for his friend.

But this was not a moment to feel fear. Beauchampe was a man of courage. His talent was active, his mood fiery, his imagination very prompt and energetic. He, too, was meant to be an orator; but he had gone through no such school of preparation as that of the man whom he was to answer. But this did not discourage him. If he lacked the exquisite finish of manner, and the logical relation of part with part, which distinguished the address of his opponent, he had an irresistible impulse of expression. Easily excited himself, he found little difficulty in exciting those whom he addressed. If Calvert was the noble steed of the middle ages, caparisoned in chain-armor, and practised to wheel, and bound, and rear, and recoil, as the necessities of the fight required — then was Beauchampe the light Arabian courser, who, if he may not combat on equal terms with his opponent, at least, by his agility and unremitting attack, keeps him busy at all points in the work of defence. If he gives himself no repose, he leaves his enemy none. Now here, now there, with the rapidity of lightning, he fatigues his heavily-armed foe by the frequency of his evolutions — he himself being less encumbered by weight and armor, and being at the same time more easily refreshed for a renewal of the fight.

Such was the nature of their combat which lasted, at intervals, throughout the day. Beauchampe had made his debut with considerable eclat. His heart was bounding with the excitement of the conflict. The friends of Colonel Sharpe were in ecstacies. They had been dashed by the superior eloquence of the new assailant. They feared and felt the impression which Calvert had made; and, expecting nothing from so young a beginner as Beauchampe, they naturally exaggerated the character of his speech, when they found it so far to exceed their expectations. The compliments which he received were not confined to the friends of Colonel Sharpe. The opposition confessed his excellence, and Calvert himself was the first, when it was over, to come forward, make the acquaintance, and offer his congratulations.

Colonel Sharpe arrived that night. As soon as this fact was ascertained, Beauchampe prepared to return home. Sharpe had brought with him two friends, both lawyers, men of some parts, who rendered any further assistance from our young husband unnecessary. The resolution of the new bridegroom so soon to leave the field, provoked the merriment of the veterans.

" And so you are really married ? And what sort of a wife have you got, Beauchampe ?" demanded Sharpe.

" You can readily guess," said Barnabas, " when you find him so eager to get home without waiting to see the end of the business here."

" Is she young and handsome, Beauchampe ?"

" And what are her moral possessions, as defined by Whisker-Ben ?" was the demand of Barnabas.

The tone of these remarks, and inquiries was excessively annoying to Beauchampe. There was something like gross irreverence in it. It seemed as if his sensibilities suffered a stab with every syllable which he was called upon to answer. Besides, it was only when examined in reference to the age, appearance and name of his wife, that he became vividly impressed with the painful consciousness of what must be concealed in her history. The burning blush on his cheeks, when he replied to his companions, only served to subject his unnecessary modesty to the usual sarcasms which are common in such cases.

" And you *will* go ?" said Sharpe.

" I promised my wife to return as soon as you came, and she will expect me."

" I must see that wife of yours who has so much power over you. Is she so very handsome, Beauchampe ?"

" *I* think so."

" And what did you say was her name before marriage ?" was the further inquiry.

He was answered, though with some hesitation.

"Cooke, Cooke! You say in your letter that she's wonderfully smart! But, Barnabas, we must judge for ourselves, both the beauty and the wit. Hey, boy! are we not a committee on that subject?"

"To be sure we are—for that matter, Beauchampe could only marry with our consent. He will have to be very civil in showing us the lady, to persuade us to sanction this premature affair."

"Do you hear, Beauchampe?"

"I do not fear. When you have seen her, the consent will not be withheld, I'm sure."

"You believe in your princess, then?"

"Fervently!"

"You are very young, Beauchampe—very young! But we were all young, Barnabas, and have paid the penalties of youth. An age of unbelief for a youth of faith. Thirty years of skepticism for some three months' intoxication. But how soon that gristle of credulity hardens into callousness! How long do you give Beauchampe before he gains his freedom?"

"That," said Barnabas, "will depend very much on how much he sees of wife, children, and friends. If he were now to set off alone and take a voyage to Canton, the probability is he would be quite as much a victim until he got back. Three weeks at home would probably give him a more decided taste for the Canton voyage, and he would take a second, and stay abroad longer. Beyond that there is no need to look; the story always ends in the same way. I never knew a tale which had so little variety."

There was more of this dialogue which we do not care to record. The moral atmosphere was not grateful to the tastes of the young man. Sharpe saw that, and changed the subject.

"You have made good fight to-day—so they tell me. I knew you would. But you should keep it up. Take my

word, another day here would be the making of you. Oue
speech proves nothing if it produces no more."

"I shall only be in the way," said Beauchampe. "You
have Barnabas and Mercer."

"Good men and true, but the more the merrier. Hotv
know I whom the opposition will bring into the field?"

"They will scarcely get one superior to Calvert."

"So, you like him then?"

"I do—very much. He will give you a hard fight."

"Will he, then?" said Colonel Sharpe, with some appearance of pique; "well! we shall see—Heaven send
the hour as soon as may be."

"Be wary," said Beauchampe, "for I assuré you he is a
perfect master of his weapon. I have seldom even fancied
a more adroit or able speaker."

"Do I not tell you you are young, Beauchampe?"

"Young or old, take my counsel as a matter of prudence,
and be wary. He will certainly prove to you the necessity
of looking through your armory."

"By my faith but I should like to see this champion who
has so intoxicated you. You have made me curious, ana
I must see him to-night. Where does he lodge?"

"At the Red Heifer."

"Shall we go to him, or send for him? What say you,
Barnabas?"

"Oh, go to him, be sure. It will have a good effect. It
will show as if you were not proud."

"And did not fear him! Come, Beauchampe, if you will
not stay and do battle for us any longer, pen a billet of in-
troduction to this famous orator. Say to him, that your
friends, Messieurs Sharpe and Barnabas, of whom you may
say the prettiest things with safety, will come over this
evening to test the hospitality of the Red Heifer. Be sure
to state that it is your new wife that hurries you off, or the
conceited fellow may fancy that he has made you sick with
his drubbing. Ho! Sutton—landlord! what ho! there!"

The person summoned made his appearance.

"Ha! Sutton! How are you, my old boy?—hav'n't seen you since the last flood—and what's to be done down here? What are you going to do? Is it court or country party here—Tompkins or Desha?"

"Well, kurnel, there's no telling to a certainty, till the votes is in the box and counted; but I reckon all goes right, jist now, as you'd like to find it."

"Very good—and you think Beauchampe did well to-day?"

"Mighty onexpected well. He'll be a screamer yet, I tell you."

"There's a promise of fame for you, Beauchampe, which ought to make you stay a day longer. Think now of becoming a screamer! You said a screamer, Sutton, old fellow, didn't you?"

"Screamer's the word, kurnel; and 'twon't be much wanting to make him one. He did talk the boldest now, I tell you, considerin' what he had to work ag'in."

"What! is this Mr. Calvert a screamer too?"

"Raal grit, kurnel—no mistake. Talks like a book."

"And so, I suppose," said Sharpe, in the manner of a man who knows his strength and expects it to be acknowledged, "and so I suppose you look for me to come out in all my strength? You will require me to talk like two books?"

"Jist so, kurnel, the people's a-looking for it; and it's an even bet with some, that you can't do better than this strange chap, Calvert."

"But there are enough to take up such a bet? Are there not, old fellow?"

"Well, I reckon there are; but you know how a nag has to work when the odds are even."

"Ay, ay! We must see this fellow, that's clear. We must measure his height, breadth, and strength, beforehand.

No harm to look at any one's enemy the night before fighting him, Sutton, is there ?"

"None in natur', kurnel. It's a sort o' right one has to feel the heft of the chap that wants to fling him."

"Even so, old boy — so get us pen, ink, and paper, here, while Beauchampe writes him a sort of friendly challenge. I say, Sutton, the Red Heifer is against us, is she ?"

"I reckon it's the Red Heifer's husband, kurnel," said the landlord, as he placed the writing materials. "If 'twas the Red Heifer herself, I'm thinking the vote would be clear t'other way."

"Ha! ha! you wicked dog!" exclaimed Sharpe, with a chuckle of perfect self-complacence; "I see you do not easily forget old times."

"No, no, kurnel!—a good recollection of old times is a sort of Christian duty: it sort o' keeps a man in memory of friends and inimies."

"But the Red Heifer was neither friend nor enemy of yours, Sutton ?"

"No, kurnel, but the Heifer's husband had a notion that 'tworn't any fault of mine that she worn't."

"Ah, you sad dog!" said Sharpe, flatteringly.

"A leetle like my customers, kurnel," responded the landlord, with a knowing leer.

"I would I could see her, though for a minute only.'

"That's pretty onpossible. He's strict enough upon her now-a-days; never lets her out of sight, and watches every eye that looks to her part of the house. He'd be mighty suspicious of *you*, if you went there."

"But he has no cause, Sutton!"

"Well, *you say so*, kurnel, and I'm not the man to say otherwise; but he thinks very different, I can tell you. He ain't the man to show his teeth; but, mark me, his eye won't leave you from the time you come, to the time you quit."

" We'll note him, Sutton. Ready, Beauchampe ?"

The youth answered by handing the note to the landlord, by whom it was instantly despatched according to its direction. A few moments only had elapsed, when an answer was received, acknowledging the compliment, and requesting to see the friends of Mr. Beauchampe at their earliest leisure.

" This is well," said Sharpe. " I confess my impatience to behold this formidable antagonist. Bestir yourself, Barnabas, with that toddy, over which you seem to have been saying the devil's prayers for the last half-hour ! Be sure and bring a hatful of your cigars along with you. The Red Heifer, I suspect, will yield us nothing half so good. Ho, Beauchampe ! are you sleeping ?"

A slap on the shoulder aroused Beauchampe from something like a waking dream, and he started to his feet with a bewildered look. He had been thinking of his wife, and of the cruel portions of her strange history — to which, as by an inevitable impulse, the equivocal dialogue between Sharpe and the landlord seemed to carry him back.

" Dreaming of your wife, no doubt ! Ha ! ha !—Beauchampe, how long will you be a boy ?"

Why did these words annoy Beauchampe ? Was there anything sinister in their signification ? Why did those tones of his friend's voice send a shudder through the youth's veins ? Had he also his presentiments ? We shall see. At all events, his dream, whatever may have been its character, was thoroughly broken. He turned to the landlord, and ordered his horse to be got instantly.

" You will go, then ?" said Sharpe.

" Yes ; you do not need me any longer."

" You are resolved, then, not to be a screamer ! What a perverse nature ! Here is Fame, singing like the ducks of Mrs. Bond, ' Come and catch me'— and d—l a bit he stirs for all their invitation ! But he's young, Barnabas, and has a young wife not five weeks old. We must be indulgent, Barnabas. We must not be too strict in our examination."

" We were young ourselves once," said Barnabas, kindly looking to Beauchampe.

" But do not be precipitate, old fellow. Though mercifully inclined, it must be real beauty, and genuine wit, that shall save our brother. Our certificate will depend on that. Beauchampe, look to see us to dinner day after to-morrow."

" I shall expect you," said Beauchampe, faintly, as, bidding them farewell, he left the room.

" Ha! ha! ha! poor fellow!" said Sharpe. " His treasures make him sad. He is just now as anxious and apprehensive as an old miser of seventy."

" Egad, he little dreams, just now, how valuable the club will be to him a few months hence," said Barnabas.

" Everything to him. Let us drink ' The club,' Barnabas." And they filled, and bowed to each other, *hob-a-nob.*

" *The* club!"

" The *pope!*"

" And the pope's wife!"

" No go, that!" said Sharpe. " Antiques are masculine only. She's dead to us; she's too old."

" What say you to this wife of Beauchampe, then?"

" We won't drink *her* until we see her; though I rather suspect she must be pretty, for he has an eye in his head. But what a d——d fool to leap so hurriedly, without once looking after the consideration! That was a woful error! —only to be excused by her superexcellence. We shall see in season; though, curse me, if I do not fancy he'd rather see the devil than either of us! He's jealous already. Did you observe how faintly he said, ' Good-night' —and how coldly he gave his invitation? But we'll like his wife the better for it, Barnabas. ' When the husband's jealous, the wife's fair game.' Thus saith the proverb."

"And a wholesome one! But—did we drink? I'm not sure that we have not forgotten it."

And the speaker explored the bottom of the pitcher, and knew not exactly which had deceived him, his memory or his palate.

CHAPTER XVII.

THE SAGE AND HIS PUPIL.

In one of the apartments of the Red Heifer, wo persons were sitting about this time. One of these vas the orator whose successes that day had been the theme of every tongue. The other was a man well stricken in years, of commanding form, and venerable and intellectual aspect. His hair was long and white, while his cheeks were yet smooth and even rosy, as if they spoke for a well-satisfied conscience and gentle heart in their proprietor.

The eyes of the old man were settled upon the young one. There was a paternal exultation in their glance, which sufficiently declared the interest which he felt in the fortunes and triumphs of his companion. The eyes of the youth were fixed with something of inquiry upon the note of Beauchampe, which he still turned with his fingers. There was something of doubt and misgiving in the expression of his face; which his companion noted, to ask :—

"Is there nothing in that note, William, besides what you have read ? It seems to disturb you."

"Nothing, sir ; nor can I say that it disturbs me exactly. Perhaps every young beginner feels the same disquieting sort of excitement when he is about to meet his antagonist for the first time. You are aware, sir, that this gentleman, Colonel Sharpe, is the Coryphæus of the opposition. He is the right-hand man of Desha, and has the reputation of being one of the ablest lawyers and most popular orators in the state."

"You need not fear him, my son," said the elder; "I am now sure of your strength. You will not fail—you can not. You have your mind at the control of your will; and it needs only that you should go and be sure of opposition. Had that power but been mine—but it is useless now! I enjoy my own hoped-for triumphs in the certainties of yours."

"So far, sir, as the will enables us to prove what we are, and have in us, so far I think I may rely upon myself. But the mere will to perform is not always—perhaps not often—the power. This man Sharpe brings into the field more than ordinary talents. Hitherto, with the exception of this young man Beauchampe, all my opponents have been very feeble men—mere dealers in rhodomontade of a very commonplace sort. Beauchampe, who is said to have been a pupil of Colonel Sharpe, was merely put forward to-day to speak against time. This fact alone shows the moderate estimate which they put upon his abilities: and yet what a surprising effect his speech produced—what excitement, what enthusiasm! Besides, it was evidently unpremeditated; for it was, throughout, an answer to mine."

"But it was no answer: it was mere declamation."

"So it was, sir; but it was declamation that sounded very much like argument, and had the effect of argument. It is no small proof of a speaker's ability, when he can enter without premeditation upon a subject—a subject, too, which is decidedly against him—and so discuss it—so suppress the unfavorable and so emphasize the favorable parts of his cause—as to produce such an impression. Now, if this be the pupil of Colonel Sharpe, and so little esteemed as to be used simply to gain time, what have we to expect, what to fear, from the presence of the master?"

" Fear nothing, William ! nay, whatever you may say here, in cool deliberate moments, you can not fear when you are there ! That I know. When you stand before the people, and every voice is hushed in expectation, a different spirit takes possession of your bosom. Nothing then can daunt you. I have seen the proofs too often of what I say ; and I now tell you that it is in your power to handle this Colonel Sharpe with quite as much ease and success as you have handled all the rest. Do not brood upon it with such a mind, my son — do not encourage these doubts. To be an orator you must no more be liable to fear than a soldier going into battle."

" Somehow, sir, there are certain names which disturb me — I have met with men whose looks had the same effect. They seem to exercise the power of a spell upon my mind and frame."

" But you burst from it ?"

" Yes, but with great effort."

" It matters nothing. The difficulty is easily accounted for, as well as the spell by which you were bound. That spell is in your own ardency of imagination. Persons of your temperament, for ever on the leap, are for ever liable to recoil. Have you never advanced impetuously to grasp the hand of one who has been named to you, and then almost shrunk away from his grasp, as soon as you have beheld his face ? He was a phlegmatic, perhaps ; and your warm nature recoiled with a feeling of natural antipathy from the repelling coldness of his. The man who pours forth his feelings under enthusiastic impulses is particularly liable to this frigid influence. A deliberate matter-of-fact question, at such a moment — the simplification into baldness of the subject of his own inquiry, by the lips of a cynic — will quench his ardor, and make him shrink within his shell, as a spirit of good may be supposed to recoil from the approach of a spirit of evil. Now, you have just enough of this enthusiasm to be sensible ordinarily to this influence.

You acknowledged it only on ordinary occasions, however At first, I feared its general effect upon you. I dreaded lest it should enfeeble you; but I soon discovered that you had a will, which, in the moment of necessity, could overcome it quite. As I said before, when you are once before the crowd, and they wait in silence for your utterance, you are wholly a man! I have no fears for you, William — I believe in no spells — none, at least, which need to trouble you. I know that you have no reason to fear, and I know that you will not fear when the time comes. Let me predict for you a more complete triumph to-morrow than any which has happened yet."

"You overrate me, sir. All I shall endeavor to do will be to keep what ground I may have already won. I must not hope to make any new conquests in the teeth of so able a foe."

"That is enough. To maintain your conquests is the next thing to making them; and is usually a conquest by itself. But you will do more — you can not help it. You have the argument with you, and that is half the battle. Nay, it is all the battle to a mind so enthusiastic as yours in the cause of truth. The truth confers a strange power upon its advocate. Nay, I believe it is from the truth alone that we gather the last best powers of eloquence. I believe in the realness of no eloquence unless it comes from the sincerity of the orator. To make me believe, the speaker must himself believe."

"Or seem to do so."

"I think I should detect the seeming. Nay, after a little while, the people themselves detect it, and the orator sinks accordingly. This is the fate of many of our men who begin popularly. With politics, *for a profession*, no man can be honest or consistent long. He must soon trade on borrowed capital. He soon deals in assignats and false papers. He endorses the paper of other men, sooner than not issue; and in doing business at all hazards, he soon inours the last—bankruptcy! Political bankruptcy is of all sorts the worst. There is some chance of regaining caste, where it is lost by dishonesty—but never where it follows from a blunder. The knave is certainly one thing, but the blunderer may be both. The fool and knave united are incorrigible. Such a combination is too monstrous for popular patience. And how many do we see of this description. I do not think there is in any profession under the sun such numerous examples of this combination. Every day shows us persons who toil for power and place with principles sufficiently flexible to suit any condition of things; and yet they fail, and expose themselves. This is the wonder—that, unfettered as they make themselves at the beginning, they should still become bondsmen, and so, convict! They seem to lack only one faculty of the knave—and that the most necessary—art."

"Their very rejection of law enslaves them. That is the reason. They set out in a chain, which increases with every movement—which seems momently to multiply its own links and hourly increase its weight. Falsehood is such a chain. You can not convict a true man, for the simple reason that his feet are unimpeded from the first. A step in error is a step backward, which requires two forward before you can regain what is lost. How few have the courage for this. It is so much easier to keep on—so difficult to turn! This chain—the heavy weight which error is for ever doomed to carry—produces a stiffness of the limbs—a monstrous awkwardness—an inflexibility, which exposes its burdens whenever it is checked, compelled to leap aside, or attempt any sudden change of movement. This was the great difficulty of this young man, Beauchampe, in the discussion to-day: he scarcely knew it himself, because, to a young man of ingenuity, the difficulties of the argument on the wrong side, are themselves provocations to error. By exercising ingenuity, they appeal flatteringly to one's sense of talent; and, in proportior as he may succeed in plausibly relieving himself from these difficulties of the subject, in the same proportion will he gradually identify himself with the side he now espouses. His mind will gradually adopt the point of view to which its own subtleties conduct it; and, in this way will it become fettered, possibly to the latest moment of his existence. There is nothing more important to the popular orator than to have Truth for his ally when he *first* takes the field. Success, under such auspices, will commend her to his love, and the bias, once established, his faith is perpetual."

" True, William, but you would make this alliance accidental. It must be the result of choice to be worth anything. We must love Truth, and seek her, or she does not become our ally."

" I wish it were possible to convince our young beginners everywhere, not only that Truth is the best ally, but the only one that, in the long run, can possibly conduct us to permanent success."

" This is not so much the point, I think, as to enable them to detect the true from the false. Very few young men are able to do this before thirty. Hence the error of forcing them into public life before that period. You will seldom meet with a very young person who will deliberately choose the false in preference to the true, from a selfish motive. They are beguiled into error by those who are older. It is precisely in politics as in morals. The unsuspecting youth, through the management of some cold, cunning debauchee, into whose hands he falls, finds himself in the embrace of a harlot, at the very moment when he most dreams of beatific love. The inner nature, not yet practised to defend itself, becomes the prey of the outer; and strong indeed must be native energies which can finally recover the lost ground, and expel the invader from his place of vantage."

" The case is shown in that of this young man, Beauchampe. It is evidently a matter of no moment to him on

which side he enlists himself just now. There is no truth
involved in it, to his eyes. It is a game of skill carried
on between two parties; and his choice is determined simply by that with which he has been familiar. He is used
by Sharpe, who is an older man, and possessed of more experience, to promote an end. He little dreams that, in
doing so, he is incurring a moral obligation to maintain the
same conflict through his whole career."

CHAPTER XVIII.

THE MEETING OF THE WATERS — AN EXPLOSION.

AT this stage of the conversation, the two companions were interrupted by the sudden entrance of a sly-looking little deformity of a man, the landlord of the Red Heifer, who, in somewhat stately accents, announced the approach of Colonel Sharpe and his friend Mr. Barnabas. The two gentlemen rose promptly, expressed their pleasure at the annunciation, and begged the landlord to introduce the visiters.

In a few moments this was done, though it was found that they were not the only guests. They were followed closely by a group of ten or a dozen substantial yeomen of the neighborhood — persons who never dreamed, in the unsophisticated region of our story, that they were guilty of any trespass upon social laws in thus pressing uninvited into a gentleman's private apartments. Our simple republicans supposed that, because they had a motive, they had also a sufficient plea in justification. Their object was, to be present at the first meeting of the rival candidates, when, they fancied, that there would be a keen encounter of wits, and such a display of the respective powers of the opponents as would enable them to form a judgment in respect to the parties, for one or other of whom they would be required to cast their votes.

The intrusion was of a sort to offend nobody. The public men were used to such familiarities, particularly at public hotels; and the *people* somewhat presumed upon the dependence of the candidates upon their support, which would make them quite careful neither to take nor to give offence.

The two gentlemen, accordingly, as the crowd made its appearance, welcomed all parties; while the yeomen, ranging themselves about the entrance, suffered the invited guests to pass beyond them into the centre of the room.

William Calvert, our young orator, felt a rising emotion at his heart, which was not, as he fancied, exactly the result of his mental humility. It was, on the contrary, rather the proof of a strong craving, an intense ambition, which, aiming at the highest, naturally felt some misgivings of its own strength and securities when about to measure, for the first time, with a champion who was already famous. We have seen how these misgivings had troubled him in the previous dialogue, and have heard how his venerable companion had endeavored to strengthen him against them.

The labor was perhaps an unnecessary one. The young man's quailing was from his own extreme standards, rather than from the height and dimensions of his rival. But the issue between them was not destined to be one of intellect, and, in respect to the keen encounter of the rival wits, our yeomen were doomed to disappointment. But there was to be a trial between them, nevertheless, which probably compensated the hungering expectants for what was withheld.

The huge, beefy landlord of the opposition house, Sutton, now bustled forward, having the arm of Colonel Sharpe within his own. The little, deformed representative of the Red Heifer—*our* house—stationing himself beside Calvert, confronted the rival landlord with an air which exhibited something more of defiance than cordiality. Very bitter, from time immemorial, had been the feuds between the two houses—not so bloody, perhaps, but quite as angry, bitter, and enduring, as those which sundered the factions of York and Lancaster. Of course, the quarrel between them being generally understood, the defiant demonstrations of the two commanded but little notice. All eyes were rather addressed to the rival politicians who were about to meet.

Mr. Barnabas, with bow and smirk, drew near to the elder Calvert, who extended his hand to him very courteously, received his gripe, and with him turned to the younger Calvert, to whom Colonel Sharpe was approaching at the same time. As the parties were about to meet, the colonel, shaking off the arm of his landlord, extended his hand to the rival :—

"Mr. Calvert, I believe. I am Colonel Sharpe."

The hand of William Calvert was extended to receive that of Sharpe, when it was suddenly drawn back. The light was now streaming full on the face of Sharpe. In that of William Calvert, the expression instantly became one of mingled astonishment and loathing. His hands were thrown behind his back, while, drawing his person up to its fullest height, he exclaimed, with a voice of equal surprise and scorn—

"You, sir, Colonel Sharpe—you !"

The effect was a mute wonder in the circle.

Sharpe started, his cheek paling, his eye flashing, at the unexpected reception. The audience was confounded to expecting silence. Sharpe himself was so surprised as not to be able to recover speech immediately. He did, however, in a moment after, and said :—

"What is this ? I *am* Colonel Sharpe. And you, sir—are you not Mr. Calvert ?"

"Ay, sir ; and, as Mr. Calvert, I can not *know* Colonel Sharpe."

These words were spoken in hoarse, almost choking accents, but full of determination. The heart of the speaker was swelling with indignation ; his brain was fired with terrible reminiscences ; his cheek was flushed with inexpressible passion; his eyes darted glances of most withering scorn, hate, loathing, full in the face of his opponent.

And thus stood the two for a moment. For that space, all was mute consternation in the circle. At length, old Calvert found his voice, though almost in a whisper, and, drawing close to the young man, he said:—

"What do you mean, my son? Wherefore this strange anger? Who is this man, and why—"

Young Calvert had only time to say—"What, sir! do you not see?—" when Sharpe, fully recovered from his momentary surprise, came forward with Barnabas, and, with rising accents, formally demanded an explanation.

"You must explain, sir—explain!" said Mr. Barnabas. "Why, sir, do you say that you can not know my friend?"

"For the simple reason, sir, that I know him too well already," was the answer, made with a successful effort to speak in distinct and resolute tones.

"Ha!" exclaimed Sharpe—"know *me?*"

"Ay, sir! as a villain—a base, consummate villain!"

All was confusion again.

Sharpe, with prompt fury, darted upon the speaker, putting forth all his strength of sinew for the grapple. But he was not the man, physically, to deal with Calvert. The latter seized him with a gripe of iron, and, with a moderate effort of muscle, flung him off, staggering, among the group near the door. This performance exhibited such a degree of strength as amply satisfied all the spectators that Calvert might well scorn such an assailant in that sort of encounter.

Sharpe did not fall—was perhaps saved from falling by the interposing crowd. He soon recovered himself, and was rushing forward to renew his hopeless attempt, when his friend Barnabas threw his arms around him, and held him back.

"Unhand me, Barnabas! unhand me, I say! Shall I submit to a blow?"

"Surely not, Sharpe. But this is not the way."

For a moment, as if slowly recovering thought, Sharpe paused, then said huskily, and in low tones :—

"You are right. There must be blood! See to it!"

"Stand back! I will see to it."

Then advancing to the other party, Barnabas said :—

"Mr. Calvert, we must have an apology, or a meeting. And the apology must be ample, sir; and it must be public, as is the offence."

"Apology, sir!—to that worthless scoundrel? You mistake me, sir, very much, if you suppose that I shall apologize to him, of all men living, whatever the offence! It is possible, too, sir, that you somewhat mistake your friend. He will scarcely demand one—will certainly not *need* one —when he knows *me*—when he recalls the features of one who has already taught him what to fear from an avenger!"

"What does all this mean?" demanded Barnabas; while Sharpe eagerly stretched forward, bewildered—with curious eyes, seeking to distinguish the features of the speaker —a study not much facilitated by the dim light of the two tallow-candles which stood upon the mantel-place.

"Who, then, are you, sir?" continued Barnabas.

"Nay, sir," answered the other, "speak for your friend! Your Colonel Sharpe has, I fancy, as many *aliases* as any rogue of London! Let Colonel Sharpe—if such be, in truth, his name—"

"It is his name, sir, I assure you. Why should you doubt it?"

"I have known him by another, and one associated with the foulest infamy!"

"Ha!" cried Sharpe—beginning, perhaps, to recall an unhappy past.

Calvert turned full toward him.

"Look at me, Alfred Stevens—for such I must still call you—look at me, and behold one who is ready to avenge the dishonor of Margaret Cooper! Ha! villain! do you start? do you shrink? do you remember now the young preacher of Charlemont?—the swindling, smooth-spoken rogue, who sought out the home of innocence to rob it of peace and innocence at a blow? Once, before this, we stood opposed in deadly strife. Do you think that I am less ready now? Then, your foul crime had not been consummated: would to God I had slain you then!

"But it is not too late for vengeance! Apology, indeed! Will you fight, Alfred Stevens? Say—are you as ready now as when the cloth of the preacher might have been a protection for your cowardice? If you *are*, say to your friend here that apology between *us* is a word of vapor, and no meaning. Atonement—blood only—nothing less will suffice!"

Sharpe, staggered at the first address of the speaker, had now recovered himself. His countenance was deadly pale. His eyes wandered. He had been stunned by the suddenness of Calvert's revelations. But the eyes of the crowd were upon him. Murmurs of suspicion reached his ears. It was necessary that he should take decided ground. Your politician must not want audacity. Nay, in proportion to his diminished honesty, must be his increase of brass. To brazen it out was his policy; and, by a strong effort, regaining his composure, he quietly exclaimed, looking round him as he spoke:—

"The man is certainly mad. I know not what he means."

"Liar! this will not serve you. You shall not escape me. You do not deceive *me*. You *shall not* deceive these people. Your words may deny the truth of what I say, but your pallid cheeks confess it. Your hoarse, choking accents, your down-looking eyes, confess it. The lie that is spoken by your tongue is contradicted by all your other faculties. There is no man present who does not see that you tremble in your secret soul; that I have spoken nothing but the truth; that you are the base villain—the destroyer of beauty and innocence—that I have pronounced you!"

"This is strange, very strange!" said Mr. Barnabas.

The man is certainly mad," continued Sharpe, "or this is a political charge intended to destroy me. A poor, base trick, this of yours, Mr. Calvert. It will have no effect upon the people. They understand that sort of thing too well."

"They *shall* understand it *better*," said Calvert. "They shall have the whole history of your baseness. Political trick, indeed! We leave that business to you, whose very life has been a lie. My friends—"

"Stay, sir," said Barnabas. "There is a shorter way to settle this. My friend has wronged you, you say. He shall give you redress. There need be no more words between us."

"Ay, but there must. The redress, of course; but the words shall be a matter of course, also. You shall hear my charge against this man renewed.—I pronounce him a villain, who, under the name of Alfred Stevens, five years ago made his appearance in the village of Charlemont, and, pretending to be a student of divinity, obtained the confidence of the people; won the affections of a young lady of the place, dishonored and deserted her. This is the charge I make against him, which will be sustained by this venerable man, and for the truth of which I invoke the all-witnessing Heaven. Alfred Stevens, I defy you to deny this charge."

"It is all false as hell!" was the husky answer of the criminal.

"It is true as heaven!" said Calvert, and his asseveration was now confirmed by that of the aged man by whom he was accompanied.

Nor were the spectators unimpressed by the firm, unbending superiority of manner possessed by Calvert over that of Sharpe, who was wanting in his usual confidence.

and who, possibly from the suddenness of the charge, and possibly from a guilty conscience, failed in that promptness and freedom of utterance which, in the case of his accuser, was greatly increased by the feeling of scorn and indignation which was so suddenly reawakened in his bosom.

The little landlord of the Red Heifer, about this time, made himself particularly busy in whispering around that it was precisely five years ago that Colonel Sharpe had taken a trip to the south with his uncle, and was absent two thirds of the year.

How much more the Red Heifer might have said—for he had his own wrongs to stimulate his hostility and memory—can only be conjectured; for he was suddenly silenced by the landlord of the opposition-house, who threatened to wring his neck if he again thrust it forward in the business.

But the hint of the little man had not fallen upon unheeding ears. There were some two or three persons who recalled the period of Sharpe's absence in the south, and found it to agree with Calvert's statements. The buzz became general among the crowd, but was silenced by the coolness of Barnabas.

"Mr. Calvert," said he, "you are evidently mistaken in your man. My friend denies your story as it concerns himself. We do not deny that some person looking like my friend may have practised upon your people; but that he is not the man he insists. There is yet time to withdraw from the awkward position in which you have placed yourself. There is no shame in acknowledging an error. You are clearly in error: you can not persevere in it without injustice. Let me beg you, sir, for your own sake, to admit as much, and shake hands upon it."

"Shake hands, and with him? No, no, sir! this can not be. I am in no error. I do *not* mistake my man. He is the very villain I have declared him. He must please himself as he may with the epithet."

"I am sorry you persist in this unhappy business, Mr. Calvert. My friend will withdraw for the present. May I see you privately within the hour?"

"At any moment."

"I am very much obliged to you. I like promptness in such matters. But, once more, sir, it is not too late. These gentlemen will readily understand how you have confounded two persons who look something alike. But there is a shade of difference, as you see, in the chin, the forehead, perhaps, the color of the eyes. Look closely, I pray you, for truly I should be sorry, for your own sake, to have you persist in your error."

Mr. Barnabas, in order to afford Calvert the desired opportunity of discerning the difference between the charged and the guilty party, took the light from the mantel and held it close to the face of Sharpe.

"Pshaw!" said the latter, somewhat impatiently, "the fellow is a madman or a fool. Why do you trouble yourself further? Let him have what he wishes."

The voice of Calvert, at the same moment, disclaimed every doubt on the score of the criminal's identity.

"He is the man! I should know him, by day and by night, among ten thousand!"

"You won't confess yourself mistaken, then?" said Barnabas; "a mere confession of error — an inaccuracy of vision — the smallest form of admission!"

Calvert turned from him scornfully.

"Very well, sir, if it must be so! Good people — my friends — you bear us witness we have tried every effort to obtain peace. We are very pacific. But there is a point beyond which there is no forbearance. Integrity can keep no terms with slander. Not one among you but would fight if you were called Alfred Stevens. It is the name, as you hear, of a swindler — a seducer — a fellow destined for the high sessions for Judge Lynch. We shall hear of him under some other *alias*. We have assured the young gentle-

9*

man here that we are not Alfred Stevens, and prefer not to
be called by a nickname; but he persists, and you know
what is to follow. You can all retire to bed, therefore,
with the gratifying conviction that both gentlemen, being
bound for it, and good Kentuckians, will be sure to do their
duty when the time comes. Good-night, gentlemen—and
may you sleep to waken in the morning to hear some famous arguments. I sincerely trust that nothing will happen to prevent any of the speakers from attending; but life
is the breath in our nostrils, and may go out with a sneeze.
Of one thing I can assure you, that it will be no fault of
mine if you do not hear the eloquence, at least, of Mr.
Barnabas."

"Hurra for Barnabas! hurra!" was the cry.

"Hurra for Barnabas!" the echo.

"Calvert for ever!" roared the trombone in the corner;
and the several instruments followed for Sharpe, Calvert,
and Barnabas, according to the sort of pipes and stops
with which Providence had kindly blessed them.

CHAPTER XIX.

BILLETS FOR BULLETS — HOW WRITTEN.

"I KNOW that this is unavoidable. I know not well, my son, how you could have acted otherwise than you did; and yet the whole affair is very shocking."

Thus began the elder Calvert to the younger, when they again found themselves alone together.

"It is: but crime is shocking; and death is shocking; and a thousand events that, nevertheless, occur hourly in life, are shocking. Our best philosophy, when they seem unavoidable, is, to prepare for them as resolutely as we prepare for death."

"*It may* be death, my son!" said the other with a shudder.

"And if it were, sir, I should gladly meet death, that I might have the power of avenging *her!* O God! when I think of her — so beautiful, so proud, so bright — so dear to me then — so dear to me even now — I feel how worthless to me are all the triumphs of life — how little worth is life itself!"

And a passionate flood of tears concluded the words of the speaker.

"Give not thus way, my son. Be a man."

"Am I not? God! what have I not endured? what have I not overcome? Will you not suffer a moment's weakness — not even when I think of her? O Margaret! but for this serpent in our Eden, what might we not have been! How might we have loved! how happy might have passed those days which are now toil and hopelessness to me, which are shame and desolation to you! But for this serpent, we had both been happy."

" No, my son, that would have been impossible. But the speculation is useless now."

" Worse than useless!"

" Why brood upon it, then ?"

" For that very reason ; as one broods over his loss, who does not value his gain. It is thus I think of *her*, and cease to think of these successes. What are they to me ? Nothing! Ah! what might they not have been had she been mine? O my father! I think of her—her beauty, her genius—as of some fallen angel. I look upon this wretch as I should regard the fiend. The hoof is wanting, it is true, but the mark of the beast is in his face. It can surely be no crime to slay such a wretch: murder it can not be !"

" You think not of yourself, William."

" Yes!—he may kill me ; but thinking of her, the fallen —and of him the beguiler—I have no fear of death—I know not that I have a love of life—I think only of the chance accorded me of avenging her cruel overthrow."

The re-entrance of Mr. Barnabas, interrupted the dialogue. He came to make the necessary arrangements.

" Very awkward business, Mr. Calvert—too late now for adjustment. May I have the pleasure of knowing the name of your friend."

Calvert named Major Hawick, a young gentleman of his party ; but the old man interfered.

" *I* will act for you, William."

" You !" said the young man.

" You, old gentleman !" exclaimed Mr. Barnabas.

" Yes," replied old Calvert, with spirit, " shall I be more reluctant than you to serve my friend. This, sir, is my son by adoption. I love him as if he were my own. I love him better than life. Shall I leave him at the very time when life is perilled. No—no! I am sorry for this affair, but will stand by him to the last. Let us discuss the arrangements."

" You've seen service before, old gentleman," said Barnabas, looking the eulogium which he did not express.

" I, too, have been young," said the other.

" True blue, still," said Barnabas ; " and though I'm sorry for the affair, yet, it gives me pleasure to deal with a gentleman of the right spirit. I trust that your son is a shot."

" He has nerve and eye !"

" Good things enough — very necessary things, but a spice of practice does no harm. Now, Sharpe has a knack with a pistol that makes it curious to see him, *if you be only a looker-on*."

" Let me stop you, young gentleman," said old Calvert ; " when I was a young man, such a remark would have been held an impertinence."

" Egad !" said Barnabas, " you have me ! Are we agreed then ? Shall it be pistols ?"

" Yes : at sunrise to-morrow."

" Good !"

" Distance, when we meet," said Calvert.

The place of meeting was soon agreed on, and the parties ceparated ; Barnabas taking his leave by complimenting the " old gentleman," as a " first-rate man of business."

" Of course," said he, " after he had reported to Sharpe the progress of the arrangements ; " of course you *were* the said Stevens. I saw that the fellow's story was true at the first jump. It was so like you."

" How if I deny it ?"

" I shouldn't believe you. 'Twas too natural. Besides, Whisker-Ben blew you long ago, though he could not tell the girl's name. Where's she now—what's become of her ?"

" That's the mystery I should give something handsome
to find out; but you may guess, from the spirit this fellow
has shown, that it wouldn't do for me to go back to Charlemont. She was a splendid woman !"

" Was she though ? I reckon this fellow loved her. He
must have done so. He looked all he said."

" He did ! The wonder is equally great in his case. He
was a sort of half-witted rustic in Charlemont—Margaret
despised him—he wanted to fight me before, on her account, and we were within an ace of it. His name was
Hinkley—to think that I should meet *in him* the now
famous Calvert. Look you, Barnabas ! the pistol is a way
we had not thought of for laying our orator on his back."

" Will you do it ?"

" I must ! He leaves me no alternative. He will keep
no terms—no counsel. If he goes on to blab this business
—nay, he can prove it, you see—he will play the devil
with my chances."

" Wing him ! That will be enough. The fellow has
pluck ; and for the sake of that brave old cock, his father,
I'd like him to get off with breath enough to carry him
farther."

" No, d—n him, let him pay the penalty of his impcrti-
nence ! Who made him the champion of Margaret Cooper ?
Were he her husband now—nay, had she even tolerated
him—I think I should let him off with some moderate hurt ;
but I owe him a grudge. You have not heard *all*, Barnabas !"—the tone of the speaker was lowered here, and a
deep crimson flush suffused his face as he concluded the
sentence—" He struck me, Barnabas—he laid cowskin
over my back !"

" The d—l he did !"

" He did—I must remember *that !*"

" So you must ! So you must !"

" I will *kill* him, Barnabas ! I am resolved on it ! I feel
the sting of that cowskin even now ?"

" So you must, but somehow, d—n the fellow, I'd like to get him off."

" Pshaw! you are getting old. Certainly you are getting blind. We have a thousand reasons for not letting him off. He's in our way—he's a giant among the opposition—the crack man they have set up against *me*. Even if I had not any personal causes of provocation, do you not see how politic it would be to put him out of the field. It's he or me. If Desha succeeds, I am attorney-general; if Tompkins, Calvert! No—no! The more I think of it, the more necessary it becomes to kill him."

" But, what if he shoots ?"

" That he does not—he *did* not at least. You must, at all events, secure me *my* distance. I suppose you will have little difficulty in this respect. The old man will scarcely know anything about these matters."

" You're mistaken—he talks as if he had been at it all his life. I reckon he has fed on fire in his younger days. The choice, of course, is his."

" A little adroitness, Barnabas, will give us what we want. You can *insinuate twelve* paces."

" Yes, that can be done, but ten is more usual. Suppose he adopts ten ?"

" That is what I expect. He will scarcely accept *your* suggestion. He will naturally suppose, from what you say, that I practise at *twelve*. This will, very probably, induce him to say ten, and then I have him on my own terms. I shall easily bottle him at that distance."

" And you will really commission the bullet ? You *will* kill him ?"

" Must !"

" Sleep on that resolution first, Sharpe !"

" It will do no good. It will not change me. This fellow was nothing to Margaret Cooper, and what right had he to interfere ? Besides—you forget the cowskin."

"Oh! true—d—n that cowskin! That's the worst part of the business."

"Good night, Barnabas," said Sharpe. "See that I do not oversleep myself.'

"No fear. Good night! Good night! D—n the fellow. Why did he use a cowskin? A hickory had not been so bad. Now will Sharpe kill him to a dead certainty. He's good for any button on Calvert's coat; and there he goes, yawning as naturally as if he had to meet, to-morrow morning, nothing worse than his *hominy!*"

CHAPTER XX.

"FIVE PACES—WHEEL AND FIRE."

It was something of a sad sight to see good old Mr. Cal-vert, till a late hour that night, brushing up the murderous weapons, adjusting bullets, and cutting out patches, with all the interested industry of a fire-eater. It was in vain that his son—his adopted son, rather, for the reader should know by this time with whom he deals—it was in vain that he implored him to forego an employment which really made him melancholy, not on his own, but the venerable old man's account. Old Calvert was principled against duelling, as he was principled against war; but he recognised the necessity in both cases of employing those modes by which, to prevent wrong, society insists upon avenging it. He would have preferred that William Calvert should not go into the field on account of Margaret Cooper; but, once invited, he recognised in all its excellence the good counsel of Polonius to his son:—

> "Beware
> Of entrance to a quarrel : but being in,
> Bear it that the opposer may beware of thee."

He at least was resolved that William should not go un-prepared and unprovided, in the properest manner, to do mischief. In the hot days of his own youth, he had acquired some considerable knowledge of the weapon, and the laws, rather understood than expressed, which govern personal combat as it is, or was, practised in our country. His care was now given, not simply to the condition of the weapons, but the mind of the combatant. The modes by which the imagination is rendered obtuse—the hardening of the nerves—the exercise of the eye and arm—could not be resorted to in the brief interval which remained before the appointed hour of conflict—and something was due to slumber, without which, all exercise and instruction would be only thrown away. But there is much that a judicious mind can do in acting upon the moral nature of the party; and the conversation of old Calvert was judiciously addressed to this point. The young man, who had by this time learned to know most of the habitual trains of thought by which his tutor was characterized, readily perceived his object.

"You mistake, my dear sir," he said, smiling, after the lapse of an hour, which had been consumed as above described; "you mistake if you think I shall fail in nerve or coolness. Be sure, sir, I never felt half so determined in all my life. The remembrance of Margaret Cooper—the sense of former wrong—the loathing hate which I entertain for this reptile—exclude every feeling from my soul *but one*, and that is the deliberate determination to destroy him if I can."

"This very intensity, William, will shake your nerves. No man is more cool than he who obeys no single feeling. Single feelings become intense and agitating from the absence or absorption of all the rest."

"Feel my arm, sir," he said, extending the limb.

"It is firm, *now*, William; but if you do not sleep, will it be so in the morning?"

"Yes—I have no fear of it."

"But you will go to sleep now? You see I have every thing ready."

"No! I can not, sir. I must write. I have much

say, which, to leave unsaid, would be criminal. Do you retire. Hawick will soon be here, who will complete what you have been doing. He is expert at these matters, and will neglect nothing. I have penned him a note to that effect. He will accompany us in the morning. Do you go to bed now. *You* can not, at your time of life, do without sleep and not suffer. It can not affect me—nay, if I did go to bed, it would be impossible, with these thoughts in my mind—these feelings in my heart—that I should close my eyes. I should only toss and tumble, and become nervous from very uneasiness."

Having finished, the old man prepared to adopt the suggestion of the young one. He rose to retire, but the " good night" faltered on his lips. Young Calvert, who was walking to and fro, was struck by the accents. Suddenly turning he rushed to the venerable man, and fell upon his neck.

"Father!—more than father to me!" exclaimed the youth—" forgive me if I have offended you. I feel that I have often erred, but through weakness only, not wilfulness. You have succored and strengthened—you have taught, counselled, and preserved me. Bless me, and forgive me, my father, if in this I have gone against your wishes and will—if I have refused your paternal guidance. Believe me, I have but one regret at this moment, and it grows out of the pain which I feel that I inflict on you. But you will forgive—you will bless me, my dear father, and should I survive this meeting, I will strive to atone—to recompense you by the most fond service, for this one wilfulness!"

" God bless you, my son—God preserve you!" was the only reply which the old man could make. His heart seemed bursting with emotion, and sobs, which he vainly strove to repress, rose in his throat with a choking, suffocating rapidity. His tears fell upon the young man's shoulder while he passionately kissed his check.

" God *will* save you," he continued, as he broke away ·

and, sobbing as he went from sight, his broken accents might still, for a few seconds, be heard in the reiteration of this one sentence of equal confidence and prayer.

" *That* is done—*that* is over !" said the youth, sinking into a seat beside the table where the writing materials were placed: his hands covered his face for a few moments, as if to shut from sight the image of the old man's agony.

" That word of parting was my fear, good old man !" he continued, after the pause of a few moments—" what a Spartan spirit does he possess ! Surely he loves me quite as well as father ever loved son before. Yet, with what strength of resolution he prepares the weapon—prepares to lose me perhaps for ever. I can not doubt that the loss will be great to him. It will be the loss of all. His hope, and the predictions of his hope, are all perilled by this ; yet he complains not—he has no reproaches !

" Surely, I have been too wanton—too rash—too precipitate in this business ! What to me is Margaret Cooper ! Her beauty, her talents, and that fair fame of which this reptile has for ever robbed her ! She loved me not—she hearkened not to my prayer of love—to that love which can not perish though the object of its devotion, like a star gone suddenly from a high place at night, has sunk for ever into darkness. I am not pledged to fight her battles—to repair her shame—to bruise the head of the reptile by which she was beguiled.

" Alas ! I can not reason after this cold fashion. Is it not because of this reptile that she is nothing to me—and does not this make her defence everything—heighten the passion of hate, and make bloody vengeance a most sacred virtue ?

" It does—it must. Alfred Stevens, I can not choose but seek thy life. The imploring beauties of Margaret Cooper rise before me, and command me. I will try ! So help me God. as I believe, that the sacrifice of the reptile that crawls to the family altar to leave its slime and venom is a duty with man—due to the holiest hopes and affec tions of man—and is praiseworthy in the sight of God! I can not choose but believe this. God give me strength to convert desire into performance!"

He raised the pistol, unconsciously, as he spoke. He pressed it to his forehead. He lifted it in the sight of Heaven, as if, in this way, he solemnized his oath. The grasp of the weapon in his hand suggested a new train of emotion.

"I may fall—I may perish! The hopes of this good old man—my own hopes—may all be set at naught. Can it be that in a few hours I shall be nothing? This voice be silent—this arm cold, unconscious, upon this cold bosom. Strange, terrible fancy!—I must not think of it. It makes me shudder! It is too late for thoughts like these. I must be a man now—a man only. The mere pang—*that* is nothing. But *he*—thrice a father—he will feel three-fold pangs which shall be more lasting. Yet, even with him, they can not endure long. Who else? My poor, poor mother!"

He paused—he drew the paper before him—a tear fell upon the unwritten sheet, and he thrust it away.

"There is one other pain! One thought!" he murmured. "These high hopes—these schemes of greatness—these dreams of ambition—stopped suddenly—like rich flowers blooming late, cut down at midnight by the premature frost! Oh! if I perish r w, how much will be left un-done?"

Once more the youth started to his feet and paced the chamber. But he soon subdued the rebellious struggles of his more human nature. Quieted once more he sought to baffle thought by concentrating himself upon his tasks. Resuming his place at the table, he seized his pen. Letter after letter grew beneath his hands; and the faint gray light of the dawn peeped in at the windows before he had yet completed the numerous tasks which required his industry.

A tap at the door drew his attention and he opened it to receive his friend, Major Hawick.

"You are ready," said Hawick—"but you seem not to have slept. How's this? You promised me——"

"But *could not* keep my promise. I had much to do, and felt that I could not sleep. I was too much excited."

"That is unfortunate!"

"It will do no harm. With *my* temperament I do things much better when excited than not. The less prepared, the better prepared."

"Where's the old gentleman?"

"He sleeps still. We will not disturb him. We will steal out quietly, and I trust everything will be over before he wakens. I have left a note for him with these letters."

But few moments more did they delay.

William Calvert remedied to a certain extent the fatigue of his night of unrest, by plunging his head into a basin of cold water. The preparations of the party were already made; and they issued forth without noise, and soon found themselves on the field. Their opponents appeared a few moments after.

"A pleasant morning, gentlemen," said Mr. Barnabas. "But how is it I do not see my old friend here, eh? I had a fancy he would not miss it for the world!"

A rustling among the bushes at a little distance, at this moment, saved William Calvert from the necessity of answering the question. There was the old man himself.

"Ah, William!" he said reproachfully, "was this kind?"

"Truly, sir, it was meant to be so. I would have spared you this scene if possible."

"It was *not* kind, William, but you meant kindly. You did not know me, my son. Had I not been here with you, in the moment of danger, I should always have felt as if I had suffered shame."

The youth was touched, and turned aside to conceal his emotion. The friends of the parties approached in conference. The irregularity of Major Hawick's attendance being explained, and excused under the circumstances, he remained as a mere spectator. The arrangements then being under consideration, Mr. Barnabas said casually, and seemingly with much indifference—

"Well, I suppose, sir, we will set them at twelve paces."

"Very singular that you should offer a suggestion on this subject!" was the sharp reply of Mr. Calvert; "this point is with us."

"Oh, surely, surely—but, this being about the usual distance—"

"It is not *ours*, sir," said the other coolly.

"What do you propose, then?"

"Five paces, sir—back to back—wheel and fire within the words one and two."

Colonel Sharpe, who heard the words, started, and grew suddenly pale.

"A most murderous distance, sir, indeed!" said Mr. Barnabas gravely. "Are you serious, sir? Do you really mean to insist on what you say?"

"Certainly, sir: if I ever jested at all, it should not be on such an occasion. These are our terms."

"We must submit, of course," said the other, as he proceeded to place his principal. While doing this, Colonel Sharpe was observed to speak with him somewhat earnestly. Mr. Barnabas, immediately after, again advanced to Mr. Calvert, and said :-

"In consenting to your right, sir, on the subject of distance, I must at the same time protest against it. The consequences, sir, must lie on your head only. I have no doubt that both parties will be blown to the devil!"

Hawick also approached, and whispered the elder Calvert, in earnest expostulation against this arrangement.

"It is impossible for either to escape," he said; "they

are both firm men, and both will fire with great quickness. The distance is very unusual, sir; and, if the affair ends fatally, the reproach will be great."

For a moment the old man hesitated, and looked bewildered. His eye earnestly sought the form of William Calvert, who was calmly walking at a little distance. He was silent for a few seconds; but, suddenly recovering himself, he murmured, rather in soliloquy than in answer to his companion :—

"No, no! it must be so : we must take *this* risk, to avoid a greater. I see through these men ; there is no other way to baffle them."

He advanced to Mr. Barnabas.

"I see no reason to alter my arrangement. To a brave man, the nearer the enemy the better."

"A good general principle, sir, but liable to abuse," said Barnabas ; "but as you please. We toss for the word."

The word fell to Calvert. The parties were placed, back to back, with a space of some ten feet between — space just enough for the grave of one. With the word, which was rather gasped than syllabled by the old man, William Calvert wheeled. The first instant glance that showed him his enemy drew his fire, and was followed by that of his foe.

In the first few moments after, standing himself, and seeing his enemy still stood, he fancied that no harm had been done. Already the words were on his lips to call for the other pistol, when he felt a sudden sickness and dizziness ; his right thigh grew stiffened, and he lapsed away upon the earth, just as the old man drew nigh to his assistance.

The bullet had entered the fleshy part of his hip, and had lodged there, narrowly avoiding the bone.

These particulars were afterward ascertained. At first, however, the impression of the old man, and that of Major Hawick, was, that the wound was mortal. We will not seek to describe the mental agony of the former. It was now that his conscience spoke in torturous self-upbraidings ; and, throwing himself beside the unconscious youth, he moaned as one who would not be comforted, until assured by the more closely-observing Hawick, who, upon inspecting the wound, gave him hope of better things.

Colonel Sharpe was more fortunate. He was uninjured, but he had not escaped untouched. His escape, though more complete than that of Calvert, had been even yet more narrow — the bullet of the former actually barking his skull just above the ear, and slightly lacerating the skin over his organ of destructiveness. So narrow an escape made him very anxious to avoid a second experiment, which William Calvert, feebly striving to rise from the ground, readily offered himself for. But, while the youth spoke, his strength failed him, and he soon sunk away in utter unconsciousness.

Thus ended an affair that promised to be more bloody in its results Perhaps it would have been, but for the arrangements which old Calvert insisted on. Had the ten paces been acceded, there is little doubt that Sharpe, secure in his practice, would have inflicted a death-wound on his opponent. The alteration of distance, the necessity of wheeling to fire, and a proximity to his enemy so close as to leave skil it few if any advantages, served to disorder his aim, and impair his coolness. It was with no small degree of satisfaction that he departed, leaving his enemy *hors de combat*. We, too, shall leave him, and follow the progress of the more fortunate party ; assured, as we are, that the wound of our young hero, though serious, is not dangerous, and that he is in the hands of those who will refuse sleep to their eyelids so long as he needs that they should watch.

It will not materially affect the value of this narrative to omit all further account of that political canvassing by which these parties were brought into a juxtaposition so fruitful of unexpected consequences. It will suffice to say

10

that, with Calvert removed from the stump, Colonel Sharpe remained master of it. His eloquence that day seemed far more potential, indeed, than on ordinary occasions. No doubt he tried his best, in order to do away with what Calvert had previously succeeded in doing; but there was an *éclat* about his morning's work which materially assisted the working of his eloquence. The proceedings of the previous night, and the duel which succeeded it, were pretty well bruited abroad in the space of a few hours; and when a man passes with success from the field of battle to the field of debate, and proves himself equally the master in both, vulgar wonder knows little stint, and suffers little qualification from circumstances. Nay, the circumstances themselves are usually perverted to suit the results; and, in this case, the story, by the zeal of Sharpe's friends, so far from showing that the quarrel grew from the facts which *did* occasion it, was made to have a political origin entirely —Sharpe being the champion of one, and Calvert of the other party.

It may be readily conjectured that Sharpe himself gave as much encouragement to this report as possible. Bold as he might be, he was not altogether prepared to encounter the odium to which any notoriety given to the true state of the case would necessarily subject him. His partisans easily took their cue from him, and were willing to accept the affair as a sign of promise in the political contest which was to ensue. We may add that it was no unhappy augury. The friends of Sharpe were triumphant; and Desha—one of those *mauvaise sujets* which a time of great moral ferment in a country throws upon the surface, like scum upon the waters when they are broken up by floods, and rush beyond their appointed boundaries—was elevated, most unhappily, to the executive chair of the state.

Thus much is perhaps essential to what should be known of these matters in the progress of our story. How much of this result was due to the unfortunate termination of

Calvert's affair with Sharpe, is difficult to determine. The friends of the former ascribed their defeat to his wounds, which disabled him from the prosecution of that canvass through the state which had been so profitably begun. They were baffled and dispirited. Their strong man was low; and, gratified with successes already won, and confident of the future, Colonel Sharpe closed the night at Bowling-Green by communicating to Beauchampe, by letter, his purpose of visiting him on his return route—an honor which, strange enough to Beauchampe himself, did not afford him that degree of satisfaction which it seemed to him was only natural that it should.

CHAPTER XXI.

THE SPECK OF CLOUD UPON THE SKY OF HAPPINESS.

BEAUCHAMPE and his wife sat together beside the open window. It was night — a soft mellowing light fell upon the trees and herbage, and the breeze mildly blew in pleasant gushes about the apartment. In the room was no light. Her hand was in his. Her manner was thoughtful, and, when she spoke, her words were low and subdued as if, in her abstract mood, it needed some effort of her lips to speak.

Beauchampe himself was more moody than his wont. There is always, in the heart of one conscious of the recent possession of a new and strongly-desired object, a feeling of uncertainty. Even the most sanguine temperament, feels, at times, unassured of its own blessings. Perhaps, such feelings of doubt and incertitude are intended to give us a foretaste of those final privations to which life is everywhere certainly subject; and to reconcile us, by natural degrees, to the last dread separation in death. At all events nothing can be more natural than such feelings. Our hearts faint with fear in the very moment when we are revelling in the sober certainty of waking bliss! When Love, hooded and fettered, refuses to quit his cage — when every dream appears satisfied; when peace, fostered by security, seems to smile in the conviction of a reality which promises fullest permanence; and the imagination knows nothing to crave, and even egotism loses its strong passion for complaint; even then we shudder, as with an instinct that teaches much more than any thought, and knocks more loudly at the door of the heart, than any of its more reasonable apprehensions.

This instinct was at work, at the same moment, in both their bosoms.

"I know not why it is," said Beauchampe, "but I feel as if something were to happen. I feel unaccountably sad and apprehensive. It is not a fear — scarcely a doubt, that fills my mind — nay, for that matter my mind is silent — I strive to think in vain. It is a sort of voice from the soul — a presentiment of evil — more like a dream in its approaches, and yet, in its influence, more real, more emphatic, than any actual voice speaking to my outward ears. Do you ever have such feelings, Anna?"

"I have them *now!*" she answered in low tones.

"Indeed! it is very strange!"

He put his arm about her waist as he spoke, and drew her closer to himself. Her head sunk upon his shoulder. He did not behold them, but her eyes were filled with tears.

How strange were such tears to her! How suddenly had she undergone a change — and such a change! She who had never known fear, was now timid as a child. Love is, before all, the great subduer. It was in an unknown condition of peace and pleasure that the wife of Beauchampe had become softened. Apprehension necessarily succeeds to conquest. There is no courage so cool and collected as that which has nothing to lose; and timidity naturally grows from a consciousness of large, valuable, and easily endangered possessions. Such was the origin of the fear in the bosoms of both.

Certainly they had much to lose! Happiness is always an unstable possession, and we know this by instinct. The union of the two had perfected the union of the two families. Mrs. Beauchampe, the elder, in the very obvious and re-

markable change of manner, which followed the marriage
of Miss Cooke with her son, had become reconciled — nay,
pleased with the match. Mary Beauchampe was of course
all joy and all tears ; and even Jane, escaped from the first
danger of being swallowed up, was gradually brought to
see the intellectual beauties, and the personal also, of her
brother's wife, without beholding her sterner aspects.

For the present, Beauchampe lived with his wife's mother,
but the two families were together daily. They walked,
rode, sang, read, and played together. They made a little
world to themselves, and they were so happy in it! The
tastes of Beauchampe gradually became more and more refined and elevated under the nicer sway of feminine taste,
and those delicacies of direction which none can so well
impart as a highly-intellectual woman. He no longer
dreamed of such ordinary distinctions as make up the small
hopes of witling politicians. To be the great bell-wether
of a clamorous flock, for a season, did not now constitute
the leading object of his ambition. Far from it. A short
month of communion with an enthusiastic, high-souled
woman — unhappy, perhaps, that she was so — had wrought
as decided a change in his moral nature, as the love which
he brought had operated upon hers. They were both
changed. But it needs not that we should dwell upon the
power of Love to tame, and subject, and elevate the base
and stubborn nature. Surely it is no mere fable, rightly
read, which makes him lead the lion with a thread. Briefly,
there is no human beast that he can not, with the same
ease, subdue.

Before meeting with his wife, however, Beauchampe was
superior in moral respects to his associates. This must be
understood. He had strength of mind and ambition ; he
was generous, free in his impulses, and usually more gentle
in their direction than was the case with his companions.
His rudenesses were those of the rustic, whose sensibilities
yet sleep in his soul, like the undiscovered gold in the dark

places of the sullen mountain. It was for Love to detect the slight vein leading to these recesses, and to refine the treasure to which it led. Great, in matters of this sort, is that grand alchemist. The model of refiners is he! No Rosicrucian ever did so much to turn the baser metal into gold. Unhappily, as in the case of other seekers after *projection*, it is sometimes the case that the grand experiment finishes *in fumo*, and possibly with a loud explosion.

But it does not become us to jest in this stage of our narrative. Too sad, too serious, are the feelings with which we now must deal. If Beauchampe and his wife are happy, they are so in the activity and excitement of those sensibilities which are the most liable to overthrow. In proportion to the exquisite sweetness of the sensation, is its close approximation to the borders of pain. The joy of the soul which is the source of all the raptures of love, is itself a joy of sadness, and yearning and excessive apprehension. Soon does this apprehension rise to cloud the pleasure and oppress the hope. This is the origin of those presentiments, which say what our thoughts can not say, and in spite of our thoughts. They grew in the bosom of Beauchampe and his wife, along with the necessity which he felt and had declared, of assuming vigorously the duties of his profession. These duties required that he should move into a more busy sphere, and this duty involved the removal of his wife from that seclusion in which, for the last five years, her sensibilities had found safety. This, to her, was a source of terror; and she trembled with a singular fear lest, in doing so — in going once more out into the world she had left, she should encounter her betrayer.

Very different now were her feelings toward Alfred Stevens. For five years had she treasured the one vindictive hope of meeting him with the purpose of revenge. For five years had she moulded the bullets, and addressed them to the mark which symbolized his breast. Her chief prayer in all this time, was, that she might behold him with power

to employ upon him the skill which she had daily shown
upon the insensible trees of the forest. To kill him, and
then to die, was all that she had prayed for—and now the
difference!

In one little month all this had undergone a change. Her
feelings had once more been humanized—perhaps we should
say *womanized;* for, in these respects, women are more
capricious than men, and the transitions of love to hate, and
hate to love, are much more rapid in the case of a grown
woman than in that of a grown man. As for boys, until
twenty-five, they are perhaps little more than girls in
breeches—certainly they are quite as capricious. The experience of five years after twenty-five does more to harden
the sensibilities of a man, than any other ten years of his
life.

Great, indeed, was the change in this respect which
Beauchampe's wife had undergone. *Not* to meet Stevens
was now her prayer. True, she had sworn her husband,
if they did meet, to take his life. But that had been the
condition of her hand—that was *before* he had become her
husband—before she well knew his value—before she
could think upon the risks which *she* herself would incur,
by the danger which, in the prosecution of this pledge,
would necessarily accrue to *him.* Nor was her change of
character less decided in another grand essential. In
learning to forget and forgive, she had also learned to forego
the early dreams with which her ambitious mind com-
menced its progress.

"You speak of fame, Beauchampe," she said, even while
sitting as we have described, in the darkness, looking forth
upon the faint light which the stars shed upon the garden-
shrubbery: "you speak of fame, Beauchampe—oh! how I
once dreamed of it! Now, I care for it nothing. Rather,
indeed, should I prefer, if we could remain here, out of the
world's eye, living to ourselves, and secure from that opinion which we are too apt to seek; upon which we too much

depend—which does net confer fame, and but too often robs us of happiness. It is my presentiment, on this very subject, which makes me dread the removal to Frankfort which you contemplate."

"And yet," said he, "I know not how we can avoid it. It seems necessary."

"I believe it, and do not mean to urge you against it. I only wish that it were not necessary. But, being so, I will go with you cheerfully. I am not daunted by the prospect, though it oppresses me. How much more happy, if we could live here always!"

"No, no, Anna, you would soon sicken of this. You would ask, 'Why have I married this rustic?' You will hear of the great men around, and will say, 'He might have been one of them.' Your pride is greater than you believe; you are not so thoroughly cured of your ambition as you think."

"Oh, indeed, I am! I look back to the days when I had a passion for fame as to a period when I was under monomania. Truly, it was a monomania. O Beauchampe, had you known me then!"

"Why had I not? We had been so happy then, Anna— we had saved so many days of bliss, and then—but it is not too late! Anna, there is no good reason why a genius such as yours should be obscured—lost for ever. The world must know it, and worship it!"

"The world?—oh, never!" she exclaimed, with a shudder. "The world is my terror now. Would we could never know it!"

"But why these scruples, dearest?"

"Why? Can you ask, Beauchampe? Do you forget what I have been—what I am?"

"*You are my wife, and I am a man.* Do you think the world will venture to speak a word which shall shame or annoy you?"

"It is not in its speech, but in its *knowledge!*"

"But what will it know?   Nothing.'

"Unless we meet with *him!*"

"And if we do?—"

"Ah! let us speak of it no more, Beauchampe."

"One word only!   If we meet with *him, he dies, and is* thus silenced!   Will it be likely that *he* will speak of *that,* which only incurs the penalty of death?"

"Enough! enough!   The very inquiry—the conjecture which you utter, Beauchampe—is conclusive with me that I should not go into the world.   With you, as your wife— humble, shrinking out of sight, solicitous only of obscurity, and toiling only for your applause and love—I shall be permitted to pass without indignity—without waking up that many-tongued slanderer that lies ever in wait, dogging the footsteps of ambition.   Were I now to seek the praises which you and others have thought due to my genius, I should incur the hostility of the foul-mouthed and the envious.   No moment of my life would be secure from suspicion, no movement of my mind safe from the assaults of the caviller.   It is one quality of error—nay, even of misfortune—to betray itself wherever it goes.   The proverb tells us that murder will have a tongue: it appears to me, that *all* crimes will reveal themselves in some way, some day or other.   Better, Beauchampe, that I remain unseen, unknown, than be known as I am!—"

"Better?—but this can not be; you must be seen—you will be known!   The world will seek you, to admire.   Remember, Anna, that I have friends—numerous friends; among them are some of the ablest men of our profession— of any profession.   There is no man better able than this very gentleman, Colonel Sharpe, to appreciate a genius such as yours."

"Do not mock me with such language, Beauchampe! Instead of thinking of the world's admiration, I should be thinking only of its possible discoveries.   As for Colonel Sharpe, somehow I have an impression --gathered, I know not how, but possibly from his letters — that he lacks sincerity.   There is a tone of skepticism and levity about his language which displeases and pains me.   He lacks heart. I only wonder how you should have sought your professional knowledge at his hands."

"You forget, Anna, that I sought nothing at his hands *but* professional knowledge ; and most persons will tell you that I could scarcely have sought it anywhere with greater prospect of finding it.   He is one of our best lawyers.   As a man, frankly I confess to you, he is not one whom I admire.   You seem to me to have hit his right character. He has always seemed to lack sincerity ; and this impression, which he made upon me at a very early period, has always kept me from putting more of my heart within his power than was absolutely unavoidable."

"Ah, Beauchampe, a man of your earnest temperament knows not how much he gives.   You carry your heart too much in your eyes — in your hand.   This is scarcely good policy."

"With *you*, dearest, it was the *only* policy," he said, with a smile, while he pressed her closer to his bosom.

"Ah! with me ? — But that is yet to be determined. You know not yet."

"What! are you not mine ?   Do I not feel you in my arms ? do I not embrace you ?"

"It may be that you embrace death, Beauchampe !"

"Speak not so gloomily, my love.   Why should you yield yourself to such vague and nameless apprehensions ? There is nothing to cloud our prospect, which, when I think, seems all bright and cloudless as the night we gaze on !"

"Ah! *when you think*, Beauchampe : but thought is no seer, though an active speculator.   You forget these instincts, Beauchampe — these presentiments !"

"I *have* forgotten mine," he answered, livelily.

"Ah! but mine depart not so soon.   They rise still, and will continue to rise."

" You brood over—you encourage them."

" No! but they seem a part of me.   I have always had
·them, even in the days of my greatest exultation; when, in
truth, I had no cares to suggest them.   They have marked
and preceded, like omens, all my misfortunes.   Should I
not fear them, then?"

" Not now: it is only the old habit of your mind which
is now active.   Gloomy thoughts and complaining accents
become habitual; and, even when the sun shines, the eye,
long accustomed to the cloud, still fancies that it beholds
it gathering blackly in the distance.   Now, you are secure.
Your cloud is gone, dearest—never, never to return."

" See where it rises, Beauchampe, an image on the night!
How ominous, were these days of superstition, would that
dark image be of our fortunes!   Even as you spoke, with
such constant assurance, the evening-star grew faint.   Love's
own star waned in the growing darkness of the west; love's
own star seemed to shroud itself in gloom at the prediction
which so soon may be rendered false.   Look how fast i
the ascent of that gloomy tabernacle of the storm!   Not
one of the lovely lights in that quarter of the sky remains
to cheer us.   Even thus, have the lights of my hope for
ever gone out.   That first light of my soul, which was the
morning-star of my being—its insane passion for fame—
was thus obscured.   Then, the paler gleams of evening,
which denoted love; and how fast, after, followed all that
troop of smaller lights which betokened the dreams and
hopes of a warm and throbbing heart!   Ah, Beauchampe!
faded, stricken out, not one by one, as the joys and hopes
of others, but with a sudden eclipse that swept all their
delusive legions at a moment out of sight—never, never to
return!"

" Say not, never!"

" Ah! it is my fear which speaks—the long sense of
desolation and dread which has made up so many years of
my life!—it is this which makes me speak, from a convic-

tion of the past, with a dark, prophetic apprehension of the
future.   True, that the love blesses me now—a delusive
image of which defrauded me before—but how, with the
sudden rising of that cloud before my eyes, even in the
hour of your boastful speech and perhaps my no less boastful
hope—how can I else believe than that another delusion, no
less fatal than the past, though now untouched with shame,
has found its way to my heart, beguiling me with hope, only
to sink me in despair?"

"Ah! why such speech, Anna? *my love* is no delusion,"
said the husband reproachfully.

"I meant not that, Beauchampe—I believe not that.
Heaven knows I hold it as a truth—and the sweetest
truth that my soul has ever known in its human experience.   But for its permanence I feared.   I doubted not
that the light was pure and perfect; but, alas! I knew not
how soon it might go out.   I felt that it was a bright star
shining down upon my soul; but I also feel that there is a
gloomy storm rising to obscure the star, and leave me in a
darkness more complete than ever.   O Beauchampe! if we
should ever meet that man—"

"He dies, Anna!"

"Oh, no! I mean not that."

"Have I not sworn?"

"Yes! but the exaction of that oath was in my madness
—it was impious : I shudder but to think of it.   May you
never, *never* meet with him."

"Amen! I trust that we may never!"

"Could I but be sure of that!"

"Let it not trouble you, dearest: we *may never* meet
with him."

"Ay, but we *may;* and the doubt of that dreadful possibility, flings a gloomy shadow over the dear, sweet reality
of the present."

"Be of better cheer, my heart.   You are mine.   You
know that nothing is left for me to learn.   You look to me

for love—you depend not upon the world, but upon me. That world, as it can teach me nothing of your value, that can make the smallest approach to the certainties which I feel, so it can report nothing in your disparagement which your own lips have not already spoken. Why then should you fear? At the worst, we can only sink out of the world's sight when its looks irk, or its tones annoy us."

"Ah! that is not so easy, Beauchampe. Once out of the world's eye, nothing is so easy as to remain so. But the world pursues the person who has challenged its regard; and haunts the dwelling where it fancies it may find a spot of shame. Besides, is not *your fame* precious to me as well as to yourself. This profession of yours, more than any other in our country, is that which concentrates upon itself the public gaze. When you have won this gaze, Beauchampe, when you have controlled the eager ears of an audience, and commanded the admiration of an admiring multitude—if, at this moment, some slanderous finger should guide the eye of the spectator from the commanding eminence of the orator to the form of her who awaits him at home, and say, 'What pity!' Ah! Beauchampe!—"

"Speak of it no more," said Beauchampe, and there was a faintness in his accents while he spoke, that made it certain that he felt annoyance from the suggestion. Unwittingly, she sighed, as her keen instinct detected the feeling which her words had inspired. Beauchampe drew her closer to him, forced her upon his knee, and sought, by the adoption of a tone and words of better assurance, to do away with the gloomy presentiments under which her mood was evidently and painfully struggling.

"I tell you, Anna, these are childish fancies!—at the worst, mere womanish fears! Believe me, when I tell you, that the days shall now be bright before you. You have had your share of the cloud. There is no lot utterly void and dark. God balances our fortunes with singular equality None are all prosperous—none are all unfortunate. If the

youth be one of gloom and trial, the manhood is likely to be
bright and cheerful ; while he, who in youth has known
sunshine only, will, in turn, most probably be compelled to
taste the cup of bitterness for which he is wholly unprepared. It is perhaps fortunate for all to whom the bitterness of this cup becomes, in youth, familiar. At the worst,
if still compelled to drink of it, the taste is more certainly
reconciled to its ungracious flavor. That you have had
this poisoned chalice commended to your lips in youth, is
perhaps something of a guaranty that you shall escape the
draught hereafter. So far from the past, therefore, fling-
ing its huge dark shadow upon the future, it should be regarded as a solemn background, which, by contrast, shall
reflect more brightly than were it not present, the gay,
gladdening lights which shall gather and burn about your
pathway. I tell you, dearest, I *know* this shall be the case.
You have outlived the storm — you shall now have sunny
skies and smooth seas. Neither this beauty which I call
my own, nor these talents which are so certainly yours,
shall be doomed to the obscurity to which your unnecessary
fears would assign them. I tell you I shall yet behold you,
glowing among, and above, the ambitious circle. I shall
yet hear the rich words of your song floating through the
charmed assembly, at once startling the soul and soothing
the still ear of admiration. Come, come — fling aside this
shadow from your heart, and let it show itself in all its
glory. Look your best smiles, my love — and — will you
not sing me now one of those proud songs, which you sang
for me the other night — one of those which tell me how
proud, how ambitious was your genius in the days of your
girlhood? Do not deny me, Anna. Sing for me — sing
for me one of those songs."

She began a strain, though with reluctance, which declared all the audacious egotism which is usually felt, if not
always expressed, by the ardent and conscious poet. The
fame for which she had once yearned — the wild dreams

which once possessed her imagination and influenced her
hope — were poured forth in one of those irregular floods
of harmony — at once abrupt and musical — which never
issue from the lips of the mere instructed minstrel. Truly,
it might have awakened the soul under the ribs of death ;
and the heart of Beauchampe bounded and struggled within him, not capable of action, yet full, as it seemed, of a
most impatient discontent. Wrought up to that enthusiasm of which his earnest nature was easily susceptible, he
caught her in his arms almost ere the strain was ended, and
the thought which filled his mind, arising from the admiration which he felt, was that which told him what a sin it
would be, if such genius should be kept from its fitting utterance before admiring thousands. The language of eulogy
which he had used to her a few moments before was no
longer that of hyperbole ; and, releasing her from his
grasp; while she concluded the strain, he paced the floor
of the apartment, meditating with the vain pride of an
adoring lover, upon the sensation which such a song, and so
sung, would occasion in the souls of any audience.

The strain ceased. The silence which followed, though
deep and breathless, was momentary only. A noise of approaching horses was heard at the entrance ; and the prescient heart of the wife sunk within her. She felt as if
this visit were a foretaste of that world which she feared ;
and, hurrying up to her chamber, while Beauchampe went
to the entrance, she endeavored, by a brief respite from the
trials of reception — and in solitude — to prepare her mind
for an encounter, the anticipated annoyance from which
was, however, of a very different character from that to
which she was really destined.

CHAPTER XXII.

THE SNAKE ONCE MORE IN THE GARDEN.

SHE was not suffered to remain long in suspense. The first accents of the strange voice addressing her husband at the door, and which reached her ears in her chamber, proved the speaker to be no stranger. Fearfully her heart sank within her as she heard it. The voice was that of Alfred Stevens! Five years had elapsed since she had heard it last, yet its every tone was intelligible; clear as then; distinct, unaltered—in every syllable the same utterance of the same wily assassin of innocence and love!

What were her emotions? It were in vain to attempt to describe them—there is no need of analysis. There was nothing compounded in them—there was no mystery! The pang and the feeling were alike simple. Her sensations were those of unmitigated horror. "One stupid moment, motionless, she stood," then sunk upon her knees! Her hands were clasped—her eyes lifted to heaven—but she could not pray. "God be with me!" was her only broken ejaculation, and the words choked her.

The trial had come! Her head throbbed almost to bursting. She clasped it with her cold hands. It felt as if the bony mansion could not much longer contain the fermenting and striving mass within. Yet she had to struggle. It was necessary that the firm soul should not yield, and hers was really no feeble one. Striving and struggling to suppress the feeling of horror which every moment threatened

to burst, she could readily comprehend the relief that nature
could afford her — could she only break forth in hysterical
convulsions. But these convulsions would be fatal — not to
herself — not to life, perhaps, for that was not now a subject of apprehension. It would endanger her secret! That
was now her fear.

To preserve her equilibrium — to suppress the torments
and the troubles of her soul — to keep Beauchampe from the
knowledge that the man he had sworn to slay was his
friend, and was even now a guest upon his threshold — this
was the important necessity. It was this necessity that
made the struggle so terrible.

She shook like an aspen in the wind. Her breast heaved
with spasmodic efforts that were only not convulsions; her
limbs trembled — she could not well walk — yet she could
not remain where she knelt. To kneel without submission,
while her soul still struggled with divided impulses, was to
kneel in vain. The consolation of prayer can only follow
the calmness of the soul. That was not hers — could not
be. Yet it was necessary that she should appear calm.
Terrible trial! She tottered across the room to the mirror,
and gazed upon its placid surface. It was no longer placid
while she gazed. What a convulsion prompted each muscle
of her face! The dilation of those orbs, how could that be
subdued? Yet it must be done.

"Thy hand is upon me now! — God be merciful!" she
exclaimed, once more sinking to her knees.

"Bitterly now do I feel how much I have offended. Had
these five years been passed in prayers of penitence rather
than of pride — in prayers for grace rather than of vengeance — it had not been hard to pray now. Thy hand had
not been so heavy! Spare me, Father. Let this trial be
light. Let me recover strength — give me composure for
this fearful meeting!"

She started to her feet. She heard a movement in her
mother's apartment. That restless old lady, apprized of

the arrival of the expected visiters, was preparing to make her appearance below. It was necessary that she should be forewarned, else she might endanger everything. With this new fear, she acquired strength. She hurried to her mother's apartment, and found her at the threshold. The impatient old lady, agog with all the curiosity of age, was preparing to descend the stairs.

"Come back with me an instant," said the daughter, as she passed into the chamber.

"What's the matter with you, Margaret? You look as if your old fits were returning!"

"It is likely: there is occasion for them. Know you who is below?"

"To be sure I do. Colonel Sharpe and Mr. Barnabas. Who but them?"

"Alfred Stevens is below! Colonel Sharpe and Alfred Stevens are the same person!"

"You don't say so! Lord, if Beauchampe only knew!" exclaimed the old lady, in accents of terror.

"And if you rush down as you are, he *will* know!" said the daughter sternly. "For this purpose I came to prepare you. You must take time and compose yourself. It is no easy task for either of us, mother, but it must be done. You do not know, for I have not thought it worth while to tell you, that, before I consented to marry Beauchampe, I told him all—I kept no secrets from him."

"You didn't, sure, Margaret?"

"As I live, I did!"

"But that was very foolish. Margaret."

"No!—it was right—it was necessary. Nothing less could have justified me; nothing less could have given me safety."

"I don't see—I think 'twas very foolish."

"Be it so, mother—it is done; and I must tell you more, the better to make you feel the necessity of keeping your countenance. Before I became the wife of Beauchampe, he

swore to revenge my wrong. He pledged himself before
Heaven to slay my betrayer whenever they should meet.
They have met — they are below together!"

"Lord have mercy, what a madness was this!" cried the
old lady, with uplifted hands, and sinking into a chair. Her
anxiety to get below was effectually quieted.

"It was no madness to declare the truth," said the daughter gloomily; "perhaps it was not even a madness to demand such a pledge."

"And you're going to tell Beauchampe that his intimate
friend and Alfred Stevens are the same — you're going to
have blood shed in the house?"

"No, not if I can help it! When I swore Beauchampe
to slay this villain, I was not the woman that I am now. I
knew not then my husband's worth. I did not then do justice to his love, which was honorable. My purpose now is
to keep this secret from him, if you do not betray it, and if
the criminal himself can have the prudence to say nothing.
From his honor, were that my only security, I should have
no hope. I feel that he would manifest no forbearance,
were he not restrained by the wholesome fear of vengeance.
Even in this respect I have my doubts. There is sometimes
such a recklessness in villany, that it grows rash in spite
of caution. I must only hope and pray for the best. Ah!
could I pray!"

Once more did the unhappy woman sink upon her knees.
She was now more composed. Her feelings had become
fixed. The necessity of concentrating her strength, and
composing her countenance, for the approaching trial, was
sufficiently strong to bring about, to a certain extent, the
desired results; and the previous necessity of restraining
her mother, or at least of preparing her for a meeting, which
otherwise might have provoked a very suspicious show of
feeling or excitement, had greatly helped to increase her
own fortitude and confirm her will. But, from prayer, she
got no strength. Still she could not pray. The empty

words came from the lips only. The soul was still wandering elsewhere — still striving, struggling in a moral chaos,
where, if all was neither void nor formless, all was dark,
indistinct, and threatening.

But little time was suffered even for this effort. The
voices from below became louder. Laughter, and occasionally the words and topics of conversation, reached their
ears. That Alfred Stevens should laugh at such a moment,
while she struggled in the throes of mortal apprehension on
account of him, served to strengthen her pride, and renew
and warm her sense of hostility. What a pang it was to
hear, distinctly uttered by his lips, an inquiry, addressed
to *her* husband, on the subject of *his* wife! What feelings
of pain and apprehension were awakened in her bosom by
the simple sounds—

"But where's your wife, Beauchampe? we must see her,
you know. You forget the commission which we bear—
the authority conferred by the club. Unless we approve,
you know—"

What more was said escaped her, but a few moments
more elapsed when Beauchampe was heard ascending the
stairs. She rose from where she knelt, and, bracing herself to the utmost, she advanced and met him at the head
of the stairs.

"Come," said he, "and show yourself. My friends wonder at your absence. They inquire for you. Where's your
mother?"

"I will inform her, and she will probably follow me
down."

"Very good: come as soon as possible, for we must get
them supper. They have had none."

He returned to his guests, and she to her chamber. Her
mother was weeping.

"If you do not feel strong enough, mother, to face these
visiters to-night, do not come down. I will see to giving
them supper. At all events, remember how much depends

on your firmness. I feel now that I shall be strong
enough; but I tremble when I think of you. Perhaps you
had better not be seen at all. I can plead indisposition
for you while they remain, which I suppose will only be
to-night."

The mother was undecided what to do. She could only
articulate the usual lamentation of imbecility, that things
were as they were.

"It was so foolish to tell him anything!"

The daughter looked at her in silence and sorrow. But
the remark rather lifted her forehead. It was, indeed, with
the pride of a high and honorable soul that she exulted in
the consciousness that she *had* revealed the truth — that she
had concealed nothing of her cruel secret from the husband
who had the right to know. With this strengthening conviction that, if the worst came, she at least had no conceal-
ments which could do her harm, she descended to the fearful encounter.

Never was the rigid purpose of a severe will, in circumstances most trying, impressed upon any nature with more
inflexibility than upon hers. Every nerve and sensibility
was corded up to the fullest tension. She felt that she
might fall in sudden convulsion — that the ligatures which
her will had put upon brain and impulse might occasion
apoplexy; but she felt, at the same time, that every muscle
would do its duty — that her step should not falter — that
her eye should not shrink — that no emotion of face, no
agitation of frame, should effect the development of her fearful secret, or rouse the suspicions of her husband that there
was a secret.

She achieved her purpose! She entered the apartment
with the easy dignity of one wholly unconscious of wrong,
or of any of those feelings which denote the memory of
wrong. But she did not succeed, nor did she try, to impart
to her countenance and manner the appearance of indifference. On the contrary, the solemnity of her looks amount-

ed to intensity. She could not divest her face of the tension which she felt. The tremendous earnestness of the encounter—the awful seriousness of that meeting on which so much depended—if not clearly expressed on her countenance, left there at least the language of an impressiveness which had its effect upon the company.

Beauchampe was aware of enough to be at no loss to account for the grave severity of her aspect. Mr. Barnabas, without knowing anything, at least felt the presence of much and solemn character in the eyes that met his own. As for Colonel Sharpe, he was too much surprised at meeting so unexpectedly with the woman he had wronged, to be at all observant of the particular feelings which her features seemed to express.

He started at her entrance. Looking, just then, at his wife, Beauchampe failed to note the movement of his guest. Sharpe started, his face became suddenly pale, then red; and his eyes involuntarily turned to Beauchampe, as if in doubt and inquiry. His *congé*, if he made any, was the result of habit only. Never was guilty spirit more suddenly confounded, though perhaps never could guilty spirit more rapidly recover from his consternation. In ten minutes after, Colonel Sharpe, *alias* Alfred Stevens, was as talkative as ever—as if he had no mortifications to apprehend, no conscience to quiet: but, when the eyes of Beauchampe and Barnabas were averted, his might be seen to wander to the spot where sat the woman he had wronged!

What was the expression in that glance? What was the secret thought in the dishonorable mind of the criminal? Though momentary only, that glance was full of intelligence: but the recognition which it conveyed found no response from hers; though—not unfrequently, at such moments—as if there were some fascination in his eyes, they encountered those of the person whom they sought, keenly fixed upon them!

CHAPTER XXIII.

THE BITTER PARLE.

AND thus, after five long years of separation — years of triumph on the one hand, years of degradation and desperation on the other — they met, the destroyer and his victim. The serpent had once more penetrated into the garden. Its flowers had been renewed. Its Eden, for a brief moment, appeared to be restored. If the sunshine was of a subdued and mellowed character, it was still sunshine! Alas for the woman! she gazed upon her destroyer, and felt that the whole fabric of her peace was once more in peril. She saw before her the same base spirit which had so profligately triumphed in her overthrow. She felt, from a single glance, that he had undergone no change. There was an expression in his look, when their eyes encountered, which annoyed her with the familiarity of its recognition. She turned from it with disgust.

"At all events," she thought, "he will keep his secret; he will not willingly incur the anger of a husband. A day will free us from his presence, and the danger will then pass for ever!"

Filled with doubts, racked with apprehension, but still succored by this hope, the woman yet performed the duties of the household with a stern resoluteness that was admirable. No external tokens of her agitation were to be seen. Her movements were methodical, and free from all precipitation. Her voice, though the tones were low, was clear, distinct, and she spoke simply to the purpose. Even her enemy felt, or rather exercised, a far less degree of coolness and composure. His voice sometimes faltered as he gazed upon, and addressed her ; and there was, at moments, a manifest effort at ease and playfulness, which the ready sense of Beauchampe himself did not fail to discriminate. It was something of a startling coincidence that, after fighting with William Calvert about Margaret Cooper, he should, the very next night, be the favored guest of her husband ! Colonel Sharpe brooded over the fact with some superstitious misgivings ; but the progress of supper soon made him forgetful of his fears, if he had any ; and, before the evening was far advanced, he had recovered very much of his old composure.

When the supper-things were removed, Mr. Barnabas brought up the subject of horses, in order, as it would seem, to advert to the condition of his favorite roan, which had struck lame that evening on their way from Bowling-Green. The question was a serious one whether he suffered from snag, or nail, or pebble ; and the worthy owner concluded his speculations by declaring his wish, at an early moment, to subject the animal to fitting inspection. Beauchampe rose to attend him to the stables.

"Will you go, colonel ?" asked Mr. Barnabas.

"Surely not," was the reply. "My taste does not lie that way. I will remain with Mrs. Beauchampe, in the hope to perfect our acquaintance."

The blood rose in the brain of the person spoken of ; her heart strove to suppress the rising feeling of indignation. At first, her impulse was to rise and leave the room. But the next moment determined her otherwise. A single reflection convinced her that there would be no good policy in such a movement — that it would be equivalent to a confession of weakness, which she did not feel ; and she was resolved that her feelings of aversion should not give her enemy such an advantage over her.

11

"He must be met, at one time or other; and perhaps the sooner the issue is over, the better."

This reflection passed through her mind in very few seconds. They were now alone together. The lantern, which the servant carried before Beauchampe and Mr. Barnabas, was already flickering faintly at a distance as seen through the window-pane beside her, when Colonel Sharpe started from his seat and approached her.

"Can it be that I again see you, Margaret?" he exclaimed; "have my prayers been granted — am I again blessed with a meeting with one so dearly loved, so long and bitterly lamented?"

"You see the wife of Orville Beauchampe, Colonel Sharpe!" was the expressive reply.

"Nay, Margaret, it is my misfortune that you are *his* wife, or the wife of any man but one. Hear me—for I perceive that you think that I have wronged you—"

"Think, sir, think!—but no more of this!" was her indignant answer, as she rose from her chair and prepared to leave the room; "it can matter little to you, sir, what my thoughts of your conduct and character may be, as it is now small matter to me what they ever have been. It is enough for you to know that you are the guest of my husband; and that, in his ignorance of your crime, lies your only safety. A word from me, sir, brings down his vengeance upon your head! You yourself best know whether that is to be feared or not."

"But you will not speak that word, Margaret!"

"Will I not?" she exclaimed, while a fiery scorn seemed to gather in her eyes.

"No, Margaret, no! I am sure you can not. For the sake of the past, you will not."

"Be not so sure of that! It is for the sake of the future that I am silent. Were it for the past only, Alfred Stevens, not only should my lips speak, but my hands act. I should not ask *of him* to avenge me: my own arm should right my wrong; my own arm should, even now, be uplifted in the work of vengeance, and you should never leave this house alive!"

He smiled as he replied:—

"I know you better, Margaret. If you ever loved—"

"Stay, sir—stay, Alfred Stevens—if you would not have me so madden as to prove to you how little you have known or can know of me! Do not speak to me in such language. Beware—for your own sake, for my sake, I implore you to forbear!"

"For your sake, Margaret—anything for your sake. But be not hasty in your judgment. You wrong me—on my soul you do! If you knew the cruel necessity that kept me from you—"

"O false!" she exclaimed—"false, and no less foolish than false! Do not hope to deceive me by your base inventions. I heard all—know all! I know that I was the credulous victim of your subtle arts—that my conquest and overthrow was the subject of your dishonest boast."

"It is false, Margaret! The villain lied who told you this."

"No, Alfred Stevens, no!—he spoke the truth. The veracity of the two Hinkleys was never questioned. But your own acts confirmed the story. Why did you not keep your promise? why did you fly? Where have you been for five bitter years, in which I was the miserable mock of those whom I once looked on with contempt—the desperate, the fearful wretch—on the verge of a madness which, half the time, kept the weapons of death within my grasp—which I only did not use upon myself, because there was still a hope that I should meet with you!"

"I am here now, Margaret. If my death be necessary to your peace, command it. I confess that I owe you atonement, though I am less guilty than you think. Take my life, if that will suffice: I offer no entreaty; I utter no complaint."

" One little month go, Alfred Stevens, and you had not
needed to make this offer—you had not made it a second
time in vain. But that time has changed me. Go—live!
Leave this house with the morning's sun, and forget that
you have ever known me! Forget, if possible, that you
know my husband! It is for his sake that I spare you—
for his sake I entreat your silence of the past—your utter
forgetfulness of him and me."

" For *his* sake, Margaret!" he answered with an incredulous smile while offering to take her hand. She repulsed
him.

" No, no, Margaret! it is impossible that this young man
can be anything *to you*. You can not be so forgetful of
those dear moments, of that first passion, consecrated as it
was by those stolen joys—"

" Remind me not—man or devil!—remind me not.
Remind me not of your crime—remind me not of my sworn
vengeance—sworn, day by day, every day of bitterness and
death which I have endured since those dark and damning
hours. Hark ye, Alfred Stevens!"—her voice here suddenly lowered almost to a whisper—" hark ye, you are not
a wise man! You are tempting your fate. You are in the
very den of danger. I tell you that I spare your life, though
the weapon is shotted—though the knife is whetted. I
spare your life, simply, on condition that you depart. Linger longer than is absolutely needful—vex me longer with
these insolent suggestions—and you wake into fury the
slumbering hatred of my soul, which, for five years, has
known no moment's sleep till now. See!—the light returns—a word—a single word more by way of warning—
depart by the dawn to-morrow. Linger longer, and you
may never depart again!"

" Why, Margaret, this is downright madness!"

" So it is; and I *am* mad, and can not be otherwise than
mad, while you remain here. Do you not fear that my
madness will turn upon and rend you."

" No !" he said quietly, but earnestly and in subdued tones, for the light was now rapidly approaching. " No, Margaret, for I can not believe in such sudden changes from love to hate. Besides, if it were true, of what profit would it be to take this vengeance ? It would forfeit all the peace and happiness which you now enjoy !"

" Do I not know it ? Is not this what I would tell you ? Do I not entreat you to spare me, for this very reason ? To rend and destroy *you* might gratify *my* vengeance, but it would overthrow the peace of others who have become dear to me. I ask you to spare *them* — to spare *me* — not to provoke me to that desperation which will make me forgetful of everything except the wrong I have suffered at your hand and the hate I bear you."

" But how do I this, Margaret ?"

" Your presence does it."

" I can not think you hate me."

" Ha ! indeed ! you can not ? Do not, I pray you, trust to that. You deceive yourself. You do ! Leave this house with the morrow. Break off your intimacy with Beauchampe. Forget me ! Look not at me ! Provoke me not with your glance — still less with your accents ; for, believe me, Alfred Stevens, I have had but a single thought since the day of my dishonor — but a single prayer — and that was for the moment and the opportunity when I might wash my hands in your blood. Your looks, your words, revive the feeling within me. Even now I feel the thirst to slay you arising in my soul. I do not speak to threaten. To speak, at all, I must speak this language. I obey the feeling whatever it may be. Let me then implore you, be warned while there is time. Another day, and I may not be able to command myself — I can scarcely do so now ; and in doing so, the effort is not made in your behalf — not even in my own. It is for him — for Beauchampe only. He comes — be warned — beware !"

The approach of the light and the sounds of voices from

without, produced their natural effect. They warned the
offender much more effectually than even the exhortation
of the woman, stern, vehement, as it was. Nay, he did not
believe in the sincerity of her speech. His vanity forbade
that. He could not easily persuade himself of the revolu-
tion which she alleged her mind to have undergone, in his
case, from love to hate; and was not the man to attach any
very great degree of faith to asseverations of such hostility
at any time on the part of a creature usually so unstable
and capricious as he deemed woman to be. It is certain
that what she said had failed to affect him as it was meant
to have done. The unhappy woman saw that with an increased feeling of care and apprehension. She beheld it
in the leer of confident assurance which he still continued
to bestow upon her even when the feet of Beauchampe were
upon the threshold; and felt it in the half-whispered words
of hope and entreaty with which the criminal closed the
conference between them at the same moment.

Truly bitter was that cup to her at this moment — fearful and bitter! Involuntarily she clasped her hands, with
the action of entreaty, while her eyes once more riveted
themselves upon him. A meaning smile, which reawakened
all her indignation, answered her, and then the muscles of
both were required to be composed and inexpressive, as the
husband once more stood between them.

CHAPTER XXIV.

THE BLIND SEEKER AFTER FATE.

THE necessity of the case brought a tolerable composure to the countenances of both the parties as Beauchampe and his companion re-entered the room. An instant after, the wife left it and hurried up to her chamber. Beauchampe's eye followed her movements curiously. In truth, knowing the dread and aversion which she had avowed, at mingling again in society, he was anxious to ascertain how she had borne herself in the interview with his friend.

" Truly, Beauchampe," said the latter, as if in answer to his thoughts, " your wife is a very splendid woman."

" Ah! do you like her? Did she converse freely with you? She speaks well, but does not like society much."

" Very—she has a fine majestic mind. Talks admirably well. Did you meet with her *here?*"

" Yes," said the other, though with some hesitation. " This farm upon which we live is her mother's."

" Her mother! ah! what was her maiden-name, Beauchampe? I think you mentioned it in your letter, but it escapes me now?"

" Cooke: Miss Anna Cooke."

" Cooke, Cooke—I wonder if she is of the Cookes of Sunbury? I used to know that family."

" I think—I believe not—I am not sure, however. I really can not say."

The reply of Beauchampe was made with some trepida-

tion. The inquiry of Sharpe, which had been urged very
gravely, aroused the only half-latent consciousness of the
husband, who began to feel the awkwardness of answering
any more particular questions. Sharpe did not perceive
the anxiety of Beauchampe—he was himself too much absorbed in the subject of which he spoke.

"Your wife is certainly a very splendid woman in per
son, Beauchampe; and her mind appears to be original and
well informed. But she seems melancholy, Beauchampe;
quite too much so, for a newly-made bride. Eh! what can
be the matter?"

"She has had losses—misfortunes—her mother, too, is
an invalid, and she has been compelled to be a watcher for
some time past."

"And how long have they been neighbors to your mother?
If I recollect, you never spoke of them before?"

"You forget, I have been absent from home some years,"
replied Beauchampe evasively.

"True; I suppose they have come into the neighborhood
within that time? You did not know your wife in boyhood,
did you?"

"No—I did not. I never saw her till my present visit."

"I thought not! Such a woman is not to be passed over
with indifference. Her person must attract—and her intellect must secure and fascinate. I should say no man
was ever more fortunate in his choice. What say you, Barnabas? We must give Beauchampe a certificate?"

"I suppose so, if you say so; but I can only judge of
Mrs. Beauchampe by appearances. I have had none of the
chat. I agree with you that she is a splendid woman to
the eye, and will take your judgment for the rest."

"You will be safe in doing so. But how do you find
your horse?"

"Regularly lame. I'm afraid the cursed brute's snagged
or has a nail in his foot. The quick's touched somehow, for
he won't lay the foot to the ground."

" That's bad !   What have you done ?"

" Nothing !   We can see to do nothing to-night ; but by the peep of day I must be at him.   I must have your help, Beauchampe—with your soap and turpentine, and whatever else may be good for such a case ?"

Beauchampe answered with readiness, perhaps rather pleased than otherwise that the subject should be changed.

" With your permission, then, I will leave you," said Barnabas, " and get my sleep while I may.   Let your boy waken me at dawn, if you please, for I am really anxious about the animal.   He is a favorite—a nag among a thousand."

" As every man's nag is," said Sharpe.   " You can always tell a born egotist.   He has always the best horse and the best gun, the best ox and the best ass, of any man in the country.   He really believes it.   But ask Barnabas about the best wife, and ten to one he says nothing of his own.   He has no boasts, strange to say, about his own rib —bone of his bone, and flesh of his flesh."

" You are cutting quite too close," said Barnabas.

" As near to the quick, in your case, as in that of your nag."

" Almost ! but the quick in that region is getting callous."

" High time, Barnabas ; it has been subject to sufficient induration."

" At all events, I have no dread of your knife ; its edge is quite too blunt to do much hurt.   Good-night: try it on Beauchampe.   A young man and a young wife—I have very little doubt you can find the quick in him with a little probing."

The quick in Beauchampe's case had already been found. Good Mr. Barnabas little knew on what delicate ground he was trespassing.

" A good fellow, that Barnabas," said Sharpe, " but a dull one.   He really fancies, now, that his nag is a creature of great blood and bottom; and a more sorry jade

never paddled to a country muster-ground. He will scarcely
sleep to-night, with meditating upon the embrocations, the
fomentations, the fumigations, and whatever else may be
necessary. But a truce to this, Beauchampe. I have a
better subject. Seriously, my dear boy, I have never been
more pleasantly surprised than in meeting with your wife.
Really, she is remarkably beautiful; and, though she is
evidently shy of strangers, yet, as you know I have the art
of bringing women out, I may boast of my ability to say
what stuff she is made of. She speaks with singular force
and elegance. I have never met with equal eloquence in
any woman but one."

"And who is she?"

"Nay, I can not tell you *that*. It is years since I knew
her, and she is no longer the same being: but your wife
very much reminds me of her."

"Was she as beautiful as Anna?"

"Very near. She was something younger than your
wife—a slight difference—a few years only; but the advantage, if this were any, is compensated by the superior
dignity and the lofty character of yours. She I allude to
—but it matters not now. Enough that your wife brings
her to my mind as vividly as if the real, living presence
were before me, whom I once knew and admired, years
ago."

Thus, with a singular audacity, did Colonel Sharpe dally
with this dangerous subject. He did not this perversely—
with wilful premeditation. It seemed as if he could not
well avoid it. Evil thoughts have in them that faculty of
perversely impelling the mind and tongue which is possessed by intoxicating liquors. At moments, the wily assassin strove to avoid the subject, but he returned to it
again almost the instant after, even as one who recoils suddenly from the edge of some unexpected precipice, again
and again advances once more to gaze, with fascinated
vision, down into its dim and perilous depths.

A like fascination did this subject possess over the mind of Beauchampe. The feeling of confidence, amounting to defiance, which he expressed to his wife, before their guests had arrived, and whenever the two had spoken of going into the world, no longer seemed to sustain him. The moment that a stranger's lip spoke her name, and those inquiries were made, which are natural enough in such cases from the lips of friends, about the connections and history of the woman he had married, then did Beauchampe, for the first time, perceive the painful meshes of deception into which the unfortunate events in his wife's life would necessarily involve his utterance. Yet still, with the restlessness of discontent, did he himself incline his ear to the smallest reference which his companion made to this subject. His pride was excited to hear her praises, and the rather barefaced and bald compliments which had been paid to her intellect and beauty were dear to him as the lover and the worshipper of both. If love be timid, of itself, in the utterance of eulogium upon the beauties which it admires, it is equally certain that no subject, from the lips of another, can be more really grateful to its ear. It was perhaps this sort of pleasure which Beauchampe derived from the subject, and which made him incline to it whenever his companion employed it.

Still, in the language of Mr. Barnabas, there was an occasional touching of the *quick* in what Sharpe said, at moments, under which his sensibilities winced. It was, therefore, with a mixed or rather divided feeling, neither of pain nor pleasure, or a compounded one of both, that Beauchampe conducted his friend to the chamber which was assigned him — returning afterward to his own, in a state of mind highly excited, almost feverish — dissatisfied with himself, his friend — with every person *but* his wife. With her he had no cause of quarrel. No doubt of her, no sense of jealousy, no regret, no apprehension, disturbed that devoted passion which made him resolve, under all circumstances.

to link her with his life. If anything, the effect of the
evening's interview was to make him look with eyes of
greater favor upon her taste for privacy, and the life of
seclusion in which, up to this period, his moments of superior happiness had been known. But this subject does not
concern us now.

Colonel Sharpe was shown into the same chamber which
had been allotted to Mr. Barnabas. In our frontier country,
it need scarcely be stated, that the selfishness which insists
upon chamber and bed to itself is apt to be practically rebuked in a manner the most decided. In some parts, two
in a bed would be thought quite a liberal arrangement; and
may well be thought so, when it is known that four or five
is not an uncommon number — the fifth man being occasionally placed crosswise, in the manner of a raft-tie, rather, it
would seem, to keep the rest from falling out, than with the
view to making him unnecessarily comfortable.

Messrs. Sharpe and Barnabas were too well accustomed
to the condition of country-life to make any scruple about
that arrangement which placed them in the same apartment
and couch; and, under existing circumstances, the former
was rather pleased with it than otherwise. He had scarcely entered the room before he carefully fastened the door;
listened for the retreating steps of Beauchampe, till they
were finally lost; and, while Barnabas was wondering at,
and vainly endeavoring to divine the reason of this mystery,
he approached the bed where the other lay, and seated
himself upon it.

"You are not asleep, Barnabas?" he said in a whisper.

"No," replied the other, with tones made rather husky
by a sudden tremulousness of the nerves. "No! what's
the matter?"

"Matter enough — the strangest matter in the world!
Would you believe it, that Margaret Cooper — the girl
whose seduction was charged upon me by Calvert — and
Beauchampe's wife are one and the same person!"

"The devil they are!" exclaimed the other, in his surprise rising to a sitting posture in the bed.

"True as gospel!"

"Can't be possible, Sharpe!"

"Possible, and true. They are the same. I have spoken with her as Margaret Cooper; the recognition is complete on both sides. We talked of nothing else while you and Beauchampe were at the stables."

"Great God! how awkward! What's to be done?"

"Awkward? where's the awkwardness? I see nothing awkward about it. On the contrary, I regard this meeting as devilish fortunate. I was never half satisfied to lose her as I did, and to find her again is like finding one's treasure when he had given up the hope of it for ever."

"But what do you mean, Sharpe? Are you really insensible to the danger?"

"What danger?"

"Why, that she'll blow you to her husband!"

"What wife would do that, d'ye think? No, no, Barnabas; she's no such fool! Of course, she kept her secret when she married him. She'll scarcely blab it now."

"But won't this affair of Calvert get to his ears?"

"What if it does? It can do no mischief. Had you listened to my examination of Beauchampe—but you're a dull fellow, Barnabas! Didn't you hear me ask what his wife's maiden name was?—maiden name, indeed!—Did you hear the answer?"

"Yes—he said the name was Cooke."

"To be sure he did—Ann, or Anna Cooke—his Anna! Ha! ha! ha! *His* Anna!"

"But don't laugh so loud, Sharpe; they'll hear you and suspect."

"Pshaw, you're timid as a hare in December. Don't you see that she has imposed upon him a false name. Let him hear till doomsday of Margaret Cooper and myself, and it brings him not a jot nigher to the truth. But, of course,

you must tell him of my affair with Calvert, and give the
political version. He can scarce hear any other version
from any other source : political hacks will scarcely ever
deal in truth when a lie may be had as easily, and can serve
their turn as well. We are representatives of our several
parties and principles, you know ; treating each other
roughly — too roughly — without gloves, and, as usual in
such cases, exchanging shots by way of concluding an ill-
adjusted argument. There's no danger of anything, but
what we please, meeting Beauchampe's ears about this affair
with Calvert."

"But, by Jove, Sharpe, this is a d——d ticklish situation
to be in. I'd rather you were not here in his house. I'd
rather be elsewhere myself."

"You are certainly the most timid mortal. Will you set
off to-morrow with your lame horse ?"

"If he can hobble at all, I will, by Jove! I don't like
the situation we're in at all."

"And by Venus, friend Barnabas, if such be your determination, you set off alone. I'm not going to give up my
treasure the moment I find it, for any Beauchampe or Barnabas of you all. No — no! my most excellent, but most
apprehensive friend — having seen her, how can you think
it ? But you have neither eyes nor passion. By Heavens,
Barnabas, I am all in a convulsion of joy! I see her before
me now — those dilating eyes, wild, bright, almost fierce
in their brightness, like those of an eagle ; those lips, that
brow, and that full and heaving bosom, whose sweets—"

"Hush! you are mad ; if you must feel these raptures,
Sharpe, for God's sake say nothing about them. They will
hear you in the adjoining room."

"No — no! it is your silly fears, Barnabas. I am speaking in a whisper."

"D—n such whispers, say I. They can be heard by
keen ears half a mile. But you say you spoke with her —
what did she say ? Did she abuse you ?"

" No ! indeed !"

" Is it possible — the b —"

" Hush ! hush ! You do not understand her. She i'd not abuse me, for of Billingsgate she knows nothing. You must not think of her as of your ordinary town wenches. She is too proud for any such proceeding. She threatened me."

" Ah ! How ?"

" With her own vengeance and that of her husband. Told me she had the weapon for me ready sharpened, and the pistol shotted, and had kept them ready for years."

" The Tartar ! and what did you say ?"

" Laughed, of course ; and, but for the coming of the lantern and the husband, I should have silenced her threats by stopping her mouth with kisses."

" You're a dare-devil, Sharpe, and you'll have your throat cut some day by some husband or other."

" Your whiskers will be gray enough before that time comes. You know husbands quite as little as you know wives. Now, as soon as Margaret Cooper began to threaten me, I knew I was safe."

" Devilish strange sort of security that."

" True and certain, nevertheless. People who threaten much seldom perform. But I have even better security than this."

" What's that ?"

" She loves me."

" What ! you think so still, do you ? You're a conceited fellow."

" I know it ! That first passion, Barnabas, is the longest lived. You can not expel it. It holds on, it lasts longer than youth. It is the chief memory of youth. It recalls youth, revives it, and revives all the joys which came with youth — the bloom, the freshness and the fragrance. Do you think that Margaret Cooper can forget that it was my lips that first gave birth to the passion of love within her

bosom—that first awakened its glow, and taught her—
what before she never knew—that there were joys still
left to earth, which could yet restore all the fabled bliss of
Eden ? Not easily, *mon ami!* No, Barnabas—the man
who has once taught a woman how to love, may be, if he
pleases, the perpetual master of her fate. She can not
help but love him—she must obey—and none but a fool or
a madman can forfeit the allegiance which her heart will
always be ready to pay to his."

"I don't know, Sharpe—you always talk these things
well ; but I can't help thinking that there's danger. There's
something in this woman's looks very different from the ordinary run of women."

"She *is* different, so far as superiority makes her different, but the same nature is hers which belongs to all. Love
is the fate that makes or unmakes the whole world of
woman."

"Maybe so ; but this woman seems as proud, and cold,
and stately—"

"Masks, my boy—glorious masks, that help to conceal
as much fire and passion, and tumultuous love, as ever
flamed in any woman's breast."

"She awes me with her looks, and if she threatened you,
Sharpe, she seems to me the very woman to keep her
threats."

"If she had *not* threatened me, Barnabas, I should have
probably set out to-night."

"It will be a wise step to do so in the morning."

"No—no! my dear fellow. Neither you nor I go in the
morning. Fortune favors me ! She has thrown in my way
the only treasure which I did not willingly throw aside myself, and which I have so long sighed, but in vain, to recover. Shall I now refuse to pick it up and enshrine it in
my breast once more ? No—no! Barnabas ! I am no
stoic—I am no such profligate insensible !"

"Why, you don't mean—"

The inquiry was conveyed, and the sentence finished by a look.

"Do I not! Call me slave, ass, dotard—anything that can express contempt—if I do not. And hark ye, Barnabas, you must help me."

"I help you? I'll be d——d if I do! What! to have this fellow, Beauchampe, slit my carotid? Never! never!"

"Pshaw, you are getting cowardly in your old age."

"I tell you this fellow, Beauchampe, is a sort of Mohawk when he's roused."

"And I tell you, Barnabas, there's no sort of danger—none at least to you. All that you will have to do will be to get him out of the way. You wish to ride round the country—I do not. You wish to try the birds—nay, he can even get up an elk-hunt for you. He knows that I have no passion for these things, and it will seem natural enough that I should remain at home. Do you take? At the worst, I am the offender—and the danger will be mine only. But there will be *no* danger. I tell you that Margaret Cooper has only changed in name. In all other respects she is the same. There can be no danger if Beauchampe chooses to remain blind, and if you will assist me in keeping him so."

"I don't half like it, Sharpe."

"Pshaw! my good fellow, there's no good reason why you should like or dislike. The simple question is, whether, in a matter which will not affect you one way or the other, you are willing to serve your friend. That is the true and only question. You see for yourself that there can be no danger to you. I am sure there's no danger to anybody. At all events, be the danger what it may, and take you what steps you please, I am resolved on mine. Reconcile to yourself, as you may, the desertion of your friend, in consequence of a timidity which has no cause whatever of alarm."

Sharpe rose at this moment, kicked off his boots, and

prepared to undress. The effect of a strong will upon a feeble one was soon obvious. Barnabas hesitated still, hemmed and ha'd, dilated once more upon the danger, and finally subsided into a mood of the most perfect compliance with all the requisitions of his friend. They carried the discussion still farther into the night, but that is no reason why we should trespass longer upon the sleeping hours of our readers.

CHAPTER XXV.

THE SERPENT AT HIS OLD SUBTLETIES.

IT was no difficult matter, in carrying out the design of
Sharpe, to send Barnabas abroad the next morning in charge
of Beauchampe. Sharpe had a convenient headache, and
declined the excursion; proposing, very deliberately, to the
husband, to console himself for his absence in the company
of the wife.

The latter was not present when the arrangement was
made. It took place at the stables, after breakfast, while
they were engaged in the examination of the injured horse
of Mr. Barnabas; and this gentleman, with his *cicerone*, set
forth from the spot, leaving Sharpe, at his own leisure, to
return to the house.

Having seen them fairly off, he did so with the deliberation of one having a settled purpose. For his reappearance,
alone, Mrs. Beauchampe was entirely unprepared. As he
entered the room where she was sitting, she rose to leave
it, though without any symptoms of haste or agitation. He
placed himself between her and the door, and thus effectually prevented her egress.

She fixed her eye keenly and coldly upon him.

"Alfred Stevens," she said, "you are trifling with your
fate."

"Call it not trifling, dear Margaret. *You* are my fate,
and I never was more earnest in my life. Do not show

yourself so inflexible. After so long a separation, such coldness is cruel—it is unnatural."

"You say truly," she replied; "I *am* your fate. I have long felt the persuasion that I would be; and I had prepared myself for it. Still, I would it were not so. I would not have your blood either on mine or the hands of Beauchampe. I implored you last night to spare me this necessity. It is not yet too late. Trifle not with your destiny—waste not the moments which are left you. Persevere in this course of madness for a day longer, and you are doomed! Hear me—believe me! I speak mildly and with method. I am speaking to you the convictions of five dreary years."

The calm, even, almost gentle manner and subdued accents of the woman, had the effect of encouragement rather than of warning to the vain and self-deceiving *roué*. He was deceived by her bearing. He was not so profound a proficient as he fancied himself in the secrets of a woman's heart; and, firmly persuaded of the notion that he had expressed to Barnabas, in the conversation of the previous night, that women are never so little dangerous as when they threaten, he construed all that she said into a sort of *ruse de guerre*, the more certainly to conceal her real weakness.

"Come, come, Margaret," he said, "it is you that trifle, not me. This is no time for crimination and complaint. Let me atone to you for the past. Believe me, you wrong me if you suppose I meant to desert you. I was the victim of circumstances as well as yourself—circumstances which I can easily explain to you, and which will certainly excuse me for any seeming breach of faith. If you ever loved me, dear Margaret, it will not be difficult to believe what I am prepared to affirm."

"I do not doubt, sir, that you are prepared to affirm anything. But I ask you neither for proofs nor oaths. Why should you volunteer them unasked, undesired? I have no wish to make you add a second perjury to the first."

"It is no perjury, Margaret; and you *must* hear me.   I claim it for my own justification."

"I *will not* hear you, sir!   If you are so well assured of your justification, let that consciousness content you.   I do not accuse—I will not reproach you.   Go your ways— leave me to mine.   Surely, surely, Alfred Stevens, it is the least boon that I could solicit at your hands, that, having trampled me to the dust in shame—having robbed me of peace and pride for ever—you should now leave me, without further persecution, to the homely privacy which the rest of my life requires."

"Do not call it persecution, Margaret.   It is love—love only!   You were my first love—you shall be my last.   I can not be deceived, dear Margaret, when I assume that I was yours.   We were destined for each other; and when I recall to your memory those happy hours—"

"Recall them at your peril, Alfred Stevens!" she exclaimed vehemently, interrupting him in the speech; "recall them at your peril!   Too vividly black already are those moments in my memory.   Spare me—spare yourself!   Beware! be warned in season!   O man! man! blind and desperate, you know not how nearly you stand on the brink of the precipice!"

He regarded her with eyes full of affected admiration.

"At least, Margaret, whatever may be the falling off in your love, your genius seems to be as fresh and vigorous as ever   There is the same high poetical enthusiasm in your words and thoughts, the same burning eloquence—"

"Colonel Sharpe, these things deceive me no longer.   I regard them now as the disparaging mockeries of a subtle and base spirit, meant to beguile and abuse the confidence of a frank and unsuspecting one.   I am no longer unsuspecting.   I am no longer the blind, vain country-girl, whom with ungenerous cunning you could deceive and dishonor

Shame and grief, which you brought to my dwelling, have
taught me lessons of truth and humiliation, if not wisdom.
What you say to me now, in the way of praise, does not
exhilarate — can not deceive me — and may exasperate!
Once more I say to you, beware!"

"Ah, Margaret! are you sure that you do not deceive
yourself also in what you say? Allow that you care nothing for praise — allow that your ear has become insensible
to the language of admiration — surely it can not be insensible to that of love."

"Love! — *your* love!"

"Yes, Margaret — *my* love. You were not insensible to
it once."

"I implore you not to remind me!"

"Ah, but I must, Margaret. Those moments were too
precious to me to be forgotten; the memory of those joys
too dear. Bitter was the grief which I felt when compelled
to fly from a region in which I had taught, and been learned
myself, the first true mysteries which I had ever known of
love. Think you that I could forget those mysteries —
those joys? Oh, never! nor could you! On that conviction my hope is built. Wherever I fled, that memory was
with me still. It was my present solace under every difficulty — the sweetening drop in every cup which my lips
were compelled to drink of bitter and annoyance. Margaret, I can not think that you did not love me; I can not
think that you do not love me still. It is impossible that
you should have forgotten what we both once knew of rapture in those dear moments at Charlemont. And having
loved me then — having given to me the first youthful emotions of your bosom — you surely can not love this Beauchampe. No, no! love can not be so suddenly extin
guished. The altar may have been deserted; the fire,
untended, it may have grown dim; but it is the sacred fire
that can never utterly go out. I can understand, dearest
Margaret, that it is proper, that, having formed these new

ties, you should maintain appearances; but these appearances need not be fatal to Love, though they may require prudence at his hands. Have no fear that my passion will offend against prudence. No, dearest Margaret, the kiss will be the sweeter now, as it was among the groves of Charlemont, from being stolen in secret."

She receded a few steps while he was yet speaking, and at the close sunk into a chair. He approached her. She waved him off in a manner that could not be set at naught. A burning flush was upon her face, and the compression of her lips denoted the strong working of a settled but stifled resolution. She spoke at length:—

"I have heard you to the close, Alfred Stevens. I understand you. You speak with sufficient boldness now. Would to God you had only declared yourself thus boldly in the groves of Charlemont! Could I have seen then, as I do now, the tongue of the serpent, and the cloven foot of the fiend, I had not been what I am now, nor would you have dared to speak these accursed words in my ears!"

"Margaret—"

"Stay, sir! I have heard you patiently. The shame which follows guilt required thus much of me. You shall now hear *me!*"

"Will I not, Margaret? Ah! though your words continue thus bitter, still it is a pleasure to hearken to *your* words."

A keen, quick flash of indignation brightened in her eyes.

"I suppress," she said, "I suppress much more than I speak. I will confine my speech to that which seems only necessary. Once more, then, Colonel Sharpe, I understand your meaning. I do not disguise from you the fact that nothing more is necessary to a full comprehension of the foul purposes which fill your breast. But my reply is ready. I can not second them. I hate you with the most bitter loathing. I behold you with scorn and detestation—as a

creature equally malignant and contemptible—as a villain
beyond measure—as a coward below contempt—as a traitor to every noble sentiment of humanity—having the mal-
ice of the fiend without his nobleness, and with every characteristic of the snake but his shape! Judge, then, for
yourself, with what prospect you pursue your purpose with
me, when such are the feelings I bear you—when such are
the opinions which I hold you in."

"I can not believe you, Margaret!" and his mortified
vanity showed itself in his angry visage. The truth was
equally strange and terrible to his ears.

"God be witness that I speak the truth!"

"Margaret, it is you that trifle with your fate. If, in
truth, you despise my love, you can not surely despise my
power. It is now my turn to give you warning. I do not
threaten, but—beware!"

She started to her feet, and confronted him with eyes
that flashed the defiance of a spirit above all apprehension.

"Your power! your power! you give me warning—you
threaten! Do I rightly hear you? Speak out! I would
not now misunderstand you! No, no! never again must I
misunderstand you! . What is it you threaten?"

"You do misunderstand me, Margaret: I do not threaten.
I seek to counsel only—to warn you that I have power;
and that there can be no good policy in making me your
enemy."

"You *are* mine enemy: you have ever been my *worst*
enemy! Heaven forbid that I should again commit the
monstrous error of thinking you my friend!"

"I *am* your friend, and would be. Nay, more, in spite
of this scorn which you express for me, and which I can
not believe, I love you, Margaret, better, far better, than I
have ever loved woman."

"You have a wife, Colonel Sharpe?"

"Yes—but—"

"And children?"

" Yes—"

" For their sakes—I do not plead for myself, nor for you—for *their* sakes, once more I implore you to forbear this pursuit. Persecute me no longer. Do not deceive yourself with the vain belief that I have any feeling for you but that which I now express. I hate and loathe you—nay, am sworn, and again swear, to destroy you, unless you desist—unless you leave me, and leave me for ever!"

Her subdued tones again deceived him. He caught her hand, as she waved it in the utterance of the last sentence. He carried it to his lips; but, hastily withdrawing it from his grasp, she smote him upon the mouth in the next instant, and, as he darted toward her, threw open the drawer of a table which stood within arm's length of her position, and pulling from it a pistol, confronted him with its muzzle. He recoiled, more perhaps with surprise than alarm. She cocked the weapon, thrust it toward him with all the manner of one determined upon its use, and with the ease and air of one to whom the use of the weapon is familiar.

There was a pause of a single instant, in which it was doubtful whether she would draw the trigger or not—doubtful even to Sharpe himself. But, with that pause, a more human feeling came to her bosom. Her arm sunk—the weapon was suffered to fall by her side, and she said, with faltering voice:—

" Go! I spare you for the sake of the unhappy woman, your wife. Go, sir: it is well for you that I remembered her."

" Margaret! this from you?"

" And from whom with more propriety? Know, Alfred Stevens, that this weapon was prepared for you last night; nay, more, that mine is no inexpert hand in its use. For five years, day by day, have I practised this very weapon at a mark, thinking of you only as the object upon whom it was necessary I should use it. Think you, then, what you escape, and return thanks to Heaven that brought to my

12

thought, in the very moment when your life hung upon the smallest movement of my finger, the recollection of your wife and innocent children! Judge for yourself who has most to fear, you or myself."

" Still, Margaret, there is a cause of fear which you do not seem to see."

" What is that ?"

" Not the loss of life, perhaps. *That*, I can readily imagine, is not likely to be a cause of much fear with a proud, strong-minded woman like yourself. But there are subjects of apprehension infinitely greater than this, particularly to a woman, a wife, and to you more than all — your husband !"

" What of my husband ?"

" A single word from me to him, and where is your peace, your security ? Ha ! am I now understood ? Do you not see, Margaret, do you not feel, that I have power, with a word, more effectually to destroy than even pistol-bullet could do it ?"

" And this is your precious thought !" she said, with a look of bitter, smiling contempt ; " and, with the baseness which so completely makes your nature, you would lay bare to my husband the unhappy guilt in which, through your own foul arts, my girlish innocence was lost ! What a brave treachery would this be !"

" Nay, Margaret, but I do not threaten this. I only declare what might be the effect of your provoking me beyond patience."

" Oh ! you are moderate — very moderate. I look on you, Alfred Stevens, from head to foot, and doubt my eyes that tell me I behold a man. The shape is there — the outside of that noble animal, but it is sure a fraud. The beast-fiend has usurped the nobler carcass, himself being all the while unchanged."

" Margaret, this scorn—"

" Is due, not less to your folly than your baseness, as you

will see when I have told you all. Know then, that when I gave this hand to Orville Beauchampe—nay, before it was given to him, and while he was yet at liberty to re-nounce it—I told him that it was a dishonored hand."

"You did not! You could not!"

"By the God that hears me, I did. I told him the whole story of my folly and my shame. Oh! Alfred Stevens, if in truth you had loved me as you professed, you would have known that it was not in my nature to stoop to fraud and concealment at such a time. Could you think that I would avail myself of the generous ardor of that noble youth to suffer him, unwittingly, to link himself to possible shame? No—no! His magnanimity, his love, the warmth of his affections, the loftiness of his soul, his genius—all—all de-manded of me the most perfect confidence ; and I gave it him. I withheld nothing, except, it seems, the true name of my deceiver!"

"I can not, believe it, Margaret—Beauchampe never would have married you with this knowledge."

"On my life, he did. Every syllable was spoken in his ears. Nay, more, Colonel Sharpe—and let this be another warning to you to forbear and fly—I swore Beauchampe on the Holy Evangelists, ere he made my hand his own, to avenge my dishonor on my betrayer. I made *that* the con-dition of my hand !"

"And why now would you forbear prosecuting this ven geance ? Why, if you were so resolved upon it—why do you counsel me to fly from the danger ? Do you mean to declare the truth to Beauchampe when I am gone ?"

"No ! not if you leave me, and promise me never again to seek either me or him."

"No—no! Margaret, this story lacks probability. I can not believe it. I am a lawyer, you must remember. These inconsistencies are too strong. You swear your husband on the Holy Evangelists to take my life, and the next mo-ment shield me from the danger ! Now, the ferocious hate

which induced the first proceeding can not be so easily
quieted, as in a little month after, to effect the second.
The whole story is defective, Margaret—it lacks all probability."

"Be it so. You are a lawyer, and no doubt a wise one.
The story may seem improbable to you, but it is true nevertheless. However strange and inconsistent, it is yet not
unnatural. The human ties which bind me to earth have
grown stronger since my marriage, and, for this reason, if
for no other, I would have the hands of my husband free
from the stain of human blood, even though that blood be
yours! For this reason I have condescended to expostulate with you—to implore you! For this reason do I still
implore and expostulate. Leave me—leave this house the
moment your friend returns. Avoid Beauchampe as well
as myself. There are a thousand easy modes for breaking
off an intimacy. Adopt any one of these which shall seem
least offensive. Spare me the necessity of declaring to my
husband that the victim he is sworn to slay, is the person
who has pretended to be his friend."

The philosophical poet tells us, that he whom God seeks
to destroy he first renders a lunatic. In the conceit of his
soul, in the plenitude of his legal subtlety, and with that
blinding assurance that he could not lose, by any process,
the affections he had once won, Sharpe persisted in believing that the story to which he listened, was in truth, nothing more than an expedient of the woman to rid herself of
the presence and the attentions which she rather feared
than disliked. He neither believed that she had told the
truth to Beauchampe, nor that she loathed him as she had
declared. Himself of a narrow and slavish mind, he could
not conceive the magnanimity of soul, which, in such a case
as that of Margaret Cooper, would declare her dishonor to
a lover seeking her hand—still less was he willing to believe in the further stretch of magnanimity, on the part of
Beauchampe, in marrying any woman in the teeth of such

a revelation. We may add, that, with such a prodigious degree of self-esteem as he himself possessed, the improbability was equally great that Margaret should ever cease to regard him with the devotedness of love. He had taken for granted that it was through the medium of her affections that she became his victim, though all his arts were made to bear upon other characteristics of her moral nature, entirely different from those which belong to the tender passion. A vain man finds it easy to deceive himself, if he deceives nobody else. Here, then, was a string of improbabilities which it required the large faith of a liberal spirit to overcome. Sharpe was not a man of liberal spirit, and such men are usually incredulous where the magnanimity of noble souls is the topic. Small wits are always of this character. Skepticism is their shield and even sevenfold coat-of-mail, and incredulity is the safe wisdom of timidity and self-esteem. Such men neither believe in their neighbors or in the novel truths which they happen to teach. They pay the penalty in most cases by dying in their blindness.

Will this be the case with the party before us ? Time will show. At all events, the earnest adjurations of the passionate and full-souled woman were entirely thrown away upon him. What she had said had startled him at first ; but with the usual obduracy of self-esteem, he had soon recovered from his momentary discomposure. He shook his head slowly, while a smile on his lips declared his doubts.

" No, Margaret, it is impossible that you should have told these things to Beauchampe. I know you better, and I know well that he could never have married you, having a knowledge of the truth. You can not deceive me, Margaret, and wherefore should you try ? Why would you reject the love which was so dear to you in Charlemont ; and if *you* can do this, *I* can not ? I love you too well, Margaret — remember too keenly the delights of our first union,

and *will not* believe in the necessity that denies that we
should meet. No — no! Once found, I will not lose you
again, Margaret. You are too precious in my sight. We
must see and meet each other often. Beauchampe shall
still be my friend — his marriage with you has made him
doubly dear to me. So far from cutting him, I shall find
occasions for making his household a place of my constant
pilgrimage; and do not sacrifice yourself by vain opposition
to this intimacy. It will do no good and may do harm. I
can make his fortune; and I will, if you will hear reason.
But you must remove to Frankfort — be a dutiful wife in
doing so; and — for this passion of revenge — believe that
I was quite as much afflicted as yourself by the necessity
that tore us asunder — as was the truth — and you will forgive the involuntary crime, and forget everything but the
dear delights of that happy period. Do you hear me, Margaret — you do not seem to listen!"

She regarded him with a countenance of melancholy
scorn, which seemed also equally expressive of hopelessness
and pity. It seemed as if she was at a loss which sentiment most decidedly to entertain. Looking thus, but in
perfect silence, she rose, and taking the pistol from the
table where it had lain, she advanced toward the door of
the apartment. He would have followed her, but she
paused when at the door, and turning, said to him : —

"If I knew, Colonel Sharpe, by what form of oath I
could make you believe what I have said, I would assev-
erate solemnly its truth. I am anxious for your sake, for
my sake, and the sake of my husband, that you should believe me. As God will judge us all, I have spoken nothing
but the truth. I would save you, and spare myself the
necessity of any further revelations. Life is still dear to
me — peace is everything to me now. It is to secure this
peace that I suppress my feelings — that I still implore you
to listen to me and to believe. Be merciful. Spare me!
Spare yourself. Propose any form of oath which you con-

sider most solemn, most binding, and I will repeat it on my knees, in confirmation of what I have said ! for on my soul I have spoken nothing but the truth !"

He laughed and shook his head, as he advanced to where she stood.

"Nay, nay, Margaret—the value of oaths in such cases is but small. No form of oath can be very binding. Jove, you know, laughs at the perjuries of lovers; and if we are lovers no longer—which I can not easily believe—the business between us, is so certainly a lover's business, that Jove will laugh none the less at the vows we violate in carrying it on. You take it too seriously, Margaret—it is you that are not wise. You can not deceive me—you are wasting labor."

She turned from him mournfully, with a single look, and in another moment was gone from sight.

CHAPTER XXVI.

DOOMED.

MR. BARNABAS and Beauchampe returned from their morning ride in excellent spirits; but there was some anxiety and inquiry in the look of the former as his eye sought that of his confederate. He gathered little from this scrutiny, however, unless it were the perfect success of the latter in the prosecution of his criminal object. The face and manner of Colonel Sharpe wore all the composure and placid satisfaction of one equally at peace with all the world and his own conscience. His headache had subsided. He seemed to have nothing on his mind to desire or to regret.

"Lucky dog!" was the mental exclamation of his satellite. "He never fails in anything he undertakes. He does as he pleases equally with men and women."

Beauchampe had his anxieties also, which were a little increased as he noted a greater degree of sadness on his wife's countenance than usual. But his anxiety had no relation whatever to the real cause of fear—to the real source of that suffering which appeared in her looks. Not the slightest suspicion of evil from his friend Colonel Sharpe had ever crossed his mind, even for an instant.

Dinner came off, and Colonel Sharpe was in his happiest vein. His jests were of the most brilliant order; but, unless in the case of Mr. Barnabas, his humor was not contagious. Mrs. Beauchampe scarcely seemed to hear what was addressed to her; and Beauchampe, beholding the increasing depth of shade on his wife's countenance, necessarily felt a corresponding anxiety, which imparted similar shadows to his own.

At dinner, Mr. Barnabas said something across the table to his companion, in reference to the probable time of departure.

"What say you—shall we ride to-morrow?"

"Why, how's your nag?"

"Better; not absolutely well, but able to go, when going homeward."

"*You* may go," said Sharpe, abruptly; "but I shall make a week of it with Beauchampe. The country, you say, is worth seeing, and there may be votes to be won by showing one's self. I see no reason even for you to hurry; and I dare say Beauchampe's hospitality will scarcely complain of our trespass for two days longer."

The speaker looked to Beauchampe, who, as a matter of course, professed his satisfaction at the prospect of keeping his friends. The eye of Sharpe glanced to the face of the lady. A dark-red spot was upon her forehead. She met the glance of her enemy, and requited it with one of deep significance; then, rising from the table, at once left the apartment.

The things were removed, and Mr. Barnabas, counselled by a glance from his companion, proposed to Beauchampe to explore the farm.

"I can't bear the house when I can leave it—that is, when I'm in the country. A country-house seems to me an intolerable bore. Won't you go, Sharpe?"

But the person addressed had already disposed himself in the rocking-chair, as if for the purpose of taking a nap. He answered, drowsily:—

"No, no, Barnabas; take yourself off! I would enjoy my *siesta* merely. With you, I should be apt to sleep soundly.

Take him off, Beauchampe, and suffer me to make myself at home."

" Oh, certainly, if you prefer it."

" I do! I take the world composedly — detest sight-seeing, and believe in Somnus. This habit of mine keeps me out of mischief, into which Barnabas is for ever falling. Away, now, my good boys, and enjoy the world and one another !"

The *roué* was alone. Ten minutes had not passed, when Mrs. Beauchampe re-entered the apartment. This was an event which Colonel Sharpe had scarcely anticipated. He had remained, simply to be in the way of what he would esteem some such fortunate chance ; hoped for it ; and, be-lieving that the lady was playing only a very natural femi-nine game, did not think it improbable that the desired opportunity would be afforded him. So early a realization of his wishes was certainly unexpected — not undesired, however. The surprise was a pleasurable one, and he started into instant vivacity on her appearance, rising from his seat and approaching her with extended hand as if to conduct her to it.

" Stay, Colonel Sharpe! I come but for a moment."

" Do not say so, Margaret."

" A moment, sir, will suffice for all that I purpose. You speak of remaining here till the close of the week ? Now, hear me! `Your horses must be saddled after breakfast to-morrow. You must then depart. I must hear you express this determination when we meet at the breakfast-table. If you do not, sir — on the word of a woman whom you have made miserable, and still keep so, I shall declare to Mr. Beauchampe the whole truth !"

" What! expel me from your house, Margaret ? No, no ! I as little believe you can do this as do the other. This, my dear girl, is the merest perversity !"

He offered to take her hand. She recoiled.

" Colonel Sharpe, your unhappy vanity deceives you.

What do you see in my looks, my conduct, to justify these doubts of what I say, or this continued presumption on your part? Do I look the wanton? do I look the pliant damsel whose grief is temporary only—which a smile of deceit, or a cunning word, can dissipate in a moment? Look at me well, sir. *My* peace, and *your* life, depend upon the wisdom which Heaven at this moment may vouchsafe you. Oh, sir, be not blind! See, in these wobegone cheeks and eyes, nothing but the misery, approaching to despair, which my bosom feels! See, and be warned! You can not surely doubt that I am in earnest. For the equal sake of your body and soul, I implore you to believe me!"

Cassandra never looked more terribly true to her utterance—to the awful predictions which her lips poured forth—but, like Cassandra, Margaret Cooper was fated not to be believed. The unhappy man, blinded by that flattering self-esteem which blinds so many, was insensible to her expostulations—to the intense wo, expressing itself in looks of the most severe majesty, of her highly-expressive countenance.

The effect of her intensity of feeling was to elevate the style of her beauty, and this was something against the success of her entreaty. Vain and dishonorable as he was, Sharpe gazed on her with a sincere admiration. Unhappily, he was not one to venerate. That refining agent of moral worship was wanting to his heart; and in its place a selfish lust after the pleasures of the moment was the only divinity which he had set up.

It would be idle to repeat his answer to the imploring prayer of the half-distracted woman. He had as little generosity as veneration: he could not forbear. His mind had become inflexible, from the too frequent contemplation of its lusts; and what he said was simply what might have been said by any callous, clever man, who, in the prosecution of a selfish purpose, regards nothing but the end in view. He answered with pleasantry that we which was so much more expressively shown in her looks than in her utterance. Pleasantry at such a moment!—pleasantry addressed to that painfully-excited imagination, whose now-familiar images were of death, and despair, and blood! She answered him by clasping her hands together.

"We are doomed!" she exclaimed, while a groan forced its way, at the close of her sentence, as if from the very bottom of her heart.

"Doomed, indeed, Margaret! How very idle, unless *you* doom us!"

"And I do! *You* are doomed, and doomed by *me*, Alfred Stevens, unless you leave this house to-morrow!"

"Be sure I shall do no such thing!"

"Your blood be upon your own head! I have warned you, counselled you, implored you—I can do no more!"

"Yes, Margaret, you can persuade me, beguile me, subdue me—make me your captive, slave, worshipper, everything—as you have done before—by only loving me as you did then. Be not foolish and perverse. Come to me let us renew those happy hours that we knew in Charlemont, when you had none of these gloomy notions to affright others and to vex yourself with!"

"Fool! fool! Blind and vain! With sense neither to see nor to hear!—Alfred Stevens, there is yet time! But the hours are numbered. God be merciful, so that they be not yours! We meet at the table to-morrow morning for the last time."

"Stay, Margaret!" he exclaimed, seeing her about to leave the room.

"To-morrow morning for the last time!" she repeated, as she disappeared from sight.

"Devilish strange! But they are all so—perverse as the devil himself! There is nothing to be done here by assault. We must have time, and make our approaches with more caution. My desertion sticks in her gorge. I must mollify her on that score. Work slowly, but surely

I have been too bold—too confident. I did not make sufficient allowances for her pride, which is diabolically strong. I must ply her with the sedatives first. But one would have thought that she had sufficient experience to have taken the thing more coolly. As for her blabbing to Beauchampe, that s all in my eye! No, no, you can not terrify me by such a threat. I am too old a stager for that: nay, indeed, how much of your wish to drive me off arises from your dread that *I* shall blab! Ha! ha! ha! but you too shall be safe from that. My policy is 'mum,' like your own. To be frightened off by such a threat would prove a man as sorry a fool as coward. We sha'n't go to-morrow, fair Mistress Margaret, doom or no doom!"

Such were the muttered meditations of Colonel Sharpe after Mrs. Beauchampe had left him. Perhaps they were such as would be natural to most men of the same character. His estimate of the woman, also, was no doubt a very just estimate of the ordinary woman of the world, placed in similar circumstances, after having committed the same monstrous and scarcely remediable lapse from virtue and place.

But we have shown that Margaret Cooper was no ordinary woman! He knew *that*, himself; but he did not believe her equal to the purpose which she threatened, nor did he believe her when she informed him of the magnanimous course which she had already pursued in relation to Beauchampe. Could he have believed *that*, indeed?

But it was not meant that he should believe. The destiny that shapes our ends was not to be diverted in his case. As his victim had declared, with solemn emphasis, on leaving him, he was, indeed, doomed—doomed—doomed!

CHAPTER XXVII.

BITTER TEARS OF PREPARATION.

We pass, with hurried progress, over the proceedings of
that night. The reader will please believe that Colonel
Sharpe was, as usual, happy in his dialogue, and fluent in
his humor. Indeed, by that strange contradiction in the
work of destiny, which sometimes so arranges it that death
does the work of tragedy in the very midst of the marriage
merriment, the spirits of the doomed man were never more
elastic and excitable than on that very night. He and
Barnabas kept his host, till a late hour, from his couch.
The sounds of their laughter penetrated the upper apartments, and smote mournfully upon the ears of the unhappy
wife, to whom all sounds, at that moment, came laden with
the weight of wo. One monotonous voice rang through her
senses and the house, as in the case of Macbeth, and cried,
" Sleep no more!" Such, at least, was the effect of the
cry upon her. Precious little had been her sleep, in that
house, from the moment that bad man entered it. Was she
ever to sleep again? She herself believed not.

The guests at length retired to their chamber, and Beauchampe sought his. At his approach, his wife rose from
her knees. Poor, striving, struggling, hopeless heart! she
had been laboring to beat down thought, and to wrestle
with prayer. But thought mingled with prayer, and obtained the mastery. Such thoughts, too — such thoughts
of the terrible necessity before her!

Oh, how criminal was the selfish denial of that man! Life had become sweet and precious. Her husband had grown dear to her in proportion as he convinced her that she was dear to him. Permitted to remain in their obscurity, life might still be retained, and would continue, with length of days, to become more and more precious. But the destroyer was there, unwilling to spare — unwilling to forego the ravages he had begun. Not to tell her husband the whole truth — to listen to the criminal any longer without denouncing him — would not only be to encourage him in his crime, but to partake of it. If he remained another day, she was bound by duty, and sworn before the altar, to declare the truth; and the truth, once told, was only another name for utter desolation — blood upon the hands, death upon the soul! With such thoughts, prayer was not possible. But she had striven in prayer, and that was something. Nay, it was something gained, even to think in the position of humility — upon her knees.

She rose, when she heard her husband approach — took a book, and seating herself beside the toilet, prepared to read. She composed her countenance, with a very decided effort of will, so as to disperse some of the storm-clouds which had been hanging over it. Her policy was, at present, not to alarm her husband's suspicions, if possible, in relation to her guests. It might be that Sharpe would grow wiser with the passage of the night. Sleep, and quiet, and reflection, might work beneficial results; and if he would only depart with the morning, she trusted to time and to her own influence over Beauchampe, to break off the intimacy between the parties without revealing the fatal truth.

"What! not abed, Anna?" said Beauchampe. "It is late; do you know the hour! It is nigh one!"

"Indeed, but I am not sleepy."

"I am; what with riding and rambling with Barnabas I am completely knocked up. Besides, he is such a dull fel-

low.   Now Sharpe has wit, humor, and other resources,
which make a man forgetful of the journey and the progress
of time."

"Has Colonel Sharpe said anything about going?" demanded the wife with some abruptness.

"Yes—"

"Ah!"—with some eagerness—"when does he go?"

"At the close of the week.   He is disposed to see something of the neighborhood."

She drew a long breath, scarcely suppressing the deep
sigh which struggled for utterance; and once more fixed
her eyes on the book.   It need not be said that she read
nothing.

"Come to bed, dearest," said Beauchampe tenderly; "you
hurt your eyes by night reading.   They have been looking
red all day."

She promised him, and, overcome with fatigue, the husband soon slept, but the wife did not rise.   For more than
two hours she sat, the book still in her hands; but her
eyes were unconscious of its pages, her thoughts were not
in that volume.   She thought only of that coming morrow,
and the duties and dangers which its coming would involve.
She was seeking to steel her mind with the proper resolution, and this was no easy effort.

Imagine the task before her—and the difficulty in the
way of acquiring the proper hardihood will easily be understood.   Imagine yourself preparing for the doom which is
to follow in twelve hours; and conjecture, if you can, the
sort of meditations which will come to you in that dreary
but short interval of time.   Suppose yourself in health, too
- -young, beautiful, highly endowed, intensely ambitious,
with the prospect—if those twelve hours can be passed in
safety—of love, long life, happiness, and possibly, " troops
of friends" all before you, smiling, beckoning, entreating
in the sunny distance!   Imagine all this in the case of that
proud, noble-hearted, most lovely, highly intellectual, but

wo-environed woman, and you will not wonder that she did not sleep. Still less will it be your wonder that she could not pray. Life and hope were too strong for sufficient humility. The spirit and the energy of her heart were not yet sufficiently subdued.

Dreary was the dismal watch she kept—still in the one position. At length her husband moved and murmured in his sleep. In his sleep he called her name, and coupled with it an endearing epithet. Then the tide flowed. The proper chords of human feeling were stricken in her heart. The rock gushed. It was stubborn no longer. But the waters were bitter, though the relief was sweet. Bitter were the tears she wept, but they *were* tears, human tears; and like the big drops that relieve the heat of the sky and disperse its unbreathing vapors, they took some of the mountain pressure from her heart, and left her free to breathe, and hope, and pray.

She rose and stepped lightly beside the bed where Beauchampe slept. She hung over him. Still he murmured in his sleep. Still he spoke her name, and still his words were those of tenderness and love. Mentally she prayed above him, while the big drops fell from her eyes upon the pillow. One sentence alone became audible in her prayer — that sentence of agonizing apostrophe, spoken by the Savior in his prescience of the dreadful hour of trial which was to come : " If thou be willing, Father, let this cup pass by me !"

She had no other prayer, and in this vain and useless repetition of the undirected thoughts, she passed a sad and comfortless night. But she had been gaining strength. A stern and unfaltering spirit—it matters not whence derived —came to her aid, and with the return of sunrise she arose, with a solemn composure of soul, prepared, however gloomily, to go forward in her terrible duties.

CHAPTER XXVIII.

THE BOLT SPED.

BEAUCHAMPE rose refreshed and more cheerful than usual.
The plans for the day, which had been discussed by himself and friends the previous night, together with the lively
dialogue which had made them heedless of the progress of
the hours, were recalled to his memory, and he rose with
an unwonted spirit of elasticity and humor.

But the lively glance of his eye met no answering pleasure in that of his wife. She was up before him. He did
not dream that she had not slept—that for half the night
she had hung above his sleep engaged in mental prayer that
such slumbers might still be spared to him, even if the
dreary doom of such a watch was still allotted to her. He
gently reproached her for the settled sadness in her looks,
and she replied only by a sigh. He did not notice the intense gleams which, at moments, issued from her eyes, or
he might have guessed that some terrible resolution was
busy working at the fiery forge within her brain. Could he
guess the sort of manufacture going on in that dangerous
workshop? But he did not.

The party was assembled at the breakfast-table; and, as
if with a particular design to apprize Mrs. Beauchampe, that
her warnings were not heeded, Colonel Sharpe dwelt with
great deliberation upon the best modes before them of con-
suming the rest of the week with profit.

"What say you, Beauchampe, to a morning at your
friend Tiernan's—he will give us a rouse, I'm thinking;
the next day with Coalter, and Saturday, what ho! for an
elk-hunt! at all events, Barnabas must go to Coalter's—he's
a client of his, and will never forgive the omission; and it
is no less important that you should give him the elk-hunt
also; he has a taste for hard riding, and it will do him
good. He's getting stoutish, and a good shaking will keep
his bulk within proper bounds. Certainly, he must have an
elk-hunt."

"A like reason will make it necessary that you should
share it also, colonel," said Beauchampe. "You partake,
in similar degree, of the infirmity of flesh which troubles
Mr. Barnabas."

"Ay, ay, but I am no candidate for the red-hat, which is
the case with Barnabas, and which the conclave will reli-
giously refuse to a man with a corporation."

"But you are after the seat of attorney-general," said
Mr. Barnabas, with the placable smile of dullness.

"Granted; and for such an office a good corporation may
be considered an essential, rather than anything else. It
confers dignity, Hal. Now, the red-hatted gentry of the
club are not expected to be dignified. The humor of the
thing forbids it; and as a candidate for that communion,
it is necessary that you should live on *soup maigre*, and
'seek the chase with hawk and hound,' as Earl Percy did.
Besides, Beauchampe, he has a passion for it."

"I a passion for it?" said Barnabas.

"Yes, to be sure—what were all those stories you used
to tell us of hunting in Tennessee; stories that used to set our
hair on end at your hairbreadth escapes. Either we must
suppose you to have grown suddenly old and timid, or we
must suppose, that, in telling those stories of your prowess,
you were amusing us with some pleasant fictions. That's
a dilemma for you, Barnabas, if you disclaim a passion for
an elk-hunt now."

"No! by Jupiter, I told you nothing but the truth," said Barnabas, solemnly.

"I believe it," said Sharpe, with equal solemnity, "I oelieve it, and believe that the passion continues."

"Well," said the other, "I can't altogether deny that it does, but it has been somewhat cooled by other pursuits and associations."

"It must be warmed again," responded Sharpe; "remember, Beauchampe, be sure to make up a party for Saturday."

"We include you in it?" asked Beauchampe.

"Ay, ay—if I happen to be 'i' the vein.' But, you know, like Corporal Nym, I'm a person of humors. I may not have the fit upon me, or I may have some other fit; and may prefer remaining at home to read poetry with our fair hostess."

The speaker glanced significantly at Mrs. Beauchampe as he said these words. Their eyes encountered. Hers wore an expression of the soberest sadness. As if provoked by the speech and the glance, she said, in the most deliberate language, while her look was full of the most rebukeful and warning expression:—

"I thought you were to leave this morning for Frankfort, Colonel Sharpe. I derived that impression somehow from something that was said last evening."

Beauchampe turned full upon his wife with a stern look of equal astonishment and inquiry. Mr. Barnabas was aghast; and Colonel Sharpe himself for a moment lost his equilibrium, and was speechless, while his eyes looked the incertitude which he felt. He was the first, however, to recover; and, with a sort of legal dexterity, assuming as really having been his own the determination which she had suggested as being made by him, he replied:—

"True, my dear madam, that was my purpose yesterday; but the kind entreaties of our host, and the pleasant projects which we discussed last night, persuaded me to yield to the temptation, and to stay till Sunday."

The speaker bowed politely, and returned the severe glance of the lady with a look of mingled conciliation and doubt. For the first time, he began to feel apprehensive that he had mistaken her, and perhaps himself. She was a woman of prodigious strength of soul, indomitable resolution, and the courage of a gigantic man. Never did words proceed more deliberately, more evenly, from human lips, than did the reply from hers :—

"That can not be, Colonel Sharpe. It is necessary that you should keep your first resolution. Mr. Beauchampe can no longer accommodate you in his dwelling."

"How, Mrs. Beauchampe!" exclaimed the husband, starting to his feet, and confronting her. She had risen while speaking, and was preparing to leave the room. She looked on him with a countenance mournful and humble— very different from that which she wore in addressing the other.

"Speak, Anna—say, Mrs. Beauchampe!" exclaimed the husband, "what does this mean? This to my guests—to my friend!"

"He is not your friend, Beauchampe—nor mine! But let me pass—I can not speak here!"

She left the room, and Beauchampe, with a momentary glance at Sharpe, full of bewilderment, hurried after his wife.

"What's this, Sharpe, in the devil's name?" demanded Barnabas in consternation.

"The devil himself, Barnabas!" said Sharpe. "I'm afraid the Jezebel means to blow me, and tell everything!"

"But you told me last night that all was well and going right."

"So I thought! I fear I was mistaken! At all events, I must prepare for the worst. Have you any weapons about you?"

"My dirk!"

"Give it me: my pistols are in the saddle-bags."

" But what shall I do ?"

" *You* are in no danger. Give me t ie dirk, and hurry out and have our horses ready. D—n the woman!—who could have believed it!"

" Ah, you're always so sanguine!" began Barnabas; but the other interrupted him :—

" Pshaw! this is no time for lecturing. Your wisdom is eleventh-hour wisdom! It is too late here. Hurry, and prepare yourself and the horses, while I go to the room and get the saddle-bags ready. If I am blown, my start can not be too sudden."

Barnabas, always pliant, disappeared instantly; and Sharpe, concealing the dirk in his bosom, with the handle convenient to his clutch, found himself unpleasantly alone.

" Who the d—l could have thought it? What a woman! But it may not be as bad as I fear. She may invent something to answer the purpose of getting me off. She certainly can not tell the whole. No, no! that would be to suppose her mad. And mad she may be: I had not thought of that! Now, I think of it, she looks cursedly like an insane woman. That wild, fierce gleam of her eye—those accents—and, indeed, everything since I have been here! Certainly, had she not been mad, it must have been as I wished. I *could* not have been deceived—never *was* deceived yet—by a sane woman! It must be so; and, if so, it *is* possible that she may blurt out the whole. I must be prepared. Beauchampe s as fierce as a vulture when roused. I've seen that in him before. I must get my pistols— though, in going for them, I may meet him on the stairs. Well, if I do, I am armed! He is scarcely more powerful than myself. Yet I would not willingly have him grapple with me, if only because he is *her* husband. The very thought of *her* makes me half a coward! And yet I must be prepared. It must be done!"

Such were his reflections. He advanced to the entrance. The footsteps of Beauchampe were heard rapidly striding across the chamber overhead. The criminal recoiled as he heard them. A tremor shot through his limbs. He clutched the dagger in his bosom, set his teeth firmly, and waited for a moment at the entrance.

The sounds subsided above. He thrust his head through the doorway, into the passage, and leaned forward in the act of listening. The renewed silence which now prevailed in the house gave him fresh courage. He darted up the steps, sought his chamber, and with eager, trembling hands caught up and examined his pistols. Both were loaded, and he thrust them into the pockets of his coat; then seizing his own and the saddle-bags of his companion, he darted out of the chamber, and down the stairs, with footsteps equally light and rapid.

Once more in the hall, and well armed, he was more composed, but as little prepared, morally, for events as before. There was a heavy fear upon his spirit. The consciousness of guilt is a terrible queller of one's manhood. He waited impatiently for the return of Barnabas. At such a moment, even the presence of one whom e estimated rather humbly, and with some feelings of contempt, was grateful to his enfeebled spirit; and the appearance of the horses at the door, and the return of his friend, had the effect of re-enlivening him to a degree which made him blush for the feeling of apprehension which he had so lately entertained.

"All's ready!—will you ride?" demanded Barnabas, picking up his saddle-bags. The worthy coadjutor was by no means audacious in his courage. Sharpe hesitated.

"It may be only a false alarm, after all," said he; "we had better wait and see."

"I think not," said the former. "There was no mistaking the words, and as little the looks. She's a very resolute woman."

Colonel Sharpe was governed by the anxieties of guilt as well as its fears. The painful desire to hear and know

to what extent the revelations of the wife had gone — a
half confidence that *all* would not be told — that some loop-
hole would be left for retreat — and the further conviction
that, at all events, whatever was the nature of her story to
her husband, it was quite as well that he should know it at
one moment as another — encouraged him to linger; and
this resolve, with the force of an habitual will, he impressed
upon his reluctant companion.

Leaving them to their suspense below, let us join the
husband and wife above stairs.

CHAPTER XXIX.

EXPLANATION — THE OATH RENEWED.

" Take the dagger —
The victim waits !   Thy honor and my safety
Demand the stroke !" — *Old Play.*

" In the name of God, Mrs. Beauchampe !" — such was
the address of her husband as he joined her in their chamber — " what is the meaning of all this ?"

She silently took from the toilet a pair of pistols, and
offered them to him.

" What mean you by these — by this treatment of my
friends ?"

" Your friends are villains !   Colonel Sharpe and Alfred
Stevens are the same person !"

" Impossible !" he replied, recoiling with horror from the
proffered weapons.

" True as gospel, Beauchampe !"

" True ?"

" True ! before Heaven, I speak the truth, my husband !
— a dreadful, terrible truth, which I would not speak were
it possible not to do so !"

" And why has not this been told me before ?   Why has
he been suffered to remain in your presence — nay, to be
alone with you for hours — since his coming ?   Did you
know him from the first to be the same man ?"

" From the first !"

" Explain, then ! — for God's sake, explain !   You blind
13

me — you stun me! I am utterly unable to see this thing!
How, if you knew him from the first, suffer for a moment
the contagion of his presence?"

"This I can easily answer you, my husband. Bear with
me patiently while I do so! I will lay bare to you my
whole soul, and show you by what motives of forbearance
I was governed, until driven to the course I have pursued
y the bold insolence of this uncompromising villain."

She paused — pressed her head with her hands as if to
subdue the tumult which was striving within; then, with
an effort which seemed to demand her greatest energies,
she proceeded with her speech.

She entered into an explanation of that change in her
feelings and desires which had been consequent upon her
marriage. She acknowledged the force of those new domestic ties which she had formed, in making her unwilling
that any event should take place which should commit herself or husband in the eyes of the community, and bring
about a disruption of those ties, or a further development
of her story — which would be certain to follow, in the
event of an issue between her husband and her seducer.
With this change in her mood, prior to the appearance of
this person and his identification with Colonel Sharpe, she
had prayed that he might never reappear; and when he
did — when he became the guest of her husband, and was
regarded as his friend — it was her hope that a sense of
his danger would have prompted him to make his visit
short, and prevent him from again renewing it. Her own
deportment was meant to be such as should produce this
determination in his breast. But when this failed of its
effect; when, in despite of warning, in defiance of danger,
in the face of hospitality and friendship, the villain presumed to renew his loathsome overtures of guilt; when no
hope remained that he would forbear; when it was seen
that he was without generosity, and that neither the rebuke
of her scorn nor the warnings of her anger could repel his

insolent advances — then it was that she felt compelled to speak — then, and not before!

She had deferred this necessity to the last moment; she had been purposely slow. She had given the seducer every opportunity to withdraw in safety, and made the condition of his future security easy, by asking only that he would never seek or see her again!

She had striven in vain; and, failing to find the immunity she sought from her own strength and firmness, it was no longer possible to evade the necessity which forced her to seek it in the protection of her husband. It was now necessary that he should comply with his oath, and for this reason she had placed the weapons of death in his hands. Henceforth, the struggle was his alone. Of the sort of duty to be done, no doubt could exist in either mind!

Such was the narrative which, with the coherence not only of a sane but a strong mind, and a will that no pain of body and pang of soul could overcome, she poured into the ears of her husband. We will not attempt to describe the agony, the utter recoil and shrinking of soul, with which he heard it. There is a point to which human passion sometimes arrives when all language fails of description; as, in a condition of physical suffering, the intensity of the pain is providentially relieved by utter unconsciousness and stupor. But, such was the surprise with which Beauchampe received the information of that identity between Alfred Stevens and his friend — his friend! — that the impression which followed from what remained of his wife's narrative was comparatively slight. You might trace the accumulation of pang upon pang, in his heart, as the story went on, by a slight convulsive movement of the lip — but the eye did not seem to speak. It was fixed and glassy, and so vacant, that its expression might have occasioned some apprehension in the mind of the wife, had her own intensity of suffering — however kept down — not been of so blinding and darkening a character.

When she had ended, he grasped the pistols, and hurried to the entrance, but as suddenly returned. He laid the weapons down upon the toilet.

"No!" he exclaimed—"not here! It must not be in this house. He has eaten at our board—he is beneath our roof. This threshold must not be stained with the blood of the guest!"

He looked at her as he spoke these words. But she did not note his glance. Her eyes were fixed; her hands were clasped; she did not seem to note his presence, and her head was bent forward as if she listened. A moment was passed in this manner, when, as he still looked, she turned suddenly and seemed only then to behold him.

"You are here!" she said; "where are the pistols?"

He did not answer; but, following the direction of his eye, she saw them on the toilet, and, striding toward them, fiercely and rapidly she caught them up from the place where they lay.

"What would you, Anna?" he asked, seizing her wrists.

"The wrong is mine!" she exclaimed. "My hand shall avenge it. It is sworn to it. I am prepared for it. Why should it be put upon another?"

"No!" he cried—while his brow gathered into a cloud of wrinkles—"no, woman! *You* are mine, and *your wrongs* are mine—mine only! *I* will avenge them: but I must avenge them as I think right—after my own fashion —in my own time. Fear not that I will. Believe that I am a man, with the feelings and the resolution of a man, and do not doubt that I will execute my oath—ay, even were it no oath—to the uttermost letter of the obligation! Give me the weapons!"

She yielded them. Her whole manner was subdued— her looks—her words.

"O Beauchampe, would that I could spare you this!"

"Do I wish it, Anna? Would I be spared? No, my wife! This duty is doubly incumbent on me now. This reptile has made your wrong doubly that of your husband. Has he not renewed his criminal attempt under my own roof? This, this alone, would justify me in denying him its protection; but I will not. He shall not say he was entrapped! As the obligation is a religious one, I shall execute its laws with the deliberation of one who has a task from God before him. I will not violate the holy pledges of hospitality, though he *has* done so. While he remains in my threshold, it shall protect him. But fear not that vengeance shall be done. Before God, my wife, I renew my oath!"

He lifted his hand to heaven as he spoke, and she sunk upon her knees, and with her hands clasped his. Her lips parted in speech, and her murmurs reached his ears, but what she spoke was otherwise inaudible. He gently extricated himself from her embrace — went to the basin, and deliberately bathed his forehead in the cold water. She remained in her prostrate position, her face clasped in her hands, and prone upon the floor. Having performed his ablutions, Beauchampe turned and looked upon her steadfastly, but did not seek to raise her; and, after a moment's further delay, left the chamber and descended the stairs.

Then his wife started from her feet, and moved toward the toilet, where the weapons lay. Her hand was extended as if to grasp them, but she failed to do so, and staggered forward with the manner of one suddenly dizzy with blindness. With this feeling she turned toward the bed, and reached it in time to save herself a fall upon the floor. She sank forward, face downward, upon the couch; and while a husky sound — a feeble sort of laughter, wild and hysteric — issued from her throat, she lost all sense of the agony that racked her soul and brain, in the temporary unconsciousness of both; and which, but for the relief of this timely apathy, must have been fatal to life.

CHAPTER XXX.

REPRIEVE AND FLIGHT.

WHEN Colonel Sharpe heard the descending footsteps of Beauchampe as he came down the stairs, he asked Barnabas to go into the passage-way and meet him—a request which made the other look a little blank.

"There is no sort of danger to you, and you hear he walks slowly, not like a man in a passion. I doubt if she has told him *all;* perhaps she has told him nothing. At all events, you will be decidedly the best person to receive intelligence of what she has told. I'm thinking it's a false alarm after all; but, whether true or false, it can in no manner affect you. *You* are safe—go out, meet him, and learn how far I am so."

It has been seen that the will of the superior man, in spite of all first opposition, usually had its way with the inferior. Mr. Barnabas, however reluctant, submitted to the wishes of his companion, and with some misgivings, and with quite slow steps, left the room in order to meet with the husband, of whose rage such apprehensions were formed in both their minds. Sharpe, though he had expressed himself so confidently, or at least so hopefully, to Barnabas, was really full of apprehension. The moment that the latter left the room, he took out his pistols, deliberately cocked them, and placing them behind his back, moving backward a little farther from the entrance; preparing himself in this

manner for the encounter — if that became inevitable — with
the angry husband.

But the danger seemed to have passed away. Silence
followed. The steps of Beauchampe were no longer heard,
and, moving toward one of the front windows, the criminal
beheld the two, already at a distance, and about to disappear behind the copse of wood that spread itself in front.

Sharpe breathed more freely, and began to fancy that
the cloud had dispersed, that the danger was overblown.
He was mistaken. Let us join Beauchampe and his companion.

"Mr. Barnabas," said the former, "I speak to you still
as to a gentleman, as I believe you have had no knowledge
of the past crime of Colonel Sharpe, and no participation
in his present villany."

"Such was the opening remark of Beauchampe, when he
had led the other from the house. Mr. Barnabas was
prompt in denial and disclaimer.

"Crime — Beauchampe — villany! Surely, you can not
think I had any knowledge — any participation — ah! — do
you suppose — do you think I knew anything about it —"

"About *what?*" demanded the suspicious Beauchampe,
coolly fixing his eyes, with a keen glance, upon the embar-
rassed speaker.

"Nay, my dear Beauchampe — that's the question," said
the other. "You speak of some crime, some villany, as I
understand you, of which our friend Sharpe has been guilty.
If it be true, that he has been guilty of any, you are right
in supposing that I know nothing about it. Nay, my dear
fellow, don't think it strange or impertinent, on my part, if
I venture a conjecture — mark me, my dear fellow, a mere
supposition — that there must be some mistake in this matter. I can't think that Sharpe, a fellow who stands so high,
whom we both know so well and have known so long, such
an excellent fellow in fact, so cursed smart, and so clever
a companion, can have been such a d——d fool as to have

practised any villany, at least upon a gentleman whom we both love and esteem so much as yourself."

"There's no mistake, Mr. Barnabas!" said the other, gravely. "This man is a villain, and has been practising his villany to my dishonor, while in my house and enjoying my confidence and hospitality."

"You don't say so! it's scarce possible, Beauchampe! The crime's too monstrous. I still think, I mean, I still hope, that there's some very strange mistake in the matter which can be explained."

"Unhappily, sir, there is none. There is no mistake, and nothing needs explanation!"

"That's unfortunate, very unfortunate! May I ask, my dear fellow, what's the offence?"

"Surely, of this I drew you forth to tell you, in order that you might tell him. I do not wish to take his life in my own dwelling, though his crime might well justify me in forgetting the sacred obligations of hospitality — might justify me, indeed, in putting him to death even though his hands grasped the very horns of the altar. He has busied himself, while in my dwelling, in seeking to dishonor its mistress. While we rode, sir, and in our absence, he has toiled for the seduction of my wife. That's his crime! You will tell him that I know all!"

"Great God! What madness, what folly, what could have made him do so? But, my dear Mr. Beauchampe, as he has failed, not succeeded, eh?"

The speaker stopped. It was not easy to finish such a sentence.

"I can not guess what you would say, Mr. Barnabas, nor, perhaps, is it necessary. You will please to go back to your companion, and say to him that he will instantly leave the dwelling which he has endeavored to dishonor. I see that your horses are both ready — a sign, sir, that Colonel Sharpe has not been entirely unconscious of this necessity. I would fain hope, Mr. Barnabas, that, in pro-paring to depart yourself, you acknowledge no more serious obligation to do so, than the words of my wife, conveyed at the breakfast-table!"

The sentence was expressed inquiringly, and the keen, searching glance of Beauchampe, declared a lurking suspicion that made it very doubtful to Barnabas whether the husband did not fully suspect the auxiliary agency which he had really exhibited in the dishonorable proceedings of Sharpe. He felt this, and could not altogether conceal his confusion, though he saw the necessity of a prompt reply.

"My dear Beauchampe, was it not enough to make a gentleman think of trooping, with bag and baggage, when the lady of the house gives him notice to quit."

" but the notice was not given to *you*, Mr. Barnabas."

" Granted; but Sharpe and myself were friends, you know, and came together, and being the spokesman in the case, you see—"

" Enough, Mr. Barnabas; I ask no explanation from you. I do not say to you that it is necessary that you should quit along with Colonel Sharpe, but as your horse is ready, perhaps it is quite as well that you should."

" Hem! such was my purpose, Mr. Beauchampe."

" Yes, sir; and you will do me the favor for which I requested your company, to say to him that the whole history of his conduct is known to me. In order that he should have no further doubts on this subject, you will suffer me to intrude upon you a painful piece of domestic history."

" My dear Beauchampe, if it's so very painful—"

" I perceive, Mr. Barnabas, that what I am about to relate will not have the merit of novelty to you."

" Indeed, sir, but it will—I mean, I reckon it will. I really am very ignorant of what you intend to mention. I am, sir, upon my honor, I am!"

Beauchampe regarded the creature with a cold smile of the most utter contempt, and when he had ended, resumed:—

13*

" Tell Colonel Sharpe, if you please, that, before I married Mrs. Beauchampe, she herself told me the whole history of Alfred Stevens and her own unhappy frailty, while she swore me to avenge her dishonor. Tell him that I *will* avenge it, and that he must prepare himself accordingly. My house confers on him the temporary privilege of safety. He will leave it as soon as convenient after you return to it. I will seek him only after he has reached his own; and when we meet it is with the one purpose of taking his life or losing my own. There can be no half struggle between us. There can be no mercy. Blood, alone! the blood of life—the life itself—can acquit me of my sworn obligation. It may be his life, or it may be mine; but he must understand, that, while I live, the forfeit stands against him, not to be redeemed but in his blood! This is all, sir, that I have to say."

" But, my dear Beauchampe—"

" No more, Mr. Barnabas, if you please. There can be nothing more between us. You will understand me further, when I tell you that I am not assured of your entire freedom from this last contemplated crime of Colonel Sharpe. I well know your subserviency to his wishes, and but for the superior nature of his crime, and that I do not wish to distract my thoughts from the sworn and solemn purpose before me, I should be compelled to show you that I regard the weakness which makes itself the minister of crime as a quality which deserves its chastisement also. Leave me, if you please, sir. I have subdued myself with great difficulty, to the task I have gone through, and would not wish to be provoked into a forgetfulness of my forbearance. You are in possession of all that I mean to say—your horses are ready—I suspect your friend is ready also! Good morning, sir!"

The speaker turned into the copse, and Mr. Barnabas was quite too prudent a person to follow him with any further expostulations. The concluding warning of Beau-

champe was not lost upon him; and, glad to get off so
well, he hurried back to the house, where Sharpe was awaiting him with an eagerness of anxiety which was almost
feverish.

"Well—what has he to say? You were long enough
about it!"

"The delay was mine. He was as brief as charity. He
knows all."

"All! impossible!"

"All—every syllable! Nay, says he knew the whole
story of Alfred Stevens and of his wife's frailty before he
married her. Begs me particularly to tell you *that*, and
to say, moreover, that he was sworn to avenge her wrong
before marriage."

"Then she told me nothing but the truth! What a blind
ass I have been not to know it, and believe her! I should
have known that she was like no other woman under the
sun!"

"It's too late now for such reflections: the sooner we're
off the better!"

"Ay, ay! but what more does he say?"

"That you are safe till you reach your own home; but,
after that, never! It's your life or his! He swears it!"

"But was he furious?"

"No—by no means."

"Then I'm deceived in the man as well as the woman!
If *he* lets me off now, I suspect there's little to fear."

"Don't deceive yourself. He looked ready to break out
at a moment's warning. It was evidently hard work with
him to contain himself. Some fantastic notion about the
obligations of hospitality alone prevented him from seeking
instant redress."

"Fantastic or not, Barnabas, the reprieve is something.
I don't fear the cause, however bad, if I can stave it off
for a term or two. Witnesses may die, in the meantime;
principals become unsettled; new judges, with new *dictâ*,

come in, and there is always hope in conflicting authorities. To horse, *mon ami!*—a reprieve is a long step to a full pardon."

" It's something, certainly," said the other, " and I'm sure I'm glad of it; but don't deceive yourself. Be on your guard. If ever there was a man seriously savage in his resolution, Beauchampe is."

"Pshaw! Barnabas!—you were ever an alarmist!" replied Sharpe, whose elasticity had returned to him with the withdrawal of the momentary cause of apprehension.

" We shall tame this monster, however savage, if you only give us time. Let him come to Frankfort, and we'll set the whole corps of ' Red-Hats,' yours among 'em, at work to get him to the conclave ; and one Saturday's bout, well plied, will mellow body and soul in such manner that he will never rage afterward, however he may roar. I tell you, my lad, time is something more than money. It subdues hate and anger, softens asperity, wakens up new principles, makes old maids young ones—ay, my boy, and"— here, looking up over his horse, which he was just about to mount, at the windows of Beauchampe's chamber, and closing the sentence in a whisper—" ay, my boy, and may even enable me to overcome this sorceress—this tigress, if you prefer it—make her forget that she is a wife—forget everything, but the days when I taught her her first lessons in loving !"

" Sharpe," exclaimed the other in a sort of husky horror, " you are a perfect dare-devil, to speak so in the very den of the lion ?"

" Ay, but it is while thinking of the lioness."

" Keep me from the claws of both !" ejaculated Barnabas, with an honest terror, as he struck spurs into the flanks of his horse.

" I do not now feel as if I feared either !" replied the other.

"Don't halloo till out of the woods!"

"No!—but, Barnabas, do you really think that this woman is sincere in giving me up?"

"Surely! How can I think otherwise?"

"Ah, my boy, you know nothing of the sex."

"Well—but she has told him all. How do you explain that?"

"She has had her reasons. She perhaps finds, or fancies, that Beauchampe suspects. She hopes to blind him by this apparent frankness. She's not in earnest."

"D—n such manœuvring, say I!"

"Give us time, Barnabas—time, my boy, and I shall have her at my feet yet! I do not doubt that, with the help of some of our boys, I shall baffle *him;* and I will never lose sight of *her* while I have sight. I have felt more passion for that woman than I ever felt for any woman yet, or ever expect to feel for another; and, if scheme and perseverance will avail for anything, she shall yet be mine!"

"If such were your feelings for her, why didn't you marry her in Charlemont?"

"So I would have done—if it had been necessary; but who pays for his fruit when he can get it for nothing?"

"True," replied the other, evidently struck by the force of this *dictum* in moral philosophy—"that's very true; but the fruit has its Argus now, if it had not then; and the paws of Briareus may be upon your throat, if you look too earnestly over the wall. My counsel to you is, briefly, that you arrive with all possible speed at the faith of the fox."

"What! sour grapes? No, no, Barnabas!—the grapes *are sweet*—as I do not think them entirely out of reach. As for the dragon, we shall yet contrive to 'calm the terrors of his claws.'"

So speaking, they rode out of sight, the courage of both

rising as they receded from the place of danger. Whether
Sharpe really resolved on the reckless course which he
expressed to his companion, or simply sought, with the
inherent vanity of a small man, to excite the wonder of the
latter, is of no importance to our narrative. In either
case, his sense of morals and of society is equally and
easily understood.

CHAPTER XXXI.

CHALLENGE.

COLONEL SHARPE sat, one pleasant forenoon, in the snug parlor of his elegant mansion in the good city of Frankfort. It was a *dies non* with him. He had leisure, and his leisure was a leisure which had its sauce. It was a satisfactory leisure. The prospect of wealth with dignity was before him. Clients were numerous; fees liberal; his political party had achieved its triumph, and his own commission as attorney-general of the state was made out in the fairest characters. The world went on swimmingly. Truly, it was a blessed world. So one may fancy, with the wine and walnuts before him. Ah, how much of the beauty of this visible world depends on one's dessert—and digestion!

Colonel Sharpe's dessert was excellent, but his digestion not so good. Nay, there were some things that he could not digest; but of these, at the pleasant moment when we have thought proper to look in upon him, he did not think. His thoughts were rather agreeable than otherwise; perhaps we should say, rather exciting than agreeable. They were less sweet than piquant; but they were such as he did not seek to disperse. A man of the world relishes his bitters occasionally. It is your long-legged lad of eighteen who purses his lips while his eyes run water, as he imbibes the acrid but spicy flavor. Colonel Sharpe was no such boy. He could linger over the draught, and sip, with a sense of relish, from the mingling but not discordant elements. He was no milksop. He had renounced the natural tastes at a very early day.

He thought of Margaret Cooper—we should say Mrs. Beauchampe, but that, when he recalled her to his memory, she always came in the former, never in the latter character. He did not like to think of her as the wife of another. The reflection made him sore; though, to think of her was always a source of pleasure in a greater or less degree. But he had not forgotten the husband; and now, in connection with the wife, he felt himself unavoidably compelled to think of him. His countenance assumed a meditative aspect. There was a gathering frown upon his brow in spite of his successes. At this moment a rap was heard at the door, and Mr. Barnabas was announced.

"Ha! Barnabas—how d'ye do?"

"Well—when did you get back?"

"Last night, after dark."

"Yes—I looked in yesterday and you were not here then. What news bring you?"

"None! Have you any here?"

"As little. It's enough to know that all's right. We are quite joyful here—nothing to dash our triumph."

"That's well, and our triumph *is* complete; but"—with an air of abstraction—"what do you hear of Beauchampe?"

"Not a word—but he's in Frankfort!"

"Ha! indeed!"

"Was here two days ago. Haven't you heard from him?"

"Not a syllable."

"But how could you—going to and fro, and so brief a time in any place, it was scarcely possible to find you!"

"I doubt if he'll do anything, Barnabas. The affair will be made so much worse by stirring. He'll not think of it—he's very proud—very sensitive—very sensible to ridicule!"

" I don't know. I hope he won't. But he's as strange an animal as the woman, his wife; and, I tell you, there was a damned sour seriousness about him when he spoke to me on the subject, that makes me apprehensive that he'll keep his word. The ides of March are not over yet."

Sharpe's gravity increased. His friend rose to depart.

" Where do you go ?"

" To Folker's. I have some business there. I just heard that you were here, and looked in to say how happy we all are in our successes."

" You will sup with me to-night, Barnabas. I want you: I feel dull."

" The devil you do — what, and just made attorney-general!"

" Even so! Honors are weighty."

" Not the less acceptable for that. Glamis thou art — Cawdor shalt be — and let me be your weird sister, and proclaim, yet further — ' Thou shalt be king hereafter!' governor, I mean."

" Ah! you are sharp, this morning, Barnabas," said Sharpe. his muscles relaxing into a pleasant smile. " I shall expect you to-night, if it be only to hear the repetition of these agreeable predictions."

" I will not fail you! addio!"

Colonel Sharpe sat once more alone. Pleasant indeed were the fancies which the words of Mr. Barnabas had awakened in his mind. He murmured in the strain of dramatic language, which the quotation of his friend had suggested, as he paced the apartment to and fro:—

> " 'I know I'm thane of Glamis,
> But how of Cawdor —
> — And to be king,
> Is not within the prospect of belief.'

Ay, but it does !" he proceeded in the more sober prose of his own reflections; " The steps are fair and easy. Barnabas is no fool in such matters, though no wit. He knows the people. He can sound them as well as any man. This suggestion does not come from himself. No — no! It comes from a longer head. It must be Clay! Hem! this is to be thought upon! *His* word against a thousand pounds! If he thinks so, it is as good as done ; and Barnabas is only an echo, when he says, ' Thou shalt be king hereafter!' Poor Barnabas! how readily he takes his color from his neighbor."

A rap at the door arrested these pleasant reflections. The soliloquist started and grew pale. There was surely a meaning in that rap. It was not that of an ordinary acquaintance. It wanted freedom, rapidity. It was very deliberate and measured. One — two — three! — you could count freely in the intervals. A strange voice was heard at the door.

" Colonel Sharpe is in town — is he at home!"

The servant answered in the affirmative, and appeared a moment after, followed by a stranger — a gentleman of dark, serious complexion, whose face almost declared his business. The host felt an unusual degree of discomposure for which he could not so easily account.

" Be seated, sir, if you please. I have not the pleasure of your name."

" Covington, sir, is my name — John A. Covington."

" Covington — John A. Covington! I have the pleasure of knowing a gentleman whose name very much resembles yours. I know John W. Covington."

" I am a very different person," answered the stranger. — " I have not the honor of being ranked among *your* friends.

The stranger spoke very coldly. A brief pause followed his words, in which Colonel Sharpe's discomposure rather underwent increase. The keen eye of Covington observed his face, while he very deliberately drew from his pocket a paper which he handed to Sharpe, who took it with very sensible agitation of nerve.

"Do me the favor, sir, to read that. It is from Mr. Beauchampe. He tells me you are prepared for it. It is open, you see: I am aware of its contents."

"From Beauchampe—"

"*Mr.* Beauchampe, sir," said the visiter, coolly correcting the freedom of the speaker.

"This paper, as you will see by the date, sir, has beer some time in my hands. Your absence in the country, alone prevented its delivery."

"Yes, sir"—said Sharpe, slowly, and turning over the envelope—"yes, sir; this, I perceive, is a peremptory challenge, sir?"

"It is."

"But, Mr. Covington, there may be explanations, sir."

"None, sir! Mr. Beauchampe tells me that this is impossible. He adds, moreover, that you know it. There is but one issue, he assures me between you, and that is life or death."

"Really, sir, there is no good reason for this. Mr. Covington, you are a man of the world. You know what is due to society. You will not lend yourself to any measure of unnecessary bloodshed. You have a right, sir—surely you have a right, sir, to interpose, and accept some more qualified atonement—perhaps, sir—an apology—the expression of my sincere regret and sorrow, sir—"

The other shook his head coldly—

"My friend leaves me none."

"But, sir, if you knew the cause of this hostility—if—"

"I do sir!" was the stern reply.

"Indeed! But are you sure that you have heard it exactly as it is. There are causes which qualify offence—"

"I believe, Mr. Beauchampe, sir, in preference to any other witness. This offence, sir, admits of none. You will permit me to add, though extra-official, that my friend deals with you very magnanimously. The provocation is of a sort which deprives you of any claim of courtesy. May I ave your answer, sir, to the only point to which this letter relates ! Will you refer me to your friend ?"

" Sir — Mr. Covington — I will not fight Mr. Beauchampe !"

" Indeed, sir ! — can it be possible !" exclaimed Covington, rising from his chair and regarding the speaker with surprise.

" No, sir ! I *can not* fight him. I have wronged him too greatly. I can not lift weapon against his life !"

" Colonel Sharpe — this will never do ! You are a Kentuckian ! You are regarded as a Kentucky gentleman ! I say nothing on the score of your claim to this character. Let me remind you of the penalties which will follow this refusal to do my friend justice."

" I know them, sir — I know them all. I defy them — will bear them, but I can not fight Beauchampe !"

" You will be disgraced, sir : I must post you !"

Sharpe strode the apartment hastily. His cheek was flushed. He felt the humiliation of his position. In ordinary matters, in the usual spirit of society, he was no coward. We have seen how readily he fought with William Calvert. But he could not meet Beauchampe — he could not nerve himself to the encounter.

" I can not, will not fight Beauchampe !" was his muttered ejaculation. " No ! I have wronged him — wronged her ! I dare not meet him. I can never do it !"

" Be not rash, Colonel Sharpe," said the other. " Think of it again before you give me such an answer. I will give you three hours for deliberation : I will call again at four."

" No, sir — no, Mr. Covington — the wrongs I have done to Beauchampe are known — probably well known. The world will understand that I can not fight him — that my offence is of such a nature, that, to lift weapon against *him*, would be monstrous. You may post me, sir; but no one who knows me will believe that it is fear that makes me deny this meeting. They will know all; they will acquit me of the imputation of cowardice."

"And how should they know," demanded Covington sternly, "unless you make them acquainted with the facts, and thus add another to my friend's causes of provocation?"

"Nay, Mr. Covington, he himself told Mr. Barnabas."

"True, sir; but that was in a special communication to yourself, which implied confidence, and must have secrecy. My friend will have his remedy against Mr. Barnabas, if he does not against you, if *he* speaks what he should not. There is a way, sir, to muzzle your barking dogs."

"It is known to others—Mr. William Calvert, with whom I fought on this very quarrel."

"Ah! that is new to me; but as you fought in this very quarrel with Mr. Calvert, it seems to me that your objection fails. You must fight with Mr. Beauchampe also on the same quarrel."

"Never, sir! You have my answer—I will not meet *him!*"

"Do not mistake your position with the public, Colonel Sharpe. The extent of the wrong which you have done to Beauchampe only makes your accountability the greater. Nobody will acquit you on this score; nay, any effort to make known to the people the true cause of Mr. Beauchampe s hostility will make it obvious that you seek rather to excuse your cowardice, than to show forbearance, or to make atonement. Truly, they will regard that as a very strange sort of remorse which publishes the shame of the wife in order to justify a refusal to meet the husband!"

"I will not publish it—Beauchampe has already done so."

"It is known to two persons, sir, through him. It need not be known to more. Colonel Calvert is a friend of mine.

He is not the man to speak of the affair. Besides, I will communicate to him on the subject, and secure his silence. You shall have no refuge of this sort."

"I have answered you, Mr. Covington," said Sharpe, doggedly.

"I must post you, then, as a scoundrel and a coward!"

Sharpe turned upon the speaker with a look of suddenly-roused fury in his face, but, swallowing the word which rose to his lips, he turned away. The other proceeded coolly:—

"This shall be done, sir; and I must warn you that the affair will not end here. Mr. Beauchampe will disgrace you in the public streets."

The sweat trickled from the brows of Sharpe in thick drops such as precede the torrents of the thunderstorm. He strove to speak, but the convulsive emotions of his bosom effectually baffled utterance; and, with dilated eyes and laboring breast, he strode the floor, utterly incapable of self-control. Covington lingered.

"You will repent this, Colonel Sharpe. You will recall me when too late. Suffer me to see you this afternoon for your answer."

The other advanced to him, then turned away; once more approached, and again receded. A terrible strife was at work within him; but, when he did find words, they expressed no bolder determination than before. Covington regarded him with equal pity and contempt, as he turned away evidently dissatisfied and disappointed.

He was scarcely gone when the miserable man found words:—

"God of heaven, that I should feel thus!—that I should be so unmanned! Why is this? why is the strength denied me—the courage—which never failed before? It is not too late. He has scarcely left the step! I will recall him. He shall have another answer!"—and, with this late resolution, he darted to the entrance and laid his hand upon the knob of the door; but the momentary impulse had already departed. He left it unopened. He recoiled from the entrance, and, striking his hands against his forehead, groaned in all the novel and unendurable bitterness of this unwonted humiliation.

"And this is the man—Cawdor, Glamis, all!—king hereafter, too, as Mr. Barnabas promised—echoing, of course, the language of that great political machinist, Mr. Clay. Ha! ha! ha!"

Did some devil growl this commentary in the ears of the miserable man? He heard it, and shuddered from head to foot.

CHAPTER XXXII.

PROGRESS OF PASSION.

LET nobody imagine that a sense of shame implies remorse or repentance. Nay, let them not be sure that it
implies anything like forbearance in the progress of offence.
It was not so with our attorney-general. The moment he
recovered, in any fair degree, his composure, he despatched
a messenger for his friend Barnabas. He, good fellow,
came at the first summons. We will not say that his footsteps were not absolutely quickened by the recollection
that it was just then the dinner-hour; and, possibly, some
fancy took possession of his mind, leading him to the strange
but pleasant notion that Sharpe had suddenly stumbled
upon some *bonne bouche* in the market-place, of particular
excellence, of which he was very anxious that his friend
should partake. The supper, be it remarked, was no less
an obligation still! Conceptive Mr. Barnabas! Certainly,
he had some such idea. The *bonne bouche* quickened his
movements. He came seasonably. The dinner was not
consumed; perhaps not quite ready: but, for the *bonne
bouche* — alas! *Sic transit gloria mundi!*

Such is the inscription, at least, upon this one pleasant
ope of our amiable philosopher. There was a morsel for
his digestion, or rather for that of his friendly entertainer;
but, unhappily, it was one that neither was well prepared
to swallow. Mr. Barnabas was struck dumb by the intelligence which he heard. He was not surprised that Beau-

champe had sent a challenge: his surprise, amounting to utter consternation, was that his friend should have refused it. He was so accustomed to the usual bold carriage of Colonel Sharpe—knew so well his ordinary promptness—nay, had seen his readiness on former occasions to do battle, right or wrong, with word or weapon—that he was taken all aback with wonder at a change so sudden and unexpected. Besides, it must be recollected that Mr. Barnabas was brought up in that school of an earlier period, throughout the whole range of southern and western country, which rendered it the point of honor to yield redress at the first summons, and in whatever form the summoner pleased to require. That school was still one of authority, not merely with Mr. Barnabas, but with the country; and the loss of caste was one of those terrible social consequences of any rejection of this authority which he had not the courage to consider without absolute horror. When he did speak, the friends had changed places. They no longer stood in the old relation to each other. Instead of Colonel Sharpe's being the superior will, while that of Barnabas was submission, the latter grew suddenly strong, almost commanding.

"But, Sharpe, you *must* meet him. By Jupiter, it won't do! You're disgraced for ever, if you don't. You can't escape. You must fight him."

"I can not, Barnabas! I was never so unnerved in my life before. I can not meet him. I can not lift weapon against the husband of Margaret Cooper."

"Be it so; but, at all events, receive his fire."

"Even for this I am unprepared. I tell you, Barnabas, I never felt so like a cur in all my life. I never knew till now what it was to fear."

"Shake it off; it's only a passing feeling. When you're up, and facing him, you will cease to feel so."

The other shook his head with an expression of utter despair and self-abandonment.

14

"By God, I know better!" exclaimed Barnabas warmly; "I've seen you on the ground — I've seen you fight. There was that chap Calvert—"

"Barnabas, it is in vain that you expostulate. I *have* fought—have been in frequent strifes with men, and brave men too — but never knew such feelings as oppress me now, and have oppressed me ever since I had this message. Do not suppose me insensible to the shame. It burns in my brain with agony; it rives my bosom with a choking and continual spasm. A hundred times, since Covington has been gone, have I started up with the view to sending him a message, declaring myself ready to meet his friend; but as often has this cursed feeling come upon me, paralyzing the momentary courage, and depriving me of all power of action. I feel that I can not meet Beauchampe — I feel that I dare not."

"Great God! what are we to do? Think, my dear fellow, what is due to your station — to your position in the party! Remember, you are just now made attorney-general: you are the observed of all observers. Everything depends upon what exhibition you make now. Get over this difficulty — man yourself for this meeting — and the rest is easy. Another year puts you at the very head of the party."

"I have thought of all these things, Barnabas; and one poor month ago, had an angel of heaven come and assured me that they would have failed to provoke me to the encounter with any foe, however terrible, I should have flouted the idle tidings. Now, I can not."

. "You must! What will they say at the club? You'll be expelled, Sharpe — think of that! You'll be cut by every member. Covington will post you. Nay, ten to one but Beauchampe will undertake to horsewhip you."

"I trust I shall find courage to face him then, Barnabas, though I could not now. Look you, Barnabas — something can be done in another way. Beauchampe can be acted on."

" How—how can that be done ?"

" Two or three judicious fellows can manage it It is only to show him that any prosecution of this affair necessarily leads to the public disgrace of his wife. It is easy to show him that, though he may succeed in dishonoring me, the very act that does it is a public advertisement of her shame."

" So it is," said the other.

" Something more, Barnabas. It might be intimated to Covington that, as Margaret Cooper had a child—"

" Did she, indeed ?"

" So I ascertained by accident. She had one before leaving Charlemont."

" Indeed !—well ?"

" Well—it might have the effect of making him quiet show him that this child was—"

The rest of the sentence was whispered in the ears of his companion.

" The d—l it was !" exclaimed the other. " But is that certain, Sharpe ?—for, if so, it acquits you altogether. The color alone would be conclusive."

" Certainly it would. Now, some hint of this kind to Covington, or to Beauchampe himself—"

" By Jupiter, I shouldn't like to be the man to tell him, however ! He's such a bulldog !"

" Through his friend, then. It might be done, Barnabas ; and it can't be doubted that the dread of such a report would effectually discourage him from any prosecution of this business."

" So it might — so it would ; but—"

" Barnabas, you must get it done."

" But, my dear colonel—"

" You must save me, Barnabas—relieve me of this difficulty. You know my power—my political power—you see my strength. I can serve you—you can not doubt my

willingness to serve you; but if this power is lost—if I
am disgraced by this fellow—we are all lost."

"True—very true. It must be done. I will see to it.
Make yourself easy. I will set about it as soon as dinner's
over."

Here the politic Mr. Barnabas looked round with an
anxious questioning of the eye, which Colonel Sharpe understood.

"Ah! dinner—I had not thought of that, but it must be
ready. Of course, you will stay and dine with me."

"Why, yes—though I have some famous mutton-chops
awaiting me at home."

"Mine are doubtlessly as good."

We shall leave the friends to their pottage, without any
unnecessary inquiry into the degree of appetite which they
severally brought to its discussion. It may not be impertinent, however, to intimate, as a mere probability, that
Mr. Barnabas, in the discussion of the affair, was the most
able analyst of the two. The digestion of Colonel Sharpe
was, at this period, none of the best. We have said as
much before.

For that matter, neither was Beauchampe's. The return
of Covington, with the wholly unexpected refusal of Colonel
Sharpe to meet and give him redress, utterly confounded
him. Of course, he had the usual remedies. There was
the poster—which may be termed a modern letter of credit
—a sort of certificate of character, in one sense—carrying
with it some such moral odor as, in the physical world, is
communicated by the whizzing of a pullet's egg, addled in
June, directed at the lantern visage of a long man, honored
with a high place in the public eye, though scarcely at ease
(because of his modesty), in the precious circumference of
the pillory.

Beauchampe's friend was bound to post Colonel Sharpe.
Beauchampe himself had the privilege of obliterating his
shame, by making certain *cancelli* on the back of the

wrong-doer, with the skin of a larger but less respectable animal.

But were these remedies to satisfy Beauchampe? The cowskin might draw blood from the back of his enemy; but was that the blood which he had sworn to draw? His oath! his oath! that was the difficulty! The refusal of Colonel Sharpe to meet him in personal combat left his oath unobliterated—uncomplied with. The young man was bewildered by his rage and disappointment. This was an unanticipated dilemma.

"What is to be done, Covington?"

"Post him, at the courthouse, jail, and every hotel in town."

"Post him—and what's the good of that?"

"You disgrace him for ever!"

"That will not answer—that is nothing!"

"You can go further. Horsewhip him—cowskin him—cut his back to ribands, whenever you meet him in the open thoroughfare!"

"Did you tell him that I would do so?"

"I did!"

"It did not move him? What said he then?"

"Still the same! He would not fight *you*—could not lift weapon against *your* life."

"The villain!—the black-hearted, base, miserable villain? Covington, you will go with me?"

"Surely! You mean to post him, or cowhide him—or both?"

"No, no! That's not what I mean. I must have his blood—his life!"

"That's quite another matter, Beauchampe. I do not see that you can do more than I have told you. He is a coward: you must proclaim him as such. Your poster does that. He is a villain—has wronged you. You will punish him for the wrong. Your horsewhip does that! You can do no more, Beauchampe."

"Ay, but I must, Covington. Your poster is nothing, and the whip is nothing. I am sworn to take his life or lose my own!"

"I can do no more than I have told you. I will back you to this extent—no further."

"I can force him to fight me," said Beauchampe.

"In what way?"

"By assaulting him with my weapon, after offering him another."

"How, if he refuses to receive it?"

"He can not—surely—he *will* not refuse."

"He will! I tell you, he will refuse. The man is utterly frightened. I never witnessed such unequivocal signs of cowardice in any man."

"Then is he wonderfully changed."

A servant entered at this moment, and handed Beauchampe a letter. It was from his wife. Its contents were brief:—

. . . . "I do not hear from you, Beauchampe—I do not see you. You were to have returned yesterday. Come to me. Let me see you once more. I tremble for your safety." . . . .

The traces of an agony which the words did not express were clearly shown in the irregular, sharp lines of the epistle.

"I will go to her at once. I will meet you to-morrow, Covington, when we will discuss this matter further."

"The sooner you take the steps I propose, the better," said Covington. "The delay of a day to post him, is, perhaps, nothing; but you must not permit the lapse of more."

"I shall *not* post him, Covington. That would seem to mock my vengeance, and to preclude it. No, no! posting will not do. The scourging may; but even that does not satisfy me *now*. To-morrow—we shall meet to-morrow."

Let us go with the husband and rejoin Mrs. Beauchampe. A week had wrought great changes in her appearance. Her eyes have sunken, and the glazed intensity of their stare is almost that of madness. Her voice is slow—subdued almost to a whisper.

"It is not done!" she said, her lip touching his ear—her hands clasping his convulsively.

"No! the miserable wretch refuses to fight with me." She recoiled as she exclaimed—

"And did you expect that he would fight you? Did you look for manhood or manly courage at his hands?"

"Ay, but he *shall* meet me!" exclaimed Beauchampe, who perceived, in this short sentence, the true character of the duty which lay before him. "I will find him, at least, and you shall be avenged! He shall not escape me longer. His blood or mine."

"Stay! go not, Beauchampe! Risk nothing. Let me be the victim still. Your life is precious to me—more precious than my own name. Why should you forfeit station, pride, peace, safety—everything for me? Leave me, dear Beauchampe—leave me to my shame—leave me to despair!"

"Never! never! *You are* my life. Losing you I lose more than life—all that can make it precious! I will not lose you. Whatever happens, you are mine to the last."

"To the last, Beauchampe—thine—only thine—to the last—the last—the last!"

She sunk into his arms. He pressed his lips upon hers, and drawing the dirk from his bosom, he elevated it above her head, while he mentally renewed his oath of retribution. This done, he released her from his grasp, placed her in a seat, and, once more, pressing his lips to hers, he darted from the dwelling. In a few seconds more the sound of his horse's feet were heard, and she started from her seat, and from the stupor which seemed to possess her faculties. She hurried to the window. He had disappeared.

" He is gone !" she exclaimed, pressing her hand upon
her forehead, " He is gone ! gone for what ? Ha ! I have
sent him. I have sent him on this bloody work. Oh !
surely it is madness that moves me thus ! It must be madness. Why should he murder Alfred Stevens ? What good
will come of it ? What safety ? What— But why should
he not ? Are we never to be free ? Is he to thrust himself into our homes for ever—to baffle our hopes—destroy
our peace—point his exulting finger to the hills of Charlemont, and cry aloud, ' Remember—there' ? No ! better he
should die, and we should all die ! Strike him, Beauchampe ! Strike and fear nothing ! Strike deep ! Strike
to the very heart—strike ! strike ! strike !"

Why should we look longer on this mournful spectacle.
Yet the world will not willingly account this madness. It
matters not greatly by what name you call a passion which
has broken bounds, and disdains the right angles of con-
vention. Let us leave the wife for the husband.

CHAPTER XXXIII.

THE AVENGER.

Was Beauchampe any more sane — we should phrase it otherwise — was he any less mad than his wife?

Perhaps he was more so. The simple inquiry which Mrs. Beauchampe had made, when he told her that Sharpe refused to fight him, had opened his eyes to all the terrible responsibility to which his unhappy oath had subjected him. When he had pledged himself to take the life of her betrayer, he had naturally concluded that this pledge implied nothing more than the resolution to meet with his enemy in the duel. That a Kentucky gentleman should shrink from such an issue did not for a moment enter his thoughts; and it is not improbable but that, if he could have conjectured this possibility, he had not so readily yielded to the condition which she had coupled with her consent to be his wife.

But, after this, when in his own house, and under the garb of friendship, Colonel Sharpe labored to repeat his crime, still less could he have believed it possible that the criminal would refuse the only mode of atonement, which, according to the practices of that society to which they both were accustomed, was left within his power to make. Had he apprehended this, he would have chosen the most direct mode of vengeance — such as the social sense everywhere would have justified — and put the offender to death upon the very hearth which he had striven to dishonor.

14*

That he had not done so, was now his topic of self-reproach. An idea, whether true or false, of what was due to a guest, had compelled him to forbear, and to send the criminal forth, with every opportunity to prepare himself for the penalties which his offences had incurred.

Still, up to this moment, he had not contemplated the necessity of lifting his weapon except on equal terms, with the enemy whose life he sought. In fair fight he had no hesitation at this; but, as a murderer, to strike the unde-fended bosom — however criminal; however deserving of death — was a view of the case equally unexpected and painful. It was one for which his previous reflections had not prepared him; and, the excitement under which he labored in consequence, was one, that, if it did not madden him deprived him at least of all wholesome powers of re-flection.

While he rode to Frankfort, he went as one in a cloud. He saw nothing to the right or the left. The farmer, his neighbor, spoke to him, but he only turned as if impatient at some interruption, but, without answering, put spurs again to the flanks of his horse, and darted off with a wilder speed than ever. An instinct, rather than a purpose, when he reached Frankfort, carried him to the lodgings of his friend Covington.

"And what do you mean to do?" demanded the latter.

"Kill him — there is nothing else to be done!"

"My dear Beauchampe — you must not think of such a thing."

"Ay, but I must: why should I not? Tell me that. Shall such a monster live?"

"There are good reasons why you should not kill him. If you do, unless in very fair fight, you will not only be tried, but found guilty of the murder."

"I know not that. His crime—"

"Deserves death and should have found it at the time! Had you put him to death when he was in your house, and made the true cause known, the jury must have justified you; but you allowed the moment of provocation to pass."

" Such a moment can not pass."

" Ay, but it can and does! Time, they say, cools the blood !"

" Nonsense! When every additional moment of thought adds to the fever."

" They reason otherwise. Nay, more—just now that feeling of party runs too high, Already, they have trumpeted it about that Calvert sought to kill Sharpe on the score of his attachment to Desha. They made the grounds of that affair political, when, it seems to have been purely your own; and if you should attempt and succeed in such a thing, he would be considered a martyr to the party, and you would inevitably become its victim."

" Covington, do you think that I am discouraged by this? Do you suppose I fear death? No! If the gallows were already raised—if the executioner stood by—if I saw the felon-cart, and the gloating throng around, gathered to behold my agonies, I would still strike, strike fatally, and without fear !"

" I know you brave, Beauchampe; but such a death might well appal the bravest man !"

" It does not appal me. Understand me, Covington, I *must* slay this man !"

" I can not understand you, Beauchampe. As your friend I will not. I counsel you against the deed. I counsel you purely with regard to your own safety."

" As a friend, would you have me live dishonored ?"

" No! I have already counselled you how to transfer the ish-nor from your shoulders to his. Denounce him for his crime—disgrace him by the scourge !"

" No! no! Covington—this is no redress—no remedy. His blood only can wipe out *that* shame."

" I will have nothing to do with it, Beauchampe."

" Will you desert me ?"

"Not if you adopt the usual mode. Take your horse-whip, arm yourself; give Sharpe notice to prepare; and it is not impossible, then, that he will be armed, and the rencontre may be as fatal as you could desire it. I am ready for you to this extent."

"Be it so, then! Believe me, Covington, I would rather a thousand times risk my own life than be compelled to take his without resistance. But understand one thing. He or I must perish! We can not both survive."

"I will strive to bring it about," said the other; and, urged by the impatience of Beauchampe, he proceeded, a second time, to give Colonel Sharpe the necessary notice.

But Sharpe was not to be found. He was denied at his own dwelling as in town; and Covington took the way to the house of his arch-vassal Mr. Barnabas. The latter gentleman confirmed the intelligence. He stated, not only that Sharpe had left town, but had proceeded to Bowling-Green.

Covington did not conceal his object. Knowing the character of Barnabas, and his relation to Sharpe, he addressed himself to the fears of both.

"Mr. Barnabas, it will be utterly impossible for Colonel Sharpe to avoid this affair. Beauchampe will force it upon him. He will degrade him daily in the streets of Frankfort: he will brand him with the whip in the sight of the people. You know the effect of this upon a man's character and position."

"Certainly, sir; but, Mr. Covington, Mr. Beauchampe will do so at his peril."

"To be sure—he knows that; but, with such wrongs as Mr. Beauchampe has had to sustain, he knows no peril He will certainly do what I tell you."

"But, Mr. Covington—my dear sir—can not this be avoided? Is there no other remedy? Will no apology— no atonement of Colonel Sharpe—suppose a written apol-

ogy—most humble and penitent—to Mr. and Mrs. Beauchampe—"

"Impossible! How could you think that such an apology could atone for such an offence?—first, the seduction of this lady, while yet unmarried; and, next, the
abominable renewal of the attempt when she had become a
wife "'

" But nobody believes this, Mr. Covington. It is generally understood that the first offence is the only one to
be laid at Sharpe's door, and this is to be urged only
on political grounds. Beauchampe supported Tompkins
against Desha, and the friends of Tompkins revive this
stale offence only to discredit Sharpe as the friend of the
former."

" Mr. Barnabas, *you* know better. You *know* that Beauchampe was the friend of Sharpe, and spoke against Calvert in his defence. *We* also know, as well as you, that
Calvert and Sharpe fought on account of this very lady;
though Desha's friends have contrived to make it appear
that the combat had a political origin."

" Well, Mr. Covington, *my* knowledge is one thing—
that of the people another. I can only tell you that it is
very generally believed that the true cause of the affair is
political."

"And how has this general knowledge been obtained,
Mr. Barnabas?" remarked Covington rather sternly. " As
the friend of Beauchampe, and the only one to whom he has
confided his feelings and wishes, I can answer for it that
no publicity has been given to this affair by us."

" I don't know," said Barnabas, hurriedly, " how the
report has got abroad. I only know that it is very general."

Mr. Covington rose to depart.

" Let me, before leaving you, Mr. Barnabas, advise you,
as one of the nearest friends of Colonel Sharpe, what he is
to expect. Mr. Beauchampe will *take the road* of him, and

will horsewhip him through the streets of Frankfort on the
first occasion — nay, on every occasion — till he is prepared
to fight him.   I am free to add, for the benefit of any of
Colonel Sharpe's friends, that I will accompany him when
ever he proposes to make this attempt."

And, with this knightly intimation, Mr. Covington took
his departure.

When Beauchampe heard that Sharpe had left town, and
gone to Bowling-Green, he immediately jumped on his hors
and went off in the same direction.

That very afternoon, Mr. Barnabas sat with his friend
Colonel Sharpe over a bottle, and at the town-house of the
latter!   It had been a falsehood by which Beauchampe was
sent on a wild-goose chase into the country.   The object
was to gain time, so as to enable the friends of both parties, or rather the friends of the criminal, who were members of the club, to interpose and effect an arrangement of
the affair, if such a thing were possible ; and, in the natural
gratification which Sharpe felt that the danger was parried,
though for a moment only, the spirits of the criminal rose
into vivacity.   The two made themselves merry with the
unfruitful journey which the avenger was making ; not considering the effect of such manœuvring upon a temper so
excitable, nor allowing for the accumulation of those passions which, as they can not sleep, and can not be subdued,
necessarily become more powerful in proportion to the delay in their utterance, and the restraints to which they are
subjected.

Of course, Mr. Barnabas made a full report to his principal of all that Covington had told him.   There was little
in this report to please the offender ; but there were other
tidings which were more gratifying.   The members of the
club were busy to prevent the meeting.   Mr. Barnabas had
already sent a judicious and veteran politician to see Covington ; and, having a great faith himself in the powers of
the persons he had employed to bring the matter to a

peaceable adjustment, he had infused a certain portion of his own faith into the breast of his superior.

And the bowl went round merrily; and the hearts of the twain were lifted up, for, in their political transactions, there was much that had taken place of a character to give both of them positive gratification. And so the evening passed until about eight o'clock, when Mr. Barnabas suddenly recollected that he had made an appointment with some gentleman which required his immediate departure. Sharpe was unwilling to lose him, and his spirits sunk with the departure of his friend; nor were they much enlivened by the entrance of a lady, in whose meek, sad countenance might be read the history of an unloved, neglected, but uncomplaining wife. He did not look up at her approach. She placed herself in the seat which Mr. Barnabas had left.

"You look unwell, Warham. You seem to have been troubled, my husband," she remarked with some hesitation, and in a faint voice. "Is anything the matter?"

"Nothing which you can help, Mrs. Sharpe," he replied in cold and repelling accents, crossing his legs, and half wheeling his chair about so as to turn his back upon her. She was silenced, and looked at him with an eye full of a sad reproach and a lasting disappointment. No further words passed between them, and a few moments only elapsed when a rap was heard at the outer entrance.

"Leave the room," he said; "I suppose it is Barnabas returned. I have private business with him. You had better go to bed."

She rose meekly, and did as she was commanded. He also rose, and went to the door.

"Who's that—Barnabas?" he demanded, while opening the door.

He was answered indistinctly; but he fancied that the words were in the affirmative, and the visiter darted in the moment the door was opened. The passage-way being dark, he could not distinguish the person of the stranger.

except to discover that it was not the man whom he expected. But this discovery was made almost in the very instant when the intruder entered, and with it came certain apprehensions of danger, which, however vague, yet startled and distressed him. Under their influence he receded from the entrance, moving backward with his face to the stranger, till he re-entered the sitting-apartment. The moment that the light fell upon the face of the visiter, his knees knocked against one another. It was Beauchampe.

"Beauchampe!" he involuntarily exclaimed, with a hollow voice, while his dilated eyes regarded the fierce, wild aspect of the visiter.

"Ay, Beauchampe!" were the echoed tones of the other —tones almost stifled in the deep intensity of mood with which they were spoken—tones low, but deep, like those of some dull convent-bell, echoing at midnight along the gray rocks and heights of some half-deserted land! As deep and soul-thrilling as would be such sounds upon the ear of some wanderer, unconscious of any neighborhood, did they fall upon the sudden sense of that criminal. His courage instantly failed him. His knees smote each other; his tongue clove to his mouth; he had strength enough only to recede as if with the instinct of flight. Beauchampe caught his arm.

"You can not fly—you must stay! My business will suffer no further postponement."

Beauchampe forced him into a chair.

"What is the matter, Beauchampe? what do you mean to do?" gasped the trembling criminal.

"Does not your guilty soul tell you what I *should* do?" was the stern demand.

"I *am* guilty!" was the half-choking answer.

"Ay! but the confession alone will avail nothing. You must atone for your guilt!"

"On my knees, Beauchampe?"

"No!—with your blood!"

"Spare me, Beauchampe! oh! spare my life. Do not murder me—for I can not fight you on account of that injured woman!"

"This whining will not answer, Colonel Sharpe. You must fight me. I have brought weapons for both. Choose!"

The speaker threw two dirks upon the floor at the feet of the criminal, while he stood back proudly.

"Choose!" he repeated, pointing to the weapons.

But the latter, though rising, so far from availing himself of the privilege, made an effort to pass his enemy and escape from the room. But the prompt arm of Beauchampe arrested him and threw him back with some force toward the corner of the apartment.

"Colonel Sharpe, you can not escape me. The falsehood of your friend, which sent me from the city, has resolved me to suffer no more delay of justice. Will you fight me? Choose of the weapons at your feet."

"I can not! spare me, Beauchampe—my dear friend— for the past—in consideration of what we have been to each other—spare my life!"

"You thought not of this, villain, when, in the insolence of your heart, you dared to bring your lust into my dwelling."

"Beauchampe, hear me for your own sake, hear me."

"Speak! speak briefly. I am in no mood to trifle."

"My crime was that of a young man—"

"Stay! your crime was the invasion of my family—of its peace."

"Ah!—that *was* a crime—if it were so."

"What, do you mean to deny? Dare you to impute falsehood to my wife?"

"Beauchampe, she is your wife; and for this reason, I will not say, what I might say, but—"

"Oh! speak all—speak all! I am curious to see by what new invention of villany you hope to deceive me."

"No villany—no invention, Beauchampe—I speak only

the solemn truth.   Before God, I assure you it is the truth
only which I will deliver."

" You swear ?"

" Solemnly."

" Speak, then — but take up the dirk."

" No! If you will but hear me, I do not fear to convince you that there needs none either in your hands or
mine."

" You are a good lawyer, keen, quick-witted, and very
logical ; but it will task better wits than yours to alter my
faith that you are a villain, and that you shall perish by
this hand of mine."

Beauchampe stooped and possessed himself of one of
the weapons.

" Speak now! what have you to say ?   Remember Colonel Sharpe, you have not only summoned God to witness
your truth, but you may be summoned in a few moments to
his presence to answer for your falsehood. I am sent here,
solemnly sworn, to take your life!"

" But only because you believed me a criminal in respects
in which I am innocent. If I show you that I never approached Mrs. Beauchampe, while your wife, except with
the respect due to herself and you—"

" Liar! but you can not show me *that!*   I tell you, I
believe what she has told me. I know her truth and your
falsehood."

" She is prejudiced, my dear friend.   She hates me—"

" And with good reason: but hate you as she may, she
speaks, and can speak, nothing in your disparagement but
the truth."

" She has misunderstood—mistaken me, in what I said."

" Stay!" approaching him. " Stay! do not deceive yourself, Colonel Sharpe : you can not deceive me.   She has
detailed the whole of your wild overtures—the very words
of shame and guilt, and villanous baseness which you employed."

" Beauchampe, my dear friend, arc you sure that she *has* told you all ?"

Here the criminal approached with extended hand, while he assumed a look of mysterious meaning, which left something for the other to anticipate.

" Sure that she told me all ? Ay! I *am* sure! What remains ? Speak out, and leave nothing to these smooth, cunning faces. Speak out, while the time is left you."

" Did she tell you of our first meeting in Charlemont ?"

" Ay, did she—*that!* everything !"

" I seek not to excuse my crime, *there*, Beauchampe— but that was not a crime against *you!* I did not know you then. I did not then fancy that you would ever be so *?* lied to—"

" Cease that, and say what you deem needful."

" Did she tell you of the child ?"

" Child! what child ?" demanded Beauchampe, with a start of surprise.

The face of Sharpe put on a look of exultation. He felt that he had gained a point.

" Ah! ha! I could have sworn that she did not tell **you** *all!*"

The eyes of Beauchampe glared more fiercely, and the convulsive twitching of the hand which held the dagger, and the quivering of his lip, might have warned his companion of the danger which he incurred of trifling with him longer.

But Sharpe's policy was to induce the suspicions of Beauchampe in relation to his wife. He fancied, from the unqualified astonishment which appeared in the latter's face, as he spoke of the child, that he had secured a large foothold in this respect, for it was very clear that Mrs. Beauchampe, while relating everything of any substantial importance which concerned herself, had evidently omitted that portion of the narrative which concerned the unhappy and short-lived offspring of her guilty error.

It does not need to inquire why she had forborne to include this particular in her statement to her husband.
There may have been some superior pang in the recollection of that gloomy period which had followed her fall; and
it was not necessary to the frank confession which she had
freely offered of her guilt.

But, though unimportant, Colonel Sharpe very well knew,
that there is a danger in the suppression of any fact, in a
case like this, where the relations are so nice and sensitive,
which is like to involve an appearance of guilt, and to lead
to its presumption. Like an experienced practitioner at
the sessions, he deemed it important to dwell upon this particular.

"I could have sworn!" he repeated, "that she had not
told you of that child. "Ah! my dear friend, spare me
the necessity of telling you what she has forborne. She is
now your wife. Her reputation is yours—her shame
would be yours also. Believe me, I repent of all I have
done—for your sake, for hers—believe me, moreover,
when I assure you that she mistook my language, when she
fancied that I meant indignity in what I said lately in your
house."

"But *I* could not mistake that, Colonel Sharpe."

"No! but did you hear it rightly reported?"

"Ay! she would not deceive me. You labor in vain.
This dirty work is easy with you; but it does not blind
me! Colonel Sharpe, what child is this that you speak
of?"

"Her child, to be sure!"

"Her child! Had she a child?"

"To be sure she had. Ask her: she will not deny it,
perhaps, and if she does, I can prove it."

"Her child!—and yours?"

"No—no! No child of mine!"

"Ha! not your child! Whose—whose then?"

"Go to her, my dear friend! Ask her of that child."

" Where is the child ?"

" Dead !"

" Dead ! well ! what of it then ?"

" Go to her—ask *her* whose it was?　Ah ! my dear Beauchampe, let *me* say no more.　Press me no further to speak.　She is *your* wife !"

The eye of Beauchampe settled upon him with a suddenly-composed but stony expression.

" Say *all !*" he said deliberately.　" Disburthen yourself of all ! I request it particularly, Colonel Sharpe—nay, I command it."

" My dear friend, Beauchampe, I really would prefer not —ah ! it is an ugly business."

" Do not trifle, Colonel Sharpe—speak—you do not help your purpose by this prevarication.　What do you know further of this child ?　It was not yours, you say— whose was it then ?"

" It was not mine ! and to say whose it was is scarce so easy a matter, but—" and he drew nigh and whispered the rest of the sentence, some three syllables, into the ears of the husband.

The latter recoiled.　His face grew black, his hand grasped the dagger with nervous rigidity, and, while the look of cunning confidence mantled the face of the criminal, and before he could recede from the fatal proximity to which, in whispering, he had brought himself with the avenger, the latter had struck.　The sharp edge of the dagger had answered the shocking secret—whatever might have been its character—and the terrible oath of the husband was redeemed !—redeemed in a single moment, and by a single blow.

The wrongs of Margaret Cooper were at last avenged !

But were her sorrows ended ?

How should they be ?　The hand that is stained with human blood, in whatever cause—the soul that has prompte the deed of blood—what waters shall make clean ?

"Vengeance is mine!" saith the Lord—meaning "mine only!" Wo, then, for the guilty soul that usurps this sublime privilege of Deity! It must bide a dreary destiny before the waters of heavenly mercy shall flow to cleanse and sweeten it. We may plead the madness of the criminals, and this alone may excuse what we are not permitted to justify. Certainly, they had been stung to madness. The very genius of Margaret Cooper made the transition to madness easy!

But—Colonel Sharpe fell, prone on his face, at the feet of the avenger!

A single blow had slain him!

CHAPTER XXXIV.

HUE AND CRY.

"Now that we have the food we so have longed for,
    Let us talk cheerily! We'll think of pleasures
    That never shall grow surfeit—of joys of Death,
    Whose reign wraps earth in its eternal grasp,
    And feeds eternity! Oh, we'll be joyful now!"—*Old Play.*

A MURDER in a novel, though of very common occurrence, is usually a matter of a thousand very thrilling minutiæ. In the hands of a score of our modern romancers, it is surprising what capital they make of it! How it runs through a score of chapters!—admits of a variety of details, descriptions, commentaries, and conjectures! Take any of the great *raconteurs* of the European world—not forgetting Dumas and Reynolds—and see what they will do with it! How they turn it over, and twist it about, as a sweet morsel under the tongue! In either of these hands, it becomes one of the most prolific sources of interest; which does not end with the knife or bludgeon stroke, or bullet-shot, but multiplies its relations the more it is conned, and will swallow up half the pages of an ordinary duodecimo. As they unfold the long train of consequences, in interminable recital, you are confounded at the dilating atmosphere of the deed; at the long accumulation of dreary details, the fact upon fact—whether of moment or value to the progress, or not, is not necessary to be asked here—which grows out of the crime on every hand. How it spreads, as the radiating circles in the water, from a pebble plunged

nto the axe. There you see the good old butler or porter
of the household, or it may be the cook or hostler—Saunders Maybin, or Richard Swopp, by name—going forth at
dawn, having been troubled during the night with sundry
uneasinesses, the consequence of a hearty supper of lobster
or salt cod, and suddenly encountering a blood-spot upon
the sward!

That mysterious blood-spot!—

At the sight of it, the said Saunders or Richard recoils,
puts his finger to his nose dubitatingly, shakes his noddle
s gnificantly, and mutters—quoting Shakspere without a
consciousness: "This is miching malico! It means mischief!"

And, so saying, he goes on nosing—all nose from that
moment—till he finds more *sign*, in the parlance of the
Indian, and is at length conducted, step by step, till he
stumbles over the lopped members of a human carcass jut-
ting out from a dunghill!

Nay, it may not be so easily found—may require some
circuitous turns of the nose before full discovery; and then
it may not be in a dunghill that it is hidden. It may be in
the bushes or in the sands; but no matter where: you shall
be a whole summer day in making the discovery, for our
authors will not suffer you to lose a single detail in the
progress; and, by the time the search is ended, it is to be
hoped that you will believe that your author as well as
conductor has a valuable nose!

But, whatever the particulars of search and discovery,
you must have 'em all; you will be bated not a hair, not
an item, not an atom: how many are the drops of blood;
ow large the puddle; whether first seen on grass or sand;
ow the body lies when found; what the shape and size of
the wound; whether by a sharp or rusty blade, smooth shil-
lelah or knotted hickory: there must be a regular inven-
tory! Such is equally crowner's quest and novelist's law!

And the "crowner's quest" itself—*that* is always an

inquisition of rare susceptibilities, and nice details and discriminations; amplifications of the old case of Ophelia, as to whether the woman went to the water, or the water went to the woman! The differences of vulgar opinion; the array of vulgar prejudices; the free use of legal technicalities; and a thousand other abominable little niceties, that ought to be gathered up at a grasp, all spread out to the utmost stretch — like the shirt of Cæsar — scored with bloody gashes, each having name and number! To crown all, and to render the "miching malico" more endurable and desirable, you are always sure to have some poor devil of an innocent in the way — just where he ought not to be — looking very much like the guilty one, and behaving with such pains-taking stupidity, that nobody doubts that he is; and he is accordingly laid by the heels, and clapped up in prison, to answer to the crime. The genius of the novelist then goes to work, in right good earnest, to see how he can be got out of the darbies! This is the notable way to relate such a history usually; and one might think it a tolerably good way, indeed, were it not that most people find it abominably tedious.

Having seen, for ourselves, how Sharpe was murdered, who was the murderer, and how the blow was struck, we shall not fatigue the reader in showing how many versions of the affair got abroad among those who were, of course, more and more positive in their conjectures in proportion to the small knowledge which they possessed. We make short a story which, long enough already, we apprehend, might, by an ingenious romancer, be made a great deal longer.

Suspicion fell instantly on Beauchampe. On whom else should it fall? He had announced his purpose to take the life of the criminal; and, wherever Sharpe's offence had got abroad, people expected that he would commit the deed.

In our country, a great many crimes are committed to gratify public expectation. Most of our duels are fought

15

to satisfy the demands of public opinion; by which is understood the opinions of that little set, batch, or clique, of which some long-nosed Solomon—some addle-pated leader of a score whose brains are thrice addled—is the sapient lawgiver and head. Most of the riots and mobs are instigated by half-witted journalists, who first goad the offender to his crime, and, the next day, rate him soundly for its commission! He who, in a fit of safe valor, the day before, taunted his neighbor with cowardice for submitting to an indignity, lifts up his holy hands with horror when he hears that the nose-pulling is avenged, and, as a conscientious juryman, hurries the wretch to the halter who has only followed his own suggestions in braining the assailant with his bludgeon! All this is certainly very amusing, and, with proper details, makes a murder-paragraph in the newspaper which delights the old ladies to as great an extent as a marriage does the young ones. It produces that pleasurable excitement which is the mental brandy and tobacco to all persons of the Anglo-Saxon breed—for both of which the appetite is tolerably equal in both Great Britain and America.

In the case of Beauchampe, the " Hue and Cry" knew, by a sort of conventional instinct, exactly in what quarter to turn its sagacious nostrils.

" It is Beauchampe that has done this!" was the common voice, as soon as the deed was known. And, by-the-way, when public expectation so certainly points to the true offender, it is highly probable that it gave the clue to the offence in the first instance. It said: " Do it!—it ought to be done!"

Beauchampe did not much concern himself about the " Hue and Cry," or even about that great authority " Public Opinion." He returned to his own dwelling; but not with the feet of fear—not even with those of flight. His journey homeward was marked with the deliberation of one who feels satisfied that he has performed a duty, the neglect of which had long been burdensome and painful to his conscience.

It is, of course, to be understood that he was laboring under a degree of excitement which makes it something like an absurdity to talk of conscience at all. The fanaticism which now governed his feelings, and had sprung from them, possessed his mind also. With the air of one who has gone through a solemn and severe ordeal, with the feeling of a martyr, he presented himself before his wife.

The deliberation of monomania is one of its most remarkable features. It is singularly exemplified by one portion of Beauchampe's proceedings. On leaving her to seek the interview with Sharpe, he had informed her, not only on what day, but at what hour, to look for his return; and he reached his dwelling within fifteen minutes of the appointed moment.

Anxiously expecting his arrival, she had walked down the grove to meet him. On seeing her, he raised his handkerchief, red with the bloody proofs of his crime, and waved it in the manner of a flag. She ran to meet him, and, as he leaped from his horse, she fell prostrate on her face before him. Her whole frame was convulsed, and she burst into a flood of tears.

"Why weep, why tremble?" he exclaimed. "Do you weep that the deed is done—the shame washed out in the blood of the criminal—that you are avenged at last?"

His accents were stern and reproachful. She lifted her hands and eyes to heaven as she replied:—

"No! not for this I weep and tremble; or, if for this, it is in gratitude to Heaven that has smiled upon the deed."

But, though she spoke this fearful language, she spoke not the true feeling of her soul. We have already striven to show that she no longer possessed those feelings which would have desired the performance of the deed. She no longer implored revenge. She strove to reject the memory of the murdered man, as well as of the wanton crime by which he had provoked his fate; and the emotion which she expressed, when she beheld the bloody signal waving from her husband's hands, had its birth in the revolting of that feminine nature which, even in her, after the long contemplation which had made her imagination familiar with the crime, was still in the ascendant. But this she concealed. This she denied, as we have seen. Her motive was a noble one. It is soon expressed :—

"He has done the deed for me — in my behalf! Shall I now refuse approbation? shall I withhold my sympathy? No! let his guilt be what it may, he is mine, and I am his, for ever!"

And, with this resolve, she smiled upon the murderer, kissed his bloody hands, and lifted her own to Heaven in seeming gratitude for its sanction of the crime.

But a new feeling was added to those which, however conflicting, her words and looks had just expressed. She rose from the ground in apprehension.

"But are you safe, my husband?" she demanded.

"What matters it?" he replied. "Has he not fallen beneath my arm?"

"Yes; but if you are not safe!—"

"I know not what degree of safety I need," was his reply. "I have thought but little of that. If you mean, however, to ask whether I am suspected or not, I tell you I believe I am. Nay, more — I think the pursuers are after me. They will probably be here this very night. But what of this, dear wife? I have no fears. My heart is light. I am really happy — never more so — since the deed is done. I could laugh, dance, sing — practise any mirth or madness — just as one, who has been relieved of his pain, throws by his crutch, and feels his limbs and strength free at last, after a bondage to disease for years."

And he caught her in his arms as he spoke, and his eye danced with a strange fire, which made the woman shudder to behold it. A cold tremor passed through her veins.

"Are you not happy too?—do you not share with me this joy?" he demanded.

"Oh, yes, to be sure I do!" she replied, with a husky apprehension in her voice, which, however, he did not seem to observe.

"I knew it—I knew you would be! Such a relief, ending in a triumph, should make us both so happy! I never was more joyful, my dear wife. Never! never!"—and he laughed—laughed until the woods resounded—and did not heed the paleness of her cheek; did not feel the faltering of her limbs as he clasped her to his breast; did not note the wildness in her eye as she looked stealthily backward on the path over which he came.

She, at least, was now fully in her senses, whatever she may have been before. She stopped him in his antics. She drew him suddenly aside, into the cover of the grove—for, by this time, they had come in sight of the dwelling—and, throwing herself on her knees, clasped his in her arms, while she implored his instant flight.

But he flatly refused, and she strove in vain, however earnestly, to change his determination. All that she could obtain from him was, a promise to keep silent, and not, by any act of his own, to facilitate the progress of those who might seek to discover the proofs of his criminality. Crime, indeed, he had long ceased to consider his performance. The change, in this respect, which had taken place in her feelings and opinions, had produced none in his. His mind had been wrought up to something like a religious frenzy. He regarded the action, not only as something due to justice—an action appointed for himself particularly—but as absolutely and intrinsically glorious.

Perhaps, indeed, such an act as his should always be estimated with reference to the sort of world in which the performer lives. What were those brave deeds of the middle ages - the avenging of the oppressed, the widow, and the orphan—by which stalwart chiefs made themselves famous? Crimes, too, and sometimes of the blackest sort, but that they had their value as benefits at a period when society afforded no redress for injury, and consequently no protection for innocence.

And what protection did society afford to Margaret Cooper, and what redress for injury? Talk of your action for damages—your five thousand dollars—and of what avail to such a woman, robbed of innocence; mocked, persecuted; followed to the last refuge of her life, the home of her mother and her husband: and, afterward, thrice-blackened in fame by the wanton criminal, by slanders of the most shocking invention!

Society never yet could succeed in protecting and redressing all its constituents, or any one of them, in all his or her relations. There are a thousand respects where the neighbors must step in; where, to await for law, or to hope for law, is to leave the feeble and the innocent to perish. You hear the cry of "Murder!" Do you stop, and resume your seat, with the comforting reflection that, if John murders Peter, John, after certain processes of evidence, will be sent to the stateprison or the gallows, and make a goodly show, on some gloomy Friday, for the curious of both sexes? Law is a very good thing in its way, but it is not everything; and there are some honest impulses, in every manly bosom, which are the best of all moral laws, as they are the most certainly *human* of all laws. Give us, say I, Kentucky practice, like that of Beauchampe, as a social law, rather than that which prevails in some of our pattern cities, where women are, in three fourths the number of instances, the victims—violated, mangled, murdered—where men are the criminals—and where (Heaven kindly having withdrawn the sense of shame) there is no one guilty—at least none brave enough or manly enough to bring the guilty to punishment! What is said is not meant to defend or encourage the shedding of blood. We may not defend the taking of life, even by the laws. We regard life as an express trust from Heaven, of which, as we should not divest ourselves, no act but that of Heaven should divest us: but there is a crime beyond it, in the shedding of that vital soul-blood, its heart of hearts, life of all life, the fair fame, the untainted reputation; and the one offence which provokes the other should be placed in the opposing balance, as an offset, in some degree. to the crime by which it is avenged.

CHAPTER XXXV.

THE DUNGEON.

WE could tell a long story about the manner in which Beauchampe was captured; but it will suffice to say that when the pursuers presented themselves at his threshold, he was ready, and with the high, confident spirit of one assured that all was right in his own own bosom, he yielded himself up at their summons, and attended them to Frankfort.

Behold him, then, in prison. The cold, gloomy walls are around him, and all is changed, of the sweet, social outer world, in the aspects which meet his eye.

But the woman of his heart is there with him; and if the thing that we love is left us, the dungeon has its sunshine, and the prison is still a home. The presence of the loved one hallows it into home. Amidst doubt, and privation—the restraint he endures, and the penal doom which he may yet have to suffer—her affection rises always above his affliction, and baffles the ills that would annoy, and soothes the restraint which is unavoidable. She has a consolation such as woman alone knows to administer, for the despondency that weighs upon him. She can soothe the dark hours with her song, and the weary ones with her caress and smile.

But not to ordinary appeals like these does the wife of *his* bosom confine her ministry. Her soul rises in strength corresponding to the demands of his. Ardent in his nature,

little used to restraint, the circumscribed boundary of his
prison grows irksome, at moments, beyond his temper to
endure. At such moments his heart fails him, and doubts
arise — shadows of the solemn truth which always haunt the
soul of the wrong-doer, however righteous to his diseased
mind may seem his deeds at the moment of their performance — doubts that distress him with the fear that he may
still have erred.

To the pure heart — to the conscientious spirit — there is
nothing more distressing than such a doubt; and this very
distress is the remorse which religion loves to inspire, when
it would promote the workings of repentance. It is a misplaced and mistaken kindness that the wife of Beauchampe
undertakes to fortify his faith, and strengthen him in the
conviction that all is right. We can not blame her, though
pity 'tis 'twas so. She no longer speaks — perhaps she no
longer thinks — of the deed which he has done, as an event
either to be deplored, or to have been avoided. She speaks
of it as a necessary misfortune. As she found that he derived his chief consolation from the conviction that the deed
was laudable, she toils, with deliberate ingenuity and industry, to confirm his impressions. Through the sad, slow-
pacing moments of the midnight, she sits beside him and
renews the long and cruel story of her wrong. She sup-
presses nothing *now*. That portion of the narrative relating
to the child, from her previous suppression of which, the
unhappy man whom he had slain, had striven to originate
certain doubts of her conduct, and to infuse them into the
mind of Beauchampe — was all freely told, and its previous
suppression explained and accounted for. The wife seemed
to take a singular and sad pleasure in reiterating this painful narrative; and yet, every repetition of the tale brought
to her spirit the pang, as keenly felt as ever, of her early
humiliation. But she saw that the renewal of the story
strengthened the feeling of self-justification in the mind of
her husband! That was the rock upon which he stood, and

15*

to confirm the solidity of that support, was to lighten the restraints of his prison, and all the terrors which might be inspired by the apprehension of his doom. Of the mere stroke of death, he had no fears ; but there is something in the idea of a felon death by the halter, which distresses and subjugates the strongest nerves. This idea sometimes came to afflict the prisoner, but the keen instincts of his wife enabled her very soon to discover the causes of his depression, and her quick, commanding intellect provided her with the arguments which were to combat them.

" Do not fear, my husband," she would say. " I know that they must acquit you. No jury of men—men who have wives, and daughters, and sisters, but must not only acquit you of crime, but must justify and applaud you for the performance of a deed which protects their innocence, and strikes terror into the heart of the seducer. You have not been my champion merely, you are the champion of my sex. The blow which your arm has struck, was a blow in behalf of every unprotected female, of every poor orphan — fatherless, brotherless, and undefended—who otherwise would be the prey of the ruffian and the betrayer. No, no! There can be no cause of fear. I do not fear for you. I will myself go into the court, and, if need be, plead your cause by telling the whole story of my wrong. They shall hear me. I will neither fear nor blush—and they shall believe me when they hear."

But to this course the husband objected. The heart of a man is more keenly alive to the declared shame of one he truly loves, than to the loss of life or of any other great sacrifice which the social man can make. Besides, Beauchampe knew better than his wife what would be permitted, and what denied, in the business of a court of justice. Still, it was necessary that steps should be taken for his defence. At first, he proposed to argue his own case ; but he was very soon conscious, after a few moments given to reflection on this subject, that his feelings would enter too largely into his mind to suffer it to do him or itself justice. While undetermined what course to pursue, or who to employ, his friend Covington suggested the name of Calvert, as that of a lawyer likely to do him more justice by far than any other that he could name.

"I know Colonel Calvert," said the young man, "and I can assure you he has no superior as a jury pleader in the country. He is very popular — makes friends wherever he goes, and is beginning to be accounted, everywhere, the only man who could have taken the field against Sharpe."

"But what was it that you told me of his fighting with Sharpe on my account!" was the inquiry of Beauchampe, now urged with a degree of curiosity which he had neither shown nor felt, when the fact was first mentioned to him.

"Of that I can tell you little. It is very well known that Sharpe and Calvert quarrelled and fought, almost at their first meeting. The friends of Sharpe asserted that the quarrel arose on account of offensive words which Calvert made use of in disparagement of Desha."

"Yes, I heard *that* — now I remember — from Barnabas himself."

"Such was the story; but Sharpe assured me that the affair really took place on account of Mrs. Beauchampe."

"Mrs. Beauchampe!" exclaimed the husband.

The wife, who was present, looked up inquiringly, but said nothing. Mr. Covington looked to the lady and remained silent, while, with a face suddenly flushed, Beauchampe motioned to his wife to leave them. When she had done so, Covington repeated what had been said by Sharpe concerning his duel with Calvert.

"It was only some lie of his, intended to help his evasion. It was to secure the temporary object. I never heard of Calvert from my wife."

Such was Beauchampe's opinion. But Covington thought otherwise.

"A rumor has reached me since," he added, "which

leads me to think that the story is not altogether without foundation. At all events, whether there be anything in it or not, Calvert will be your man for the defence. If anything is to be done, he will do it. But really, Beauchampe, if you have stated all the particulars, they can establish nothing against you."

"Ah! the general persuasion that I ought to kill Sharpe, will produce testimony enough. I think I shall escape, Covington, but it will be in spite of the testimony. I will escape, because of the sentiment of justice, which, in the breast of every honest man, will say, that Sharpe ought to die, and that no hand had a better right to take his life than mine. But you know the faction. They are strong—his friends and relatives are numerous. They will strain every nerve—spare no money, and suborn testimony enough to effect their object. They will fail, I think: I can scarcely say I hope, for, of a truth, my dear fellow, it seems to me that I have done the great act of my life. I feel as if I had performed the crowning achievement. I could do nothing more meritorious if I lived a thousand years; and death, therefore, would not be to me *now* such a misfortune as I should have regarded it a month ago. Still, life has something for me. I should like to live. The thought of losing *her*, is a worse pang than any that the mere loss of life could inflict."

The prisoner was touched as he said these words. A big tear gathered in his eye, and he averted his face from his companion. Covington rose to depart. As he did so he asked:—

"Shall I see Calvert for you, Beauchampe?"

"I will think of it, and let you know to-morrow," was the reply.

"The sooner the better. Your enemies are busy, and Calvert lives at some distance. He must be written to, and time may be lost, as he may be on the road now somewhere. I will look in upon you in the morning."

"**Do** so. I shall then be better able to say what should be done. I will think of it to-night: but, of a truth, Covington, I do not feel disposed to do anything. I prefer to remain inactive. For what should I say? Speak out? That would be against all legal notions of making a defence. And yet, I know no mode properly of defending myself, than by declaring the act my own, and justifying it as such. To myself — to my own soul — it is thus justified. God! — if it were not! But, in order to make this justification felt by the jury, they must know my secret. They must hear all that damning tale of *her* trial and over-throw, and the serpent-like progress of him whose head I have bruised for ever! How can *I* tell *that?* That is impossible!"

Covington agreed with the speaker. who proceeded thus:

"Well, then, I am silent. The general issue is one of form, pleading which I am not supposed to be guilty of any violation of the laws of morals — though what an absurdity is that! — I plead it, and keep silent. The *onus probandi* lies with the state—"

"And it can prove nothing, if your statement be correct."

"*Non sequitur*, my good fellow. My statement *is* correct. Nobody saw me commit the deed. The clothes which I wore are sunk to the bottom of the Kentucky river; the dirk is buried; and I know that, with the exception of the great Omniscient, my proceedings were hidden from the eyes of all. But it does not follow from this that there will be no evidence against me. I suspect there will be witnesses enough. The friends and family of Sharpe will suborn witnesses. There are hundreds of people, too, who readily believe what they fancy; and conjecture will make details fast enough, which the vanity of seeming to know will prompt the garrulous to deliver. I am convinced that vanity makes a great many witnesses, who will lie for the sake of having something to say, and will swear to the lie for the sake of having an audience who are compelled to

listen to them. With a little management, you can get
anything sworn to. You have heard of the philosopher
who, under a bet, with some previous arrangement, collected a crowd in the street to see certain stars at noonday,
which soon became visible to as many as looked. Some
few did not see so many stars as others, nor did they seem
to these so bright as to the rest; but all of them saw the
stars — they were there — that was enough; and some of
your big-mouthed observers booked a few incipient moons
or comets, and, of course, were more conspicuous themselves
in consequence of their conspicuous sight-seeing. If I have
any fear at all, it will be from some such quarter. The
friends of Sharpe have already turned upon me as the
criminal, and other eyes will follow theirs. Those who
know the crime of Sharpe, will conclude that the deed is
mine, from a conviction which all have felt that it should
be mine; and, not to look to the political manœuvrers for
interference, I make no question but they will find the very
dagger with which the deed was done — perhaps half-a-dozen
daggers — each of which will have its believer, and each
believer will be possessed of as many leading circumstances
to identify the murderer."

"I believe that they will try to convict you, Beauchampe,
but I can not think, with you, that witnesses are so easy to
be found."

"We shall see — we shall see."

"At all events, a good lawyer, who will probe such witnesses to the quick, will be the best security against their
frauds, whether these arise from vanity or malevolence;
and I can not too earnestly recommend you to let me see
or write to Calvert."

"On that point I will give you my answer hereafter,"
said Beauchampe evasively.

"In the morning," suggested the other.

"Ay, perhaps so: at least, Covington, let me see you then."

The other promised, and, taking a kind farewell, departed. When he had gone, the wife of Beauchampe reappeared, and, with some earnestness of manner, he directed her to sit beside him upon his pallet.

"Anna," said he, "you never told me anything of a Mr. Calvert. Do you know any such person, and how are you interested in him?"

"I know but one person of the name—an old gentleman who taught school at Charlemont. But I have neither seen nor heard of him for years."

"An old gentleman! How old?"

"Perhaps sixty or sixty-five."

"Not the same! But, perhaps, he had a son? Now, I remember, that, when I went to Bowling-Green, there was an old gentleman, with a very white head, who seemed intimate with Colonel Calvert."

"He had no son—none, at least, that I ever saw."

"It is strange!"

"What is strange, Beauchampe?" she asked.

He then told her all that he had learned from Covington. She concurred with him that it was strange, if true; but declared her belief that the story was an invention of Sharpe, by which he hoped to effect some object which he might fancy favorable to his safety.

"But, at all events, husband, employ this Colonel Calvert, of whom Mr. Covington and the public seem to think so highly. You have spoken very highly of him yourself"

"Yes," was the reply; "but somehow, Anna, I am loath to do anything in my defence. I hate to seek evasion from the dangers of an act which I performed deliberately, and would again perform, were it again necessary."

"But this is a strange prejudice, surely, Beauchampe. Why should you not defend yourself?"

"I would, my wife, if defence, in this case, implied justification."

"And does it not?" demanded the wife anxiously.

"No, nothing like it. It implies evasion—the suppres-

sion of the truth, if not the suggestion of the falsehood.
You are no lawyer, Anna.   The truth would condemn me."

"What! the *whole* truth!"

"No—perhaps not; but it would be difficult to get the
whole truth before a jury: and, even if this could be done,
could I do it?"

"And why not, my husband?" she demanded earnestly,
approaching him at the same moment, and laying her hand
impressively upon his shoulder, while her eyes were fixed
upon his own—

"And why not?   The day of shame—shame from this
cause—has gone by from us.   We are either above or below the world.   At least, we depend not for the heart's
sustenance upon it.   Suppose it scorns and reviles us—
suppose it points to me as the miserable victim of that
viperous lust which crawled into our valleys with a glozing
tongue—I, that know how little I was the slave of that foul
passion, in my own breast, will not madden, more than I
have done, at its contumelious judgment.   They can not
call me harlot.   No, Beauchampe! I fell; I was trampled
in the dust of shame; I was guilty of weakness, and vanity,
and wilfulness; but, believe me, if ever spirit felt the remorse and the ignominy which belong to virtuous repentance of error, that spirit was mine!"

"I know it—do I not know it, dearest?" he said, tenderly taking her in his arms.

"I believe you know and feel it; and this conviction,
Beauchampe, strengthens me against the world.   In your
judgment I fixed my proper safety for the future.   Let the
world know all—the whole truth—if that will anything
avail for your justification.   Let them speak of me hereafter as they please.   Secure in myself—secure from the
self-reproach of having fallen a victim to the harlot-appe-
tite (though the victim to my own miserable vanity and
folly)—doubly secure in your conviction of the truth of
what I say, and am—I can smile at all that follows: I can

do more, Beauchampe—endure it with patience and fortitude, and without distressing you or myself with the langage of complaint. Do not, therefore, dear Beauchampe, refuse the justification which the truth may bring, through any wish to save me from the further exposure. Hear me, when I assure you, solemnly, in this solemn midnight— with no eye upon us in this cold, gloomy dungeon, but that of Heaven—hear me solemnly affirm that though you should resolve to spare me, I will not spare myself. If need be, I will go into the courthouse—before the assembled judges, before the people—and with my own tongue declare the story of my shame. Base should I be, indeed, if, to save these cheeks from the scarlet which would follow such a recital, I could see them hale you to the ignominious gallows!"

" And sooner would I die a thousand deaths on that gallows, than suffer you to do yourself such cruel wrong!"

Such was the answer spoken with effort, with husky accents, which the criminal made to the strong-minded woman, whose high-souled, and seemingly unnatural resolution— however opposed to his—yet touched him really as a proof of the most genuine devotion. He did not say more ; he did not offer to dispute a resolution which he well knew he could not overthrow ; but he determined, inly, to practise some becoming artifice, to deprive her, when the crisis of his fate was at hand, of any opportunity of meddling in its progress.

Thus the night waned—the long, dark night, in that gloomy dungeon. Not altogether gloomy! Devotion makes light in the dark places. Love cheers the solitude with its own pure star-lighted countenance. Sincerity wins us from the contemplation of the darkness ; and with the sweet word of the truthful comforter in our ear, the fever subsides from the throbbing temples, and the downcast heart is lifted into hope. That night, and every night, she shared with him his dungeon !

CHAPTER XXXVI.

DIFFERENT PHILOSOPHIES OF LOVE.

THE arguments of Covington, to persuade Beauchampe to employ the services of Calvert, were unavailing. He, at length, gave it up in despair. The very suggestion which Sharpe had made, that Calvert had some knowledge already of the wife's character, and that the duel between himself and Calvert had originated in the knowledge of his wrong to her—however curious it made Beauchampe to learn what relation the latter could have had to his wife—was also a cause, why, in the general soreness of his feelings on this subject, he should studiously avoid the professional assistance of the other. The wife, when Covington took his departure, renewed the attempt. The arguments of the latter had been more imposing to her mind than they were to that of the husband; but, repeated by her, they did not prove a jot more successful that when urged by Covington. To these she added suggestions of her own, a sample of which we have seen in a previous chapter; but the prisoner remained stubborn. The wife at length ceased to persuade, having, with the quick perception and nice judgment which distinguished her character, observed the true point of difficulty—one not to be easily overcome—and which was to be assailed in a manner much more indirect. She resolved to engage the services of Calvert herself.

Her own curiosity had been raised in some degree by what she had heard in respect to this person; and though she did not believe the story which Covington got from Sharpe, touching the causes of the duel between himself and rival, yet the fact that they had fought, and that Calvert had been wounded in the conflict with her enemy, of itself commended the former to her regard. As the period for her husband's trial drew nigh, her anxieties naturally increased, so as to strengthen her in the resolution which she had already formed to secure those legal services which Beauchampe had rejected. Accordingly, concealing her purpose she absented herself from the prison, and, having secured the necessary information, set forth on her mission.

Of the prosperous fortunes of William Calvert, some glimpses have already been given to the reader in the course of this narrative. These glimpses, we trust, have sufficed to satisfy any curiosity, which the story of his youth and youthful disappointments might have occasioned in any mind. We understand, of course, that thrown upon his own resources, driven from the maternal petticoats, which enfeeble and destroy so many thousand sons, the necessities to which he was subjected, in the rough attrition of the world, had brought into active exercise all the materials of his physical and intellectual manhood. He had plodded over the dusky volumes of the law with unrelaxing diligence. He had gone through his probationary period without falling into any of those emasculating practices which too often enslave the moral sense and dissipate the intellectual courage of young men. He had graduated with credit; had begun practice with an unusual quantity of business patronage, and had made his debût with a degree of eclât, which, while it put to rest all the apprehensions of the good old man who had adopted him, had effectually recommended him to the public, as one of the strong men to whom they could turn with confidence, to represent the characteristics and maintain the rights of the people.

Of his success, some idea may be formed, if we remember the position in which he stood in the conflict with Colonel

Sharpe. If the latter was the Coryphæus of one party,
William Calvert was regarded by all eyes as the most
prominent champion of the other; and though the other
party might be in the minority, it was not the less obvious
to most, that, if the success of the party could be made entirely to depend upon the relative strength of the representative combatants, the result would have been very far
otherwise. The best friends of Sharpe, as we have already
seen, endeavored to press upon him the belief, which they
really felt, that, with such an opponent as William Calvert
in the field against him, it would require the exercise of
his very best talents in order to maintain his ground. We
need not dwell longer on this part of our subject.

But, with the prominence of position, taken of necessity
by William Calvert, in the political world, was an accumulation of legal business which necessarily promised fortune.
In the brief space of three years which followed his admission to the bar, his clients became so numerous as to render it necessary that he should concentrate his attentions
upon a more limited circuit of practice. Other effects followed, and the good old man whose name he had taken,
leaving Charlemont, like his protégé, for ever, had come to
live with him in the flourishing town where he had taken
up his abode. Here their united funds enabled them to buy
a fine house and furnish it with a taste which, day by day,
added some object of ornament or use.

The comforts being duly considered, the graces were necessarily secured, as the accumulation of means furnished
the necessary resources. Books grew upon the already-
groaning shelves; sweet landscapes and noble portraits
glowed from the walls. With no wife to provide, in those
thousand trifles for which no funds would be altogether
adequate, in the shocking and offensive style of expendi-
ture which has recently covered our land with sores and
spangles, shame and frippery — the income of William Calvert was devoted to the cultivation of such tastes as are

legitimate in the eyes of a truly philosophical judgment.
He sought for no attractions but such as gave employment
either to the sense of beauty or the growth of the under
standing.

The contemplation of the forms of beauty produces in the
mind a love of harmony and proportion, which, in turn, establish a nice moral sense, that revolts with loathing at
what is mean, coarse, or brutal; and, with this impression,
our young lawyer, whenever his purse permitted such out-
lay, despatched his commission to the Atlantic city for the
speaking canvass or the eloquent and breathing bust. In
tastes like these his paternal friend fully sympathized with
him. In fact they had been first awakened in him by his
venerable tutor, during the course of his boyish education.
Thus co-operating, and with habits, which, in other respects, were singularly inexpensive, it is not surprising that
the dwelling of William Calvert should already be known,
among the people of ——, as the very seat of elegance and
art. His pictures formed a theme among his acquaintance
—and even those who were not—which every new addition contributed to revive and enlarge; and, in the innocent pursuit of such objects of grace and beauty—with
books, the philosophies and songs, of the old divines of Nature—her proper priesthood—the days of the youth began
to go by sweetly and with such soothing, that the memory
of Margaret Cooper, though it never ceased to sadden, yet
now failed entirely to sting. He had neither ceased to
love nor to regret; but his disappointment did not now occasion a pang, nor was his regret such as to leave him insensible to the genial influences which life everywhere
spreads generously around for the working spirit, and the
just and gentle heart.

But, as we have seen, William Calvert was not permitted, either by his own nature and pursuits, or by the exactions of society, to indulge simply in the elegancies of life.
The possession of active talents of any kind, and in all

regions, implies a proper impulse to their use. This is more particularly the case in our country, where the field is more free than in all others, more open to all comers, and where the absence of hereditary distinctions and a prescriptive social *prestige* compels ambition to strain every nerve in the attainment of position.

The profession of the law itself implies government among us, and politics are apt to lay their talons upon all who exhibit the possession of oratorical powers in connection with the pursuit of law. William Calvert, somewhat in spite of his own tastes and wishes—for he well knew how slavish and degrading were the conditions of public favor in a democracy like ours—was forced to buckle on the armor of party, and take the field in a great local contest, which contemplated federal as well as state politics.

We have seen how suddenly his career was arrested and suspended for a season, by the bullet, at five paces, of his political rival.

His wound—probable owing to the bold course adopted by his venerable counsellor—was not a serious one, though it laid him up for a space, during which his party was defeated; a result which many of its able men were pleased to ascribe mostly to the fact that their chief speaker was thus *hors de combat*. This conviction strengthened his claims in the future, though the immediate battle was lost in which he had been engaged at the time. The defeat was temporary only—that they all felt; and all parties were equally persuaded that the next struggle must eventuate in the elevation of William Calvert to the full supremacy over his own.

The brief period during which he was confined to his chamber by his hurt was one which was crowded with ample testimonies of his popularity with the many, and the grateful esteem with which he was regarded by the select and sacred few. The sturdy yeomen thronged to inquire about his progress with an interest which showed how deeply he had made his way into the common heart. Nor were the men of mark less earnest and considerate — less solicitous of the fate of one who, as a dangerous rival, must either be denounced or conciliated. Higher and more honorable motives were at work, however, in the breasts of others — too far above the crowd to suffer such as these to abridge their sympathies; and the bedside of our young lawyer was honored by the visits of such great men as Clay and Crittenden. His wound, though rendering his thigh a somewhat sore precinct for a while, was yet productive of much balm and soothing for his mind and heart.

But there was one visiter, over all, whose unexpected presence was eminently grateful, bringing with it not only a true devotion and a genuine sympathy, but recalling so many dear and pleasant passages in a past of various sad and sweet experiences. As soon as his cousin Ned Hinkley heard of his disaster, he hastened off to see and tend upon him, bringing with him nothing but a carpet-bag, with a few changes of linen, his violin, and a pair of pistols, consecrated in the family affections by a grandsire's use of them in Revolutionary periods.

Ned Hinkley, though a good fellow, was inveterate as a violinist. Ned relieved the violin by occasional practice with the pistols. Ned's boast was that he could draw an equally good sight and bow; and Ned was especially anxious to take up the game with Colonel Sharpe — to whom he owed an old grudge as Alfred Stevens — just where his cousin had ended it. Ned's conscience troubled him, too, as being somewhat the occasion of William's present sufferings, as he felt and said, very logically :—

"For you see, Willie, if I had shot that fellow Stevens, five years ago, as I ought to have done, he wouldn't have been able to put an ounce bullet into your bacon!"

It was no fault of Ned, we assure you, that he did not shoot Stevens. He had every disposition to do that oily politician some such touching service.

Ned Hinkley was a good companion. He was lively, garrulous, full of quip and crank; could make his fiddle speak when his own tongue was tired; was a very loving kinsman, and no humbug. He was as sincere as sunshine.

He was soon installed beside the couch of the wounded man, relieving old Mr. Calvert of his watch, and sharing with him the grateful employment of amusing the invalid, which he did after a fashion of his own. We give a sample of his quality in this sort of performance :—

" And how does it feel, Willie ?"

" How does what feel ?"

" Why, the bullet in your hip."

" There is no bullet there now, Ned. It is extracted."

" Well, I know that! What I mean to ask is, what is the sort of sensation which it leaves behind it? Rather a pleasant one, I suppose !"

" Indeed ! a curious supposition, Ned."

" Not so ! In small wounds, such is the case usually when they are in a way to heal. I have so found it in my own case. When I was getting better of that ugly gash I got at muster six years ago—you remember—from Ralph Byers, I was really delighted by the sensation. There was a sort of pleasant tickling going on all the time, as Nature was taking up the old threads and reuniting them. So, when I shot off that finger, trying Tom Curtis's little double barrel—after the first pain of the thing was over, I began to feel a sort of pleasure in the sensation; and I suppose there's good reason for it. Nature, as a matter of course, like a good surgeon, will do her best to soothe one's hurts on such an occasion, by some secret remedial processes of er own. The fact is, I always found so much pleasure in etting well on such occasions, that I found myself always pulling and picking at the wound, just to keep up a sort of irritation, so as to prolong the duration of the cure."

" Comical ! On the same plan, if you found a medicine, however nauseous, doing its work effectually, you will re quire that the dose should be doubled, and take some of the physic daily, with the same object—the prolongation of the benefit."

"Not so—no! The analogy fails, Willie. The skin, or flesh, is one thing; but the stomach is another—quite. No tampering with that! It is sacred to fish, flesh, fowl, and physic is its abomination. I don't believe in physic, though I do in the pleasure of flesh-wounds."

The tuning of the fiddle followed this philosophy; and, under the sedative influences of an original fantasia which might have afforded some new ideas to Ole Bull, William Calvert sank off into a pleasant slumber, leaving Ned in the midst of a backwoods commentary on the nature, the sources, and the methods of music, particularly of violin-music, which he held to be the proper foundation of every other sort.

Ned Hinkley thus, alternating between his sister's farm-stead and the house of his cousin—the two places being some twelve miles apart—continued to visit and console William Calvert through the month of his confinement.

And this was no small sacrifice on the part of Ned, when we are told that, in addition to the fatigue of such a ride some three or four times a week, he was busily engaged in all the rigors of a warm courtship. Of course, he told his cousin the whole history of his wooing.

"Well—but, Ned, how is it that you have forborne all description of Miss Bernard?"

"Sallie Bernard is indescribable, Willie."

"What! so very beautiful?"

"No! I don't think that even a lover would call her beautiful."

"Is she so wise, then—so highly endowed with intellect, and the graces and accomplishments?"

"No, I can t say that either! The fact is, Willie, that Sallie is nothing more than a clever country-girl—a good girl, a loving girl, a gentle girl, and a willing girl—and

16

that word *willing* goes a great ways with me in a woman.
I don't go for wisdom, and learning, and great talents, and
great beauties, and charms, and graces, in a wife, Willie;
I go for a woman—a true woman—that knows she's the
weaker vessel, and knows what's due to her lord and master.　I am after a wife, not a philosopher in petticoats.　I
want a wife who will be the mother of my children; not a
conceited fool, who is perpetually trying to show the world
that she is more of a man than her husband, as is the case
generally with all that sort of people, of whom your famous
Margaret Cooper was a particularly superb brimstone example."

"Nothing of *her*, Ned," said the other sadly.　"Tell me
of your Sallie Bernard."

"Well, perhaps I'd better tell you in poetry.　You know
that I too have written verses, and was no small fish at it,
as you remember.　I am half disposed to think that my
verses were sometimes quite as good as yours.　You remember the lines I wrote upon the old mill at Charlemont?"

"Yes: they were really very good, Ned."

"To be sure they were!　I doubt if you could do better,
try your best.　Then there was the epitaph I made on poor
old Wolf, my bull-terrier.　'Gad!　I liked it better than
Lord Byron's on his Newfoundland pup.　But I've done
better things since, that I never showed you; and some of
my lines about Sallie are, to my thinking, quite good enough
to be put into a magazine."

"Very likely, Ned—and yet not make you sure of cedar-
oil immortality.　But let's have your metrical portrait of
Miss Sallie."

"You shall!　I'm not squeamish about it; and these
verses are just about the proper answer to your question.
They tell you just why I love Sallie, and for what a man
ought to seek a wife.　They're rough yet, for I haven't had
time to pass the smoothing-iron over them.　But I'll work

'em out in ship-shape yet, and make a spiggot or spoil a horn. Now, don't you begin to find fault, and stop me, whenever you fancy there's a hitch in the verse. I'll bring it all right when I turn in to smoothing out."

William Calvert gave the required assurance; and, with few more preliminaries — for Ned Hinkley was a downright, to-the-purpose, matter-of-fact fellow — with little nonsense or conceit about him, and no affectations — he recited, or rather chanted, the following rude ballad, which, for the backwoods muse, Calvert was inclined to think a very creditable performance; and we quite agree with him, and could wish to see it married to corresponding harmonies by some such priest in music as Mr. Russell:—

I.

"You ask me why I love her —
   Why my heart, no longer free,
Is no more a wingéd rover,
   Like the forest-bird or bee:
Ah! love still hath its season,
   For the heart as for the tree;
Would you have a better reason,
   Then my love loves me!
      I know it well, I know it —
      My love loves me!

II.

"You say she is not beautiful,
   And it may be so to you;
But she's very fond and dutiful,
   And she's very kind and true:
And there's beauty in the tenderness
   That every eye can see,
And something more than loveliness
   In the love she feels for me!
      I know it well, &c.

III.

"She's no strong-minded woman,
   And in weighty things unwise;
But a loving heart, all human,
   Is to me a dearer prize:

And there's a sovereign wisdom
　In much loving, do you see;
And a pure young soul, in a loving breast,
　Makes a woman wise for me!
　　I know it well, &c.

IV.

"You may talk of stately damsels,
　With keen wit and manners fine —
But a true young heart's affections
　Are the jewels dear to mine!
And I own enough of splendor,
　When her loving eyes I see;
And I hear sufficient wisdom,
　When she murmurs love to me!
　　I know it well, &c.

V.

"You may try her faith, and tell her
　Of a prouder suitor still —
One whose name and wealth may bring her
　To whatever state she will;
That I've naught to boast of power —
　Neither wealth nor fame — yet she
Will smile — so well I know her —
　And still give her love to me!
　　I know it well, &c."

"There — you have it! Now, that's what I call good sense, Willie Calvert, and no bad poetry either."

"It is positively beautiful, Ned, and contains more of the true philosophy of love and marriage than half the treatises ever written. Positively, Ned, you surprise me! Your improvement is prodigious. You must set up the poetical sign. Were you, now, in some of the great cities, following up some of the popular singers, you could have that ballad united to music which would make your name famous."

"I thought you'd like it, Willie — I knew you would. It is a good ballad, Willie — very good; and it's true, Willie. Sallie Bernard deserves it all. She's the very woman of the verses."

" And she has accepted you, Ned ?"

" On the fifteenth day of the very next November, Willie, we go into cohoot for life—-God willing, and weather permitting."

William Calvert warmly congratulated his kinsman, and closed the speech with a deep sigh from the very bottom of his heart.

" Don't sigh, William.   Your time will come yet.   Ah! if you had only fancied some such true, sweet, humble-hearted, and devoted girl as Sallie, instead of that proud, great-eyed, outlawed woman, Margaret Cooper—"

" Hush, hush, Ned!—name her not!"

The other muttered something more, no doubt expressive of the indignation which he felt at the treatment his cousin had received from Margaret Cooper.   The good fellow had never admired that damsel.   He was, in truth, afraid of her.   She was the only person that had ever fairly awed him into distance and apprehension.   While he still muttered, William Calvert said :—

" Open that desk, Ned, and hand me the book in a blue cover which you will find in it."

This was done.

" I, too, have written some verses lately, Ned, which somewhat relate to my own affections.   They are, by no means, so good as yours, but they will enforce my plea to you for forbearance in reference to Margaret."

And, without further word, William read the following apostrophe :—

> " Speak not the name, in scorn or blame,
>   Nor link her thought with aught of shame,
>   Nor ask of me, the guilt to see
>   That tore my blossom from the tree !

> " We may not crush the thought, or hush
>   The tale that still compels the blush ;
>   But we may chide the speech, and hide
>   The shame, that else would torture pride !

"Deep in the heart, a thing apart,
    We shrine the memory of the smart;
    And only gaze on happier days,
    When Love and Pride could gladly praise.

"There let me hold, nor cheap nor cold,
    The image shrined I loved of old;
    There let me know the charm, the glow,
    And not the shame, the guilt, the wo!

"Beneath that spell, still let her dwell,
    Pure, bright, as when I loved so well —
    Where, haply taught, the older thought
    Can see of fall or frailty naught.

"With Love for guest, the faithful breast
    Shuts out all entrance to the rest,
    And asks no more, from Memory's store,
    Than what the heart can still adore.

"Oh! when she grew, no more in view,
    The starlike thing that once I knew,
    I deemed her fled, I wept her dead —
    Not frail, not shamed, but lost instead.

"Her fall, though fraught with grief, has taught
    Love's lesson to the sterner thought;
    And Grief's worst moan now takes its tone
    From what young Memories loved alone!"

" Ah! Willie, that's a poetical huckleberry above my
sour rhyming persimmon. How well you do those things!
Why, that's a sort of treble-shotted verse. Now, those
cursed rhymes won't come to me when I call for 'em!—
They are as obstinate as those abominable spirits of ' the
vasty deep' that turned a deaf ear to Mr. Glendower. You
must help me, Willie, to polish my ballad, before I send it
to Sallie Bernard."

" Don't touch it, Ned; it needs no polishing. It is as
nearly perfect as you can make it. Its very carelessness
is in its favor as a song. It shows it to be an outpouring,
a gushing upward, of the fancy, which is the true proof of
a good thing for music. No, no! don't touch it. Its sim-

plicity is its secret.   One sees that the art has been entirely
subservient to Nature, as it always should be in such things.
But, go and ramble now, Ned, and leave me for a while to
slumber.   Your talk and my own, with such subjects as we
have been dealing with, have left me a little too much excited.   Go, and write to Sallie."

"'Gad! if she were here!" cried the tall fellow, stretch-
ing out his arms as if to embrace the universe—

"If she were only here—smack!"   And, so saying, he
disappeared.

CHAPTER XXXVII.

THE MEETING.

> " And do we meet again,
> After that mournful parting !   Both how changed ;
> You with new pinions — mine all soiled and broken !"

It was when William Calvert had regained his legs and
began to resume his customary vocations, that Ned Hinkley suddenly made his appearance, one day, almost bursting
with excitement.   The story of the Beauchampes had
reached his ears ; the marriage of Margaret Cooper with
Beauchampe, and the subsequent murder of Colonel Sharpe.
He was the first to reveal the whole tragedy to the Calverts.

It was a story to make them gloomy enough — to strike
them into silence.   When they could speak of the subject,
it was only in language so inadequate that the topic was
dropped as by mutual consent.

" Can we do anything for them ?" was the question of
William Calvert.

It was one which all parties strove to answer but in
vain.

Ned Hinkley alone lingered over the subject.

" It was her doings, all.   She, no doubt, beguiled the
young fool into marriage.   She prompted him to avenge
her dishonor on the head of Sharpe.   I would have done it
myself, with half an opportunity, but I would have shot myself sooner than received the reward."

William Calvert rebuked the speech in his sternest manner, and Ned Hinkley rode off, happy in the prospect of a wife who was not a strong-minded woman. He left the two Calverts to brood together over the melancholy narrative which they had heard.

We have already formed a sufficient idea of the dwelling which William Calvert occupied—a dwelling in just correspondence with his improved fortunes. The reader will please go with us while we re-enter it. Ned Hinkley has been gone some two hours. We ascend the neat and always well-swept porch, and pass through the common hall into the parlor. It has now but a single occupant. Old Calvert is there alone. His adopted son has retired to his chamber. He broods alone on the fate of Margaret Cooper, and of the wretched young man to whom she has been a fate. The old man broods also, sadly too on the same subject, but he is so happy in his own protégé, that his mind does not yield itself with any intensity, to the case of other parties, no matter what their futures. And this is a law of our nature, else we should suffer unprofitably from those afflictions, to which we can offer no relief.

Old Calvert has become older since we last painted his portrait. His hair has grown even more silvery and thin and his forehead whiter, more capacious, more polished. In other respects, however, he seems to have undergone but little change. His skin is quite as smooth as ever; but little wrinkled; the crows have not trampled very vigorously about the corners of his eyes. His heart is comparatively at ease; his eye is bright as of old—nay, even brighter than when we last saw it dilating over the valley of Charlemont: and, perhaps, with reason. His warmest hopes have been gratified; his worst doubts dissipated; his neart has become uplifted. He has realized the pride of a father without suffering the trials and apprehensions of one; and with heart and body equally in health, he is still young

for a gentle spirit in age, is not a bad beginning of the

16*

soul's immortality. He owes this state of mind and body,
to a contemplative habit acquired in youth; to the presence
of a nice governing sense of justice, and to that abstinence
which would have justified in him the brag of good old
Adam, in "As You Like It:"—

> "For in my youth I never did apply
> Hot and rebellious liquors in my blood;
> Nor did not, with unbashful forehead woo,
> The means of weakness and debility;
> Therefore my age is as a lusty winter,
> Frosty but kindly."

The old man sits in the snug, well-cushioned armchair,
with his eyes cast upward. A smile mantles upon his face.
His glance rests upon a portrait of his favorite; and as he
gazes upon the well-limned and justly-drawn features—and
as the mild and speaking eye seems to answer to his own
—the unconscious words tremble out from his lips! Good
old man!—he recalls the early lessons that he gave the
boy; how kindly they were taken—with what readiness
they were acquired; and the sweet humility which followed
most of his rebukes. Then, he renews the story of the first
lessons in law—his own struggles and defeats he recalls—
only, as it would seem, to justify the exultation which an-
nounces, under *his* guidance, the better fortunes of the
youth.

And thus soliloquizing, he rises, and mounting a chair,
dusts the picture with his handkerchief, with a solicitude that
has seen a speck upon the cheek, and fancies a fly upon the
hair! This was a daily task, performed unconsciously, and
under the same course of spiriting!

While thus engaged a servant enters and speaks. He
answers, but without any thought of what he is saying.
The servant disappears, and the door is re-opened. The
old man is still busy at the heart-prompted duty. His lips
are equally busy in dilating upon the merits of his favorite.
He still wipes and rewipes the picture; draws back to ex

amine the outline; comments upon eye and forehead; and dreams not, the while, what eye surveys his toils — what ear is listening to the garrulous eulogium that is dropping from his lips. The intruder is Margaret Cooper — Mrs. Beauchampe we should have said — but for a silent preference for the former name, for which we can give no reason and will offer no excuse.

She stands in silence — she watches the labor of the good old man with mixed but not unpleasant feelings. She recognises him at a glance. She does not mistake the features of that portrait which exacts his care. She gazes on that, too, with a very melancholy interest. The features, though the same, are yet those of another. The expression of the face is spiritualized and lifted. It is the face of William Hinkley — true — but not the face of the rustic, whom once she knew beneath that name. The salient points of feature are subdued. The roughness has disappeared, and is succeeded by the entreating sweetness and placid self-subjection which shows that the moulding hand of the higher civilization has been there. It is William Hinkley, the gentleman — the man of thought, and of the world — whose features meet her eye; and a sigh involuntarily escapes her lips. That sigh is the involuntary utterance of the self-reproach which she feels. Her conscience smites her for the past. She thinks of the young man, worthy and gentle, whom she slighted for another — and that other! — She remembers the youth's goodness — his fond devotedness; and, forgetting in what respect he erred, she wonders at herself, with feelings of increasing humiliation, that she should have repulsed and treated him so harshly. But, in those days she was mad! It is her only consolation that she now thinks so.

Her sigh arrests the attention of the old man and awakens him from his grateful abstraction. He turns, beholds the lady, and muttering something apologetically, about the rapid accumulation of dust and cobwebs, he de-

scends from the chair. A step nearer to the visiter informs
him who she is. He starts, and trembles.

"You, Miss Cooper: can it be?"

"It is, Mr. Calvert; but there is some mistake. I
sought for Colonel Calvert, the lawyer."

"My son—no mistake at all—be seated, Miss Cooper."

"Your son, Mr. Calvert?"

"Yes, my son—your old acquaintance—but here he
is!"—

William Calvert, the younger, had now joined the party.
His entrance had been unobserved. He stood in the doorway—his eye fixed upon the object of his former passion.
His cheeks were very pale; his features were full of emotion. Margaret turned as the old man spoke, and their
eyes encountered. What were their several emotions then?
Who shall tell them? What scenes, what a story, did that
one single glance of recognition recall. How much strife
and bitterness—what overwhelming passions—and what
defeat, what shame, and sorrow to the one; and to the
other—what triumph over pain—what victory even from
defeat. To her, from pride, exultation, and estimated triumph, had arisen shame, overthrow, and certain fear.
Despair was not yet—not altogether. To the other, "out
of the eater came forth meat, and out of the strong came
forth sweetness." From his defeat he was strengthened;
and from the very overthrow of his youthful passion, had
grown the vigor of his manhood.

The thought of William Calvert, as he surveyed the
woman of his first love, was a natural one: "Had she
been mine!"—but with this thought he did not now repine
at the baffled dream and desire of his boyhood. If the
memory and reflection were not sweet, at least the bitter
was one to which his lips had become reconciled by time.
Recalling the mournful memory of the past, his sorrow was
now rather for her than for himself. His regret was not
that he had been denied. but that she had fallen. He rec-

ollected the day of her pride. He recalled the flashes of
that eagle spirit, which, while it won his admiration, had
spurned his prayer. The bitter shame which followed,
when, by crawling, the serpent had reached the summits
where her proud soul kept in an eyry of its own, oppressed
his soul as he gazed upon the still beautiful, still majestic
being before him. She too had kept something of that noble spirit which was hers before she fell. We have seen
how she had sustained herself: —

> " Not yet lost
> All her original brightness, nor appeared
> Less than archangel ruined, and th' *excess*
> Of glory obscured ;"—

and still, as the youth gazed, he wondered — and as he re
membered, he could not easily restrain the impulse once
more to sink in homage. But all her story was now known
to him. Of Sharpe's murder he was aware ; and that the
wife of the murderer was the same Margaret Cooper, in
whose behalf he had himself met the betrayer in single combat, he was apprized by a private letter from Covington.

While he thus stood beholding, with such evident tokens
of emotion, the hapless woman who had been the cause,
and the victim, equally, of so much disaster — what were
her reflections at the sight of him? At first, when their
eyes encountered, and she could no longer doubt the identity of the Colonel Calvert whom she sought, with the William Hinkley whom she had so long and yet so little known,
her color became heightened — her form insensibly rose,
and her eye resumed something of that ancient eagle-look
of defiance, which was the more natural expression of her
proud and daring character. She felt, in an instant, all the
difference between the present and the past; between his
fortune and her own — and, naturally assuming that the
same comparison was going on in his mind, necessarily
leading to his exaltation at her expense, she was prepared,

with equal look and word, to resent the insolence of his triumph.

But when, at a second glance, she beheld the unequivocal grief which his looks expressed — when she saw still, that the fire in his heart had not been quenched — that the feeling there had nothing in it of triumph — but all of a deep abiding sorrow and a genuine commiseration, her manner changed — the bright, keen expression parted from her glance, and her cheek grew instantly pale. But her firmness and presence of mind returned sooner than his. She advanced and extended to him her hand.

The manner was so frank, so confiding, that it seemed to atone for all the past. It evidently was intended to convey the only atonement which, in her situation, she could possibly offer. It said much more than words, and his heart was satisfied. He took her hand and conducted her to a seat. He was silent. It was with great difficulty that he withheld the expression of his tears.

"You know me, Colonel Calvert," she at length said. "I see you know me."

"Could you think otherwise, Margaret?" he succeeded in replying. "Could I forget?"

"No! not forget, perhaps," she returned; "but you seem not to understand me. My person, of course, you know — who I was — but not who I am?"

"Yes — even that too I know."

"Then something is spared me!" she replied with the sigh of one who is relieved from a painful duty.

"I know the whole sad story, Margaret — Mrs. Beauchampe. Can I serve you, Margaret — is it for this you seek me?"

"It is."

"I am ready. I will do what I can. But it will be necessary to see Mr. Beauchampe."

"Can not that be avoided? I confess, I come to you without his sanction or authority. He is unwilling to seek assistance from the law, and proposes either to argue his own case, or to leave it, unargued, to the just sense of the community."

The youth mused in silence for a few moments, before he replied. At length : —

"I will not hide from you, Margaret — forgive me — Mrs. Beauchampe — the danger in which your husband stands. The frequency of such deeds as that for which he is indicted, has led to a general feeling on the part of the community, that the laws must be rigorously enforced. But—"

She interrupted him with some vehemence: "But the provocation of the villain he slew—"

She stopped suddenly. She trembled, for the truth had been revealed in her inadvertence.

"What have I said!" she exclaimed.

"Only what shall be as secret with me, Margaret, as with yourself—"

"Oh, more so, I trust!" she ejaculated.

"Do not distress yourself with this. Understand me. It was to gather from Mr. Beauchampe the whole truth, that I desired to see him. To do him justice, I must know from him what may be known by others, and which might do him hurt. It is to prepare for the worst, that I would seek to know the worst. I will return with you to Frankfort. I will see him. He, as a lawyer, will better understand my purpose than yourself."

"Ah! I thank you — I thank you, William Hinkley. I feel that I do not deserve this at *your* hands. You are avenged — amply avenged — for all the past!"

She covered her face with her hands. Memories, bitter memories, were rushing in upon her soul.

"Speak not thus, Margaret," replied the youth in subdued and trembling accents. "I need no such atonement as this. Believe me, to know what you were, and should have been, Margaret, and see you thus, brings to me no feelings but those of shame and sorrow. Such promise—such pride of promise, Margaret—"

"Ah! indeed! such pride—such pride!—and what a fall!—there could not be a worse, William—surely not a worse!—"

"But there is hope still, Margaret—there is hope."

"You will save him!" she said, eagerly.

"I trust," said he, "that there is hope for him. I will try to save him."

"I know you will—I know you will! But, even then, there is no hope. I feel like a wreck. Even if we founder not in this storm—even if you save us, William—it will be as if some once good ship, shattered and shivered, was carried into port by some friendly prow—only to be abandoned as then no longer worth repair. These storms have shattered me, William—shattered me quite! I am no longer what I was—strong, proud, confident. I fear, sometimes, that my brain will go wild. I feel that my mind is failing me. I speak now with an erring tongue. I scarcely know what I say. But I speak with a faith *in you*. I believe, William, you were always true."

"Ah, had you but believed so *then*, Margaret!—"

"I did! I did believe so!"

"Ah, could it have been, Margaret!—could you have only thought—"

"No more—say no more!" she exclaimed, hurriedly, with a sort of shudder. "Say no more!"

"Had it been," he continued, musingly—"could it have been, there had been now no wreck. Neither of us had felt these storms. We had both been happy!"

"No, no! speak not thus, William Hinkley!" she exclaimed, rising, and putting on a stern look and freezing accent. "The past should be—is—nothing now to us. Nor could it have been as you say. There was a fate to humble *me;* and I am here now to sue for *your* succor. *You* have nothing to deplore. You have fortune which you

could not hope, fame which you did not seek—everything
to make you proud, and keep you happy."

"I am neither proud nor happy, Margaret. You—"

"Enough!" she exclaimed. "You have promised to
strive in his behalf. Save *him*, William Hinkley—and if
prayer of mine can avail before Heaven, you will feel this
want no longer. You *must* be happy!"

"Happy, Margaret?—I do not hope for it!"

She extended him her hand. He took it, and instantly
released it, though not before a scalding tear had fallen
from his eyes upon it. Further farewell than this they had
none. She looked round for old Mr. Calvert, but he was
no longer in the apartment.

CHAPTER XXXVIII.

"GUILTY !"

WE pass over the interviews between Beauchampe and William Calvert. At none of these was the wife present. The former was satisfied to accept the services of one who approached him with the best manners of the gentleman, and the happy union, in his address, of the sage and lawyer; and he freely narrated to him all the particulars of that deed for which he was held to answer. Calvert was ut in possession of all that was deemed necessary to the defence, or rather of all that Beauchampe knew.

But, either the latter did not know *all*, or perjury was an easily-bought commodity upon his trial. There were witnesses to swear to his footsteps, to his voice, his face, his words, his knife and clothes; though he believed that no living eye, save that of the Omniscient, beheld him in his approaches to commit the deed. The knife which struck the blow was buried in the earth. The clothes which he wore were sunk in the river. Yet a knife was produced on the trial as that which had pierced the heart of the victim; and witnesses identified him in garments which he no longer possessed, and in which, according to his belief, they had never seen him !

It is possible that he deceived himself. There can be no doubt that he was just enough of the maniac, while carrying out the monomania which made him so, to be conscious of little else but the one stirring, all-absorbing

passion in his mind. Such a man walks the streets, and
sees no form save that which occupies his imagination;
speaks his purpose in soliloquy which his own ears never
heed; fancies himself alone, though surrounded by specta-
tators. His microcosm is within. He has, while the leading idea is busy in his soul, no consciousness of any world
without.

Could we record the argument of Calvert—analyze for
the reader the voluminous and not always consorting testimony, as he analyzed it for the court—and repeat, word
for word, and look for look, the exquisite appeal which he
offered to the jury—we should be amply justified in occu-
pying, in these pages, the considerable space which such a
record would require. But we dare not make the attempt;
the more particularly, as, however able and admirable, the
speech failed of its effect. Eyes were wet, sighs were audible at its close; but the jury, if moved by the eloquence
of the advocate, were obdurate, so far as concerned the
prisoner. The verdict was rendered "Guilty!" and, with
the awful word, Mrs. Beauchampe started to her feet, and
accused herself to the court, not only of participating in
the offence, but of prompting it. It was supposed to be a
merciful forbearance that Justice permitted herself to become deaf, as well as blind, on this occasion. Her wild
asseverations were not employed against her; and she failed
of the end she sought—to unite her fate, at the close, with
that of him to whom, as she warned him in the beginning,
she herself was a fate.

But, though she failed to provoke Justice to prosecution,
she was yet not to be baffled in her object. Her resolution
was taken, to share the doom of her husband. For her he
had incurred the judgment of the criminal, and her nature
was too magnanimous to think of surviving him. She resolved upon death in her own case, and at the same time
resolved on defeating, in his, that brutal exposure which
attends the execution of the laws. But of her purpose she

said nothing—not even to him whom it most concerned
With that stern directness of purpose which formed so dis
tinguishing a trait in her character, she made her prepara
tions in secret. The indulgence of the authorities permit
ted her to see her husband at pleasure, and to share with
him, when she would, the sad privilege of his dungeon
This indulgence was not supposed to involve any risk, since
a guard was designated to maintain a constant watch upon
the prisoner; and it does not seem to have entered into the
apprehensions of the jailer to provide against any danger
except that of the convict's escape.

The dungeon of the condemned was a close cell, the only
entrance to which was by a trap-door from above. Escape
from this place, with a guard in the upper chamber, was not
an easy performance, nor did it seem to enter for a moment
into the calculation or designs of either of the Beauchampes.
The husband was prepared to die; and the solemn, though
secret determination of the wife, had prepared her also.
The former considered his fate with the feeling of a martyr;
and every word of the latter was intended to confirm, in
his mind, this strengthening and consoling conviction. The
few days which were left to the criminal were not otherwise unsoothed and unlighted from without. Friends came
to him in his dungeon, and strove, with the diligence of
love, to convert the remaining hours of his life into profitable capital for the future grand investment of immortality.
Religion lent her aid to friendship; and, whether Beauchampe did or did not persist in the notion that the crime
for which he stood condemned was praiseworthy, at all
events he was persuaded by her unremitting cares and counsels that he was a sinner—sinning in a thousand respects,
for which repentance was the only grand remedy which
could atone to God for the wrongs done, and left unre-
paired, to man.

Among the friends who now constantly sought the cell of
the criminal, William Calvert was none of the least punctual

Beauchampe became very fond of him, and felt, in a short time, the vast superiority of his mind and character over those of his late tutor. The wife, meanwhile, with that fearless frankness which knows thoroughly the high value of the most superior truth—for truth has its qualities and degrees, though each may be intrinsically pure—had freely told her husband the whole history of the early devotion of William Calvert, when she knew him as the obscure William Hinkley; how, blinded by her own vanity, and the obscurity to which the very modesty of the young rustic had subjected him, she despised his pretensions; and, for the homage of the sly serpent by whom she had been deceived—beguiled with his lying tongue, and pleased with his gaudy coat—had slighted the superior worth of the former, and treated his claims with a scorn as little deserved by him as becoming in her. Sometimes, Beauchampe spoke of this painful past in the history of his wife and visiter, and the reference now did not seem to give pain, at least to the former. The reason was good: she had done with the past. The considerations which now filled her mind were all of a superior nature; and she listened to her husband, even when he spoke on this theme in the presence of William Calvert himself, with an unmoved and unabashed countenance. The latter possessed no such stoicism. At such moments his heart beat with a wildly-increased rapidity of pulsation, and he felt the warm flush pass over his cheeks as vividly and quickly now as in the days of his first youthful consciousness of love.

It was the evening preceding the day of execution. The dark hours were at hand. The guard of the prison had warned the visiters to depart. The divine had already gone. The drooping sisters of Beauchampe were about to go for the night, moaning wildly as they went, in anticipation of the day of awful moan which was approaching. Fond and fervent, and very sad, was the parting, though for the night only, which the condemned gave to these dear twin-buds of his affections. It was a pang spared to him that his poor old mother was too sick to see him. When he thought of her, and of the unspeakable misery which would be hers were she present, he felt the grief lessened which followed from the thought that their eyes might never more encounter.

But the sisters went—all went but William Calvert; and he seemed disposed to linger to the last permitted moment. His thoughts were less with the condemned man than with the wife. His eyes were fixed upon the same object. His anxiety and surprise increased with each moment of his gaze. Whence could arise that strange serenity which appeared in her countenance? Where did she find that strength which, at such an hour, could give her composure? Nor was it serenity and composure alone which distinguished her air, look, and carriage. There was a holy intentness, a sublime decision in her look, which filled him with apprehension. He knew the daring of her character—the bold disposition which had always possessed her to dare the dark and the unknown—and his prescient conjecture divined her intention.

She sat behind her husband, on his lowly pallet. Calvert occupied a stool at its foot. Beauchampe had been speaking freely with all his visiters. He was only moved by the feeling of his situation on separating from his sisters. At all other periods he was tolerably calm, and sometimes his conversation ran into playfulness. When we say playfulness, we do not mean to be understood as intimating his indulgence of mere fun and jest, which would have been as inconsistent with his general character as with the solemn responsibility of his situation. But there was an ease of heart about what he said—an elastic freedom— which insensibly colored, with a freshness and vitality, the idea which he uttered.

"Sit closer to me, Anna," he said to his wife—"sit closer. We are not to be so long together, that we can spare these moments. We have no time for distance and formality. Calvert will excuse this fondness, however annoying it might seem between man and wife at ordinary periods."

He took her hand in his as she drew nigh, and passed his arm fondly about her waist. She was silent; and Calvert, thinking of the conjecture which had been awakened in his mind by the deportment of the wife, was too full of serious and startling thoughts to be altogether assured of what Beauchampe was saying. The latter continued, after a brief pause, by a reference of some abruptness to the past history of the two:—

"It seems to me the strangest thing in the world, Anna, that you should ever have refused to marry our friend Calvert. My days," he said, turning to the latter as he spoke —"my days of idle speech and vain flattery are numbered, Calvert; and you will do me the justice to believe that I am not the man to waste words at any time in worthless compliment. Certainly I will not now. But, since I have known you, I feel that I could wish to know no more desirable friend; and how my wife could have rejected you for any other person—I care not whom—I do not exclude myself—I can not understand, unless by supposing that there is a special fate in such matters, by which our best judgments are set at naught, and our wisest plans baffled. Had she married *you*, Calvert—"

"Why will you speak of it?" said Calvert, with an earnestness of tone which yet faltered. The wife was still silent. Beauchampe answered:—

"Because I speak as one to whom the business of life is over. I am speaking as one from the grave. The passions are dumb within me. The strifes are over. The vain delicacies of society seem a child's play to me now. Besides, I speak regretfully. For her sake, how much better had it been! Instead of being, as she is now, the wife of a convict, doomed to a dog's death; instead of the long strife

through which she has gone; instead of the utter waste
of that proud genius which might, under other fortunes,
have taken such noble flights, and attained such a noble
eminence—"

The wife interrupted him with a smile:—

"Ah, Beauchampe, you are supposing that the world has
but one serpent—but one Alfred Stevens! The eagle in
his flight may escape one arrow, but who shall insure him
against the second or the third? I suspect that few persons at the end of life—of a long life—looking back, with
all their knowledge and experience, could recommence the
journey and find it any smoother or safer than at first. He
is the best philosopher who, when the time comes to die,
can wash his hands of life the soonest, with the least effort,
and dispose his robes most calmly—and so gracefully—
around him. Do not speak of what I have lost, and of
what I have suffered. Still less is it needful that you should
speak of our friend's affairs. We are all chosen, I suspect.
Our fortunes are assigned us. That of our friend was never
more favorable than when mine prompted my refusal of his
kind offer. I was not made for him, nor he for me. We
might not have been happy together; and for the best reason, since I was too blind and ignorant to see what I should
have seen—that the very humility which I despised in him
was the source of his strength, and would have been of my
security. I now congratulate him that I was blind to his
merits. He will live; he will grow stronger with each
succeeding day; fortune will smile upon his toils, and fame
will follow them. At least, we will pray, Beauchampe, that
such will be the case. At parting, William Hinkley—I
an not call you by the other name *now*—at parting, for
ever—believe this assurance. You shall have our prayers
and blessings—such as they are—truly, fondly, my friend,
for we owe much to your help and sympathy."

"For ever, Margaret!—Why should *you* say for
ever?"

Calvert fastened his eyes upon her as she spoke. She met the glance unmoved, and replied: —

"Will it not be for ever? To-morrow which deprives me of *him*, deprives me of the world. I must hide from it. I have no more business with it, nor it with me. I have still some sense of shame — some feelings of sacred sorrow — which I should be loath to expose to its busy finger. Is not this enough, William Calvert?"

"But I am not the world. Friends you will still need; my good, old father —"

She shook her head.

"I know what you would say, William: I know all your goodness of heart, and thank you from the very bottom of mine. Let it suffice that, should I need a friend after to-morrow, I shall seek none other than you."

"Margaret," said William, impressively, "you can not deceive me. I know your object. I see it in your eyes — in those subdued tones. I am sure of what you purpose."

"What purpose? what do you mean?" demanded Beauchampe.

Before he could be answered by Calvert the wife had spoken. She addressed herself to the latter.

"And if you do know it, William Hinkley, you know it only by the conviction in your own heart of what, if not unavoidable, is at least necessary. Speak not of it — give it no thought, and only ask of yourself what, to me, to such a soul as mine, would be life after to-morrow's sun has set! Go now — the guard calls. You will see us in the morning."

"Margaret — for your soul's sake —"

The expostulation was arrested by the repeated summons of the guard. The wife put her finger on her lips in sign of silence. Calvert prepared to depart, but could not forbear whispering in her ears the exhortation which he had begun to speak aloud. She heard him patiently to the end, and sweetly, but faintly smiling, she shook her head,

17

making no other answer. The hoarse voice of the guard again summoned the visiter, who reluctantly rose to obey. He shook hands with Beauchampe, and Margaret followed him to the foot of the ladder. When he gave her his hand she carried it to her lips.

"God bless you, William Hinkley!" she murmured. "You are and have been a noble gentleman. Remember me kindly, and oh! forgive me that I did you wrong, that I did not do justice to your feelings and your worth. Perhaps it was better that I did not."

"Let me pray to you, Margaret. Do not— oh! do not what you design. Spare yourself."

"Ay, William, I will! Shame, certainly, the bitter mock of the many—the silent derision of the few—deceit and fraud—reproach without and within—all these will I spare myself."

"Come! come!" said the guard gruffly, from above, "will you never be done talking? Leave the gentleman to his prayers. His time is short!"

And thus they parted for the night.

CHAPTER XXXIX.

FATAL PURPOSES.

" WHAT did Calvert mean, Anna, when he said he knew your purpose?" was the inquiry of Beauchampe, when she returned to his side; "what do you intend?—what purpose have you?"

She put her hand upon her lips in sign of silence, then looked up to the trap-door, which the guard was slowly engaged in letting down. When this was done, she approached him, and drawing a vial from her bosom displayed it cautiously before his eyes.

" For me!" he exclaimed—" poison!"

A sort of rapturous delight gathered in his eyes as he clutched the vial.

" Enough for both of us!" was the answer. "It is laudanum."

" Enough for both, Anna! Surely you can not mean—"

" To share it with you, my husband. To die with you, as you die for me."

" Not so! This must not be. Speak not—think not thus, my wife. Such a thought makes me wretched. There is no need that *you* should die."

" Ay, but there is, Beauchampe. I should suffer much worse were I to live. Where could I live? How could I live? To be the scorned, and the slandered—to provoke the brutal jest, or more brutal violence of the fopling and the fool! For, who that knows my story, will believe in.

my virtue; and who that doubts, will scruple to approach
me as if he knew that I had none! If I have neither joy
nor security in life, why should I live; and if death keeps
us together, Beauchampe, why should I fear to die? Should
I not rather rejoice, my husband?"

"Ah! but of that we know nothing. That is the doubt
—the curse, Anna!"

"I do not doubt—I can not. Our crime, if crime it be,
is one—our punishment will doubtless be one also."

"It were then no punishment. No, Anna, live! You
have friends who will protect you—who will respect and
love you. There is Colonel Calvert—"

"Do not speak of him, Beauchampe. Speak of none.
I am resolute to share with you the draught. We tread the
dark valley together."

"You shall not! It is in my grasp—no drop shall pass
your lips. It is enough for me only."

"Ah, Beauchampe! would you be cruel?"

"Kind only, dear wife. I can not think of you dying—
so young, so beautiful, and born with such endowments—
so formed to shine, to bless—"

"To kill rather—to blight, Beauchampe; to darken the
days of all whom I approach. This has ever been my fate;
it shall be so no longer. Beauchampe, you can not baffle
me in my purpose. See!—even if you refuse to share with
me the poison, I have still another resource."

She drew a knife from her sleeve and held it up before
his eyes, but beyond the reach of his arm.

"Oh! why will you persist in this, my wife? Why make
these few moments, which are left me, as sad as they are
short and fleeting."

"I seek not to do so, dear husband; nor should my resolution have this effect. Would you have me live for such
sorrows, such indignities, as I have described to you."

"You would not suffer them! Give me the knife, Anna."

"No! my husband!" She restored it to her sleeve. "I

have sworn to die with you, and no power on earth shall persuade me to survive."

"Not *my* entreaties—*my* prayers, Anna!"

"No! Beauchampe!—not even *y ur* prayers shall change my purpose."

"Nay, then, I will call the guard!"

"And if you do, Beauchampe, the sound of your voice shall be the signal for me to strike. Believe me, husband, I do not speak idly!"

The knife was again withdrawn from her sleeve as she spoke, and the bared point placed upon her bosom.

"Put it up, dearest; I promise not to call. Put it up, from sight. Believe me—I will not call!"

"Do not, Beauchampe; and do not, I implore you, again seek to disturb my resolution. Move me you can not. I have reached it only by calmly considering what I am, and what would be left me when you are gone. I have seen enough in this examination to make me turn with loathing from the prospect. I know that it can not be more so behind the curtain; and we will raise it together."

"The assurance, Anna, is sweet to my soul, but I would still implore you against this resolution. To be undivided even in death conveys a feeling to my heart like rapture, and brings back to it a renewed hope; yet I dare not think of your suffering and pain. I dread the idea of death when it relates to you."

"Think rather, my husband, that I share the hope and the rapture of which you speak. Believe me only, that I joy also in the conviction that in death we shall not be divided. The mere bitter of the draught or the pain of the stroke is not worthy of a thought. The assurance that there will be no interruption in our progress together—that death, with us, will be nothing but a joint setting forth in company on a new journey and into another country—that is worthy of every thought, and should be the only one!"

" Ay, but that country, Anna ?"

" Can not be more full of wo and bitter than this hath
been to us."

" It may ! I have read somewhere, my wife, a vivid description of two fond lovers — fondest among the fond —
born, as it were, for each other — devoted, as few have been
to one another; who, by some cruel tyrant were thrown
into a dungeon, and ordered to perish by the gnawing process of hunger. At first, they smiled at such a doom. They
believed that their tyrant lacked ingenuity in his capacity
for torture, for he had left them *together!* Together, they
were strong and fearless. Love made them light-hearted
even under restraint ; and they fancied a power of resistance in themselves, so united, to endure the worst forms of
torment. For a few days they did so. They cheered each
other. They spoke the sweetest, soothing words. Their
arms were linked in constant embrace. She hung upon his
neck, and he bore her head upon his bosom. Never had
they spoken such sweet truths — such dear assurances.
Never had their tendernesses been so all-compensating.
Perhaps they never had been so truly happy together, at
least for the first brief day of their confinement. Their
passion had been refined by severity, and had acquired new
vigor from the pressure put upon it. But as the third day
waned, they ceased to link their arms together. They recoiled from the mutual embrace. They shrunk apart. They
saw in each other's eyes, a something rather to be feared
than loved. Famine was there, glaring like a wolf. The
god was transformed into a demon ; and in another day
the instinct of hunger proved itself superior to the magnanimous sentiment of love. The oppressor looked in on the
fourth day, through the grated-window upon his victims —
and lo ! the lips of the man were dripping with the blood,
drawn from the veins of his beloved one. His teeth were
clenched in her white shoulder ; and he grinned and growled

above his unconscious victim, even as the tiger, whom you
have disturbed ere he has finished with his prey."

"Horrible! But *she* submitted—*she* repined not. Her
moans were unheard. *She* sought not, in like manner, to
pacify the baser, beastly cravings, at the expense of him
she loved. Hers *was* love, Beauchampe—*his* was passion."

"Alas! my wife, what matters it by what name we seek
to establish a distinction between the sentiments and passions? In those dreadful extremes of situation, from which
our feeble nature recoils, all passions and sentiments run
into one. *We* love!—Before Heaven, my wife, I conscientiously say, and as conscientiously believe, that I love you
as passionately as I can love, and as truly as woman ever
was beloved by man. It is not our love that fails us, in the
hour of physical and mental torment. It is our strength.
Thought and principle, truth and purity, are poor defences,
when the frame is agonized with a torture beyond what nature was intended to endure. Then the strongest man de-
serts his faith and disavows his principles. Then the purest
becomes profligate, and the truest dilates in falsehood. It
is madness, not the man, that speaks. It was madness, not
the man, that drunk from the blue veins of the beloved one
and clenched his dripping teeth in her soft white shoulder.
The very superior strength of his blood, was the cause of
his early overthrow of reflection. As, in this respect, she
was the weaker, so her mind, and consequently, the sweet
pure sentiments which were natural to her mind, the longest
maintained its and their ascendency, and preserved her
from the loathsome frenzy to which the man was driven
Ah, of this future, dear wife! This awful, unknown future! Fancy some penal doom like this—fancy some tiger
rage in me—depriving me of the reason, and the sentiments
which have made me love you, and made me what I am -
fancy, in place of the man, the frenzied beast, raging in
his bloody thirst, rending in his savage hunger—drinking the

blood from the beloved one's veins—tearing the flesh from her soft white shoulder! This thought—this fear, Anna—"

"Is neither thought nor fear of mine! God is good and gracious. I am not bold to believe in my own purity of heart, or propriety of conduct. I am a sinner, Beauchampe —a proud, stern, fierce sinner. I feel that I am—I would that I were otherwise, and I pray for Heaven's help to become otherwise—but, sinner as I am, I neither fear nor believe, that such penal dooms are reserved for any degree of sin. The love of physical torture is an attribute with which man has dressed the Deity. As such torture can not be human, so it can not be godlike. I can believe that we may be punished by privation—by denial of trust—by degradation to inferior offices—but it is the brutal imagination that ascribes to God a delight in brutal punishments. Nowhere do we see in nature such a feeling manifested. Life is everywhere a thing of beauty. Smiles are in heaven, sweetness on earth, the winds bring it, the airs breathe it, stars smile it, blossoms store and diffuse it—man, alone, defaces and destroys, usurps, vitiates, and overthrows. It was man, not God, who, in your story, was the oppressor. He made the prison, and thrust the victims into it. It was not God! And shall God be likened to such a monster? What idea can we have of the Deity to whom such characteristics are ascribed!—"

—"I go yet farther," she added, after a pause. "I do not think, even if our sins incur the displeasure of God, that his treatment of us, however harsh, will be meant as punishment. That it will be punishment, I doubt not; but this will be with him a secondary consideration. We are *his* subjects, in *his* world, employed to carry out his various purposes, and set to various tasks. Failing in these, we are set to such as are inferior—perhaps, not employed at all, as being no longer worthy of trust. I can not think of a severer moral infliction. Where all are busy—triumphantly busy—pressing forward in the glorious tasks of a life which is all soul—to be the only idle spirit—denied to share in any mighty consummation—pitied, but abandoned by the rest—the proffer of service rejected—the sympathy of joint action and enterprise denied—a spirit without wings—a sluggish personification of moral sloth, and that too, in such an empire as *God's own*—in his very sight—millions speeding beneath his eye at his bidding—all bid, all chosen, all beloved but one! Ah! Beauchampe, to a soul like mine—so earnest, so ambitious as mine has been, and is—could there be a worse doom!"

"No, dearest! But the subject is dark, and such speculations may be bold—too bold!"

"Why? Do I disparage God in them? Does it not seem that such a future could alone be worthy of such a present—of such a God, as has made a world so various and so wondrous! methinks, the disparagement is in him who ascribes to the Deity such tastes and passions as preside over the inquisitions and the thousand other plans of mortal torture, which have made man the hateful monster that we so frequently find him."

"Let us speak no more of this, Anna. The subject startles me. It is an awful one!"

Hers was the bolder spirit.

"And should not our thoughts be awful thoughts? What other should we have? The future, alone, is ours—will be ours in a short time. A few hours will bring us to the entrance. A few hours will lift the curtain, and the voice that we may not disobey will command us to enter."

"Not you, Anna—oh! not you! Let me brave it alone I can not bear to think that you too should be cut off in your youth—with all that vigorous mind—that beauty—that noble heart—all crushed, blighted—now, when blooming brightest—buried in the dust—no more to speak, or sing, or feel.'

"But they do not perish, Beauchampe. might grow coward—I might cling to this life—could I fanc, there

17*

were no other. But this faith is one of my strongest convictions. It is an instinct. No reasoning will reach the
point and establish it, if the feeling be not in our heart of
hearts. I know that I can not perish quite. I know that
I must live; and that poison-draught, or the thrust of this
sudden knife, I regard as the plunge which one makes,
crossing a frail trembling bridge, or hurrying through some
dark and narrow passage. Do not waste the moments,
which are so precious, in the vain endeavor to dissuade me
from a sworn and settled purpose. Beauchampe, we die
together!"

"Lie down by me, Anna. You should sleep—you are
fatigued. You must be weary."

"No! I am not weary. At such moments as these we
become all soul. We do not need sleep. With the passage
of this night we shall never need it again. Think of that,
Beauchampe! What a thought it is."

"Terrible!"

"Glorious, rather! Sleep was God's gift to an animal
—to restore limbs that could be wearied—to refresh spirits that could be dull! What a godlike feeling to know
that we should need it no longer!—no more yawning—no
more drowsiness—and that feebleness and blindness, which,
without any of the securities of death, has all of its incom-
petencies—when the merest coward might bind, and the
commonest ruffian abuse, and trample on us. Ah! the im-
munities-of death! How numerous—how great! What
blindness to talk of its terrors—to shrink from its glorious
privileges of unimpeded space—of undiminishing time.
Already, Beauchampe, it seems to me as if my wings are
growing. I fancy I should not feel any hurt from the
knife—perhaps, not even taste the poison on my lips."

"Sit by me, at least, if you will not sleep, Anna."

"I will sit by you, Beauchampe—nay, I wish to do so;
but you must promise not to attempt to dispossess me of the
knife. I suspect you, my husband."

" Why suspect me ?"

" I perceive it in the tones of your voice: I know what you intend. But, believe me, I have taken my resolution from which nothing will move me. Even were you now to deprive me of the weapon, nothing would keep me from it long. I should follow you soon, my husband; and the only effect of present denial would be to deprive me of the pleasure of dying with you!"

" Come to me, my wife! I will not attempt to disarm you. I promise you."

" On your love, Beauchampe ?"

" With my full heart. dearest. You shall die with me. It will be a sweet moment instead of a bitter one. For your sake only, my wife, would I have disarmed you— but my selfish desires triumph. I will no longer oppose you."

" Thanks—thanks!"

She sprang to him, and clung to his embrace.

" Will you sleep ?" he asked, as her head seemed to sink upon his bosom.

" No, no! I had not thought of that! I thought only of the moment—the moment when we should leave this prison."

" Leave it ?"

" By death! I am tired, very tired, of these walls— these walls of life—that keep us in bonds—put us at the mercy of the false and the cruel, the base and the malicious! Oh, my husband, we have tried them long enough!"

" There is time enough!" he said. " I would see the daylight once more."

" You can only see it through those bars."

" Still, I would see it. We can free ourselves a moment after."

Even while they spoke together, Beauchampe sunk into a pleasant slumber. She pillowed his head upon her bosom, but had no feeling or thought of sleep. Through the grated window she saw a few flitting stars. One by one, they came into her sphere of vision, gleamed a little while, and passed, like the bright, spiritual eyes of the departed dear ones. When she ceased to behold them, then she knew that the day was at hand; and the interval of time between the disappearance of the stars and the approach of dawn, though brief, was dark.

"Such," she mused, "will be that brief period of transition, when, passing from the dim, deceptive starlight of this life, we enter into the perfect day. That will be momentarily dark, perhaps. It must be. There may be a state of childhood—an imperfect consciousness of the things around us—of our own wants—and among these, possibly, a lack of utterance. Strange, indeed, that the inevitable should still be the inscrutable! But of what use the details? The great fact is clear to me. Even now things are becoming clearer while I gaze. My whole soul seems to be one great thought! How strange that he should sleep—so soundly, too—so like an infant! He does not fear death, that is certain; but he loves life. I, too, love life, but it is not this. Oh, of that other! Could I get some glimpses—but this is childish! I shall see it all very soon!"

Beauchampe slept late; and, bearing his head still on her bosom, the sleepless wife did not seek to awaken him. Through the intensity of her thought, she acquired an entire independence of bodily infirmities. The physical nature, completely controlled by the spiritual, was passive at her mood. But the soundness of Beauchampe's sleep, continued, as it was, after day had fairly dawned, awakened her suspicions. She searched for the vial of laudanum where she had seen him place it. It was no longer there. She found it beside him on the couch—it was empty!

But his breathing was not suspended. His sleep was natural, and, while she anxiously bent over him in doubt whether to strike at once, or wait to see what further effects might be produced on him by the potion, he awakened. His first words at awakening betrayed the still superior feelings of attachment with which he regarded her. His voice was that of exultation:—

"It is over—and we are still together! We are not divided!"

"No! but the hour is at hand!"

"What mean you, my love? I have swallowed the laudanum!—where am I?"

His question was answered as his eyes encountered the bleak walls of his dungeon, and beheld the light through the iron bars of his window.

"God! the poison has failed of its effect!"

His look was that of consternation. Her glance and words reassured him.

"We have still the knife, my husband!"

"Ah! we shall defeat them still!"

CHAPTER XL.

LAST WORDS.

"On the morning of the fifth of June, eighteen hundred and twenty-six," says the chronicle, "the drums were heard beating in the streets of Frankfort, and a vast multitude was hurrying toward the gibbet, which was erected on a hill without the town."

At the sound of this ominous music, and the clamors of that hurrying multitude, Beauchampe smiled sadly.

"Strange, that men should delight in such a spectacle — the cruel death, the miserable exposure, of a fellow-man! — that they should look on his writhings, his distortions, his shame and pain, with composure and desire! It will be cruel to disappoint them, Anna! Will it not?"

"I think not of them, my husband. Oh, my husband, could we crowd the few remaining moments with thoughts of goodness, with prayers of penitence! Oh, that I had not urged you to the death of Stevens!"

"It was right!" he answered sternly. "I tell you, Anna, the wives and daughters of Kentucky will bless the name of Beauchampe!"

"They should, my husband, for your blow has saved many from shame and suffering — has terrified many a wrong-doer from his purpose. But, though right in you to strike, I feel that it was wrong in me to counsel."

"That can not be! Do not speak thus, my wife. Let not our last moments be embittered by reproach. Let us die in prayer rather. Hark! I hear visitors—voices—some one approaches!"

"It is William Hinkley!" she exclaimed.

The guard was heard about to remove the trap-door. Beauchampe looked up, and, a moment after, he heard his wife sigh deeply. She then spoke to him, faintly but quickly: "Take it, my husband! It is not painful."

He turned to her, while a sudden coldness seized upon his heart. She presented him the knife.

"Have you struck?" he asked, in a husky whisper. The wet blade of the knife, already clotty with the coagulating blood, answered his question.

"Take me in your arms—quickly, quickly, dear husband —do not leave me! I lose you—oh, I lose you!"

"No, never! I come! I am with you. Nothing shall part us. This unites us for ever!"

And, with the words, he struck the fatal blow, laid his lips on hers, and covered her and himself with the blanket.

"This is sweet!" she murmured. "I feel you, but I can not see you, husband. Who is it comes?"

"Calvert!"

The young man descended a moment after. His apprehensions were realized. Margaret Cooper was dying—dying by her own hands.

"Was this well done, Margaret?" he asked reproachfully.

"Ay, William," she answered firmly, but in feeble tones. "It was well done! It could not be otherwise, and I find dying sweeter than living. You will forgive me, William?"

"But God, Margaret?—"

"Ah! pray for me—pray for me!—Husband—I am losing you. I feel you not. This is death!—it was for me—it was all for me! O Beauchampe!—"

"She is gone!" cried the husband.

Calvert, who had assisted to support her, now laid the inanimate form softly upon the couch. He was dumb. But the cry of Beauchampe had drawn the attention of the guard.

"What is this—what's the matter?" he demanded.

"Ha! ha! we laugh at you—we defy you!" was the exclamation of Beauchampe, holding up the bloody knife with which he had inflicted upon himself a second wound. We have slain ourselves."

"God forbid!" cried the officer, wresting the weapon from the hands of the criminal.

"You are too late, my friend: we shall spoil your sport. You shall enjoy no public agonies of mine to-day."

They brought relief—surgical help—stimulants, and bandages. They succored the fainting man, cruelly kind, in order that the stern sentence of the laws might be carried into effect. The hour of execution, meanwhile, had arrived. They brought him forth in the sight of the assembled crowd. The fresh air revived the dying man—awakening him into full but momentary consciousness. He looked up, and beheld where the windows of some of the neighboring houses were filled with female forms. He lifted his hands to them with a graceful but last effort, while he murmured:—

"Daughters of Kentucky! you, at least, will bless the name of Beauchampe!—"

This was all. He then sunk back, as they strove to lift him into the cart. Before his feet had pressed the felon-vehicle, his eyes closed. He was unconscious of the rest. Earth and its little life was nothing more to him. He had also passed behind the curtain!

And here our narrative might fitly end. We have disposed of those parties whose superior trials and struggles constituted the chief interest of our story. But custom requires something more; and the curiosity of the reader naturally seeks to know what of the fortunes of the subordinates—such of the minor persons of the drama as, by their virtues and good conduct, have established a claim upon our regards. We, perhaps, need to know whether

Ned Hinkley, for example, found his compensative happiness — as he proposed it to himself — in the affections of the fair, simple Sallie Bernard, who had so much commended herself to his love by forbearing all " strong-minded" demonstrations. Well, we may satisfy this curiosity. Ned and Sallie are still in the full enjoyment of life and a vigorous old age, with troops of young Neds and Sallies about them. We are persuaded that neither of them regrets or repents the union which they formed upon such moderate expectations of what was due to each other and the public. As they did not marry to please the public, so have they proved themselves perfectly satisfied with the simple duty of pleasing one another.

Of the mother of Margaret Cooper, the mother of Beauchampe, and his sisters, we know nothing. They wisely sheltered their bleeding hearts in obscurity.

Old Hinkley and his wife, the parents of William Calvert, returned from Mississippi to Kentucky, where they were living, at last advices, with their son. The successful career of the latter has, singularly enough, persuaded the old man to believe that William's religion was not, after all, of so doubtful a character. His own devotions are maintained with the tenacity of his nature ; but, as he is satisfied that God approves the virtues whenever he helps the fortunes of the subject — a notion which is exceedingly current among the Pharisaical, whose self-esteem is the chief guardian of their religion, and perhaps its only foe — so he leaves his son to settle his own account with the Deity, contenting himself with an unusually long grace at table, and a frequent voluntary prayer for grace before the family retires for the night.

The good old schoolmaster, who could not be lawyer or politician, though with ambition and endowment enough for both, has been gathered to his fathers. He had reached the ripe old age of eighty-one before he yielded to the sacred slumber. He subsided from life, as the withered leaf

drops from the tree in autumn, without an effort or strug
gle. He died while he slept, and no doubt in a sweet
dream, and with the far-off sounds of angelic music in his
ears, full of welcome and rejoicing. He was at peace with
he world. His last days were cheered by affectionate
ares and the most loving solicitude. All that he beheld
and heard was grateful to his matured thoughts and his
innocent desires. His pride was unselfish, like his hopes.
It was all grounded in the prosperity of another!

And that other?—

William Calvert continued to prosper. He never married. He still lives, in a green and vigorous old age, in
the midst of a noble estate, the fruit of his own well-applied
industry and honorable energies. He concentrated all his
talents upon his profession, and his profession made him
prosperous in turn. His one experiment in politics satisfied all his desires in that direction. For ever after, he
steadily refused all connection with political life. He was
wont to say that the sacrifice was quite too great for so
small an object; and that, while politics in a democracy
were admirably calculated to intoxicate and stimulate vanity, they furnished very unwholesome and unsatisfactory food
for any real, craving, honest ambition. And he was right.
He still lives—lives, as we have said, a bachelor—with
lofty frame, erect carriage, fair, round face, benevolent
heart, and a calm, sedate mind, always equal to the occasion, and seeking after nothing more. His affections were
true to his first and only love; and sometimes, as if speaking to himself rather than those about him, he will mention
the name of Margaret Cooper. This will be followed by a
deep sigh; and then, as if suddenly remembering himself, he
will hurry out of the apartment, and seek refuge in his own.

And thus he still lives, in waiting—and in hope!

Let us drop the curtain.

THE END.